"What are you hiding, Ellie?

"What makes you think I'm hiding something?" Ellie busied herself pouring the hot water into a mug.

"I get the feeling there's something in your past you don't like to talk about," Colt murmured.

"I didn't know full disclosure about all details of my life was necessary for me to get this job. Your grandmother seems satisfied."

He dipped his head in a curt nod. "Winnie is a great judge of character."

Meaning he had his doubts?

One of the reasons she liked being a bodyguard was that she could blend into the background. She kept a lock on her past—a past she didn't want to take out and reexamine.

"If you must know, the short version of my life so far is—"

"That's okay—I'm sorry. I didn't mean to bring up something painful."

"What did you mean?"

"To make sure Winnie was in good hands."

She stared into his light blue eyes. "She's in good hands. When I do a job, I do it one hundred percent."

CHRISTMAS MOUNTAIN PROTECTOR

USA TODAY BESTSELLING AUTHOR

MARGARET DALEY
&
MARY ELLEN PORTER

Previously published as *Christmas Stalking*
and *Off the Grid Christmas*

LOVE INSPIRED
INSPIRATIONAL ROMANCE

LOVE INSPIRED®

INSPIRATIONAL ROMANCE

Recycling programs for this product may not exist in your area.

ISBN-13: 978-1-335-23093-5

Christmas Mountain Protector

Copyright © 2020 by Harlequin Books S.A.

Christmas Stalking
First published in 2012. This edition published in 2020.
Copyright © 2012 by Margaret Daley

Off the Grid Christmas
First published in 2017. This edition published in 2020.
Copyright © 2017 by Mary Ellen Porter

This edition published by arrangement with Harlequin Books S.A.

For questions and comments about the quality of this book, please contact us at CustomerService@Harlequin.com.

Love Inspired
22 Adelaide St. West, 40th Floor
Toronto, Ontario M5H 4E3, Canada
www.Harlequin.com

Printed in U.S.A.

CONTENTS

Margaret Daley, an award-winning author of ninety books (five million sold worldwide), has been married for over forty years and is a firm believer in romance and love. When she isn't traveling, she's writing love stories, often with a suspense thread, and corralling her three cats, who think they rule her household. To find out more about Margaret, visit her website at margaretdaley.com.

Visit the Author Profile page at Harlequin.com for more titles.

CHRISTMAS STALKING

Margaret Daley

For if ye forgive men their trespasses,
your heavenly Father will also forgive you.
—*Matthew* 6:14

To Shaun and Kim, my son and daughter-in-law

ONE

In the dark, Ellie St. James scanned the mountainous terrain out her bedroom window at her new client's home in Colorado, checking the shadows for any sign of trouble before she went to sleep. The large two-story house of redwood and glass blended in well with the rugged landscape seven thousand feet above sea level. Any other time she would appreciate the beauty, but she was here to protect Mrs. Rachel Winfield.

A faint sound punched through her musing. She whirled away from the window and snatched her gun off the bedside table a few feet from her. Fitting the weapon into her right palm and finding its weight comforting, she crept toward her door and eased it open to listen. None of the guard dogs were barking. Maybe she'd imagined the noise.

A creak, like a floorboard being stepped on, drifted up the stairs. Someone was ascending to the second floor. She and her employer were the only ones in the main house. She glanced at Mrs. Winfield's door two down from hers and noticed it was closed. Her client kept it that way only when she was in her bedroom.

So who was on the stairs? Had someone gotten past

the dogs outside and the security system? And did that someone not care that he was being heard coming up the steps? Because he didn't intend to leave any witnesses?

The latest threat against Mrs. Winfield urged her into action. She slipped out of her room and into the shadows of the long hallway that led to the staircase. Having memorized all the floorboards that squeaked, Ellie avoided the left side of the corridor as she snuck forward—past Mrs. Winfield's door.

Another sound echoed through the hall. Whoever was on the steps was at the top. She increased her speed, probing every dark recess around her for any other persons. Near the wooden railing of the balcony that overlooked the front entrance, she found the light switch, planted her bare feet a foot apart, preparing herself to confront the intruder, and then flipped on the hall light.

Even though she expected the bright illumination, her eyes needed a few seconds to adjust to it. The large man before her lifted his hand to shield his eyes from the glare. Which gave Ellie the advantage.

"Don't move," she said in her toughest voice, a husky resonance she often used to her advantage.

The stranger dropped his hand to his side, his gray-blue eyes drilling into her then fixing on her Wilson combat aimed at his chest. Anger washed all surprise from his expression. "Who are you?" The question came out in a deep, booming voice, all the fury in his features reflected in it.

"You don't get to ask the questions. Who are—"

The click of the door opening to Mrs. Winfield's bedroom slightly behind and to the left of Ellie halted her words as she shifted her attention for an instant to make sure the man didn't have an accomplice already with her client.

"Winnie, get back," the intruder yelled.

By the time Ellie's gaze reconnected with the man, he was charging toward her. She had less than a second to decide what to do. The use of her client's nickname caused Ellie to hesitate. In that moment the stranger barreled into her, slamming her into the hardwood floor. The impact jolted her, knocking the Wilson Combat from her hand. The thud of her weapon hitting the floor behind her barely registered as she lay pinned beneath two hundred pounds of solid muscle. Pressed into her, the man robbed her of a decent breath.

Her training flooded her with extra adrenaline. Before he could capture her arms, she brought them up and struck him on the sides of his head. His light-colored gaze widened at the blow. She latched onto his face, going for his eyes with her thumbs.

"Miss St. James, stop!" Mrs. Winfield's high-pitched voice cut into the battle between Ellie and her attacker.

The man shifted and clasped her wrists in a bone-crushing grip.

Ellie swung her attention from the brute on top of her to her employer standing over them with Ellie's gun in her quivering hand. Pointed at her!

"He's my grandson," Mrs. Winfield said. "Colt, get up. She can hardly breathe."

The man rolled off her, shaking his head as though his ears rang. After her attack they probably did.

Sitting up, he stared at his grandmother who still held the weapon. "Please give me the gun, Winnie." His soft, calm words, interspersed with heavy pants, contradicted his earlier authoritative tone.

Ellie gulped in oxygen-rich breaths while he pushed to his feet and gently removed the weapon from Mrs. Winfield's hand. He dwarfed his petite grandmother by over a foot.

With her gun in his grasp, he stood next to her client and glared down at Ellie. "Now I would like an answer. Who are you?" Anger still coated each word.

She slowly rose from the floor. "Ellie St. James."

He put his arm around his grandmother, who stood there trembling, staring at Ellie as though she was trying to understand what had just happened. "What are you doing here, Miss St. James?" he asked.

With a shake of her head, Mrs. Winfield blinked then peered up at her grandson. "She's my new assistant."

"What in the world are you doing carrying a gun?"

His question thundered through the air, none of the gentle tone he'd used with his grandmother evident. He glared at her, his sharp gaze intent on Ellie's face. Although he'd lowered the gun, Ellie didn't think it would take much for him to aim it again. Fury was etched into his hard-planed face.

"My dear, why *do* you have a gun?"

Mrs. Winfield's light, musical voice finally pulled Ellie's attention from the man. Her employer had regained her regal bearing, her hands clasped together in front of her to control their trembling.

"I've lived alone for so long in a big city I've always had a gun for protection," Ellie finally answered.

Although Mrs. Winfield was her client—the person she'd been assigned to guard—the older woman didn't know it. Her lawyer and second-in-charge at Glamour Sensations, Harold Jefferson, had hired Guardians, Inc., to protect her. Ellie was undercover, posing as her new

assistant. Her cover had her growing up in Chicago—
the south side—and still living there. But in reality, at
the first opportunity she'd had she'd hightailed it out of
Chicago and enlisted in the army. When she'd left the
military, she hadn't gone back home but instead she'd
gone to Dallas to work for Guardians, Inc., and Kyra
Morgan—now Kyra Hunt.

"You don't need a weapon now. This isn't a big city.
I have security around the estate. You're safe. I prefer you do something with that gun. I don't like weapons." A gentle smile on her face, Mrs. Winfield moved
toward her as though she were placating a gun-toting
woman gone crazy.

Ellie didn't trust anyone's security enough to give
up her gun, but she bit the inside of her cheeks to keep
from voicing that thought. She would need to call Mr.
Jefferson and see how he wanted to proceed. Ellie had
wanted to tell Mrs. Winfield that her life was in danger, but he'd refused. Now something would have to
give here.

"I'll take care of it, Winnie. I'll lock it in the safe
until she can remove it from here." The grandson
checked the Wilson Combat, slipped out the ammo
clip and ejected the bullet in the chamber, then began
to turn away.

"Wait. You can't—"

He peered over his shoulder, one brow arching. "I'm
sure my grandmother will agree that this will have to
be a condition of your continual employment. If I had
any say in it, I'd send you packing tonight." He rubbed
his ears. "They're still ringing. You have a mean punch.
Where did you learn to take care of yourself?"

"A matter of survival in a tough neighborhood."

That was true, but she'd also had additional training in the army.

"As my grandmother said, that isn't an issue here. We're on a side of a mountain miles away from the nearest town. No one bothers us up here."

If you only knew. "I'm licensed to carry—"

But Mrs. Winfield's grandson ignored her protest and descended the staircase.

Ellie rushed to the railing overlooking the downstairs entrance. Clutching the wood, she leaned over and said, "That's my weapon. I'll take care of it."

"That's okay. I'm taking care of it." Then he disappeared into the hallway that led to the office where the safe was.

"I certainly understand why you got scared." Mrs. Winfield approached her at the railing and patted her back. "I did when I heard the noise from you two in the hallway. I didn't know what was happening. I appreciate you being willing to protect me, but thank goodness, it wasn't necessary."

This time. Ellie swung around to face the older woman. "Yeah, but you never know."

"The Lord watches out for His children. I'm in the best care."

"I agree, but that doesn't mean we shouldn't be proactive, Mrs. Winfield," Ellie said, hoping to convince Mr. Jefferson to tell her about the threats tomorrow.

"Please call me Winnie. Christy, my previous assistant, did. I don't like standing on formality since you'll be helping me." She smiled. "Colt gave me that name years ago, and everyone calls me that now."

"Was he supposed to visit?"

"The last I heard he wasn't going to come back this

year for Christmas. He probably heard my disappointment when we talked on the phone a few days ago. If I had known Colt was coming, I would have said something to you."

She'd read the dossier Kyra Hunt had given her on Colt Winfield, the only grandson Mrs. Winfield had. She should have recognized him, but with a beard and scruffy hair and disheveled clothes he'd looked like a bum who had wandered into the house intent on ill gains.

"He was supposed to be in the South Pacific on the research vessel through Christmas and the New Year." Mrs. Winfield gave Ellie a smile, her blue eyes sparkling. "Just like him to forget to tell me he was coming home after all for Christmas. Knowing him, it could be a surprise from the very beginning. He loves doing that kind of thing. Such a sweet grandson." She leaned close to Ellie to whisper the last because Colt Winfield was coming back up the steps.

"I wish that were the case, Winnie." Colt paused on the top stair. "But I need to get back to the *Kaleidoscope*. I managed to get a few days off before we start the next phase of our project, and I know how important it is to you that we have some time together at Christmas."

Great, he'll be leaving soon.

"Just a few days?" His grandmother's face fell, the shine in her eyes dimming. "I haven't seen you in months. Can't you take a couple of weeks out of your busy schedule to enjoy the holidays like we used to?"

Please don't, Ellie thought, rolling her shoulders to ease the ache from their tussle on the hardwood floor.

He came to the older woman and drew her into his

embrace. "I wish I could. Maybe at the end of January. The government on the island is allowing a limited amount of time to explore the leeward side and the underwater caves."

Mrs. Winfield stepped away. "You aren't the only one on the research team. Let someone else do it for a while. You're one of three marine biologists. And the other two are married to each other. They get to spend Christmas together."

"I need to be there. Something is happening to the sea life in that part of the ocean. It's mutating over time. It's affected the seal population. You know how I feel about the environment and the oceans."

"Fine." Mrs. Winfield fluttered her hand in the air as she swept around and headed for the door to her bedroom. "I can't argue with you over something I taught you. Good night. I'll see you tomorrow morning. I hope you'll at least go for a power walk with Ellie and me. Seven o'clock sharp."

"Yes, Winnie. I've brought my running shoes. I figured you'd want me to."

When her employer shut the door to her room, Ellie immediately said, "I need my gun back."

"You do? What part of your duties as my grandmother's assistant requires you to have a gun?" His gaze skimmed down her length.

Ellie finally peered down at the clothes she wore—old sweats and a baggy T-shirt. With a glance at the mirror at the end of the hall, she noticed the wild disarray of her hair. She looked as scruffy as Colt Winfield. She certainly wouldn't appear to this man as a capable and efficient bodyguard. Or a woman who knew how to use a gun when she needed to. "Ask yourself. What if you had been a burglar? Would you have wanted me to let you rob the place or do worse?"

For half a moment he just stared at her, then he started chuckling. "Since I'm not and I'll be here for a few days, you'll be safe. Didn't you wonder why the three German shepherds didn't bark?"

"I know that dogs can be good for security purposes, but they can be taken out. It shouldn't be the only method a person uses." Which Mr. Jefferson was changing—just not fast enough for her liking. A new alarm system for the house would be in place by the end of the week. But even that didn't guarantee a person was totally safe. Hence the reason why Mr. Jefferson hired her to guard Mrs. Winfield—Winnie.

"So you decided to bring a gun."

"I'm very capable. I was in the army."

"Army? Even knowing that, I'm afraid, Miss St. James, we're not going to see eye to eye on this." He swiveled around and went to pick up a duffel bag by the steps. He hadn't had that when he'd first come upstairs. He must have brought it up when he put the gun in the safe. "Good night."

Ellie watched him stride down the corridor in the opposite direction of her bedroom. When he paused before a door at the far end, he slanted a look back at her. For a few seconds the corners of his mouth hitched up. He nodded his head once and then ducked inside.

She brought her hand up to comb her fingers through her hair and encountered a couple of tangles. "Ouch!"

Moving toward her bedroom, she kept her eye on his, half expecting him to pop back out with that gleam of humor dancing in his eyes. When he didn't, something akin to disappointment flowed through her until she shoved it away. She would have to call Mr. Jefferson to tell him that Colt was here. From what she'd read about the man he was smart, with a doctorate in marine biology as well as a degree in chemistry. Currently he worked on a research vessel as the head marine biologist for a think tank formed to preserve the world's oceans.

His grandmother hadn't ever questioned why Ellie was always around, even in her lab, but she had a feeling Colt would. Then he would demand an answer.

After traveling for almost twenty-four hours the day before, Colt dragged himself out of bed at a quarter to seven in his old room where he'd grown up. Winnie hadn't changed anything in here, and he doubted she ever would. She would always think of him as her little boy. Although Winnie was his grandmother, she'd raised him when his own mother had died from a massive infection shortly after he was born. Thinking of his past brought both heartache and joy. Heartache because he'd lost so many people he cared about. But he'd rather not dwell on his past. Besides, he had Winnie. She had given him so much.

After dressing in his sweats to power walk in the crisp December air in the Colorado mountains, he made his way toward the kitchen and the scent of coffee. Just its aroma made his body crave caffeine. He'd need it if he was going to keep up with Winnie. At seventy-three, she was an amazing woman, owner of Glamour Sensations and creator of both women's and men's fragrances. Not to mention her latest development—a line of antiaging products rumored to revolutionize the cosmetic industry. This had been a dream of Winnie and his granddad for fifteen years. Although his grandfather was dead, Winnie was close to completing their vision with the development of a cream that faded scars and lines as though they had never been there in the first place.

Clean-shaven, Colt came into the kitchen to find his grandmother and her new assistant sitting at the table drinking mugs of coffee. "I thought you would be gone for your power walk by now, leaving me with the whole pot of coffee."

His grandmother glanced at the clock on the wall. "As usual, ten minutes late. Did I not tell you we would have to wait on him, Ellie?"

The pretty assistant, dressed in a navy blue jogging suit with her long curly blond hair tamed into a ponytail, gave him a sugary sweet smile, a sparkle in her brown eyes. "I tried to talk her into leaving without you, but she insisted on waiting."

He made his way to his grandmother, kissed her cheek then headed for the pot to pour some coffee.

"You won't have time for that. I have a meeting with Harold at eight-thirty, and I'm sure he would want me to shower and change before we meet in the lab." Winnie rose and took a last swallow from her mug before setting it on the table. "You can have some later."

"What if I walk off the side of the mountain because I fell asleep?" He put his empty cup on the counter.

"Dear, if you manage to fall asleep while power walking with me, I'll be surprised. Besides, we're walking inside the fence. It would stop your fall."

"Your power walking is grueling." Taking up the rear, he followed the two women out onto the wooden deck along the back of the redwood and glass house that sat in a meadow with a high fence around the premises.

As though expecting Winnie at that time of the day, the three German shepherds sat near the door, their tails wagging. Rocket, the white one, barked his greeting.

His grandmother stooped over and patted each one, saying, "I've got a treat for you later today. A juicy bone. I know how much you like that."

Lady, the only female, nudged his grandmother's hand for more scratches behind the ear. Winnie laughed. "You always demand more attention than the boys here. They may be larger, but I have a feeling they do whatever you want."

Standing next to Ellie and watching the exchange between his grandmother and the guard dogs, Colt said, "My grandfather bought Rocket and Gabe to be company and guard the place seven years ago. He was very attached to them. Winnie went out and purchased Lady from the same trainer. She wanted female representation. They love staying outside, but whenever the weather gets bad, she brings them inside, even though they have a top-of-the-line dog structure."

"I've seen it. It isn't your ordinary doghouse. I thought it might be a storage shed until I saw them going in and out."

"That's because nothing is too good for her dogs. When Granddad died, Winnie took over all three dogs' care with her caretaker's help."

When she finished greeting each pet, Winnie went through some stretches. "Colt, I don't want to hear any complaining on my walk. You're in perfectly good shape."

"I don't complain. I tease."

"I have a feeling you swim every day you have a chance on the job. Ellie, he can swim ten miles without tiring. Not to mention he can hold his breath underwater for two minutes. I think that's from growing up here in the mountains. Great lung capacity."

His grandmother's remark to her assistant slid his attention to the tall woman who lunged to the left then right. "So you're into power walking, too?"

Ellie brought her feet together, raised one leg behind her and clasped her ankle. "When I can get the chance, I usually jog, but I've been enjoying our early morning jaunts."

"Who did you work for before this?"

Pausing, she stretched her other leg. "A small company," she said finally.

Winnie didn't seem to notice the slight hesitation in Ellie's reply, but he did. Was something going on? When he got back from his power walk, he would catch Harold before he talked with Winnie. He didn't want to upset his grandmother unless there was a good reason, but who exactly was Ellie St. James? A woman who carried a gun and, based on last night, wasn't afraid to use it.

"I'm glad I caught you before you talked with Winnie." Ellie shut the library door after the lawyer entered.

"Ah, I see you've made good progress with Winnie," Harold Jefferson said. "She doesn't usually have someone call her Winnie unless she likes you."

"I think that's because she appreciated my attempt to protect her last night."

His eyebrows shot up. "Someone got in the house? Why didn't you call me?"

"Because it turned out to be her grandson."

His forehead wrinkled. "Colt's here?"

"Yes, for a few days. I thought he was an intruder

and I pulled my gun on him in the upstairs hallway. Without her knowing why I'm here, she doesn't understand why I would have a gun. It's now sitting in her safe in her office. That ties my hands protecting her. She needs to be told."

"She will stress and shut down. She's under a tight deadline with this new product she's coming up with. That's why I'm here to talk to her about the publicity campaign now that her former assistant, Christy, has agreed to be the new face for the company."

"The Winnie I've seen this past week is tough when she needs to be."

"It's all a show. I've been through a lot with her. Years ago her company nearly fell apart because of her son's death. Then she had a heart attack ten years ago, and we went through another rough patch. That was followed by her husband passing away five Christmases ago. Finally she's close to going public with Glamour Sensations and offering stock as she brings out her new line, Endless Youth. She's been working toward this for years. She feels she needs to fulfill her late husband's vision for the business."

Ellie placed her hand on her waist, trying to control her frustration and impatience. "If she is dead, she won't be able to fulfill his vision."

"That's why you're here. To keep her alive. The fewer people who know someone has sent her threats the better. She *is* the company. The brains and creative force behind it. We need the infusion of money to make a successful campaign for the new products in the spring that will lead up to the unveiling of the signature cream next Christmas."

"If the company is going public, don't you have to disclose the threats?"

"Yes. When we reach that part of the process, we'll have to disclose the threats to the investment banker and lawyers. Fortunately, we have until right after Christmas to take care of the problem."

"I can't protect her without my weapon. It's that simple."

"What if we tell Colt and have him get the gun for you? She rarely goes into the safe. I imagine she's too busy in the lab downstairs."

Ellie looked out the floor-to-ceiling window across the back at the stand of pine trees. "Yes, but what if she does?"

She'd never liked the fact that Mrs. Winfield didn't know about the threats and the danger her life was in. The former assistant had given Mr. Jefferson each threatening letter. They had become more serious over the past month, and one also included a photo of Mrs. Winfield out power walking. That was when he had contacted Guardians, Inc. He was hoping nothing would come of the letters, but he knew he had to put some kind of protection in place. That was when Ellie had entered as the new assistant to replace Christy Boland, who was going to be the spokesperson for Glamour Sensations' Endless Youth line.

"On second thought, we probably shouldn't tell Colt. I don't want anyone else to know if possible. He might let something slip to his grandmother. It's probably better that he returns to the research ship." Mr. Jefferson snapped his fingers. "I've got it. I'll get you a gun to use. I can come back out here this afternoon with whatever you want. Maybe a smaller gun that you can keep concealed."

"Fine, unless I think there's a direct threat."

"I'm hoping I can catch the person behind the letters before then. The Bakersville police chief is working on the case personally, as well as a P.I. I hired. Winnie received another letter at headquarters yesterday."

"Another picture in it?"

"No, just threats of what the person is going to do to her."

Ellie thought of the sweet lady she'd spent the past week with—a woman who toiled long hours because she knew a lot of people who worked for her counted on her. "What in the world has she done to anger someone?"

"We're looking into disgruntled employees, but she was never directly responsible for firing anyone. If she had her way, everyone would still be working for her no matter if they didn't do their job. Thankfully I run that part of the business."

Ellie sighed. "I'll need you to bring me a Glock G27. It's smaller and easily concealed. It will have to do, even though I prefer my own weapon. At least you were able to get Winnie to stay and work from home this month. That will help the situation, but this home isn't secure."

"Is any place?"

"No, but there are some things we can do."

"Like what? I'm working on a better security system."

"That's good because the one she has is at least ten years old." Ellie paced the large room with bookcases full of books. "We could use bulletproof windows. Security guards to patrol the grounds and posted at the gate. Also cameras all over the house and the property being monitored 24/7."

"She won't go for anything else. She didn't even understand why I wanted to upgrade her security system. Told me the Lord was looking out for her and that's all she needs."

Ellie believed in the power of God, but Winnie was being naive. "What if someone gets to her? I've convinced her that I enjoy power walking, and she has graciously asked me to come with her, but she likes her independence. I'm running out of reasons to tag along with her when she leaves this house."

"It's only for a couple of more weeks at best. The P.I. on the case is tracking down some promising leads. If nothing changes after she has completed the last product for this new line, I'll tell her. She's fragile when she's in her creative mode. Easily distracted. Even Colt's visit will strain her schedule."

"And Christmas won't? I get the impression she enjoys the holiday." The wide-open space outside the window made her tense. Someone could be out there right now watching their every move.

"That's just a few days." Mr. Jefferson checked his watch. "I'd better find Winnie. She starts to worry when people are late."

"I've noticed that."

"Five years ago next week, Thomas was on the way home from work and lost control of his car. It went off the cliff. The sheriff thought he'd fallen asleep at the wheel from reports by witnesses. So anytime someone is late she begins to think the worst." He covered the distance to the door. "I'll meet with Winnie in the lab then come back later with your gun."

"So let me get this straight. You don't want to tell Colt?" Another secret she would have to keep.

Looking back at her, Mr. Jefferson opened the door. "No, not right now."

"Not right now what?" Colt stepped into the entrance of the library.

TWO

Mr. Jefferson waved his hand and passed Colt quickly in the hall. "I'll let Miss St. James tell you."

Ellie balled her hands at her sides. What was she supposed to tell Colt? Even worse, had he overheard anything they had been talking about? She started forward. "I'd better go and change for work."

He gripped her arm, halting her escape. "What aren't you telling me? Why were you and Harold talking in here?"

She schooled her expression into one of innocence. She would love to get her hands on Mr. Jefferson for putting her in this situation. "He wanted to know how my first week went with Winnie. Is there a reason we shouldn't talk? After all, he hired me."

"And how are you doing?" He stepped nearer until Ellie got a whiff of his coffee-laced breath. "Does he know about the gun?"

"Yes. I saw no reason not to tell him." Her heartbeat kicked up a notch. She moved back a few inches until her back encountered the wall behind her. "Your grandmother and I are getting along well. She's a special lady. Very talented. She's easy to talk to. To work for."

"Winnie?"

Hating the trapped feeling, she sidled away. "Who else are we talking about?"

"My grandmother is a private woman. She doesn't share much with anyone."

"I haven't found her that way. Maybe something has changed, since you've been gone for so long." There, she hoped that would keep Colt quiet and less curious about her relationship with Winnie. In some of her past jobs, she'd had to play a role, but it never was her favorite way to operate.

"Then maybe you can fill me in on what's going on with my grandmother."

"What we've talked about is private. If you want to know, go ask her." Before he could stop her again, she pivoted away and hurried down the hall to the foyer.

As she mounted the stairs to the second floor, she felt his eyes on her. It was so cold it reminded her of the icy mountain stream they'd passed on their walk today. Unable to shake loose of his frosty blue gaze, she felt the chill down to her bones.

After dinner that evening Ellie followed the small group to the den, a room with a roaring fire going in the fireplace and the dark rich wood of the mantel polished to a gleaming luster that reflected the lights. She sat on the plush, tan couch before a large glass-topped coffee table. In the middle an arrangement of sweet-smelling roses vied with the fireplace for attention. She'd quickly learned Bloomfield Flower Shop in the medium-size town at the foot of the mountain delivered a fresh bouquet twice weekly because Winnie loved looking at them in the evening. Their delicate aroma wafted up to

Ellie and surrounded her in their fragrance. Since working for Winnie, she'd become attuned to the smell of things. Like breakfast in the morning or a fresh winter day with pine heavy in the air when they were power walking. Winnie always pointed out scents wherever she went.

Colt took a forest-green wingback chair across from her. She caught his glance lingering on her for a few extra seconds while the others settled into their seats. She pulled her gaze away to finish assessing the placement of everyone, along with all the exits. Harold took the other end of the couch she sat on while Winnie eased down between them. Christy Boland, the face of the new line, and her fiancé, Peter Tyler, a Bakersville dentist, occupied the love seat.

"I can't imagine living on a research vessel for months on end," Christy said, taking up the conversation started at the dinner table.

"I have to admit it does take getting used to. It was an opportunity I couldn't pass up. I don't even have a place of my own right now."

"You don't need one. You're always welcome here when you're in the country," Winnie told her grandson. "After all, you've done so much to help me with my new line, especially this last product, which will be the coup d'état."

"How so, Winnie? I don't remember doing that."

"Your research on certain sea life sparked a breakthrough for me on this project."

Colt tilted his head to the side. "Which one?"

Winnie smiled. "I'm not telling. Right now I'm the only one who knows. It's all up here." She tapped the side of her temple. "But this will keep you busy for years, Christy. Harold isn't going to be able to count the money fast enough." Her grin grew. "At least that's what I predict. And all my predictions have been right in the past." She sat back and motioned the servers to bring in dessert.

Linda and Doug Miller, the middle-aged couple who lived on the property and took care of the house, carried in two trays, one with coffee and the other with finger sweets. Doug placed the coffee down in front of Winnie while his wife served the petite desserts to each person in the room.

"I will say I miss your cooking, Linda. No one on the vessel can cook like you." Colt selected four different sweets and put them on a small plate.

By the time the caretakers retreated to the kitchen ten minutes later, everyone had a cup of coffee and dessert.

Colt raised his cup in a toast. "To Christy. Congratulations again on becoming the face of Endless Youth. This is a big change for you from being Winnie's assistant to touring the country, your photo plastered everywhere."

"Yes. I haven't traveled like you have or Winnie. About as far as I've gone was Texas and California when Winnie did."

"That will definitely change, dear," Winnie said after taking a sip of her coffee. "I'm thrilled you agreed to do this. When you tested the product and it did such wonders for you, it became obvious you were perfect for this new job." She slid a glance toward Harold. "Thankfully, Harold found a new assistant for me who is working out great."

All eyes turned to Ellie. Never wanting to be the focus of attention, she pressed herself into the couch until she felt the Glock in its holster digging into her back. Harold had brought the gun when he'd returned for dinner. Having it holstered under her jacket was a constant reminder she was on a job. "I appreciate you helping me, Christy. Answering my hundreds of questions."

Christy laughed. "I wish I had someone to answer my hundreds of questions. I've never been a model and don't know one. Poor Peter has to listen to all my questions."

"And I don't have any answers for her. Actually, she's been gone so much lately that I haven't had to listen to them." Peter covered Christy's hand that lay between them on the love seat. "I'm looking forward to some togetherness at Christmas."

Harold bent forward to pour himself some more coffee. "I just finalized some plans for Christy to start the filming of the first commercial in L.A. next week."

Christy glanced at Peter then Harold. "But I'll be here for Christmas Day, won't I? It'll be our first Christmas together."

"Yes, but since we're launching part of the line in February for Valentine's Day, your time will be very limited."

Peter picked up her hand and moved it to his lap. "We'll work out something," he said to Christy, his adoring look roping her full attention.

As Ellie listened to the conversation shift to the launch of Endless Youth, she decided to call Kyra, her employer, and have her look into everyone around Winnie, including Harold Jefferson, who ran the day-to-day operation of Glamour Sensations as the CFO. She'd learned quickly not to take anything for granted, even the person who hired her.

The threats against Rachel Winfield had started when news of Endless Youth leaked to the press. What was it about that product line that would make some-one angry with Winnie? From what Ellie had learned, the development and testing didn't upset any environ-mental groups. So did Endless Youth have anything to do with the threats or was its development and launch just a coincidence? Maybe it was a rival cosmetic com-pany. Was the industry that cutthroat? Did this involve an industrial spy?

She kneaded her hand along her nape, trying to un-ravel the knots twisting tighter in her neck. Finding the person behind the threats wasn't her priority—keeping Winnie alive and unharmed was. She needed to leave the rest to the police and Harold's P.I.

Colt entered the kitchen that gleamed with clean counters, any evidence of a dinner party gone, but the scent of the roast that Linda had cooked still lingered in the room. The Millers did wonders behind the scenes for Winnie and had worked for the family for ten years. He wasn't sure what his grandmother would do if they decided to look for another job. He didn't worry about Winnie with Linda and Doug taking care of the prop-erty and house.

He raided the refrigerator to make himself a sand-wich with the leftover roast beef. After piling it between slices of Linda's homemade bread, he turned away from the counter ready to take a bite. But he halted abruptly when he noticed Ellie hovering in the entrance, watch-ing him.

She blinked and averted her gaze. "I heard a noise and came to check it out. Winnie just went to bed."

"She stayed up later than usual, but then when Christy and Harold come to dinner, she usually does. That's the extent of her entertaining here."

"I can see that. She spends most of her day in the lab."

"My grandmother is one of the few people in the world who has a 'nose,' as they say in the perfume industry. She can distinguish different scents and has a knack for putting them together to complement each other. That comes easy for her. But this new product line is something else, more Granddad's pet project. I'll be glad when she finishes and doesn't have to work so much."

Ellie came into the room. "She's being taken care of. Linda makes sure she eats healthy. Harold doesn't let her worry about the running of Glamour Sensations, and I do all the little things she has allowed to mount up."

"So she can focus on Endless Youth. I can remember when Granddad was alive. Those two talked about the line back then. He had already started the research. Winnie is just finishing up what they began in earnest eight years ago. I think he pushed her to help her recover from her heart attack. She loves a good challenge." He held up his plate. "I can fix you one."

Her chuckles floated through the air. "I think I'll pass on that. I ate more tonight than I usually do."

He put his sandwich on the kitchen table and gestured at a chair beside him. "Join me. I hate eating alone. When you live on a small ship with fifteen others, you're rarely alone except in your tiny cabin. You would think I would cherish this time."

"You don't?" Ellie slid into the seat next to him.

He noticed she didn't wear any fragrance and wondered if Winnie would change that. "I'm used to it so it's strange when I'm not here. When I've come back here, I've felt the isolation I never felt while I was growing up here."

"Well, it won't feel isolated too much longer. Winnie has several evening events the closer we get to the holidays."

"Let me guess. Most of them have to do with the business."

"Yes, and she is the mistress of ceremony at the lighting of the Christmas tree in Bakersville in a few days. This year the town is naming the park after your grandparents."

"They've been trying to get her to light the Christmas tree for years. I'm glad she finally accepted."

A tiny frown made grooves between Ellie's eyebrows.

"You aren't?" Colt asked.

Her expression evened out. "I'm only concerned she doesn't wear herself out. She has the big gala for Endless Youth and Christy's introduction to the press a few days after that."

"Yeah, she's been trying to get me to stay an extra week."

"I can understand the demands of work."

"Is this job demanding to you? Is the isolation getting to you?"

"I love the isolation. Remember, I grew up in Chicago where everywhere I turned there were people."

"How did you find out about this job?"

Ellie rose. "I think I'll fix a cup of tea. Do you want

any? Herbal, no caffeine." She walked to the cabinet where the tea was kept and withdrew a tin of lavender tea.

"No, thanks." He waited until she put the water on to boil then continued, "Harold said something about him finding you. How? Chicago is a far piece from here."

"Harold knew my former employer. She suggested me for the job."

"She let you go?"

"Not exactly. She knew how much I love the mountains and thought this would be perfect for me."

"What did you do at your former job?"

She laughed. "I feel I'm being interviewed again, but since I already have the job, that isn't it. So why the interest?"

"Because I love Winnie and have her best interest at heart."

Gripping the counter edge with both hands, Ellie lounged back, except that there was nothing casual about her stance. Something wasn't right. Colt lived in close quarters and had learned to read people accurately and quickly. It made his life much easier and calmer.

"What are you hiding, Ellie?"

THREE

"What makes you think I'm hiding something?" Ellie busied herself pouring the hot water into a mug and dunking the tea bag.

"I get the feeling there's something in your past you don't like to talk about. If it wasn't that Harold is thorough when it comes to my grandmother, I would be concerned at your evasiveness."

"But Harold is thorough." She drew herself up straight, cupping her hands around the mug. "I didn't know full disclosure about all the details of my life was necessary for me to get this job. Winnie seems satisfied. Is this something we should bring up to her?" Lifting her chin, she clamped her jaws together to keep from saying anything else that would get her fired.

He dipped his head in a curt nod. "Duly noted. Winnie is a great judge of character."

Meaning he had his doubts? Pain shot down her neck from the tense set of her teeth grinding together. She strode to the table and took the chair across from him. Though she would rather drink her tea in peace, she knew escaping to her bedroom would only confirm that she had something to hide.

One of the reasons she liked being a bodyguard was that she could blend into the background. Most of her clients didn't engage her in casual conversation. But Winnie had been different, and it seemed to run in the family. She kept a lock on her past—a past she didn't want to take out and reexamine. No point in going over it.

"If you must know, the short version of my life so far is—"

"That's okay—"

"I grew up in Chicago," she interrupted, "in a part of town where I had to learn to take care of myself and stick up for my brother, too. People weren't kind to him. He had a mental disability and talked 'funny.' Their word, not mine. When I could get out of the neighborhood, I did." She sipped her tea, gripping the mug tighter to keep her hands steady.

"Where's your brother?"

"Dead." The word hung in the air between them for a long moment while Ellie relived the moment when Toby had slipped away from congestive heart failure.

"I'm sorry. I didn't mean to bring up something painful."

"What did you mean to do, then?"

"To make sure Winnie was in good hands."

She stared into his light, gray-blue eyes. "She's in good hands. When I do a job, I do it one hundred percent."

Another long silence stretched between them as she felt the probe of his gaze, seeking, reading between the lines.

"Did I pass?" She raised her cup and drank, relishing the warm, soothing tea.

"This wasn't a test."

"You could have fooled me." After she scooted back her chair, the scraping sound filling the kitchen, she pushed to her feet. "While I would love to continue this interrogation—I mean conversation—I'm tired and plan to go to bed. Good night."

She left the kitchen. Out in the hallway she paused, a hand braced on the wall as images of her twin brother washed through her mind—running from the neighborhood bullies, falling and scraping his palms and shins, crying because he didn't understand why they didn't like him. But the worst picture was of Toby on the floor of their small, dirty apartment, taking his last breath. He looked straight at her. She held him while they waited for the ambulance. A light brightened his eyes, and a peace she'd never seen fell over his face. Then he went limp as the sirens came down the street. She'd been thirteen.

Tears crowded her eyes. She squeezed them closed. This was why she never dwelled in the past. She did not shed tears—hadn't since she was thirteen.

She slowly crossed to the front door and checked to make sure it was locked and the antiquated security system was on. After Colt went to bed, she would make a more thorough check of the house before she slept. Until then she would prowl her bedroom, hating the situation she'd been placed in. This secrecy handicapped her doing her job.

Standing in the dark, Colt stared out his bedroom window at the yard in front of the house; the outdoor lights illuminated the circular drive. Usually by this time of year there was a lot of snow on the ground, but not so far this winter. Most Christmases as a child, he remembered it being white. This year he'd be in the middle of the Pacific Ocean with blue water as far as he could see. One morning at the beginning of the week, a day after he'd talked to Winnie, a strong urge had overcome him. He needed to see his grandmother if only for a short time. He couldn't shake the feeling all that day. By nighttime he'd made a reservation to fly back to Colorado.

He glanced at his bed. He needed to sleep. Wanted to sleep. But he couldn't. Winnie's new assistant plagued his thoughts. Something didn't fit. First, although she and Winnie seemed to get along great, Ellie wasn't his grandmother's usual type of assistant. Christy had fit the mold well for three years. Accommodating. Almost meek. A follower, not a leader.

But Ellie certainly wasn't meek. He rubbed his ear, recalling her defensive tactic last night. And accommodating? Hardly. He had thought for a minute that she was going to tackle him for her gun. But mostly she wasn't a follower. Although she'd done everything his grandmother had requested of her today, her mannerisms and actions spoke of a woman in command. A woman who wouldn't admit to a vulnerability.

A couple of hours ago, though, he'd seen a crack in her defenses when she'd talked about her childhood, her brother. That was what he couldn't get out of his mind. The glimpse of pain in her eyes he suspected she didn't realize she'd shown. Or maybe she did and couldn't control it because the hurt went so deep.

Staring at the play of light and dark surrounding the front of the house, Colt plowed his fingers through his hair. His skin felt as if he was swimming through a swarm of jellyfish, their tentacles grazing across his arms and legs, their touch sending pain through him.

Something wasn't right. He couldn't shake that feeling, just as he couldn't deny the need to come see Winnie a few days ago.

One of the German shepherds that guarded the property pranced across the drive and disappeared into the dark. Squinting, Colt tried to follow the dog's trek. Something white flashed out of the corner of his eye, so briefly he wasn't sure he'd seen anything. He shoved away from the window and headed for the door. He wasn't sure why. It was probably nothing. One of the guard dogs had white fur.

Still. He wanted to check.

A sound in the foyer caught Ellie's attention. She'd just checked that part of the house. Was Winnie up? Colt? She crept down the hallway toward the front entrance, pulling her gun from the holster under her large sweatshirt. She found Colt crossing the foyer to the exit.

Relieved it was only him, she stuck the borrowed gun back into its holster and entered the entry hall. "Is something wrong?"

With his hand reaching for the doorknob, Colt jerked and pivoted toward her. "What are you doing down here? I thought you went to bed."

"And I thought you did, too."

"I did. Couldn't sleep."

"So you're going for a walk dressed like that? Won't you get cold?" She gestured at his sweatpants, T-shirt and bare feet.

He peered down. "I thought I saw something outside." Taking a few steps toward her, he took in her similar attire except for her bulky sweatshirt to cover her weapon and her tennis shoes, in case she had to give chase. "I'm sure it was nothing now that I think about it. Probably one of the dogs. If anyone had been outside, they would be barking."

Unless they were taken out, she thought, recalling her words to Colt earlier. "Dogs aren't invulnerable."

He paused. "True. I'd better check on it."

"I can. I'm dressed for it."

"Yeah, I noticed your tennis shoes."

She started toward the front door. "I don't have slippers, and I'm not accustomed to the cold."

"But you're from Chicago," Colt said as she passed him.

"We are seven thousand feet up the side of a mountain in December, and, besides, I've never been accustomed to the cold, even being from Chicago." Glancing at the alarm system, she noticed he'd turned it off. She grasped the handle and opened the door. As she stepped out onto the front deck, Colt followed her. "I've got this." *Leave it to a pro.* The urge to say those words was strong, but she bit them back.

"You're kidding. I'm not letting you come out here alone. What if someone is here? Who do you take me for?"

"Someone who only has pants and a T-shirt on and no shoes, not even socks. That's who." She ground her teeth together, wanting to draw her gun as she checked the area out. But he was probably right about it being one of the dogs.

"I'm used to the cold. I'm coming. End of discussion."

Patience. I could use a dose of it, Lord.

"Fine. Stay close behind me."

He chuckled in her ear. "Yeah, sure." Skirting around her, he descended the steps, quickly heading into the wisps of fog snaking along the ground.

Where's a stun gun when I need one? Ellie hurried after Colt who moved quickly from the cold concrete drive to the warmer lawn. "Wait up."

He didn't slow his pace, but she caught up with him about ten yards from the house. When she glanced back and spied the unprotected place, lit with security lights, she clamped her hand around his arm.

He halted, his face unreadable in the shadows.

"Go back and make sure no one goes into the house. I'll finish checking out here." Her fingers itched to draw her gun, but Mr. Jefferson didn't want Colt to know why she was here.

"And leave you alone? This is my home, not yours. What kind of man would I be?"

"A smart one. What about leaving your grandmother alone?"

"Then you should go back and—"

Barking blasted the chilled air.

Ellie withdrew the Glock from its holster and started toward the sound to the left.

"Where did that come from?" Colt asked.

"Mr. Jefferson."

"Harold?"

"I'll explain later. Go back to the house, lock the door and don't let anyone in until I check out what caused the dog to bark. Do not follow me."

"Who are you?"

No more secrets—at least with Winnie's grandson. "A bodyguard hired to protect Winnie." She glanced over her shoulder to make sure no one was trying to get into the front of the house. "Go. Now."

In the cover of night that surrounded them, he stared at her, or at least she felt the drill of his gaze, then he whirled around and rushed back toward the deck. She moved toward where the sound had come from, retrieving her small pocket flashlight in case she needed it. Right now she let the half-moon and security lamps by the house light her path since it would be better if she didn't announce her approach if someone was inside the fence.

In the distance she heard the cry of a mountain lion. She'd seen evidence of a big cat on one of her daily power walks with Winnie. Was that what spooked the dog? She'd gone into enough situations with incomplete intel to know the heightened danger that could cause.

Her heart rate kicked up a notch as she drew closer to the perimeter on the west side of the house where the eight-foot chain-link fence was. Another roar split the air. Closer. The sound pumped more adrenaline through her body. Every nerve alert, she became hyperaware of her surroundings—a bird flying away to the right, the breeze rustling the evergreen foliage.

Away from the house the only illumination was the faint rays of the moon. Not enough. She switched on her flashlight and swept it across the area before her. Just outside a cut part of the fence, its glow fell upon the mountain lion, its big eyes glittering yellow in the dark. Her light captured the predator's menacing stance.

The rumble of a mountain lion nearby froze Colt as he mounted the last step to the front deck. He knew that sound from the many years he had lived here. He didn't know who Ellie St. James really was, how capable she was or why she would be protecting his grandmother, but he couldn't leave her out there to face a solitary predator by herself. No matter what she ordered him to do.

He rushed into the house to a storage closet where Winnie kept some of his possessions. He used to have a hunting rifle. Wrenching the door open, he clicked on the overhead light and stared at the mountain of boxes that he had stored there. He delved into the midst of the containers filled with his memories. Where was the gun?

Panic urged him deeper into the large, walk-in closet to the shelving in the back. There he saw something he could use. Not the rifle but a speargun, a weapon he was even more familiar with and actually quite good at using.

He snatched it up and raced toward the foyer, grabbing a flashlight on the way. Before leaving, he set the alarm, then locked the front door behind him. Another growl announced to anyone around that this was the big cat's territory and not to trespass.

As Colt ran toward the west side of the property, he hoped there weren't any trees the mountain lion could climb that allowed him access to the area inside the fence. Usually the eight-foot barrier kept dangerous animals out, but it had certainly sounded like it was close to the house, possibly inside the fence.

Then a yell pierced the night. "Get back. Get away."

Those words from Ellie prodded him even faster.

Ellie never took her eyes off the mountain lion. It was still on the other side of the fence with his head sticking through the part that had been cut and peeled back to allow something big—like a man—through the opening. She waved her arms around. She didn't want to shoot the animal because it was a beautiful creature. But she would if she had to.

Its snarls protested her order to leave.

Still it didn't move back. Its golden gaze seemed to assess its chances of leaping the four or five yards' distance between them.

Bracing herself, Ellie lifted her gun and shone her flashlight into its eyes. It continued to stare at her.

Behind her she heard something rushing toward her. Another mountain lion? But they were solitary animals that guarded their territory. One of the dogs? The one that had barked earlier? Where were the other two?

She was calculating her chances with the mountain lion, then the new threat, when she heard a war cry, a bloodcurdling sound. The mountain lion shifted its golden regard to her right for a few seconds, then stepped back out of the hole and sauntered away as though out for an evening stroll. Some of the tension siphoned from her.

She threw a glance over her shoulder and saw a light in the dark moving her way. Colt. An intruder wouldn't announce his presence with a flashlight or a war cry.

She spun around and started for him. "What are you doing? You were supposed to stay at the house." Her light found him in the night, carrying a speargun. "*This time* you need to stay here and guard this hole. I need to make sure Winnie is okay."

When she passed him, he clasped her arm and halted her progress. "Hold it. Winnie is fine. I set the alarm and locked the door. What's going on?"

She stared at his hand until he dropped his arm to his side. "Did you check on her?"

"Well, no. But we never went far from the house."

"I'm going to check on her, then I'll be back. Will you stay here and make sure the mountain lion doesn't come back? And this time stay where you're supposed to be. I could have shot you." She peered at his speargun. "A bit odd to be carrying around on dry land, but it should stop the cat if it returns. That is, if you can use it."

He pulled himself up straight. "I'm quite good with this. And it's very effective if you know what you're doing. Which I do." Each word was spoken with steely confidence.

"Good." She hurried away, at the moment her concern for Winnie's safety paramount.

What if this was all a diversion? What if someone got into the house when they weren't looking? Different scenarios bombarded her. All she knew was she had to lay eyes on Winnie to be reassured she was all right.

She unlocked the front door and immediately headed for the alarm to put in the code. Then she took the stairs two at a time. When she saw Winnie's door open, she finally breathed.

A strong scent of urine—probably the big cat's—pervaded the air as Colt neared the gap in the fence. He stuffed the flashlight through a chain-link hole, and its glow shone into the wooded area outside of Winnie's property. After leaning the speargun against the fence within his quick reach, he pulled the snipped sides back into place, enough that he hoped would discourage the mountain lion from plowing its way inside.

Then he examined the ground.

Footprints were barely visible on the dry ground, but about five or six feet away, tire impressions in the dead weeds and grass were clearer. Someone had pulled a vehicle up to the fence.

He swung around and swept his flashlight around his grandmother's property and then it hit him: Where were the dogs? Why weren't they over here?

Ellie entered Winnie's bedroom, her gun drawn but at her side in case the older woman was in the room unaware of what was transpiring outside. She didn't want to frighten her with a gun being waved in the air—not two nights in a row. Halting a few feet inside, Ellie stared at the messy covers spilling over onto the floor, the empty bed. As she raised her weapon, she circled the room, checking for her client. After opening the bathroom door, she noted the spacious area was empty.

As much as she would like to rush back outside and search the grounds for Winnie or any clue to her whereabouts, she had to check the house first.

As she started with the room next to Winnie's, prayers for the woman's safety flooded her thoughts. When she reached Colt's bedroom, she hesitated, feeling awkward to intrude on his privacy. But she had a job to do. She pushed open the door and looked inside.

This is ridiculous. If the man had followed her orders, she wouldn't have to do this right now. She stepped inside and made a quick tour—noting his duffel bag on a chair, his shoes on the floor, keys and some change on the dresser, pictures on the wall from when he was young.

A picture of him coming out of the darkness with a speargun in his hand crowded into her thoughts. She shook the image from her mind and turned to leave.

"What are you doing in my grandson's room with a gun in your hand?"

FOUR

"I was looking for you," Ellie said, putting the gun out of sight of Winnie in the doorway. "Someone has cut the fence and the guard dogs can't be found. I wanted to make sure you were all right." After picking up Colt's tennis shoes off the floor, she moved toward the exit.

"Where's my grandson? What are you doing with those shoes?" Winnie blocked her path.

"I'll explain everything after I call the sheriff and make sure Colt is okay. He's guarding the hole, making sure the mountain lion doesn't return. He's barefoot."

"The sheriff? A mountain lion? Colt barefoot in this weather? What in the world is going on?" What wrinkles Winnie had on her face deepened as she stepped to the side to allow Ellie to leave the room.

Ellie hurried toward the stairs, fishing for her cell in her pocket. At the top she paused and glanced at the older woman. "I'm going to set the alarm. Please stay inside."

Winnie opened her mouth but snapped it closed before saying anything.

Ellie rushed down the stairs while placing a call to the sheriff's office outside Bakersville. After reporting what happened, she hit the buttons on the keypad to set the alarm and hastened outside.

The crisp night air burrowed through the sweatshirt, chilling her. The thought of Colt without shoes spurred her faster toward the fence line. When she arrived, he stood by the hole he'd partially closed, holding his spear gun while hugging his arms against his chest.

"I thought you could use these." She thrust his shoes at him, then shined her flashlight on the area beyond the fence.

"Thanks. I will never again leave the house in winter without my shoes on."

"Why did you?" She examined the set of tire tracks and boot prints, wishing it wasn't so dark.

"To protect you."

"Someone needs to protect you from yourself."

"You can't deny I helped you. Someone needed to guard this hole. Since you're back out here, I'm assuming Winnie is all right."

"Yes, and I called the sheriff's office." Ellie backed away, realizing there was nothing she could do until morning other than talk with the deputy who was on the way up the mountain. She had half a mind to call Harold Jefferson and wake him up with the news, but she would wait and give him a full report first thing in the morning. "Do you think there's anything at the house I can use to finish closing the bottom of this hole?"

"How about rope?" Colt started for his childhood home.

"That'll do." Ellie followed him. "I'm sure the mountain lion is long gone with all this activity, but I'll feel better when we have the hole completely closed."

"You don't think the person who cut the fence is inside here?"

"Probably not. Maybe the mountain lion scared him off or maybe his intent was to take the guard dogs. He could have tranquilized them. The ground looked like something was dragged toward the car."

"Why hurt the dogs?"

"It would take a while to get trained guard dogs to replace them. Maybe it was to scare Winnie like the threatening letters. When I find him, I'll ask him."

"When *you* find him? And what threatening letters?"

She reminded herself going after the person who was trying to harm Winnie wasn't her job. "I mean when the police find him, they'll ask him."

Colt unlocked the front door and hurried to the keypad to turn off the security system. Winnie sat on the third step on the staircase, her face tensed into a frown. She didn't move when both Colt and Ellie turned toward her.

"I need to check the house then I'll explain what's going on." She peered at Colt. "Would you stay here with your grandmother?"

He held up the speargun. "Yes. But the security system was on the whole time."

"This one can be circumvented quite easily if you know what you're doing. We have to assume whoever is after Winnie knows what he's doing," Ellie said in a low voice.

Winnie pushed to her feet. "Someone's after me? Who?"

Colt took a step toward his grandmother, glancing at Ellie. "I'll take care of her. Do what you need to do."

"What is going on, young man?" Winnie asked as Ellie hastened her exit.

As she went from room to room, she heard Colt trying to explain when he really didn't know much other than what she had told him. From her responses, Winnie was clearly not happy. Ellie decided not to wait until morning to call Harold.

"What's wrong?" the chief financial officer of Glamour Sensations asked the second he answered his phone.

After she explained what happened with the dogs and the fence, she said, "Not only does Colt know, but so does Winnie. I've called the sheriff's office, and one of the deputies is on his way."

"I'm calling Sheriff Quinn. Knowing him, he'll come, too. He lives halfway between Winnie's and Bakersville. It won't take him long to get there. I'll be there as fast as I can."

"You don't need to until tomorrow morning. After the sheriff leaves, I hope to get Winnie to go back to bed." She didn't want a three-ring circus at the house with so many people coming and going. That could be hard to secure.

"She won't do that. Maybe I should call her doctor, too."

"She seems okay." Ellie looked through the dining room into the living room where Colt had taken his grandmother. "She's sitting on the couch, listening to Colt."

"Fine. I won't call the doctor, but I'll be there soon."

Ellie pocketed her cell and made her way to the pair in the living room. "The house is clear."

Winnie shifted on the couch until her glare zeroed in on Ellie. "Who are you?"

"I told her you're here to protect her. That Harold hired you. But I don't know much more than that." Colt finally sat in the chair across from his grandmother.

With a sigh, Ellie sank onto the couch at the other end from Winnie. "I work for Guardians, Inc. It's a security company out of Dallas, staffed with female bodyguards. Mr. Jefferson came to my employer about his concerns that someone was threatening you. You have been receiving notes for the past six weeks, each one more threatening. He finally knew he had to do something when one included a photo of you on your power walk, dressed in what he discovered you'd worn the day before."

"Why didn't he come to me?" Winnie's mouth pinched into a frown.

"He's on his way, and he can answer that. I believe he thought it might interrupt your creative process and since the deadline is looming, he—"

"So that man kept it from me." Winnie surged to her feet. "I am not fragile like everyone thinks. Goodness me, I've been through enough and survived. That ought to give you all a hint at how tough I can be." She pivoted toward Ellie. "Is that why he neglected to tell me my new assistant was really a bodyguard?"

Ellie nodded. "I prefer full disclosure, but he was afraid of how—"

Winnie waved her quiet. "I know. I will take care of Harold. He promised my husband he would watch out for me, and he's taking his job way too seriously."

"Winnie, I don't know that he is." Colt leaned forward, clasping his hands and resting his elbows on his thighs. "Someone did cut the fence and the dogs are missing. Not one of them came up to us while we were outside. They always do."

Winnie blanched and eased down onto the couch. "So you really think there's a threat?" She looked from Colt to Ellie.

"Yes, especially after tonight." Ellie rose at the sound of the doorbell. "I'll get it."

She let the deputy and sheriff into the house. "I'm Ellie St. James. I was hired by Harold Jefferson to protect Mrs. Winfield."

Sheriff Quinn shook her hand. "Harold called me and told me. I understand the Bakersville police chief is looking into the matter of the threatening letters."

"Yes. I believe the person has upped his game. I haven't had a chance to search the whole property outside, but I feel the dogs have been taken. I did search the house and it's secured."

The sheriff turned to his deputy and said, "Take a look outside. Miss St. James, which part of the fence was cut?"

"The west side about halfway down."

"Let me know, Rod, when you're through checking the premises and the doghouse." Then to her, the sheriff asked, "Where's Winnie?"

"In the living room."

When the sheriff entered, Winnie smiled. "I'm so glad you're here, Bill. Did Ellie tell you what went on tonight?"

"Harold filled me in. It's a good thing Miss St. James and your grandson were here." The sheriff nodded toward Colt. "You couldn't have picked a better time to be home."

Winnie blew out an exasperated breath. "It would

have been even better if they had clued me in on what was going on. Goodness, Bill, I've been out power walking. The man took a picture of me while I was."

"Maybe with all that has happened you should curtail that for the time being. It's gonna snow this weekend if the weather reports are correct." Sheriff Quinn sat on the couch where Ellie had been.

She assessed the law enforcement officer. He was probably in his early fifties but looked to be in excellent physical condition, well proportioned for his medium height with none of the potbelly she'd seen on others as they grew older and less active. She'd worked with her share of good ones and bad ones. From all of Harold's accounts, the sheriff fit into the good category. She hoped so because tonight the person after Winnie had stepped up his game.

She filled him in on what she'd seen outside. "Someone pulled a vehicle up to the fence recently. It rained hard a couple of days ago. The tracks could have been left maybe up to a day before, but they aren't deep enough for any longer than that. But I'm pretty sure it was this evening. We walk the perimeter every morning, and I haven't seen any evidence on the other side of the fence like what is there now. Also there are drag marks and a few paw prints beside those left by the mountain lion."

"So you think the tracks were made this evening?"

"Yes, Sheriff. That's the way it looks, but in the light of day we—you—might find more."

He smiled. "I'll take a look now. I've got a high-powered flashlight. I'll see where the tire tracks lead. The west side of the fence isn't the closest to the road out front."

"But it's the most isolated," Colt interjected.

Sheriff Quinn headed for the foyer. "When he gets back I'm gonna leave Rod here. I'd like you to come with me, Miss St. James."

"Would you mind, Winnie?" Ellie asked her client, eager to go with the sheriff.

"No, go. I'll be well protected with Colt and the deputy."

As Ellie left, Colt told Winnie that he'd escort her to her bedroom. Ellie chuckled when the woman said, "Not on your life. I want to know what they find out there."

The doorbell sounded again while Ellie crossed the foyer. She'd relocked the door after the deputy had left. When she answered it, Harold stood there with the young officer.

He charged inside, slowing down only long enough to ask, "Where is she?"

"In the living room."

While he went to Winnie, the deputy came into the house. "I couldn't find any signs of the dogs. They're gone, Sheriff."

Quinn grumbled, his frown deepening. "Rod, stay with Mrs. Winfield." To Ellie, he said, "I don't like this. They were excellent, well-trained guard dogs."

"Yeah, that was the only part of the security here I liked." Ellie went ahead of the man onto the front deck.

"And possibly the only threat the person behind the letters needed to get rid of."

"Maybe. Something doesn't feel right."

"Any thoughts on what?"

"No. Just a vague feeling we're missing something." Ellie slipped into the sheriff's car.

As he drove to the road then toward the west part of

the property, he said, "Harold told me the Bakersville police chief is looking into past employees. I can't believe one of them would be this angry with Winnie. She's the reason Bakersville is so prosperous. People around here love her."

"Someone doesn't. Maybe they aren't from around here. Maybe it's something we haven't thought about yet. Harold is having a private investigator look into Glamour Sensations' competition."

"Corporate sabotage?"

"It's a possibility. Winnie is the creative force behind the new line. From what I hear Endless Youth will change the playing field. It's not unheard of that a competitor will try to stop a product launch or beat a company to unveiling their own similar product."

"Mr. Winfield was the guy who talked me into running for sheriff twenty years ago. The best move I ever made. I owe the Winfield family a lot." He eased off the road and parked on the shoulder, directing a spotlight from his car toward the area where someone had driven off the highway and over the terrain toward the back of Winnie's property. "We'll go on foot from here."

Following the tire tracks led to the hole in the fence. Ellie knelt near the place where she'd seen the mountain lion's prints as well as smaller dog prints. No sign of blood or a struggle. When she had shined the light on the big cat earlier, she hadn't seen any evidence it had killed a dog. And she hadn't heard any noise to suggest that. So it meant the dogs had been taken recently by whoever drove the vehicle.

"These tire tracks look like they're from a truck or SUV. I'll have a cast made of them and see if we can narrow down the vehicle." The sheriff swung his high-powered light on the surrounding terrain. "These boot prints might help, too."

"It looks like about a size nine in men's shoes."

"Small man."

"Or a woman with large feet."

Ellie rose and searched the trees and brush. With some of the foliage gone because it was winter, she had a decent view. "No sign the dogs went that way."

"It doesn't look like it, but in the light of day we'll have better visibility and may find something. At the moment, though, I think the dogs were stolen. They're valuable. Maybe someone has kidnapped them."

"I don't think so. This is tied to the threats against Winnie somehow." Ellie ran her flashlight along the ground by the fence and caught sight of something neon green. She stooped and investigated closer. "Sheriff, I found something partially under this limb. I think it's from a dart gun. It would explain how he subdued the dogs so quickly."

The sheriff withdrew a small paper bag and gloves, then carefully picked up the long black dart with a sharp tip and a neon green cap on the opposite end. "Yup. I'll send this to the lab and see if there are any fingerprints on it. Hopefully they can tell us what was in the dart— poison or a knockout drug."

"At least there are a few pieces of evidence that might give you a lead."

As they walked back to the sheriff's car, Ellie kept sweeping her flashlight over the ground while Quinn scoured the terrain.

When he climbed into his patrol car, he said, "I have a friend who can repair the chain-link fence. I'll have him out here first thing in the morning. You don't want the return of the mountain lion."

"I'll be talking to Winnie and Harold about electrifying the fence and setting up a system to monitor the perimeter. If it hadn't been for the dogs, we might not have known about the hole in the fence for a while. That area is hidden by thick foliage from the house. We might not have seen it on our power walk in the morning, either."

"Yeah, she's definitely gonna have to beef up her security. She's been fortunate not to have problems in the past." As the sheriff returned to park in front of the main house, lights blazed from it. He chuckled. "She must have gone through and turned a light on in every downstairs room."

"I can't blame her. She all of a sudden realizes someone is after her."

Colt watched his grandmother as Harold explained his reasons for not letting her know what was going on with the letters. After he saw to Winnie, he was going to have a few words with Ellie and Harold. He should have been contacted right away when his grandmother first was threatened.

"The bottom line, Winnie, is that I didn't want you to worry about it when you have enough to deal with," Harold said.

Colt nearly laughed and pressed his lips together to keep from doing that. Harold was pulling out all the stops to persuade his grandmother not to be angry with him.

Her back stiff as a snowboard, Winnie narrowed her gaze on Harold, her hands clasped so tightly in her lap the tips of her fingers reddened. "I'm not a child, and you'd better remember that from now on, or no matter how long we have worked together, you'll be fired."

Harold swallowed hard. "My intentions were to protect you without worrying you. I have the police chief in Bakersville and a private investigator working on finding the person behind the letters."

"So you would never have told me if this hadn't happened. Was that your plan?"

Harold dropped his gaze to a spot on the carpet at his feet. Finally he nodded.

"I have to be able to trust you to inform me of *everything* that goes on at Glamour Sensations. Now I don't know if I can. What else are you keeping from me?" She lifted her chin and glared at her longtime friend.

Harold held up his hands, palms outward. "Nothing. But, Winnie, I promised Thomas I would look after you."

"I can look after myself. I have been for seventy-three years." Her rigid shoulders sagged a little.

Colt rose. "Winnie, let me escort you upstairs. We can hash this all out tomorrow."

She turned her glare on him. "Don't you start, young man. I don't need to be mollycoddled by you, too. I'll go to bed when I want to."

Harold interjected, "But you're starting the final tests tomorrow and—"

She swiveled her attention to him. "Losing a little sleep won't stop me from doing that. I'm not the fragile person you think I am. I want to hear what Sheriff Quinn has to say about the situation before I retire for the night. Or I wouldn't sleep a wink."

Colt heard the deputy greeting someone in the foyer. "I think they've returned."

Not five seconds later Ellie and Quinn came into the living room. Colt couldn't read much into Ellie's bland expression, but the sheriff's indicated there were problems, which didn't surprise him given what had happened an hour ago.

Sheriff Quinn stood at the end of the coffee table and directed his attention to Winnie. "Your guard dogs were drugged and stolen. We found a dart they used and tire tracks where they came off the main road, probably in a good-size four-wheel drive. Can't tell if it was a truck or SUV yet. A cast of the tire tracks might narrow it down for us."

Colt's gaze latched onto Ellie. She focused on Winnie, too, except for a few seconds when she slid her attention to him. But her unreadable expression hadn't changed. He saw her military training in her bearing and the way she conducted herself. Ellie had certainly performed capably tonight, but what if the person after Winnie upped his tactics to more lethal ones?

When the sheriff finished his report, Winnie shook his hand. "Thank you, Sheriff Quinn. As usual you have done a thorough job. I want to be informed of any progress." She shifted toward Harold. "I want the Bakersville police chief and the private investigator you hired to be told that, too. No more secrets. Understood?" Her sizzling stare bore into the man.

Harold squirmed on the couch but locked stares with Winnie. "Yes, on one condition."

"You aren't in a place to dictate conditions to me. For several weeks you have kept me in the dark about something that concerned me. Don't push me, Harold Jefferson."

The color leaked from Harold's face. "I won't," he bit out, his teeth snapping closed on the last word.

"Good, I'm glad we understand each other now. That goes for you, too, Ellie and Colt. Also, I don't want this common knowledge, and I certainly don't want anyone to know that Ellie is a bodyguard. She is my assistant."

"Agreed," Harold said quickly. "Sheriff, can you keep this quiet?"

"Yes. All my deputies need to know is that someone took your dogs. Nothing about the reason or who you are, Miss St. James. We'll play this down."

"I appreciate that. I don't want a media circus until I'm ready to unveil my new line, and then I want the focus on Endless Youth, not me."

The sheriff nodded toward Winnie. "We'll be leaving. I'm going to post Rod outside your house."

"You don't have to do that. I have the very capable Miss St. James." Winnie winked at Ellie.

"Humor me, ma'am, at least for tonight."

"Fine."

Colt hid his smile by lowering his head. His grandmother would have her way in the end. The deputy would be gone by the morning, but Colt planned to have some other security measures in place by tomorrow evening.

Harold stood. "I'll show you out, Sheriff, and give you the name of my P.I. working on the case."

"I'm sorry that Harold put you in the position he did. He told me you wanted to inform me from the first. We'll proceed as usual, but my grandson will return your gun. I don't like weapons, so I'll ask you to keep it out of view." His grandmother struggled to her feet.

Colt rose quickly but didn't move toward Winnie.

She would rebuke his offer to help, especially when he had made it obvious that he considered her fragile. In her mind she equated that to weak. His grandmother was anything but that. After all these years, Harold really didn't understand Winnie like Colt's grandfather had. If Harold had come to him, he would have told him his grandmother could handle anything.

He started toward the door when Winnie did.

She peered back at him. "Don't you buy into Harold's thinking I'm fragile. I hate that word. I am not going to break. Endless Youth was Thomas's project. I will complete it. I can find my own way to my bedroom. I have been doing that for years now."

Colt stopped and looked toward Ellie. Her mouth formed a thin line, but her eyes danced with merriment.

When Winnie left the room, Ellie took a seat on the couch. "I think she told you."

"It wasn't as bad as Harold got. He mismanaged this situation. All because he's in love with Winnie and doesn't really know her like he should."

"That's sad."

"I have a feeling my grandfather knew Harold has been in love with Winnie since the early days. That's why he asked Harold to watch out for her. He knew he would. But Harold envisions himself as her knight in shining armor coming to her rescue. My grandmother is not a damsel in distress."

"What happened when your grandfather died?"

"She did fall apart. She'd nursed him back to health after his bout with cancer and was planning a month long vacation with him when he fell asleep behind the wheel and went off the mountain. For a short time, I saw her faith shattered. I was worried, but Harold was frantic and beside himself. He went into protective mode and hasn't let up since then."

Hearing footsteps nearing the doorway, Colt put his finger to his lips.

Harold came through the entrance, kneading his neck. "Winnie didn't even say good-night when she went upstairs. She really is mad at me."

"I'm afraid so." Colt waved his hand at the bouquet of flowers on the coffee table. "She isn't delicate like these roses. As soon as you accept that, you might have a chance with Winnie."

"A chance?" Harold opened his mouth to say more but clamped it shut.

Colt grinned. "Just so you know it, you have my blessing to court my grandmother. I've known for a long time how you felt about her, and once this line is out, she deserves something more than working all the time. She's been driving herself for the past few years."

"What makes you think…" Harold's fingers delved into his neat hairstyle, totally messing it up.

"Because I see how you look at her when she isn't looking."

Harold's face flushed a deep shade of red. "She thinks I'm too young for her."

"You're sixty-five. That's not too young." Colt settled into his chair again. "Sit. We need to talk about securing the house and grounds."

"You stole my line," Ellie said as she angled toward Harold at the other end of the couch. "You need to electrify the fence, put in a new security system *tomorrow* and, since she doesn't want people to know what is going on, at least replace the guard dogs. That may be the biggest challenge. They need to be here with a handler right away."

Colt spoke up. "I have a high school friend who trains dogs. I'll give Adam a call tomorrow. If he has a dog for us, he only lives in Denver so he should be able to help us right away." He leaned back, trying to relax his body after the tense-filled past hour.

"This place needs a minimum of two dogs. Three would be better." Ellie looked at Harold. "How about the security system? The one in place is old and can be circumvented."

"I'll have someone here tomorrow. With the right kind of monetary incentive, I'm sure they could start right away. Maybe tomorrow afternoon. They probably could take care of the fence, too." Harold glanced toward the entrance into the living room. "Do you think Winnie will forgive my judgment call on this?"

"Her faith is strong, and she believes in forgiveness. I wouldn't be surprised if she isn't fretting right now about who she has angered enough to do this to her. Knowing her, she'll be praying for that person, whereas I would like to get hold of him and…" Colt let his words fade into silence, curling and uncurling his fists.

They didn't need to know he struggled with forgiving someone who had wronged him. He still couldn't forgive his father for all but abandoning him and going his merry way, living it up as if he didn't have a son and responsibilities. Winnie forgave his dad a long time ago, but after his mother had died, Colt had needed his only parent, and he hadn't been there for him.

"Well," Harold said, slapping his hand on the arm of the couch and pushing up, "I'd better be going. We all have a lot to do tomorrow."

"I'll walk you to the door and lock up after you leave," Ellie said, trailing after him.

Quiet settled around Colt like a blanket of snow over the landscape. Resting his head on the back cushion, he relished the silence, realizing this was what he needed after months on a small ship with cramped quarters. As thoughts of his job weaved through his mind, he knew he had to make a decision. Stay until Winnie was safe or leave and let others protect his grandmother. There wasn't really a decision, not where Winnie was concerned.

A movement out of the corner of his eye seized his attention. Ellie paused in the entrance, leaning her shoulder against the doorjamb. "Have you warmed up yet?"

"Finally I've thawed out. I may be used to living here in the winter, but remind me never to go outside in winter without shoes."

"You seemed lost in thought. I want to assure you I will do everything to protect Winnie. In the short time I've gotten to know her, I see what a special lady she is." She crossed the room and took her seat again across from him.

"We probably should follow Harold's example and get some rest, but I'm so wired right now with all that's happened."

"I know what you mean. Your adrenaline shoots up and it takes a while to come down. But when it does, you'll fall into bed."

"I imagine with your job you've had quite a lot of experience with that. I can't say I have."

"One of the fringe benefits of being a bodyguard."

He laughed. "Never looked at it like that. How long have you been a bodyguard?"

"Three years. I started after I left the army."

"What did you do in the military?"

"For the last few years of my service I was in army intelligence."

"So that's where you learned your skills."

"Yes, it comes naturally to me now. Sometimes I only had myself to rely on when I was working alone in an isolated situation."

"Which I'm sure is classified top secret."

Her brown eyes lit with a gleam. "You know the cliché. If I told you, I'd have to kill you."

"I'm curious but not that curious. What made you go from army intelligence to being a bodyguard?" She intrigued him. It wasn't every day he met a woman who protected people for a living.

She shrugged. "It was my time to re-up, and I thought I would try something different. I had a friend who put me in touch with my employer. When I met Kyra, I knew this was what I wanted to do. I like protecting people who need it. I like the challenge in security."

"Why not police work?"

"I like to go different places. Kinda like you. I have a feeling you've seen a lot of the world through your work."

"Yes, and I've enjoyed it, but I've been on a ship a large part of that time."

"Tired of life on a boat?"

Am I? He hadn't stopped long enough to think about it. "The past few years have been hectic but fulfilling. I've learned a lot about sea life aboard the *Kaleidoscope*. But if Winnie had her way, she'd want me to use my knowledge for Glamour Sensations. She tells me I've inherited her nose."

Ellie studied that part of his face and frowned. "I think you look more like your grandfather." She gestured toward the portrait over the mantel.

"But I have her supersensitive smelling ability," he said with a chuckle. "Every time I come home, I get the spiel about taking over the family business. But if she goes public, it won't be a family business anymore."

"How do you feel about that?"

"I don't know. It's good for the company, but it means we'll be in the big leagues and I don't know how Winnie will really like that. This is Harold's plan, and I understand why he is pushing to go public. The Endless Youth line will take us in a different direction. The expansion of the company will be good for this area."

Ellie tilted her head and smiled. "Do you realize you keep saying 'us' as though you are part of the company?"

"You'd make a good detective. Did you get your interview skills in the army?"

"I owe the army a lot, but I think I've always been nosy. It got me into trouble from time to time when I was growing up."

Colt yawned, the earlier adrenaline rush completely gone. "I guess that's my cue to get some sleep. Jet lag has definitely set in."

Ellie rose. "You've had two very hectic nights since you got here. This wasn't probably what you were expecting."

As he covered the distance to the foyer, he stifled another yawn before she thought it was her company. Because that was the furthest from the truth. If he wasn't so exhausted from months of nonstop work and traveling over a day to get home, he could spend hours trying to get to know Ellie St. James. And he had a feeling he wouldn't even begin to understand the woman.

He started up the stairs and she continued walking toward the dining room and kitchen area. "You're not coming upstairs?"

She peered back over her shoulder. "Not until I've checked the house again and made sure we're locked up as tight as we can be."

He rotated toward her. "Do you need company?"

Her chuckle peppered the air. "I've been doing this for a long time. It's second nature. Always know the terrain around you. In this case, this house. If I have to move around it in the dark, I need to know the layout."

"I never thought about that. I'm glad Winnie has you. See you bright and early tomorrow."

"Good night."

The smile that curved her lips zapped him. He mounted the stairs with that picture etched into his mind. He had grown up in this house. Could he move around it if the power went off and not run into every piece of furniture? Her skill set was very different from his. He could leave and be assured Winnie was in good hands.

That conclusion didn't set well with him. It niggled him as he got into bed, and it stayed with him all night.

After securing the house, Ellie ascended to the second floor. Walking toward her bedroom, she paused outside Winnie's room and pressed her ear against the door. Silence greeted her. She continued to hers two doors down. She couldn't shake the feeling they were vulnerable even with the deputy outside.

She immediately crossed the window that overlooked the front of the property. She studied the parked patrol car, glimpsing the man sitting in the front seat. She didn't leave her welfare or a client's to others. She hadn't vetted the deputy. She didn't even know him.

That thought clinched her decision. She went to her bed and gathered up a blanket and pillow then headed for the hallway. Outside Winnie's room, she spread her armload out on the floor then settled down for the night, fitting her gun close to her. This accommodation was four-star compared to some she'd had in the army.

She was a light sleeper, and anyone who wanted Winnie would have to go over her to get her client. She fell asleep with that knowledge.

Only to have someone jostle her shoulder hours later.

She gripped her gun. Her eyes inched open to find Colt stooping over her.

He leaned toward her ear and whispered, "I don't want to disturb Winnie, but Rod is gone. He's not in the car and hasn't been for a while now."

FIVE

Ellie was already on her feet, slipping on her shoes as she moved toward the stairs. "Stay here. It might be nothing but stretching his legs."

As she crept down the steps, avoiding the ones that creaked, only the light from the hallway illuminating her path, her eyes began to adjust to the darkness swallowing her at the bottom of the staircase. She saw the red glow on the security keypad across from her.

Before going outside to search for the deputy, she crept through the rooms on the first floor, using the moonlight streaming through the upper part of the windows that weren't draped. When she reached the kitchen, she had to switch on a light to inspect the area and check the back door.

When she returned to the foyer, she flipped on the light and punched the alarm off then went to the bottom of the steps. "Colt."

He appeared at the railing overlooking the foyer.

"I'm going outside and resetting the alarm. Don't leave there."

"You shouldn't go by yourself."

"I need you to stay there. Don't follow me. Understand?"

He nodded, but his jaw clamped in a hard line.

Ellie set the alarm, hurried toward the front door and slipped outside. She examined the patrol car, still empty. Rod's hat sat on the passenger's seat. That was the only evidence the man had been in the vehicle.

For the second time that night she made her way toward the west side of the property. Had the mountain lion returned and somehow got inside the fence? Earlier they had patched it the best they could. Now she noticed the rope they had tied across the opening had been cut and the fence had been parted again. Alert, she inspected the blackness beyond the property. Her eyes were fully adjusted to the dark, but a good pair of night-vision goggles would have been preferable. She swung around slowly, searching every tree and bush.

Something big lay on the ground near a group of firs. She snuck toward it. The closer she came the more sure she was that it was a body. From the size, probably a man. The body lay still, curled on his side, his face away from her. Was it the deputy? Was he dead?

Removing her small flashlight from her pocket, she increased her pace as well as her alertness in case this was a trap. Someone had cut those ropes.

The person on the ground groaned and rolled over. He tried to sit up and collapsed back. Another moan escaped him as Ellie reached his side.

"Rod? Are you okay?"

"Someone…hit me over the head." He lifted his hand to his hair and yelped when he touched his scalp. Blood covered his fingers.

"Why were you out here?"

"I heard something. I came to see what it was and found one of the dogs lying under the thick brush." He pointed beneath some large holly bushes. "The next thing I knew, I was hit and going down." He struggled to sit up.

Ellie helped him. "Take it easy. I'm phoning this in."

After she placed a call to the sheriff's office, Rod asked, "Is the dog gone?"

Using her small flashlight, Ellie inspected the bushes. "There's no dog here."

"There was a while ago. Its whimpering is what drew me."

"Whoever hit you must have taken the dog. The ropes on the fence were cut and the hole opened up again."

"They came back for the third dog?"

"I guess. Why do you say 'they'?"

"I don't know. It could have been one person or several. The dog weighed sixty or seventy pounds, so one person could have carried it, I guess."

"Or dragged it." She thought of the boot prints, about a size nine in a men's shoe, which meant probably a man of medium height or a large woman. "Can you walk back to the house?"

"Yes. I just need to take it slow."

Putting her arm around him, she assisted him to his feet. "Okay?"

"Yeah, except for a walloping headache."

She checked her watch. "Backup should be here soon."

"I didn't see that dog last night, but it was hidden by the holly bushes. I've got to admit I didn't think a dog was still here. I should have searched more thoroughly." He touched his forehead. "I've learned my lesson."

"It's only an hour or so to sunrise. We can search the whole grounds more thoroughly then."

"Why did whoever took the dogs come back for one of them? That was risky."

"Can't answer that." Although she had an idea. Last night Winnie had been extremely upset about the missing dogs. They had been special to her husband. So the person behind taking the animals might have had two reasons: to hurt the security around Winnie and to hurt her personally. "It does mean someone was watching the house for the right moment to come back."

"Except that I got to the dog before they could."

"It's looking that way."

The deputy gripped the railing as he mounted the steps to the front deck. "Does the sheriff know?"

"Probably."

Before she could unlock the door, Colt opened it. He took one look at Rod and stepped aside to let them inside. "What happened?"

Winnie hurried across the foyer, taking hold of the young man. "Come into the kitchen. Let me clean this gash."

"Ma'am, I'll be okay."

"Not until you see a doctor, and it still needs to be cleaned up. I have a first-aid kit in the kitchen." Winnie tugged the man forward.

Colt stood in Ellie's way. "What happened?"

She shut and locked the door, then faced him. "He heard a sound coming from the west side of the property and went to check it out. When he found one of your dogs on the ground under some bushes, he was hit over the head."

"One of our dogs wasn't taken?"

"It has been now, or at least I think it has. The dog was gone when I got there. The ropes were cut and the fence opened back up."

"Maybe there's another dog on the grounds?"

"In a couple of hours when it's daylight, we can search more thoroughly and see."

"We'd probably better go rescue Rod. My grandmother can get carried away with a cut or gash. Once she wrapped my calf for a small wound on the back. A bandage would have worked fine."

Ellie had taken a few steps when the doorbell rang. "I'll take care of this. It's probably the sheriff."

After looking through the peephole and seeing Sheriff Quinn, she opened the door. "The deputy should be all right, but he needs to be checked out at the hospital. He was hit over the head. Winnie is tending to him in the kitchen."

As they walked toward the room, Ellie explained where the deputy had been found and about the dog under the bushes.

Winnie glanced up when they entered. Frowning, she finished cleaning up the deputy's head wound. "Someone has stolen my dogs. Come on my property. Threatened me. And now hurt your deputy. I hardly see you, and in less than six hours you've been at my house twice. Neither a social call."

"I have one deputy outside right now and another on his way. Should be here any minute." He turned to Rod. "He can take you to the hospital. Get that head injury examined by the doc."

"Fine by me, but I want to work on this case. When this person came after me, he made it personal." Rod slowly stood and smiled at Winnie. "Thank you, ma'am, for seeing to me."

"Dear, I'm so sorry. You take care of yourself, and you're welcome back here anytime."

Before the sheriff followed his deputy from the room, he said, "If it's okay with you, Mrs. Winfield, I'd like to stay until sunrise and then thoroughly search the grounds."

"Of course. I'll get some coffee on and fix something for breakfast. I have a feeling we'll all need our energy for the day to come." Winnie washed her hands at the sink, then began making some coffee.

"I'll be back as soon as I see to Rod and post my other deputy. We need to discuss who would do this to you, Mrs. Winfield."

After the sheriff left, Winnie finished with the coffee. With her back to them, she grasped the counter on both sides of her and lowered her head.

"Winnie, are you okay?" Colt asked, coming to his grandmother's side and laying his hand on her shoulder.

The woman straightened from the counter, turned and inhaled a deep breath. "I will be once we find this person. If we get a ransom demand for the dogs, I'll pay it. I want them back. But what if…" Her bottom lip quivered, and she bit down on it.

"We'll do everything we can to get your pets back. I know how much they mean to you."

"I remember all the walks your granddad and I took with our dogs. It was our special time together. I think it was what helped me bounce back from my heart attack."

Colt embraced Winnie. "I'm not going back to the ship until this whole situation is resolved. Your safety means everything to me."

Winnie's eyes glistened. "That means so much to me. You're my only family now."

Behind her Ellie heard footsteps approaching the kitchen. She turned around, her hand on her gun in case it wasn't the sheriff returning. But when he came into the room, she dropped her arm to her side.

"Just in time for some coffee, Sheriff." Winnie stepped away from Colt and busied herself taking four mugs from the cabinet. "If I remember correctly you take yours black."

"Yes, I sure do."

Winnie poured the brew into the mugs then passed them out. "I've been trying to think of anyone who would do this to me. I can't at the moment."

"Let's all sit and talk this out. Sometimes that helps."

Ellie took a chair next to Colt while Sheriff Quinn and Winnie sat across from her. "Who have you fired recently?" she asked.

"No one." Her eyebrows scrunched together. "Well, I haven't personally. Harold and the human resources department handle those kind of things. There are days I don't even go into the office. I prefer working here. That's why I have a fully stocked lab in the basement."

"So you can't think of any disgruntled employees?" The sheriff blew on his coffee then took a sip. "Let's say in the past year."

Her head down, Winnie massaged her fingertips into her forehead. "You need to get a list from Harold. There have only been a few people I know personally who have left the company in the past year or so."

"Who?" Sheriff Quinn withdrew a small pad along with a pen from his front shirt pocket.

"About a year ago one of the chemists working with

me. I wasn't aware of this problem, but two different female employees in the lab accused him of sexual harassment. Glamour Sensations has always had a strict policy against it. Harold fired Dr. Ben Parker. He was difficult to work with but a brilliant chemist. When he came to me and complained, I supported Harold's decision. Frankly, I told him I was disappointed in him and…" Winnie averted her head and stared at the blinds over the window near the table.

"What else?" Colt slid his hand across the table and cupped his grandmother's.

"He said some ugly things to me, mostly directed at Harold and the company rather than at me. I will not repeat them." Squaring her shoulders, she lifted her chin.

The sheriff wrote down the man's name on the pad. "Okay, Winnie. We have one we can check on. Anyone else?"

"The only other who I had any contact with is the driver I used to have before my current one." She paused for a long moment. "I guess I was directly responsible for his dismissal. He came to work one day drunk. I knew he'd been having marital troubles so I was willing to give him a second chance. We all need those, but Harold was adamant that we don't. In the end I agreed with Harold."

"Harold was right. You can't be driven around by a person who has been drinking. What's his name?"

"Jerry Olson."

"Any more?" The sheriff took another drink of his coffee.

Winnie shook her head. "None. But there are a lot of departments I don't have any interaction with."

"How about someone who's been passed over for a

raise or promotion?" Ellie cradled her mug between her cold hands. "This person doesn't necessarily have to be gone from the company."

"Well…" Winnie patted her hair down, her mouth pursed. "We did have several candidates to be the spokesperson for Endless Youth. Christy actually wasn't in the running. I'm the one who decided she would be perfect. She might not be considered beautiful by a model's standard, but she conveyed what I wanted to communicate to the everyday woman. There were two young women before Christy who were in the final running for the position. Mary Ann Witlock and Lara Ulrich. I suppose neither one was happy when they weren't picked. They don't work for Glamour Sensations. Lara Ulrich lives in Denver, and Mary Ann Witlock lives in Bakersville. Several members of her family work for Glamour Sensations, but she works as a waitress at the restaurant not far from the company's main office."

The sheriff jotted down the additional names. "If you think of anyone else, give me a call. I'll be meeting with Harold and the police chief in Bakersville to see who they're looking at."

"Have you all thought this could be simply a kidnapping of my dogs?" Winnie asked. "They are valuable. But even more so to me. Anyone who knows me knows that."

Ellie nodded. "True, but they're even more valuable to you because you care for them so much. That could be the reason the person decided to steal them." She downed the last swallow of her coffee and went to get the pot and bring it back to the table. "Anyone else want some more?"

Colt held up his mug, as did the sheriff. Winnie shook her head.

The sheriff closed his notepad. "After I look around, I'll go back to the office and track down these people."

"How's an omelet for breakfast?" Winnie left her nearly untouched drink and crossed to the refrigerator.

"Wait until Linda comes to prepare breakfast." Colt pulled the blind to let in the soft light of dawn. "When she sees all the cars out front, she'll be here early."

"No, I need to keep busy. Besides, I don't get to cook like I used to. Thomas loved my omelets. Now to re-member how to make them."

"I'll help."

Colt shifted his attention to Ellie. "You cook?"

"Yes, some. I have to eat so I learned how."

One of his eyebrow arched. "A bodyguard who can cook. A woman of many talents."

"I'd love your help," Winnie said. "Be useful, Colt, and take this cup of coffee to the deputy outside."

He passed Ellie as he left with a mug and whispered, "Watch her. She once almost set the kitchen on fire. That's why Granddad insisted she hire Linda to cook."

"I heard that, young man. At least I don't go outside barefoot in winter."

Ellie slanted a look toward Colt as he left. In the doorway he glanced back and locked gazes with her. Then he winked.

Heat scored Ellie's cheeks. She'd never been around a family like the Winfields. She would have loved hav-ing the caring and the give-and-take between her and her mother. What would it have been like to grow up in a loving family? She could only imagine.

* * *

Ellie watched the last workmen leave, the black iron gates at the end of the drive shutting closed after the truck passed through the entrance to the estate. The sun disappeared completely below the western mountains, throwing a few shadows across the landscape. She surveyed the nearly fortified property, her muscles still tense from all the activity that had occurred during the day.

"What do you think?" Colt asked, coming up behind her.

"I'd rather have been in the lab with Winnie than out here supervising."

"The sheriff put a deputy on the door to the lab. Your expertise was needed making sure everything went in correctly. Winnie needed her security system updated even without the threat to her."

"I agree. She thinks being isolated keeps her protected. On the contrary, that makes her more vulnerable." She threw him a grin. "I just hate it when I need to be in two places at once. But you're right. I needed to keep an eye on the workers and the job they were doing. After tomorrow I'll breathe even easier."

"When they mount the cameras and put in the monitoring station?"

"Yes. The only one up and running right now is at the front gate. I'm glad Winnie agreed to let us use that small room off the kitchen for the monitoring station. It's a good location. Even at night we'll be able to tell what is happening outside on the grounds."

"That would have been nice last night." Colt lounged against the railing, his gaze fixed on her.

The intensity in his look lured her nearer. It took all

her willpower to stay where she was. "I'm hoping the electrified fence will keep people and large animals away. If someone tries to circumvent the power on the fence, the company monitoring it will notify the house. The jolt won't kill, but it will discourage someone or something from touching it."

"Tomorrow the two guard dogs from the trainer in Denver will arrive, but with the fence up and running and the new security system for the house, we should be all right."

He hadn't phrased it as a question, but his furrowed forehead indicated his lingering doubts. "No place can be one hundred percent safe, but this will be a vast improvement over yesterday. I wasn't sure how much they would accomplish today, but it helped that Winnie could afford to pay for a rush job."

"I got through to the *Kaleidoscope* and told them I have a family emergency. Just when you think you're indispensable, you find out they'll be all right without you. But then I figure you don't feel that way too much in your job. I know Winnie needs you. Yesterday proved that." He snapped his fingers. "I almost forgot. The sheriff called. He's on his way from Bakersville to give us an update on the people they're checking out."

"So he'll be here about the time Harold arrives. He wants us to have photos of the people Winnie mentioned and some he thought of. He wants us to convince Winnie not to attend the lighting of the Christmas tree in Bakersville tomorrow night."

Colt straightened, his movement bringing him a step closer. "I'll give it my best shot, but I don't think Winnie will change her mind. Bakersville is honoring Granddad and her at the tree lighting for all the work they've done for the town. That's important to her. Bakersville has been her home a long time since she married my granddad and came to live here."

"As important as her life?"

"My grandmother can be a stubborn woman."

"Tell me about it. She didn't want the deputy in the basement. She thought he could sit in the kitchen where he would be more comfortable. I told her that workers will have to come down there and that I can't follow every worker around. The deputy stands at the door to her lab or inside with her."

"I know she balked at that. She doesn't even like me in there. Anybody in the lab is a distraction, and she is determined to complete the project in time. She believes it's tied to who is after her. She thinks it's a competitor."

"That's still a possibility. The P.I. is looking into that. Maybe Harold will have some information."

Colt nodded his head toward the gate. "That's his car now and it looks like the sheriff is behind him."

"Nothing is assured until I check the monitor," Ellie said as she hurried inside and to the small room off the kitchen.

She examined the TV that showed the feed from the front gate. Harold waved at the camera. After clicking him through, she observed the Lexus as it passed the lower camera that gave a view of anyone in the vehicle. It appeared Harold was alone. Then she did the same thing with the sheriff.

When she glanced up, Colt stood in the doorway, his arms straight at his side while his gaze took in the bank of TV monitors. "We need someone to be in here 24/7 until this is over with."

"I agree, and I'm hoping you'll help me convince your grandmother of that in a few minutes."

"So you gathered the forces to help you?"

"Yes. She may be upset with Harold for not telling her sooner, but she trusts him. And she respects the sheriff."

"You are sly, Miss St. James, and I'm glad you are. In a week's time you have gotten to know Winnie well."

"I got a head start. On the plane ride here, I studied a file Harold provided me on her. From what he wrote, I could tell how much he cares about her. In army intelligence, I had to learn quick how to read people."

He closed the space between them. "That means you can't be fooled?"

"I'd be a fool to think that."

His chuckle resonated through the air. "Good answer. I like you, Ellie St. James."

The small room seemed to shrink as she looked at the dimple in his left cheek, the laugh lines at the corners of his eyes. She scrambled to form some kind of reply that would make sense. But as his soft gaze roamed over her features it left a tingling path where it touched as if he'd brushed his fingers over her face.

The doorbell sounded, breaking the mood.

"I'll get Winnie," he murmured in a husky voice.

She stepped to the side and rushed past him to the foyer. Her heartbeat pounded against her rib cage, and her breath was shallow as she peered through the peephole then opened the door to Harold and the sheriff.

"Colt's gone to get his grandmother," Ellie told them. "She wanted to be included in the update."

"How's she holding up?" Harold asked as they made their way into the living room.

"Fine, Harold." Winnie answered before Ellie could. "Worried? Is that why you didn't answer your private line today when I called?"

With his cheeks flushed, the CFO of Glamour Sensations faced Winnie coming down the hall. "I've been busy working with the police chief, to make sure we have a thorough list of people who could possibly be angry with you."

The older woman's usual warm blue eyes frosted. "I've always tried to treat people fairly. How many are we talking about?"

"Including the ones you gave the sheriff, in the past two years, ten."

Her taut bearing drooped a little. "That many? I've never intentionally hurt someone."

"It might not be you per se but your company. Tomorrow I'm going to look back five years."

"Why so far back?" Winnie looked from Harold to the sheriff, her delicate eyebrows crunching together.

"It's probably no one that far back, but I'd rather cover all our bases. It's better to be safe than—"

Winnie held up her hand. "Don't say it. It's been a long day. It was nearly impossible to think clearly with all the racket going on earlier. This may throw me behind a day or so. Give me the facts, and then I need to go back to the lab to finish up what should have been completed two hours ago." She came into the room as far as the wingback chair but remained standing behind it.

"Winnie, the workmen will be gone by midafternoon tomorrow. They're mounting cameras all over the estate and activating the monitoring system. The only one right now that works is the front gate." Ellie took a seat, hoping her client would follow suit. The pale cast to Winnie's face and her lackluster eyes worried Ellie.

Sheriff Quinn cleared his throat. "We've narrowed the list down to the three most likely with two maybes." He withdrew his pad. "The first one is Lara Ulrich. Although she lives in Denver, that's only an hour away, and she has been spotted in Bakersville this past month, visiting her mother. I discovered she's moving back home because she can't get enough work to support herself in Denver. Jerry Olson is working when he can but mostly he's living off his aunt, who is losing her patience with him. He's been vocal about you not giving him that second chance you're known for. The last is someone Harold brought to my attention. Steve Fairchild is back in town."

Winnie gasped.

SIX

Winnie leaned into the back of the chair, clutching it. "When?"

"A few weeks ago," Harold said, getting up and moving to Winnie.

Ellie glanced at Colt. A tic in his jaw twitched. She slid her hand to his on the couch and he swung his attention to her as she mouthed, "Who is that?"

He bent toward her and whispered, "She blamed him for causing Granddad's death."

"Why is this the first time I've heard about him?"

"Right after my grandfather died he left Bakersville to work overseas."

"Because I drove him out of town," Winnie said in a raw voice, finally taking a seat. "I said some horrible things to the man in public that I regretted when I came to my right mind." A sheen of tears shone in her eyes. "I wronged him and thought I would never have a chance to apologize. I must go see him."

"No." Colt's hand beneath Ellie's on the couch fisted. "Not when someone is after you. Not when that someone could be him."

Winnie stiffened, gripping both arms of the chair.

"Young man, I will do what I have to. I will not let this wrong go on any longer. I need to apologize—in public. My words and actions were what caused people to make his life so miserable he left town. Wasn't it bad enough that Thomas had fired him that day he died?"

"I need you to tell me what happened." Ellie rose, her nerves jingling as if she felt they were close to an answer.

"Steve Fairchild messed up a huge account for Glamour Sensations. Thomas lost a lot of sleep over what to do about him. That day he fired Steve, Thomas stayed late trying to repair the damage the man had done to the company. I blamed Steve Fairchild for my husband falling asleep behind the wheel. That was grief talking. I now realize Thomas made the choice to drive home when he could have stayed at his office and slept on the couch."

Harold pounded the arm of his chair and sat forward. "Winnie, the man was at fault. We took a hard knock when that client walked away from our company. It took us a year to get back what we lost. You only said what half the town felt, and then on top of everything, he dared to come to Thomas's funeral. You were not in the wrong."

Winnie pressed her lips together. For a long moment silence filled the room. "This is the last I'm going to say on the subject. I owe the man an apology, and I intend to give it to him." She swept her attention to the sheriff. "What about Mary Ann Witlock?"

"I'm still looking for her. She's not been seen for a week. She told her neighbor she was going to Texas to see a boyfriend. That's all I've been able to find out so far."

"And you don't think Dr. Ben Parker is a threat?"

"No, he's in a nursing home in Denver."

"He is? Why?"

"He had a severe stroke. He can't walk and has trouble talking."

"Oh, dear. I need to add him to my prayer list."

"He wouldn't leave the young women in his lab alone," Harold muttered, scowling.

Winnie tilted up her chin. "That doesn't mean I shouldn't pray for him. You and I have never seen eye to eye on praying for people regardless."

Listening to the older woman gave Ellie something to think about. She was a Christian, but was her faith strong? Could she forgive her mother for her neglect or the bullies that made her brother's life miserable? She didn't know if she had that in her, especially when she remembered Toby coming home crying with a bloodied face.

"We'll continue to delve into these people's lives. I'm just glad the police chief is handling it quietly and personally," Harold said with a long sigh. "He's trying to track down how the letters came to your office. There was no postmark. He's reviewing security footage, but there are a lot of ways to put a letter in the interoffice mail at your company. Some of them aren't on the camera."

"Fine." Winnie slapped her hands on her thighs and started to push up from her seat. "I've got a few more hours of—"

"Grandma, we have something else we need to talk to you about." Colt's words stopped her.

Ellie noticed the woman's eyebrows shoot up.

"Grandma?" Winnie asked. "Is there something else

serious you've been keeping from me? You never call me Grandma." Her gaze flitted from one person to the next.

Ellie approached Winnie. "I'm strongly recommending that you not go to the lighting of the Christmas tree tomorrow night."

"I'm going, so each of you better accept that. Knowing you, Harold, you've hired security. I wouldn't be surprised if every other person in the crowd was security. I won't let this person rob me of all my little pleasures." She stood, her arms stiff at her sides. "Just make sure they don't stand out."

Evidently Colt was not satisfied. "Grandma—"

"Don't 'Grandma' me. I will not give in to this person totally. I'm already practically a prisoner in this house, and after tomorrow, this place will be as secure as a prison." She marched toward the exit. "I'll be in my lab. Have Linda bring my dinner to me. I'm eating alone tonight."

Quiet ruled until the basement door slammed shut.

"That worked well," Colt mumbled and caught Ellie's look. "What do you suggest?"

"Short of locking her in her room, nothing. I'd say strengthen the security and pray. I won't leave her side. Harold, have you found a few people to monitor the TVs around the clock here at the house?"

"Yes. With the police chief and Sheriff Quinn's help, I have four who are willing to start tomorrow. One is a deputy and two are police officers. They need extra money. My fourth one is the retired police chief. He's bored and needs something to do. They will be discreet."

"Perfect." Although the police chief and sheriff

vouched for the men, she would have her employer do a background check on them. She'd learned to double-check everything. "I'd like a list of their names."

The sheriff jotted them down on a piece of paper. "I personally know all these men, and they will do a good job."

"That's good. Did you discover what kind of vehicle could have left those tire tracks?"

"The tire is pretty common for a SUV, so probably not a truck."

"What was in the dart?" Ellie held her breath, hoping it wasn't a poison. Winnie still thought there was a chance to get her dogs back.

Sheriff Quinn rose. "A tranquilizer. We're checking vets and sources where it can be purchased. But that will take time."

Time we might not have.

After Ellie escorted the two men to the front door then locked it when they left, she turned to see Colt in the foyer, staring at her. The scent of roasted chicken spiced the air. Her stomach rumbled. "I just realized all I had today was breakfast."

"It looks like it will be just you and me tonight."

The sudden cozy picture of them sitting before a roaring fire sharing a delicious dinner stirred feelings deep inside her she'd fought to keep pushed down. She'd purposely picked this life as a bodyguard to help others but also to keep her distance from people. She was more of an observer, not a participant. When she had participated, she'd gotten hurt—first with her family and later when she became involved with Greg, a man she had dated seriously who had lied to her.

Colt walked toward her, a crooked grin on his face.

"We have to eat. We might as well do it together and get to know each other. It looks like we'll be working together to protect Winnie."

"Working together? I don't think so. I'm the body-guard, not you. You're her grandson. You are emotion-ally involved. That can lead to mistakes, problems."

He moved into her personal space, suddenly crowd-ing her even though he was a couple of feet away. "Being emotionally involved will drive me to do what I need to protect my grandmother. Feelings aren't the enemy."

They aren't? Ellie had her doubts. She'd felt for her mother, her brother and Greg, and ended up hurt, a lit-tle bit of herself lost. "Feelings can get in the way of doing your job."

"It's dinner, Ellie. That's all. In the kitchen."

"I know that. I'm checking the house one more time, then I'll be in there to eat." She started to leave.

He stepped into her path. "I want to make it clear. I will be involved with guarding Winnie. That's not ne-gotiable."

She met the hard, steely look in his eyes. "Everything is negotiable." Then she skirted around him and started her room-by-room search, testing the windows and looking in places a person could hide. She'd counted the workmen as they'd left, but she liked to double-check.

As she passed through the house, she placed a call to her employer. "I need you to investigate some law enforcement officers who are helping with monitoring the cameras I've had installed around the estate. The sheriff and police chief vetted them."

Kyra Hunt laughed. "But you don't know if you can trust them?"

"No. You taught me well. I can remember a certain police officer being dirty on a case you took."

"I've already looked into Sheriff Quinn and the police chief. Nothing I can find sends up a red flag."

Like the background checks Kyra did on Harold Jefferson, Linda and Doug Miller, and Christy Boland. She knew nothing was completely foolproof, but she would be a fool if she didn't have these background checks done on people who came in close contact with Winnie. After she gave the four names to Kyra, she said, "Also look into Colt Winfield. He came home unexpectedly and is now staying."

"Mrs. Winfield's grandson? Do you suspect him?"

"No, not really, but then I can't afford to be wrong."

"I'll get back to you with what I find."

When Ellie finished her call, she walked toward the kitchen, the strong aroma of spices and roast chicken making her mouth water.

"Linda, I'll take care of the dishes. Go home," Colt said as Ellie came into the room.

Linda nodded. "I imagine Doug is asleep. Today was an early one, and with all that's been going on, he didn't have much chance to even sit." She removed her apron and hung it up on a peg. "Winnie said she'll bring up her dinner tray later."

Ellie crossed to the back door and locked it after the housekeeper left. She watched out the window as the woman hurried across the yard toward the guesthouse where she and her husband lived. "I haven't had a chance to tell her today that any guests she has will have to go through me first. I'll do that first thing tomorrow." She pivoted, her gaze connecting with Colt's.

"We talked about it. She's fine meeting anyone she needs in town for the time being."

"Just so long as her car is inspected when she comes back."

Surprise flashed across her face. "You think Linda might be involved?"

"No, but what if someone managed to hide in her car? Then when she drove onto the property they would be inside without us knowing. It's necessary until we know how the new dogs are going to work out."

"You have to think of everything."

"My clients depend on it. As we speak, I'm having the men who are going to monitor the security system vetted by my employer. Nothing is foolproof, but there are some procedures I can put in place to make this house safer, so Winnie won't have to worry about walking around her own home. I've had everyone who comes into close contact with Winnie on a regular basis checked out."

"Harold?

"Yes, just because he hired me doesn't make him not a suspect."

"Me?" Colt pulled out a chair for her to sit in at the kitchen table set for two.

"Yes, even you."

"I'm her grandson!"

"I know, but some murders have been committed by family members."

He took the chair across from her. "Do you trust anyone?" he asked in a tightly controlled voice.

"I'm paid to distrust."

"How about when you aren't working? Do you go around distrusting everyone?"

"I trust God."

"No one else?"

Ellie picked up the fork and speared a slice of roasted chicken. Who did she trust? The list was short. "How about you? Who do you trust?"

His intense gaze snared hers. "I trust you to protect my grandmother."

"Then why are you wanting to do my job?"

"Because I trust myself to protect my grandmother, too. Isn't two better than one?"

"Not necessarily."

After he scooped some mashed potatoes onto his plate he passed her the bowl. "You never answered my question about who you trust."

"I know." Her hand gripping her fork tight, she dug into her dinner. His question disturbed her because she didn't have a ready answer—a list of family and friends she could say she trusted. Could she trust Colt?

The chilly temperature and the low clouds in the dark night promised snow when they arrived at the tree lighting. Ellie buttoned her short coat and checked her gun before she slid from the front passenger seat of the SUV. "Winnie, wait until I open your door."

While Colt exited the car, Ellie helped his grandmother from the backseat. The whole time Ellie scanned the crowd in the park next to City Hall, her senses alert for anything out of the ordinary. Lights blazed from the two-story building behind the tree and from the string of colored lights strung from pole to pole along the street, but too many of the townspeople were shrouded in darkness where the illumination didn't reach.

Ellie flanked Winnie on the right side while Colt took the left one. "Ready?" she asked.

"I see Harold waving to us from the platform near the Christmas tree." Colt guided his grandmother toward Glamour Sensations' CFO.

"No one said anything about you standing on a platform," Ellie said. The idea that Winnie would be up above the crowd—a better target—bothered Ellie. She continued her search of the faces in the mob, looking for any of the ones the police were looking into as the possible threat to Winnie.

"Oh, yes. I have to give a speech before I flip the switch. I'll keep it short, dear."

Ellie wasn't sure Winnie took the threat against her as seriously as she should. "How about you skip the speech and go straight to turning on the lights so we can leave?"

Winnie paused and shifted toward Ellie. "I've lived a long, good life. If I go to my maker tonight, then so be it."

"Winnie," Colt said in a sharp voice that reached the people around them. They all turned to watch them. Leaning toward his grandmother, he murmured, "I'm not ready to give you up. I'd care if something happened to you."

Winnie patted his arm. "I know. But I want you two to realize I have a peace about all of this. That doesn't mean I will fire Ellie—" she tossed a look toward Ellie "—because I won't give the person after me an easy target. But, as I'm sure she knows, there is only so much you all can do. The only one who can protect me is the Lord."

"But you know He uses others to do His bidding. I

fall into that category. If I tell you to do something, just do it. No questions asked, okay?" Ellie wished she could get Winnie to take this whole situation more seriously.

"Yes, my dear."

"If I see a threat in the crowd, I'm going to get you out of here. Then later you can chalk it up to a crazy assistant getting overzealous in her job if you need to spin it for the press. Let's get this over with."

Up on the platform as Winnie approached the podium and the cheering crowd quieted, Colt whispered to Ellie, "You make this sound like we've come for a root canal."

"How about several? I don't like this at all." She gestured toward one area of the park that was particularly dark. "Why couldn't they have the lighting of the tree during the daytime?"

Her gaze latched onto a man in the front row reaching into his coat pocket. Ellie stiffened and put her hand into her own pocket, grasping her weapon. But the guy pulled out a cell and turned it off.

Five minutes later when Winnie completed her short speech thanking Bakersville for the honor to Thomas and her for naming the park after them, she stepped over to flip the first switch. Suddenly the lights went out in City Hall and the only ones that illuminated the area were the string of colorful lights along the streets and around the park. Next Winnie flipped the switch for the lights on the twelve-foot Christmas tree and their colorful glow lit the area.

"That's why it's at nighttime."

The tickle of Colt's whisper by her ear shot a bolt of awareness through Ellie. Her pulse rate accelerated, causing a flush of heat on her face. Someone in the crowd began singing "Joy to the World" and everyone joined in, including Colt and Winnie. Ellie sang but never took her attention from the people surrounding Winnie. Harold had said he would have people in plain-clothes scattered throughout the attendees in addition to the police visible in the throng.

Ellie moved closer, intending to steer Winnie back to the SUV. But before she could grasp her elbow, women, men and children swamped Winnie.

"Thank you for what you've done for Bakersville," one lady said.

Another person shook Winnie's hand. "When the economy was down, you didn't lay off anyone at the company. We appreciate that."

After five long minutes of the same kind of praises, Ellie stepped to Winnie's right while Colt took up his position on the left.

Winnie grinned. "Thank you all. Bakersville is important to me. It's my home."

People parted to allow Winnie through the crowd. Suddenly a medium-built man stepped into Winnie's path. Ellie inched closer to Winnie while she gripped her weapon.

Winnie smiled. "I'm glad to see you, Mr. Fairchild. I heard you were in town."

"Yeah. Is there a problem with me being here?" He pulled himself up straight, his shoulders back.

"No, on the contrary, I meant it. I'm glad I ran into you." She raised her voice. "I wanted to apologize to you for my behavior right after Thomas died. I was wrong. I hope you'll accept my apology."

The man's mouth dropped open. The tension in his stance eased. "I—I—"

"I would certainly understand if you don't, but I hope you'll find it in your heart to—"

"I made mistakes, too," Steve Fairchild mumbled. Then he ducked his head and hurried off.

"Let's go, Winnie," Ellie said and guided her client toward the car.

The closer they got to the SUV the faster Ellie's pace became. Her nape tingled; her breath caught in her lungs. The person behind the threats was here somewhere—she felt it in her bones. Possibly Steve Fairchild, in spite of how the encounter had turned out. Not until Winnie was safe in the backseat and Colt was pulling out of the parking space did Ellie finally exhale.

"I thought that went very well, especially with Steve Fairchild, and nothing happened at the lighting of the tree," Winnie said from the backseat.

We're not at your house yet. Ellie kept that thought to herself, but her gaze continually swept the landscape and the road before and behind the SUV.

Winnie continued to comment on the event. "The Christmas tree this year was beautiful. Not that it isn't every year, but they seemed to have more decorations and lights on it. You were here last Christmas, Colt. Don't you think it was bigger and better?"

Ellie tossed a quick glance at Colt. In the beam of an oncoming car, she glimpsed his set jaw, his focus totally on the road ahead.

"I guess so. I never thought about it."

"Isn't that just like a man, Ellie?"

"Yes, but I've found a lot of people don't note their surroundings unless there's a reason." Ellie couldn't help but notice that Winnie hadn't said much on the ride down the mountain, but now she wanted to chitchat. That was probably her nerves talking. "You'll be all right, Winnie. I won't let anything happen to you."

"I know that. I'm not worried."

"Then why are you talking so much?" Tension threaded through Colt's question.

"I'm relieved nothing happened and pleased by the kindness of the people of Bakersville. I even got my chance to apologize to Mr. Fairchild in public. I wish I could have stayed longer. I probably should call the mayor tomorrow and apologize that I couldn't linger at the end. I usually do."

Behind the SUV a car sped closer. Ellie couldn't tell the make of the vehicle from the glare of the headlights.

"I see it." Colt slowed down.

The car accelerated and passed them on a straight part of the winding road up the mountain. The Ford Focus increased its distance between them and disappeared around a curve. Ellie twisted to look behind them. A dark stretch of highway greeted her inspection.

She sat forward, her hand going to her gun. She took it out and laid it on her lap.

"Expecting trouble?" Colt asked.

Although it was dark inside the SUV, with only a few dashboard lights, Ellie felt the touch of his gaze when he turned his head toward her. "Always. That's what keeps me alert."

"Oh, my goodness, Ellie," Winnie exclaimed. "That would be hard to do all the time. When do you relax, my dear?"

"When I'm not working."

"I noticed you slept outside my bedroom again last night. You can't be getting rest."

Ellie looked back at Winnie. "Now that the security

system is totally functioning and someone is monitoring it at night, I can go back to my room. But I'm a light sleeper on the job whether in a bed or on the floor in front of a door." After checking behind the SUV, she rotated forward. "You don't need to worry about me."

"Oh, but, my dear, I do. How do you think I'd feel if anything happened to you because of me?"

Again Colt and Ellie exchanged glances. She'd never had a client worry about her. If Harold hadn't hired her, she doubted Winnie would have, even knowing about the threatening letters. That thought chilled her. The woman would have been an easy target for anyone.

As the SUV approached the next S-curve, the one where Winnie's husband went off the cliff, Colt took it slow, leaning forward, intent on the road.

When they made it through without any problem, Winnie blew out a breath. "I hate that part of the road. If I could avoid it and get down the mountain, I would. That's a particularly dangerous curve."

"It's not much farther. Which is good since they're predicting snow tonight." Colt took the next curve.

Halfway through it Ellie saw the car parked across both lanes of the road. With no place to maneuver around it, Colt slammed on his brakes and Ellie braced for impact.

SEVEN

Ellie gasped as the brakes screamed and Colt struggled to keep the vehicle from swerving. She muttered a silent prayer just before they collided with the car across the road. The crashing sound reverberated through the SUV. The impact with the side of the Ford Focus jerked Ellie forward then threw her back. The safety belt cut into her chest, holding her against the seat.

"Are you okay?" Ellie fumbled with her buckle, released it and shoved open the door.

"Yes." Colt swiveled around to look at his grandmother.

"I'm fine," she said from the backseat.

Ellie panned the crash site as she hurried toward the car. She couldn't get to the driver's door because of the SUV so she rounded the back of the vehicle and opened the front passenger's door to look inside. Emptiness mocked her.

She straightened and turned to Colt. "Have Winnie stay inside."

Standing by his car, Colt nodded and went around to Winnie's side.

"No one is in the car. Call it in." Keeping vigilant,

Ellie scanned the landscape and then made her way back to the SUV. She stood outside the vehicle.

"He said he was fifteen minutes away," Colt told her from the backseat where he sat next to his grandmother.

"Winnie, would you please get down," Ellie chided. "No sense giving anyone a target to shoot at."

"You think he's out there waiting to shoot me?"

Ellie looked around. "Could be. Someone drove this car here and left it across the road in just the right place for anyone coming around the curve to hit it. If this had been car trouble, where is the driver?"

"Walking to get help?" Winnie's voice quavered.

"But there's no reason to have it stalled across the road like this and not to leave the hazard lights flashing."

When Winnie scooted down on the floor, Colt hovered over her like a human shield.

"No, I'm not going to let you do that. I won't let you be killed in my place. Colt, sit back up."

"No. I won't make it easy for them."

"You're going back to your ship tomorrow." Anger weaved through Winnie's voice.

"We'll talk about this when we're safe at the house."

"Don't placate me. I'm your elder."

Ellie heard the back-and-forth between them and knew the fear they both were experiencing. She had a good douse of it herself. But she planted herself beside the back door, her gun raised against her chest. "Shh, you two. I need to listen."

Not another word came from inside the SUV. Ellie focused on the quiet, occasionally broken by a sound—something scurrying in the underbrush on the side of the road, a sizzling noise from under the hood, an owl's hoot. Finally a siren pierced the night. Its blare grew closer. Ellie smiled. She liked how Sheriff Quinn thought. Let whoever might be out here know that help was nearby. Through the trees on the cliff side, Ellie caught snatches of the red flashing lights as two patrol cars sped up the winding highway toward them. Help would be there in less than two minutes.

Even when the sheriff arrived at the wreck site, Ellie concentrated on her surroundings, not the patrol cars screeching to a halt and the doors slamming shut. Finally she slid a glance toward Sheriff Quinn marching toward her while three of his deputies fanned out.

"Is everyone all right?" The sheriff stopped, reaching out to open the back door.

"Yes, but I need to get Winnie to the estate." Ellie backed up against the SUV. "I don't think anyone is going to do anything now, but she isn't safe out here."

The sheriff pointed to his deputies. "One of you get behind that car. Let's see if we can push it out of the way. Wear gloves. We'll want to pull fingerprints off the steering wheel if possible. Someone left this baby out here." He waved his hand toward the car. "And I intend to find out who did this."

Colt climbed from the backseat, closing his grandmother inside and positioning his body at the door.

While the deputies moved the car off to the side of the road, the sheriff switched on his spotlight, sweeping the area. Ellie followed the beam, delving into the shadows for any sign of someone still hanging around.

Then the sheriff moved his car up along the SUV, rolled down the windows and said, "Winnie needs to get out on this side and into my car. If anyone was here, they'd be along the mountainside, not the cliff side of the highway. It's a sheer drop to the bottom."

"I'll take care of it," Ellie said to Colt. "When Winnie and I are in the sheriff's car, take the front seat."

Colt stepped to the side as Ellie slipped inside the backseat of the SUV, then he shut the door and resumed his position.

"Winnie, did you hear the sheriff?"

"It's hard not to. He was shouting."

"I'm going to follow you out of this car. We'll sit in the back of the patrol car."

"Do I hunch down in there, too?"

"It wouldn't hurt. We don't know what we're up against. Caution is always the best policy."

Winnie crawled across the floor to the other side of the backseat. She gripped the handle and pulled it down. "Here goes." The older woman scrambled out of the SUV and into the patrol car two feet away.

Ellie followed suit, and Colt jumped into the front.

The sheriff gunned his engine, maneuvering up the road with expert precision. "We had a report of a stolen Ford Focus from the parking lot near City Hall. A family came back from watching the tree lighting and found their car gone."

So someone had been at the celebration and decided not to go after Winnie in a crowd. Instead, he chose a dark, lonely stretch of road to cause a wreck. Was that someone Steve Fairchild? He had been at the tree lighting and he'd made a point to see Winnie. Was that his way of taunting her before he made his move?

If Colt hadn't been as alert as he had and his reflexes quick, the crash would have been a lot worse. Ellie peered at Winnie's face. She couldn't see the woman's expression, but she held her body rigid. Tension poured off Winnie.

Ellie felt a strong urge to comfort the woman. "You're almost home."

"Someone hates me that much. We could have gone off the road like…" Her voice melted into the silence.

"We'll find the person." Sheriff Quinn stopped at the main gate to the estate and peered back at Winnie. "This is my top priority. I'm leaving two deputies here, and I'm not going to take no for an answer."

Ellie pushed the remote button to allow them inside. As they headed for the main house, the two dogs followed the car as trained.

"Fine, whatever you think is best," Winnie said, the words laced with defeat.

Ellie covered Winnie's clasped hands in her lap. "If someone was trying to stir memories of your husband's wreck, then he would have picked the S-curve for it to happen. His intent would have been clear if he had done that. There still could be a logical explanation that has nothing to do with you. It could be kids joyriding who got scared and ditched the car."

"Do you really believe that?" Winnie asked, her hands tightening beneath Ellie's.

"It's a possibility. That's all I'm saying. Until I know for sure, I don't rule out anything." But something she said to Winnie nibbled at the edges of her mind. Was there a connection to Winnie's husband somehow? What if he didn't fall asleep at the wheel? What if it had been murder five years ago?

A couple of hours later, Ellie entered the kitchen where the sheriff and Colt sat at the table, drinking coffee and reviewing what had occurred.

"How's Winnie?" Colt walked to the carafe and poured Ellie a cup of the black brew.

She took a deep breath of the aroma. "She's bouncing back. I think the similarity to what happened to her husband is what got her more than anything."

"I agree. It worries me, too. A few threatening letters and cut-up pictures aren't nearly as menacing as trying to re-create the same kind of accident. My first instinct was to swerve and avoid the car. If I'd done that, we could have gone off the cliff." Colt slumped into his chair, releasing a sigh.

Ellie sat beside him. "That has me thinking, Sheriff. Your department handled Thomas Winfield's accident. Are you one hundred percent sure it was an accident?"

"Yes, as sure as you can be. When all this began with Winnie, I reviewed the file. Nothing to indicate he was forced off the road, no skid marks. The tire tracks on the shoulder of the road were from Thomas's car. No one else's. No stalled car like this evening. We checked for drinking and drugs, too. He had no alcohol or drugs in his system."

"He shouldn't have," Colt said. "Granddad didn't drink, and his medicine wouldn't have made him sleepy."

"I know, but there was a report of a car weaving over into the other lane a few miles from where the wreck occurred. The man who reported it honked and the driver of the other car swerved in time to miss him. That person watched that car drive off, and it was going straight, no more weaving. He called it in, anyway. His description wasn't detailed, but what he said did fit your grandfather's car."

"So you're saying in your opinion it was an accident?" Ellie took a large swallow of her coffee.

"Yes. Besides, nothing has happened in five years. Why something now? Why Winnie?"

Colt raked his fingers through his hair. "How in the world do you two sit calmly and talk about this kind of stuff?"

"Because it's good to talk about all the possibilities. Brainstorm theories." The sheriff stood. "Ellie, I'll take another look at the file, but I don't think there's a connection. While you were checking on Winnie, two of my deputies arrived after processing the scene of the wreck. The Ford Focus was towed, and we'll go over it, check for fingerprints in the front seat and door. Maybe something will turn up. Also the SUV was towed to the garage in town to be fixed. I'm posting one deputy inside at the front door and the other at the back. Don't want the two new dogs to mistake them for an intruder."

Ellie started to get up.

Sheriff Quinn waved her down. "I'll send the deputy in here and see myself out."

When he left, Colt looked at her. "Let's go into the den."

Too wired to go to sleep yet, she nodded, topped off her coffee and trailed after Colt.

In the den, he stoked the fire he'd made when they had first come home. Winnie had been cold and sat by it until she'd gone to bed. Ellie observed the strong breadth of his shoulders: his movements were precise, efficient, like the man. She liked what she saw.

When he sank onto the couch next to her, he picked up his mug and sipped his coffee. "I never thought my brief vacation was going to turn out like this."

"I can imagine. No one plans for this."

He angled so he faced her, his arm slung along the back of the couch. "What if Harold hadn't acted quickly on those letters? What if Winnie's assistant hadn't alerted Harold about the threats? I know Winnie. She would have dismissed it. She wants to think the best of everyone. This could have been totally different, especially tonight."

"We can't think about the what-ifs. It's wasted energy."

"Which is precious right now. At least the house and grounds are secure. Winnie won't be happy seeing the deputies here tomorrow morning. She's worried the press will get hold of the fact that she's been threatened and make a big deal out of it. That could jeopardize the company going public. So far the people involved have remained quiet. That won't last long. I know Harold will have to notify certain people if nothing is solved by Christmas. Maybe that is the point of all of this."

"If the news does go public, that might actually help Winnie. Most of the people in this town love Winnie and will want to help her. Someone might come forward with information they don't realize could help the police find who is behind this."

"But rumors get started and get blown all out of portion, twisted around. It happened years ago when Granddad divorced his first wife. Not long after that he married Winnie. For a while people thought she had taken him away from his first wife, but that wasn't the case. It took years for her to correct those impressions. People had to get to know her to understand she would never come between a man and his wife. It hurt her enough that when I asked her about something I'd heard, she told me what happened."

"I know. I've seen similar cases on the national level, even ones I worked behind the scenes over in the Middle East. The truth often is twisted and blatantly altered."

His hand brushed against her shoulder. "So you see why she's trying to keep all this quiet. Already too many people know about it. I'm afraid she won't be able to. Which brings me to our next problem."

The feel of his fingertips touching her lightly sent her heart racing. His nearness robbed her of coherent thought for a few seconds until she forced herself to concentrate on what he was saying. "I'm afraid to ask what."

"You afraid? All I've seen is a woman cool under pressure."

"There's nothing wrong with being afraid. It keeps me on my toes."

"This Friday night is Glamour Sensations' Christmas Gala. I know my grandmother. Even with what happened tonight, she'll insist on going. She's supposed to introduce Christy as the face of Endless Youth and tease the press with what's going to come in February and the rest of next year."

"I was hoping she would decide not to go and let Harold take care of it."

"My grandmother has always been the spokesperson for the company. Any change will fuel speculation. Glamour Sensations will need the infusion of money by going public if we're to launch and produce the new line the way it should be. If she doesn't show up, some people will think she was badly injured in the wreck."

"Do you think that could be the reason for the wreck?

Some competitor wanted to damage what the company is planning to do?"

"Could be." Colt scrubbed his hands down his face. "I wish I knew what was going on. It would make it easier to fight."

"Let me think about what we can do. I certainly don't want to drive to the gala."

"I doubt Winnie would, either, especially with the reminder of Granddad's accident. It took a long while to get over his death. Her heart attack didn't disrupt her life like his dying." He took her hands. "When this is all over with, Harold needs a raise for hiring you. Winnie trusts you. Maybe she'll listen to you about the gala."

"I'll do what I can. Meanwhile I have an idea about how to get her down this mountain without driving."

"How?"

"Use a helicopter. There's plenty of room for it to land in front of the house."

His eyes brightened and he squeezed her hands. "I like that. Winnie should agree, especially given the alternatives."

"I can talk to the sheriff tomorrow to see about who to hire in the area." Then she would have to vet the person in only a few days. But it could be done with her employer's assistance. "If there is no one in the area he'd recommend, we could check Denver or Colorado Springs."

Colt lifted one hand and cupped her face. "You're fantastic."

The gleam in his eyes nearly unraveled her resolve to keep her distance. When this was over with, she would move on to another job and he would return to his research vessel. She needed to remember that. But when his thumb caressed her cheek and he bent toward her, all determination fled in the wake of the soft look in his eyes, as though he saw her as a woman like no other. Special. To be cherished.

His lips whispered across hers before settling over them. He wound one arm around her and brought her close. Her stomach fluttered. Then he enveloped her in an embrace, plastering her against him as he deepened the kiss. Her world tilted. She could taste the coffee on his lips. She could smell his lime-scented aftershave. She could feel the hammering of his heartbeat. Heady sensations overwhelmed her, tempting her to disregard anything logical and totally give in to the feelings he stirred in her.

The realization frightened her more than facing a gunman. She wedged her hands up between them and pushed away from him. The second their mouths parted she missed the feel of his lips on hers. But common sense prevailed. She moved back, putting several feet between them.

"I know I shouldn't have kissed you," Colt said, "but I've wanted to since that first night when you attacked me in the hallway. I've never quite had that kind of homecoming before." One corner of his mouth quirked.

She rose, her legs shaky. "I need to check the house, then go to bed. There's still a lot to do tomorrow."

Before he said or did anything else, she spun on her heel and rushed toward the exit. She considered going outside for some fresh air but decided not to. Instead, she went through the house, making sure the place was secured. Heat blazed her cheeks. She'd wanted the kiss, even wished it could have continued. That would be dangerous, would complicate their situation. But she couldn't get the picture of them kissing out of her mind.

With his hands jammed into his pants' pockets, Colt stood in front of the fireplace in the den and stared at the yellow-orange flames. He'd blown it this evening. He'd had no intention of kissing Ellie, and yet he had. Against his better judgment. What kind of future could they have? He lived on a research vessel in the South Pacific. It wasn't as if he could even carry on a long-distance relationship with a woman. He'd learned from his past attempts at a relationship that he wanted a lasting one like his grandparents had had. Anything less than that wasn't acceptable.

Was that why he'd given up looking for someone? What kind of home could he give her? A berth on a ship? He didn't even call it home. This place on the side of a mountain would always be his home.

He heard her voice coming from the foyer. She said something to the deputy Colt couldn't make out. Peering at the mantel, decorated with garland and gold ribbon for the holidays, he glimpsed the Big Ben clock and the late hour. He needed to go to bed, but he waited until Ellie finished talking with the deputy. He gave her a chance to go upstairs before him because frankly he didn't know what to say to her.

He would have continued the kiss if she hadn't pulled away. His thoughts mocked his declaration to stay away from Ellie St. James, a woman who was fiercely independent and could take care of herself. He'd always wanted someone who would need him. Someone to be an equal partner but rely on him, too.

After taking care of the fire, he moved toward the

staircase. Coming home always made him reassess his life. Once he was back on the research vessel he would be fine—back on track with his career and goals.

A few days later Ellie waited for Colt and Winnie in the living room right before they were to leave for Glamour Sensations' Christmas Gala. Dressed in a long black silk gown with a slit up the right side and a gold lamé jacket that came down to the tops of her thighs, she felt uncomfortable. The only place she could put the smaller gun was in a beaded bag she would carry. After all, to the world she was Winnie's assistant, there to make things run smoothly for her employer.

A noise behind her drew her around to watch Colt enter wearing a black tuxedo. She'd only seen him in casual attire. The transformation to a sophisticated gentleman who moved in circles she didn't unless on the job only confirmed how different they were. Yes, he was working on a research ship, but he came from wealth and would inherit a great deal one day. She was from the wrong side of the tracks, a noncommissioned officer in the army for a time and now a woman whose job was to guard others.

He pulled on his cuffs then adjusted his tie. "It's been a while since I wore this. I was all thumbs tying this."

Ellie crossed to him and straightened the bow tie. "There. Perfect."

His smile reached deep into his eyes. "Sometimes I think I need a keeper. I'm much more comfortable in a wet suit or bathing suit."

His remark tore down the barriers she was trying to erect between them. "Tell me about it. I don't like wearing heels. It's hard to run in them."

"Let's hope you don't have to do that tonight."

"I talked with the police chief and his men are in place as well as security from Glamour Sensations. They're checking everyone coming into the ballroom. Thankfully that doesn't seem as out of place as it would have years ago."

She should step away from him, but before she could, he took her hand and backed up a few feet to let his gaze roam leisurely down her length. When it returned to her face, he whistled.

"I like you in heels and that black dress."

She blushed—something she rarely did. "Neither conducive to my kind of work."

"I beg to differ. The bad guy will take one look at you and be so distracted he'll forget what mayhem he was plotting."

Ellie laughed. She would not let his smooth talking go to her head. Two different worlds, she reminded herself. She could see him running Glamour Sensations one day, especially when he told her yesterday he used to work at the company until he finished his college studies.

A loud whirring sound from the front lawn invaded the sudden quiet. She used that distraction to tug her hand free and go to the window. The helicopter landed as close to the house entrance as it could. The dogs barked at it even when the pilot turned it off. Doug Miller called the two Rottweilers back. They obeyed instantly.

"Doug is great with the dogs."

"He was as excited as Granddad when he brought home Rocket and Gabe. Although I don't know if these new ones can ever replace the German shepherds in

Doug's and Winnie's hearts. I was hoping we would get a ransom demand or someone would come forward."

"So did I with the nice reward Winnie offered." Ellie rotated from the window and caught sight of the older woman behind her grandson. "You look great, Winnie."

Dignified in a red crepe gown, she walked farther into the room. "I heard the helicopter. Probably our neighbors heard it, too. Never thought of using one to go to a ball."

"It's the modern-day version of Cinderella's coach." Colt offered his arm to his grandmother.

"In that case I fit the Fairy Godmother rather than Cinderella. That role needs to go to you, Ellie."

"Which leaves me as Prince Charming." He winked at Ellie.

Fairy tales were for dreamers, not her. Ellie skirted around the couple and headed for the foyer before she let the talk go to her head. "Well, our version of the story will be altered a tad bit. This Cinderella is taking her Fairy Godmother to the ball and sticking to her side. But I definitely like the idea of us leaving by midnight."

"I may have to go, but I don't have to stay that long."

Ellie stopped and hugged Winnie. "Those were the best words I've heard in a while."

"After dinner I'll make the announcements, stay for questions then leave. We should be home by eleven. I know you aren't happy about me going to the gala, but I owe all the people who have worked years for my company. They'll benefit so much when we go public. A lot of employees will get stock in Glamour Sensations for their loyalty."

Ellie climbed into the helicopter last and searched the area. Where was the person after Winnie? Watching them here? Waiting for Winnie at the hotel or in the ballroom? She clutched her purse, feeling the outline of her gun. Was their security enough?

As employees and guests entered the ballroom, Winnie stood in a greeting line between Colt and Ellie, shaking everyone's hand and taking a moment to talk with each person attending the gala. At first Ellie wasn't thrilled with her client doing that, but it did give her a chance to assess each attendee.

When Christy moved in front of Winnie, her smile grew, and instead of shaking the woman's hand, Winnie enveloped her in a hug. "How was your trip to L.A. for the commercial?"

"A whirlwind. I never knew all that this position would involve. Peter picked me up from the airport late last night, and since I woke up this morning, I've been going nonstop. I'm going to cherish the time we sit down and have dinner tonight."

Winnie took Christy's fiancé's hand and shook it. "It's nice to see you again, Peter. Christy will be in town at least through Christmas. But afterward she'll be busy. I hope you can arrange some time to go with her on some of her trips. I never want to come between two people in love."

Dr. Tyler held Winnie's hand between his for a few extra seconds. "When it's snowing here, I plan on being on that beach when Christy shoots her second commercial next month."

"Perfect solution. I love winter in Colorado, but that beach is beginning to sound good to these old bones."

"Tsk. Tsk. You don't look old at all. It must be your products you use. You should be your own spokesperson."

Colt leaned toward his grandmother. "I've been telling her that for years. She looks twenty years younger than she is. What woman her age wouldn't like to look as youthful?" He gave her a kiss on the cheek.

As Christy and Peter passed Ellie, she said, "You two are seated at the head table. There are place cards where you're to sit."

Peter nodded his head and escorted Christy toward the front of the room, which was decorated in silver and gold. Elegance came to mind as Ellie scanned the spacious area with lights glittering among the rich decor.

Thirty minutes and hundreds of guests later, Winnie greeted the last person. "Every year this event gets bigger."

"This year we have an extra dozen media people here, including our own film crew." Harold took Winnie's arm and started for the head table.

"I guess it's you and me." Colt fell into step next to Ellie, right behind Winnie. "Did you see anyone suspicious?"

"Actually several I'm going to keep an eye on. Did you realize Mary Ann Witlock's brother is here?" Ellie asked, recalling the photo she'd seen in connection with information on Mary Ann Witlock.

"Bob Witlock? He's worked at Glamour Sensations for years."

Winnie paused and turned back. "He's in marketing and agreed that Christy would be better than his younger sister for the position. Before I made the announcement, I talked to him. I wanted him to know first. For that matter, Jerry Olson's daughter works for Glamour Sensations and is here. She's married. I won't hold someone accountable for another's actions, even a close relative."

"Who is Jerry's daughter?" The reports from the sheriff hadn't said anything about that.

"They have been estranged for years, but it's Serena Pitman. She works in the research lab."

If she'd had the time she would have run her own investigation into each of the prime suspects with grudges against Winnie, but she couldn't do everything, which meant she had to rely on information garnered from reliable sources. Sometimes, though, those sources didn't give her everything she might need.

Winnie continued her trek toward the front of the room. Ellie racked her mind with all the guests who had passed before her, trying to remember who Serena Pitman was. Her visual memory was one of her assets. Face after face flitted through her thoughts until she latched onto the one that went with the name Serena Pitman. Red hair, almost orange, large brown eyes, freckles, petite. She searched the crowd of over two hundred until she found Serena at a table three away from the head one.

When Ellie sat down, her back to the stage, she faced the attendees with a clear view of Serena and her husband. The suspects the police had narrowed down as a viable possibility had not shown up—at least they hadn't come through the greeting line. The security and hotel staff were the only other people besides the guests, and she had made her rounds checking them when she had first arrived before the doors had been opened.

Sandwiched between Winnie and Colt, Ellie assessed each one sitting at the head table. Across from her sat Christy and Peter. Next to the couple was a reporter from the Associated Press and a fashion editor from one of the industry's leading magazines. A Denver newspaper editor of the lifestyle section and a Los Angeles TV show hostess took the last two seats. Harold took his place next to Winnie.

Halfway through the five-course dinner, Colt whispered into Ellie's ear, "Is something wrong with the food?"

"No, it's delicious. I'm not that hungry." Ellie pushed her medley of vegetables around on her plate while her gaze swept over the sea of people, most intent on eating their dinner.

"Everything is going all right."

She slanted a glance at Colt, said, "For the moment," then returned her attention to the crowd.

"Remember, you're Winnie's assistant."

"One who is keeping an eye on the event to make sure it's pulled off without a hitch."

The editor from the Denver newspaper looked right at Winnie and said, "I heard someone earlier talking about a wreck you were involved in. Is that why you arrived here in a helicopter?"

Winnie managed to smile as though nothing was wrong. "A minor collision. It didn't even set off the air bags. A car left stranded in the middle of the highway. Tell me how the drive from Denver was. It was snowing when we arrived."

The man chuckled. "This is Colorado in December. We better have snow or our resort areas will be hurting."

"You're so right, Marvin. Being stranded here isn't too much of a burden. Mountains. Snow. A pair of skis. What more could you ask for?" Winnie cut into her steak.

Harold winked at Winnie. "A warm fire."

"A hot tub," the TV hostess added.

"A snowmobile since I'm probably one of the rare Coloradoans who doesn't ski," Marvin tossed back with the others at the table throwing in other suggestions.

When the conversation started to die down again, Colt asked the Denver editor, "Do you think the Broncos will go all the way to the Super Bowl?"

Ellie bent toward him. "Good question. Football ought to keep the conversation away from the wreck," she whispered.

The mischievous grin on his face riveted her attention for a few long seconds before she averted her gaze and watched the people at the table.

By dessert the conversation morphed from sports to the latest bestsellers. As Peter expounded on a thriller he'd finished, Ellie half listened as she watched the various hotel staff place the peppermint cheesecake before the attendees around the room.

Four tables away Ellie spied a woman who looked vaguely familiar. Was she in one of the photos she'd seen over the past few days? She didn't want to leave Winnie to check the woman out, but she could send a security officer standing not far from her.

"Excuse me, Winnie," Ellie leaned closer to her and whispered, "I'll be right back. I need to talk to your head of security."

Winnie peered over her shoulder at the man at the bottom of the steps that led to the presentation platform. "A problem?"

"I want him to check someone for me. Probably nothing. Be right back."

"We'll be starting our program in ten minutes. The waiters are serving the dessert and coffee."

The head of Glamour Sensations' security met Ellie halfway. "Is there a problem?"

"The dark-haired woman on the serving staff at the table two from the left wall. She looks familiar. Check her out. See who she is and if she has the proper identification."

He nodded and started in that direction. The woman finished taking a dessert plate from a man, put it on a tray and headed quickly for one of the doors the servers were using. The security chief increased his pace. Ellie slowly walked back toward Winnie, scanning the rest of the room before returning to the woman. The dark-headed lady set the tray on a small table near the door then rushed toward the exit, shoving her way through a couple of waiters. The security chief and a police officer Ellie recognized gave chase.

A couple of guests rose, watching the incident unfold.

Ellie leaned down to Winnie. "You should think about leaving. I think the lady I spotted is who we're after."

Winnie turned her head so no one at the table could see her expression or hear her whisper, "I saw. If she's gone, she can't do anything. I'll start now and run through the program then we can leave."

"Did you recognize her?"

"I couldn't tell from this distance. My eyesight isn't as good as it once was."

"Okay. Then let's get this over with. I'll be right behind you."

Winnie was introducing Christy when the head of security came back into the ballroom. He shook his head and took up his post at the foot of the steps to the platform. Ellie noted that all the doors were covered so the woman couldn't return to disrupt the presentation.

Christy came up to stand by Winnie, their arms linked around each other as they faced the audience clapping and cheering. Behind the pair, the screen showed some of the Endless Youth products being released in February. At the height of the event the confetti guns shot off their loads to fill the room with red-and-green streamers. A festival atmosphere took hold of the crowd.

Through the celebration Ellie hovered near Winnie, fixing her full attention on the crowd. Not long and they would all be back in the helicopter returning to the estate. She would be glad when that happened.

Some colorful streamers landed near Ellie, followed by a glass vial that shattered when it hit the platform. A stinking smell wafted up to her. Coughing, Ellie immediately rushed to Winnie's side as more vials mixed in with the streamers smashed against the floor throughout the ballroom, saturating the place with an awful, nauseating stench. People panicked and fled for the doors. The gaiety evolved into pandemonium almost instantly.

EIGHT

Over the screams and shouts, Colt hopped up onto the platform and reached Winnie's side just as Ellie tugged her toward the steps.

"We need to get out of here," she told them. "This would be a great time to strike in the midst of this chaos."

Colt wound his arm about his grandmother. Winnie faltered at the bottom of the stairs. He caught her at the same time Ellie turned and grabbed her, too. Their gazes met.

"We can get out this way." Ellie nodded toward a door behind the staging area. "It leads to an exit. All we have to do is get to the helicopter."

"But the announcement and celebration are ruined," Winnie mumbled, glancing back once before being ushered through the door and down a long hall.

His grandmother looked as if she were shell-shocked. He couldn't blame her. He, too, had hoped they could make it through the evening without incident.

"Once I get you home, I'll check to see what happened. Knowing the police chief and the sheriff, they are already on it." Ellie removed her gun from her purse.

The sight of the lethal weapon widened his grand-mother's eyes at the same time the color drained from her face. He tightened his arms about her. She was a remarkable woman, but anyone could hit a wall and fall apart. He was afraid she was there.

At the door that led outside, Ellie held up her hand to stop them. "Wait. Let me check the area out." She searched the long hallway. "Be right back."

He looked over his shoulder at a few people rushing down the corridor toward the exit.

A couple of seconds later, Ellie returned. "Let's go. The helicopter is around the corner. People are pouring out of the hotel, but it's clear on this side."

"Not for long." Colt tossed his head toward the people coming down the hall.

With her hand on Winnie's right arm, Ellie led the way. She'd seen the pilot in the chopper and his in-structions earlier were to start the engine the second he saw them approaching. Colt flanked his grandmother on the left and slightly behind her as though shielding her from anyone behind. Ellie did this as a job. He did it because he loved his grandmother enough to protect her with his life.

As she neared the front lawn of the hotel, Ellie slowed, panning the terrain for any sign of someone lying in wait. The woman who could have been behind what occurred in the ballroom might have planned the chaos so she could get to Winnie easier outside in the open. Ellie wouldn't allow that to happen.

Peering around the corner of the hotel, Ellie scoped out the crowd emerging from the front entrance, many with no coats on, who stood hugging themselves. The biting cold penetrated the thin layer of her lamé jacket. The people behind them in the hallway burst from the exit, their loud voices charged with fear and speculation.

"Let's go." Ellie started across the snow-covered ground.

A man hurried toward the helicopter as the blades began to whir.

Her gaze glued to the exchange between the pilot and the stranger, Ellie shortened her strides, waiting to see what transpired. When the man ran back toward the crowd, she increased her speed again. The sound of sirens blasted the chilly air.

At the chopper Colt assisted Winnie up into it while Ellie kept watch on the surroundings. After Colt followed his grandmother into the helicopter, Ellie climbed in and the pilot lifted off.

Over the whirring noise, Ellie spoke into her headset. "Who was that man?"

"Hotel security letting me know what happened in the ballroom. I figured you'd be outside soon." The pilot made a wide arc and headed toward the estate.

Ten minutes more. Ellie didn't let down her guard. Sitting forward, she scanned the terrain below. A blanket of white carpeted the ground, lighting the landscape. A helicopter ride she'd taken during one of her missions in the army flashed into her mind. Insurgents on the ground had fired on it, wounding one person in the backseat.

"Winnie, move as far over toward Colt as you can."

As her client did, Colt wrapped his arms around her. Again trying to shield her as much as he could.

Nine minutes later the pilot brought the chopper down as close to the main house as possible. Ellie scrambled out and hurried to Winnie's side to help her. The second she placed her feet on the drive, Ellie shepherded the woman toward her front door while the dogs barked at the helicopter.

Colt gave a command, and they quieted. He came up behind Ellie as they mounted the steps to the deck. Doug threw open the front door, and Ellie whisked Winnie inside.

"The sheriff called and said he's on his way," the caretaker said. "He briefly told me what happened so I came over. I figured you'd be back soon."

Through the fear that marked Winnie's face, she smiled. "I can always count on you and Linda."

"She's in the kitchen preparing some coffee. She'll bring it into the den. I'll let the sheriff in when he's at the gate."

On the way to the den, Ellie paused in the doorway of the small control room. "Have you seen anything unusual?" she asked the ex-police chief who monitored the security feed.

"Nope. Quiet."

Ellie caught up with Winnie and Colt as they entered the den. While Ellie walked from window to window, drawing the drapes, her client collapsed onto the couch, sagging back, her eyes sliding closed.

"Winnie, are you all right?" Colt sat beside her.

"No. This has got to stop. Everything was ruined tonight. Poor Christy. This was her big debut, and some mean, vicious person destroyed her moment."

Ellie positioned herself in front of the fireplace close to Winnie but facing the only entrance into the room. She still clutched her gun as though it were welded to her hand.

"I want to thank you for getting me out of there, Ellie. I'd still be standing on stage, stunned by the lengths a person will go to hurt another."

Ellie moved to the couch and sat on the other side of Winnie. Not until she took a seat did she relax her tightly bunched muscles. "I was only doing my job."

"You've done much more than that for me. The Lord sent you to me at this time." Winnie patted Colt's leg. "And you were there for me, too. I have truly been blessed having two people like you seeing to my welfare." Tears shone in her eyes.

Ellie thanked her. "I got a look at someone I suspect may be the one causing the trouble. Hopefully this might be over before Christmas. I'm still not sure from where I know that woman at the gala tonight, but when security approached, she ran. That's not the action of an innocent person." The sound of footsteps returned Ellie's attention to the door, her hand tensing again on her gun.

Linda entered with a tray of four mugs and a coffeepot. "Doug let the sheriff in the front gate. He should be here any minute. After he arrives, we'll leave unless you need me for anything, Winnie."

She shook her head, a few strands escaping her usual neatly styled silver-gray bun at her nape. "You two are up late as it is. I'm glad you didn't go to the Christmas Gala. Not after what happened."

"Doug and I felt we needed to stay here and make sure nothing went wrong from this end. He patrolled the grounds with the dogs. You know how he is when it starts snowing. He'd rather be outside than in the house." Linda placed the tray on the table in front of the couch. "Do you want me to pour the coffee?"

Colt scooted forward. "I'll do it. Tell Doug thanks."

Doug appeared in the entrance with the sheriff. Linda crossed to them and left with her husband.

Sheriff Quinn grabbed the mug Colt held out to him. "It's getting cold outside."

Winnie didn't hesitate to ask her questions. "Bill, what happened? Is everyone all right? I'm assuming since I don't feel sick that what was released into the air wasn't poisonous."

"You're right, Winnie. Thankfully they were only stink bombs. The police are still trying to determine how many. There were five confetti guns, and it looks like each one shot at least one vial out of it. Maybe more."

"Any injuries with the stampede for the doors?" Ellie cradled her hot mug between her palms. She'd been caught up in a riot once and knew how easily people could get hurt when everyone was trying to flee a place.

"Right before I arrived, the police chief called to let me know he has access to the security feed at the hotel. He said so far it looks like ten injuries, mostly minor stuff. One woman is being sent to the hospital, but I don't think she will stay long."

"It could have been a lot worse." The firm line of Colt's jaw and the extra-precise way he set his mug down attested to his tightly controlled anger.

The sheriff looked at Ellie. "The police chief wants you to look at the tapes of the event. He understands from Glamour Sensations' security head that you think you recognized someone who fled out the staff door. We need to ID that person."

"Sure. I'll do anything I can, but I don't want to leave the estate. Not when Winnie is in danger."

"I thought you would say that. We'll have access to the tapes by computer. It'll be a good time for you all to look over the footage and see if anyone is out of place."

"Anything, even watching hours of tape," Colt said. "I want this to end. My grandmother has been through enough. All I can say is that I'm glad her last product development has been concluded."

"Hon, I'm fine, especially with you and Ellie here." She patted Colt's hand. "Dear, get my laptop from my lab downstairs, will you please?"

Right before he disappeared down the hall, Colt threw a look at Ellie while Winnie and the sheriff talked. In that moment Ellie saw how worried Colt was for his grandmother. Again, she found herself wishing she had that bond with someone.

Sheriff Quinn interrupted her thoughts. "The police are rounding up the staff to question them. If we could have a picture to show them, that will help."

Ellie closed her eyes and imagined the woman from across the ballroom. "She's about five feet six inches with long dark hair. I couldn't tell her eye color specifically, but I think a light color. She was dressed as a server—even had a name tag on like the others."

"I'll let the police chief know that. See if anyone is missing a uniform. If not, it could be one of their staff even if the person wasn't supposed to work that event. Did you see who Ellie is talking about?" he asked Winnie.

"No, sorry. I was trying to keep the conversation at the table going in the right direction. As I suspected, a few rumors have been flying around. The AP reporter wanted confirmation the position of the stolen car indicated it was probably left deliberately, possibly to block our way home."

"Sheriff, did you find any fingerprints on the stalled car the other night?" Ellie leaned over, refilled her mug and poured some more coffee into Winnie's.

"The report came in. No fingerprints the owner couldn't verify weren't someone's who has been in the car lately. So no help there."

Colt came back into the den and handed the laptop to the sheriff to pull up the site with the security footage on it. When he had it, he turned it around and set it on the coffee table, then walked behind the couch to watch.

Sheriff Quinn pointed to a link. "Click on that."

Colt did and a scene from inside the ballroom popped up on the screen. They watched that angle, but Ellie couldn't find the woman or anyone else that appeared suspicious. Colt went to the next link and brought it up.

Ten minutes into it, Winnie yawned. "I'm sorry. I don't know if I can stay awake."

As her own adrenaline rush had subsided, obviously Winnie's had, too. Ellie was used to the ups and downs, but her client wasn't. "Sheriff, can she review it tomorrow morning? I may want to see them again, too."

"Sure." He turned to Winnie. "I can escort you to your room."

Colt paused the tape while Winnie struggled to her feet, sighed and stepped around her grandson. "No, you should stay. At least this person hasn't come into my home and threatened me. If I couldn't walk freely in my own house, I don't know what I would do."

When Winnie left, Ellie murmured, "I didn't have the heart to tell her there is no place one hundred percent secure."

Colt scooted over so the sheriff could sit on the couch. "You don't think it's safe here?"

"Basically it is, as much as it can be. Or I wouldn't let Winnie walk around by herself without me right there. But in any situation I've learned to be wary."

"On the research vessel we've had two run-ins with pirates in different locales, which keeps us on the watch wherever we go, but nothing like this." Colt clicked to continue viewing the security footage.

"It's sad," Ellie said, focusing again on the tape. "These kinds of things are what keep me in business."

"Pause it. That's her!" About an hour into the footage Ellie bolted forward, pointing at a dark-haired woman on the screen who was carrying a tray with coffeepots and a water pitcher. "The same height, hairstyle. Can we zoom in on her?"

Colt clicked several keys and moved in closer.

"That's who ran out of the ballroom when the security head made his way toward her. We need a still of that, and see if someone can make the photo clearer." Her image teased Ellie's thoughts.

"I'll see what I can do and bring it back to you tomorrow." Sheriff Quinn wrote down how far into that tape they were while Colt started the footage again.

On closer examination, Ellie saw surprise on the woman's face when she spied the two security men coming toward her. She glanced toward a table near the head table, then hurried toward the exit. "Back up. Who was she looking at?"

Colt found the spot and zeroed in on the table next to the one where they'd been sitting. "Take your pick who she's staring at."

"Maybe no one." The sheriff rose.

"Or maybe one of the people whose back isn't to the woman," Ellie said. "There are four men and three women. Is there any way we can find out who was sitting at the table? There were only a few tables reserved and that wasn't one of them."

"I'll see what I can find out tomorrow morning when I meet with the police chief. In the meantime, I'm leaving two deputies with you again. One is in the foyer. The other is driving up the mountain as we speak. Rod will let him in. We'll have a long day tomorrow so get some sleep. That's what I'm gonna do. I'm determined we'll find out who it is. We have a picture now. That's better than before."

"Sheriff, I love your optimism. I hope you're right. I could be home in time for Christmas." She walked with him out to the foyer where Rod stood.

"Where is home?"

"Dallas, when I'm between jobs."

"Family there?"

"No. It'll just be me, but my boss hosts Christmas dinner for anyone who's in town." Which was the closest she came to having a family during the holidays.

"I have a son coming in for Christmas with his three children. I can't wait to see them. It's been six months, and they grow up fast."

When Ellie returned to the den, Colt gathered up the closed laptop and bridged the distance between them. "I heard what you said about Christmas. Do you think this will be over by then? That we'll have a peaceful Christmas?"

"I'm hoping. Winnie has been great dealing with what's been happening to her, but it's taking its toll."

"I'm glad she's finished in the lab. She doesn't have to worry about that at least."

"But that will mean she'll focus totally on what's happening. That may be worse."

"Then we'll have to create things for her to do. We haven't decorated the house like it has been in the past. Tons of decorations are still in storage in the basement."

Ellie couldn't remember decorating for Christmas in years, and even as a child, they often didn't have a tree. Her mother didn't care about the holiday, but Toby and she had tried to make their apartment festive. Then Toby had died and Ellie hadn't cared, either. "Sure, if it will help take Winnie's mind off the threats."

"Christmas is her favorite time of year. She's been so busy she's not had the time to do what she usually does. This will be perfect." Colt strode to the staircase with Ellie.

As she mounted the steps to the second floor, she wondered what a family Christmas was really like. At the top of the stairs, she looked around and started laughing. "I can't believe I walked all the way up here when I haven't checked the house yet."

"It must have been my charm and wit that rattled you."

"I hate to burst your bubble, Colt, but it's exhaustion." The sound of his chuckles sent a wave of warmth down her length.

"I'll put this laptop in my room and come with you. I wouldn't want you to fall asleep while making your rounds." He turned toward the right.

Ellie clasped his arm. "I'll be okay. I may be exhausted, but that doesn't mean I'll fall asleep."

He swung around. His gaze intent, he grazed his fingertips down her jaw. "What keeps you from sleeping?"

She shrugged one shoulder. "The usual. Worries."

"Winnie would tell you to turn them over to the Lord."

"What would you say?"

"Winnie is right, but I've always had trouble doing that. I still want to control things."

"Me, too. I know worrying is a waste of time and energy, but I've been doing it for so long, trying to control all aspects of my life, that I don't know how to give it totally to God."

"Practice."

"Have you ever practiced and practiced and never accomplished what you set out to do?"

"Not usually." He snapped his finger. "Except ballroom dancing. I have two left feet."

"I'll remember that if you ever ask me to dance." She took a step back. "Seriously, you don't need to come with me. At least one of us should get some sleep. I'm not going to bed until the second deputy arrives, anyway."

"I can keep you company if you like."

She would, but as she stared into his face, a face she'd looked forward to seeing each morning, she knew the danger in him staying up with her. Each day she was around him she liked him more and more. The way he loved his grandmother, handled a crisis—the way he kissed. "No, I'm not going to be long." She backed up until her heel encountered the edge of the staircase.

Like the first night they met, he moved with a quickness that surprised her, hooked his arm around her and tugged her to him. He planted a kiss on her lips that melted her resolve not to be around him. Then he parted, pivoted and started down the hallway. "Good night, Ellie. I'll see you in the morning."

Why did you do that? She wanted to shout the question at him but clamped together her tingling lips that still felt the remnants of his kiss. Coupled with her stomach fluttering and her heart beating rapidly, the sensations from that brief joining left their brand on her. She hurried down the stairs, sure the only reason she was attracted to the man was because it was that time of year when she yearned for a family, for a connectedness she'd never had except with her twin brother, Toby.

As Ellie went from room to room, making sure the house was secured, she forced her mind back to the case. She visualized the picture of the woman on the computer in her mind. She'd seen her before. By the time she reached her bedroom, she strode to the photos the sheriff had shown them of the possible suspects. She flipped through the pictures until she came upon Mary Ann Witlock. Covering up the woman's long blond hair, Ellie visualized her in a dark brown wig. And that's when she knew. Mary Ann was the bogus server at the gala tonight.

"Hot chocolate for everyone," Linda announced the next afternoon as she brought in a tray with the drinks and a plate of frosted Christmas sugar cookies.

For the past couple hours Ellie had been decorating a tree with Colt and Winnie and Harold and Christy. Now she climbed the ladder to place the star at the very top. When she descended to the floor, she viewed the ten-foot tree Doug and Colt had cut down that morning. The scent of pine hung in the air.

"This is turning into a party. I love it." Winnie backed away from the tree in the living room centered in front of the large picture window. "I might not be able to leave, but I appreciate you all coming here to help cheer up an old lady. This is just what I needed."

Colt slung his arm over his grandmother's shoulders. "Old? Did I hear you admit you're old? Who has stolen my grandmother?"

Winnie punched him playfully in the stomach. "I am seventy-three."

Colt arched a eyebrow. "So?"

"Okay, I admit I've let the threats get to me. But not anymore. The sheriff is closing in on the woman who, it looks like, has been behind everything."

"I can't believe Mary Ann is behind this. If I'd known what would happen, I'd have turned down the opportunity to be the spokesperson for Endless Youth." Christy took a mug of hot chocolate and a cookie off the tray. "I didn't realize she needed the money."

Winnie frowned. "Neither did I. If she had come to me, I would have loaned her the money."

"We don't know for sure it's her behind the threats," Harold said as he planted himself in a chair. "All we know is she was disguised last night as a server and then ran from security when approached."

"That's the action of a guilty person. And why was she wearing a dark wig if she was innocent?" Linda asked as she left the room.

"What do you think, Ellie?" Winnie removed some tinsel from a box and passed it out.

"She needs money and lost a chance at making a lot. She is missing right now. The police went to her house and haven't been able to locate her. Maybe the search warrant will produce something more concrete." Ellie carefully draped a few strands of tinsel on a branch. Probably the person Mary Ann was looking at before fleeing the ballroom was her brother, sitting at the table next to them. When Winnie had identified him this morning on the video, that was at least one mystery taken care of. Sheriff Quinn was investigating Bob Witlock to make sure he had no involvement, but he didn't think the brother did because he and Mary Ann had been estranged for several years.

Colt came up beside Ellie. "At the rate you're going, Ellie, it'll be midnight before we finish decorating the tree. This is the way we do it." He took some of the tinsel and tossed it onto several limbs. "See? Effective and fast."

"But it's not neat."

"That's okay. It's fun, and our tree isn't what you would find in a magazine. It's full of our past—not fancy store-bought ornaments." Colt gave her some more tinsel. "Give it a try."

Ellie did and laughed when half ended up on the carpet. "There must be an art to it, and clearly I don't have the toss method down."

Colt stepped behind her and took her arm. "It's called losing a little control and just letting go at the right time," he whispered into her ear.

She was glad no one else could hear him; his words caused her pulse rate to accelerate.

As he brought her arm back then swung it forward, he murmured, "Let go."

In the second she did and the silvery strands landed on various branches haphazardly, but none on the floor, something inside her did let go. It had nothing to do with the activity. It had to do with the man so close to her his scent engulfed her. The brush of his breath against her neck warmed her.

Quickly she stepped away. "I have no idea when I'll use this new skill again, but thanks for showing me how to do it properly." She tore her gaze from his and swept it around the room, taking in the faces of the people, all of whom were watching them.

The chime of the doorbell cut through the silence that fell over the room. Ellie thrust the remaining tinsel into Colt's hands and hurried to answer the door. She'd let him get to her. Let him give her a little glimpse at what she was missing. And she became all soft.

She opened the door to allow the sheriff inside. "I hope you have good news for us. What did you find at Mary Ann's house?"

He faced her with a grim expression. "We found a lot of evidence that points to her being the person threatening Winnie—one letter Winnie received was on Mary Ann's computer, along with pictures of Winnie. There was also a suicide note from Mary Ann. When I turned the computer on, that was the first thing that came up."

"Suicide? You found her body?"

"No. No one has seen her since last night. The Bakersville police and my office are still searching for her. There were also a couple of large dog crates in her garage and mud-caked boots, size nine men's shoes, although that isn't the size she wears. Also, there was a stack of unpaid bills on her kitchen table. She received a foreclosure notice a week ago."

"Winnie won't be safe until Mary Ann is found. I hope alive. But what about the dogs? If she took them, where are they?" Out of the corner of her eye she glimpsed Colt coming across the foyer toward them.

"Good question," the sheriff replied. "She could have gotten rid of them or sold them perhaps to someone not from around here. She needed money, so that would be my guess."

"So there's no telling where the dogs are, then?"

Colt stopped next to her. "Winnie was concerned something has happened."

"It has. It looks like Mary Ann is the person threatening Winnie, but she's disappeared." Ellie tried not to look at Colt directly in the eyes. Something had changed between them earlier in the living room, and she didn't know what to think or what to do about it.

"Which means Winnie is still in danger."

"Afraid so," the sheriff said, removing his hat and sliding the brim through his hands.

Winnie paused in the doorway into the living room. "Bill, why are you all standing out here? Come join us. Harold is here and Christy. Peter is coming after his last patient. We're getting ready for Christmas finally."

"I hate to intrude—"

"We've got hot chocolate and Christmas cookies."

"Well, in that case, I'll stay for a little while." The sheriff made his way toward Winnie, grinning from ear to ear. "Linda makes great cookies. I bought a box of them at the cookie sale at church."

"Why, Bill Quinn, I could have made them."

Both of his eyebrows rose. "Did you?"

Winnie giggled. "No, you're safe from my cooking. Why do you think I hired Linda in the first place?"

"Your husband insisted."

As the two entered the living room and their voices

faded, Ellie hung back with Colt. "I wanted to let you know what the sheriff told me when they went to Mary Ann's house." After she explained what they found, she added, "There was a suicide note on her computer."

"But she wasn't there?"

"No. The woman isn't in her right mind. She's desperate. What she did last night is an act of a person falling apart. An act of revenge."

"And the dogs? Any idea where they are?"

"They're valuable dogs. No telling where they are now. She most likely sold them since she was in debt for thousands of dollars. The police chief is checking with the bank in Bakersville where Mary Ann had an account to see if she was paid a large amount of money lately."

"If that's the case, couldn't she take care of some of her debt, if not all?"

"I did some research on some of the suspects, and I remember she had extensive dental work six months ago. I saw a before and after picture. Her teeth and smile were perfect afterward. It made a big difference in her appearance. I wonder if she did that hoping she would get the spokesperson position for Endless Youth."

"If that were the case, I can see why Winnie wouldn't hire her. She wouldn't want anyone who'd recently had work done to her face, even dental. The press could take it and focus on that rather than on Endless Youth. I've seen it before. Where the intended message is sidetracked by something that really had nothing to do with it."

"She had a huge dental bill and her waitress salary probably barely covered her necessities."

Winnie appeared in the living room entrance and

peered at Colt. "We have guests. You two can talk after they leave. I imagine you're speculating about Mary Ann, and I would like to hear what you have to say. She needs our prayers, the troubled girl."

"Sorry, Winnie," Colt replied. "We didn't want to say anything in front of the others."

"It's only Christy and Harold. They're family. Oh, that reminds me. I've got to let the person monitoring the gate know to let Peter in when he arrives. I thought we'd have an early dinner before sending our guests down the mountain. And the sheriff is staying, too. It seems his office can run without him occasionally." Winnie hurried toward the monitoring room.

"Are you sure she is really seventy-three?" Ellie asked as she headed for the living room.

"That's what her birth certificate said. I saw it once before she whisked it away from me. That was when she wouldn't tell anyone her age."

"She should be the spokesperson for Endless Youth."

"You know Harold mentioned that to her, and she laughed in his face. I could never see my grandmother purposely putting herself in the public eye."

"Because of what happened when she married your grandfather?"

"Partly, and the fact that Winnie is really shy with most people."

"Shy? I don't see much evidence of that. Look at last night with the media before everything fell apart."

"She's learned to put on a front and can do it for short periods of time, but, believe me, the evening drained her emotionally beyond the threats and what happened with the stink bombs."

"No wonder I like her so much. She and I have a lot in common."

"I know. That's why I like you."

His words took flight in her heart until she shot them down. They didn't mean anything. Really.

Soft strains of Christmas music played in the background. The fire blazed in the hearth in the living room while the hundreds of lights strung around the tree and a lone lamp gave off the only illumination. Colt settled on the couch next to Winnie, with Harold at the other end. Ellie sat directly across from him. Cuddling as two people in love did, Christy and Peter shared an oversize lounge chair. Sheriff Quinn had left hours ago.

Cozy. Warm. Almost as if there had been no threats, no attempts on Winnie. Almost. But the thought had edged its way into Colt's mind throughout the day, souring a day meant to forget the incident at the gala and to focus on Christmas. Then he would look at Ellie and the outside world wouldn't mean anything.

Doug came into the room. "Before Linda and I leave, I thought I'd let you know that it has started snowing again. We're not supposed to get too much."

"Thank Linda for another wonderful dinner." Winnie set her coffee on a coaster on the table.

"We enjoyed sharing the celebration tonight with all of you, but I want to check on the dogs," Doug said. "We both hope they find this Mary Ann Witlock soon so this is all over with." After saying his goodbyes the caretaker left.

Colt had always felt his grandmother was in good hands with the couple who had become more a part of the family with each year. "I wish the sheriff would call us with some good news. Maybe Mary Ann fled the area."

"Sheriff Quinn said they checked the airports in the vicinity, but Mary Ann's car is gone so she might have. They have a multistate search out for the car." Ellie leaned back and crossed her long legs.

The movement drew Colt's attention, his eyes slowly making their way up her body to her face. The soft glow of the lighting in the room emphasized her beauty. What was it about Ellie that intrigued him? That she could take care of herself in just about any situation? He knew strong women, even worked with several on the research vessel, but other than respecting their intelligence, there was no draw for him—not like with Ellie.

"We all know there are plenty of places to hide in the mountains around here. Back roads to use." Peter shifted then circled his arm around Christy.

"Yeah, but it's winter and snow will make that more difficult," Harold said.

Peter came right back with, "We haven't had as much as usual so far this year. She may be long gone by now."

"True. And when you're desperate, you sometimes do things you wouldn't normally do." Ellie's gaze fixed on Colt as though there was a secret message behind her words.

"I know she was at Glamour Sensations a lot for the Endless Youth position, but she was always so quiet and reserved. I didn't really know her at all." Christy peered over her shoulder at Peter. "You did her dental work. Didn't you see her for a follow-up a few weeks ago? What do you think her frame of mind was like?"

"She was agitated. She asked me to extend the time she could pay off her bill. I did, but she still was upset when she left. If I'd thought she would commit suicide, I'd have said something, but…"

"Peter, we can't always tell what someone is thinking or is going to do. I know we all would have said something if we had known. I'm still praying the police will find her alive and hiding." Winnie's hand quivered as she brought her cup to her lips.

Colt slid his arm around his grandmother. "You'd be the first one to help her if you'd known. If she's found, I wouldn't be surprised if you pay for a good lawyer to defend her. That's one of the things I love about you."

A frown puckered Christy's forehead. "Can we change the subject? I don't want to spend any more time on this horrid situation. I feel bad enough about Mary Ann."

Winnie patted Colt's thigh, then smiled at Christy. "You're right. Let's talk about our plans for Christmas. Only three days away."

Ellie's cell rang. She looked at the number then rose, leaving the room. Colt heard her say Sheriff Quinn's name and followed her into the foyer.

As he neared her, she ended the call and lifted her gaze to his. "They found Mary Ann's body."

NINE

Ellie slipped her cell into her pocket. "Her body was found at the bottom of a cliff by cross-country skiers right before dark. Her car, parked near the top of the cliff, was found by a deputy a little later."

"Suicide?"

"That's what they think, but Sheriff Quinn will know more tomorrow after the medical examiner looks at the body and they have more time to thoroughly search the scene below and above. The preliminary processing supports a suicide, especially in light of her note and state of mind."

Colt blew out a long breath. "Then it's over with."

"It's looking that way."

"Let's go tell everyone." Colt held his hand out to her.

She took it, realizing by tomorrow or the following day she could be on her way back to Dallas. Just in time to spend a lonely Christmas at home. At least she'd have a few hours with Kyra and her husband on the twenty-fifth.

When they reentered the living room Colt sat next to Winnie. "Ellie heard from the sheriff. They found Mary

Ann's body at the bottom of a cliff. They think it was suicide but they'll make a ruling probably tomorrow."

"It's over. That's great." Standing at the fireplace, Harold dropped another log on the blaze. "The best news I've heard in a while."

"Harold! How can you say that? A young woman killed herself." Tears glittered on Winnie's bottom eyelashes.

The CFO flushed, redder than the flames behind him. "You're right. I was only thinking about you and your situation."

"She did try to kill you." Peter sat forward. "There are people last night who were hurt because of her rage. *You* could have been hurt in the stampede to leave. Or when you were outside. Surely the stink bombs were a ruse to get you outside."

Winnie pushed to her feet. "I don't care. I can't celebrate a woman's death."

Colt stood up beside her. "Grandma, I don't think Harold really meant that. He was just showing how happy he is that it's all over."

Harold crossed to Winnie and took her into his arms. "I'm sorry. I never meant to cause you any pain. Please forgive me."

She raised her chin and looked at him. "I know you didn't. I only wish I'd known what was going on in Mary Ann's head. I could have helped her."

Could she forgive like that? Ellie wondered. She still couldn't forgive her mother for her neglect as she and Toby grew up. If Toby hadn't had Ellie, he would have had no one to look out for him. He'd needed extra care, and their mother couldn't be bothered.

"I applaud you for wanting to help the woman, but

she did try to hurt you." Peter shook his head slowly. "Aren't you just a little bit angry at her? That's a natural human response to someone who does something to you."

Winnie withdrew from Harold's embrace. "Did I ever feel anger toward the person behind the threats? Of course, I did. I'm no saint. But if I let that anger take over, I'm the one who is really hurt by it."

Peter snorted. "You're really hurt if they succeed in their plan. I'm sorry. I think people should be held accountable for what they do."

"I have to agree with Peter," Colt said. "Mary Ann had choices. I can't make excuses for what she put you through. I certainly won't celebrate her death, but I'm relieved it's over with. We can all have a normal Christmas." He looked from Winnie to Ellie.

Silence hovered over the group as his gaze drew her to him. Ellie gripped the back of a chair and remained still, finally averting her eyes.

"We'd better head home. I don't want to get caught out in a snowstorm." Peter rose right after Christy and put his arm around his fiancée. "Our time is limited since Christy found out she needed to go back to L.A. for a couple of days."

"Since when?" Winnie asked.

"Since last night." Harold kneaded her shoulder. "I forgot to tell you. I meant to first thing this afternoon, then we started decorating the tree. She is going to appear on *Starr's Take*. The talk show hostess felt bad about what happened last night and wants to highlight Christy for a show at the first of the year. That is, if Christy will fly to L.A. tomorrow and tape the segment first thing the next day."

"I'll be back midafternoon Christmas Eve. I don't want to miss my first one with Peter." Christy clasped his hand. "We had plans, but he's been so good about it."

"Harold, I can't believe you didn't tell me the second you walked into my house," Winnie said.

"If you remember correctly, you dragged me over to the box of lights and told me to untangle them."

Winnie's eyes twinkled. "Oh, that's right. In that case, I know what it's like to be distracted. I've had my share of distractions these past few weeks. No more. I'm diving into Christmas. I might even persuade my grandson to go up to my cabin like we used to."

"Not unless the sheriff approves, Winnie." Harold gave her a kiss on the cheek and prepared to leave.

Winnie walked with Harold, Peter and Christy to the foyer while Colt stayed back, snatching Ellie as she started to follow his grandmother. "I can't believe this may be over."

"If it is tomorrow, when are you going back to your research vessel?"

"I'm definitely staying through Christmas now. I want to make sure Winnie is all right. She can beat herself up when she finds out someone is hurting and she didn't do anything about it. I don't want her to start blaming herself for not anticipating Mary Ann's reaction to not getting the job with Endless Youth."

"We can't control other people's reactions, only our own."

Winnie strode into the room. "You two don't have to worry about me. I'm going to be fine, especially if I can spend some time at the cabin like we used to every Christmas."

"So you really are thinking about going up the mountain?" Colt asked.

"Yes, I know we spent the day decorating the house, but all of this has made me yearn for those simpler days. Thomas and I loved to escape life by going to the cabin."

"My fondest memories are of our Christmases spent there."

"So you'll agree to go?" Winnie picked up the coffee cups and put them on the tray Doug had left earlier.

"Yes."

Winnie looked up from the coffee table. "How about you, Ellie? I'd love for you to join us. You're part of the reason I'm safe and able to go to the cabin. It would be nice to share it with you."

"I hate to intrude—"

"Nonsense. I remember you saying that you don't have family to spend the holidays with. Consider us your family this year." Winnie started to lift the tray.

Colt hurried forward and took it from her. "I agree with Winnie. After all the time you've spent protecting her, let us show our appreciation. Please."

The look he gave Ellie warmed her insides. She wasn't quite ready yet to say goodbye to him or Winnie. Which, if she thought about it, was probably a mistake. Clearly she had feelings for them—and she didn't do emotions well. Still, maybe it was time just to do something impulsive. "I'll join you, if you're sure."

"Well, then it's settled. We'll go if the sheriff thinks it's okay." Winnie walked toward the hallway. "I'm suddenly tired. It's been quite a day—actually, quite a week."

After she left to retire for the night, Colt's gaze

seized Ellie's, a smoldering glint in his gray-blue eyes. "What about you?"

"I'm surprised I'm not tired. Maybe I had one too many cups of coffee. Caffeine usually doesn't affect me, though."

"I'll be right back. I'm known around the *Kaleidoscope* as the night owl, the last to go to sleep and definitely not the first to wake up in the morning."

As Colt left with the tray, the warmth of the fire drew Ellie to the sofa nearest the fireplace. She decided that for a short time she was going to enjoy herself. Real life would return when she flew back to Dallas and took another assignment.

Settling herself on the couch, she lounged back, resting her head against the cushion. The faint sounds of "Silent Night" played in the background. She remembered a Christmas Eve service she went to years ago where at the end the lights were switched off and only candlelight glowed in the dark church. She reached over and shut off the lamp nearby, throwing the room in shadows with only the tree and fire for illumination.

With a sigh, she relaxed, though she knew she couldn't surrender her guard totally. Nothing was official concerning Mary Ann. The sheriff still had a few loose ends he wanted cleared up.

She heard Colt move across the room toward her. The air vibrated with his presence although he was quiet. The cushion gave in when he sat on the sofa only inches from her. His scent vied with the aromas of the fire and the pine tree.

"Ellie," he whispered as though he might wake her up if he spoke any louder.

"I can't fall asleep that fast." She opened her eyes and

rolled her head to the side to look at him. "I was enjoying the sound of the music and the crackling of the fire."

"I can always leave you—"

She touched her fingertips to his lips. "Shh. The sound of your voice is even better. Tell me about what it was like growing up with Winnie. What happened to your parents?"

He leaned back, his arm up against hers. "I never really knew my mother. She died shortly after I was born. A massive infection. I guess my father tried to raise me—or more like a series of nannies did. One day when I was four Winnie showed up at the house and found the nanny drinking my dad's liquor. Winnie took me home with her, and I never left after that."

"What about your father?"

"I saw him occasionally when he wanted something from his parents. Mostly I just heard about his exploits from the servants or sometimes from the news. He played fast and furious. Never cared about the family business. One day he mixed drugs and alcohol, passed out and never woke up. Winnie told me he was mourning my mother's death. According to my grandmother, he loved her very much and fell apart when she died."

"How do you feel about your dad?"

Colt tensed, sitting up. "I hardly knew the man, so how can I answer that?"

"Truthfully. You might not have known him well, but that doesn't stop you from forming an opinion, having feelings about him."

For a long moment he sat quietly, his hands clasped together tightly, staring at the coffee table. "The truth is I don't have much feeling toward him at all. He was the man who happened to sire me, but he wasn't my father. My granddad filled that position in my life. The same with Winnie. She was my mother."

"Do you blame your mother for dying?"

He turned toward her, again not saying anything, but a war of emotions flitted across his features, everything from anger to surprise to sadness. "I never really thought about it, but I guess I do carry some anger toward her. But ultimately I'm sad I didn't get to know her. My grandmother told me wonderful stories about her."

"It sounds like Winnie and your granddad were here for you."

"Yes. That's why I feel like I'm letting Winnie down."

"How so?"

"I pursued my own interests and became a marine biologist, but there's a part of me that enjoys watching my grandmother create a product. I had a double major in chemistry and marine biology, but I went on to get my doctorate in marine biology because that interested me the most. I got the chemistry degree for my grandparents, but I did like the field."

"Then why did you become a marine biologist?"

"To see what I could accomplish alone, without the Winfield name." His mouth lifted in a lopsided grin. "How about you? What were your parents like?"

She'd wanted to get to know Colt better and should have realized he would want to do the same. "I don't talk about my childhood. It's behind me. Not something I care to revisit."

One of his eyebrows rose. "I should share my whole life story with you, but yours is off-limits?"

"I said I don't talk about it, but I'll make an exception with you."

"Why?"

"Because..." She didn't know how to say what she felt was developing between them because she had never been good at relationships. She was better as a loner, and her job made that easier.

"Because of what's happening between us?"

"What is that?" *Help me to understand.*

He shifted toward her, crowding her space. "I wish I knew. I do know I'm attracted to you. That if our circumstances were different, we could be friends—good friends. Maybe..." He swallowed hard.

"More?"

He nodded. "You feel it, too?"

"Yes. But you're right. Our lives are in different parts of the world and—"

He bent forward and kissed her hard, cutting off her words, robbing her of a decent breath. But she didn't care. She returned his kiss with her own fervent feelings. Intense, overwhelming. Threatening her emotionally.

She pulled back, one part of her not wanting to end the kiss, but the sensible part of her demanding she act now before she surrendered her heart to Colt. "You know, all this talk has worn me out. I'd better do my rounds then go to bed."

She got to her feet and put some space between them before he coaxed her to stay. He wouldn't have to say much. She skirted around the coffee table and started for the hallway.

"Ellie."

She turned toward him.

"I'm a good listener. When you want to talk about your parents, I'm here."

She strode across the foyer, making sure the alarm system was on and working. Then she began with the dining room, examining the windows to verify they were locked. Not many people had ever told her they would listen to her about her past, but then she'd rarely given anyone the chance. Colt was scaling the walls she kept up around herself. Was it time to let him in?

Late the next afternoon, not long before the sun went down, Ellie propped her shoulder against a post on the porch of the mountain cabin. The Winfield place was nothing like the image of a tiny log cabin she had in her mind. Though the bottom portion was made out of logs, the three-bedroom A-frame was huge and imposing. The smoke from the huge stone fireplace, its wisps entwining with the falling snow, scented the crisp air. A large mug with Linda's delicious hot chocolate, which she'd sent with them before they'd climbed into the four-wheel-drive Jeep and trekked up to the top of the mountain, warmed her bare hands.

The cabin door opened and closed. Colt came to stand beside her with his own drink. "It's beautiful up here. The view when it isn't snowing is breathtaking."

"Will this snow be a problem?"

"The weather report says this system should move out fairly fast. We'll probably get six or seven inches. Nothing we can't handle. But we have enough food for four or five days. We always come prepared with almost twice what we need and there are staples left up here. Doug and Linda use the cabin throughout the year."

"I was glad to see you had a landline. I knew the cell

reception was nonexistent this far up the mountain. I don't want to be totally cut off from civilization."

"Mary Ann can't hurt Winnie anymore. The ME ruled it a suicide, and the sheriff couldn't find anything to indicate she wasn't working alone. Winnie is tickled they have a lead on where the dogs could have been sold."

"That'll be a nice Christmas present for Winnie if they find the dogs and they're back at the estate when she comes down off the mountain."

"If it's possible, Sheriff Quinn and Doug will make it happen."

"Winnie has a lot of people who care about her and watch out for her. That says a lot about her."

Colt's gaze snared hers. "How about you? You told me once your brother died when you were young. Do you have any more siblings?"

"Nope. It was just him and me. He was my twin."

"That had to be extra hard on you."

"Yes it was. He had a congenital heart defect that finally got the best of him."

"How old were you?"

"Thirteen."

"How were your parents?"

Suddenly the cold seemed to seep through the layers of clothing Ellie wore. She shivered, taking a large swallow of the now lukewarm chocolate. "I'd better go back inside before I freeze."

In the cabin, Winnie sat in a chair before the fire, knitting. Ellie stopped a few feet into the great room.

Winnie glanced up. "These past few years I haven't gotten to knit like I used to. I found my needles and

some yarn and decided to see if I remembered how."
A smile curved her mouth, her hands moving quickly.

"It looks like you remember."

"Yes. A nice surprise. The second I stepped inside
the cabin I felt like a new woman. My product line is
finished, at least for the time being, and the person after
me has been found. I'd say that was a wonderful Christmas gift." She lifted the patch of yarn. "And now this.
Have you ever knitted?"

Laughing, Ellie took the chair across from her. "I
wouldn't be able to sit still long enough to do it. That's
something I'll leave to others."

"I might just make this into a scarf for you. That way
you won't forget me when you get back to Dallas and
go onto another assignment."

"Forget you?" Ellie shook her head. "That's not
gonna happen. You're an amazing woman."

A hint of red colored her cheeks. "Where's my grandson?"

"Communing with nature," Ellie said with a shrug.

"I'm glad you didn't change your mind about coming." Winnie paused and leaned toward her, lowering
her voice. "I was sure you would."

"Why?"

"I saw you yesterday while we were decorating and
celebrating. You weren't totally comfortable with the
whole scene. I imagine since you go from one place
to another because of your job, you don't do much for
the holidays. Who did you spend Thanksgiving with
this year?"

"No one. I microwaved a turkey dinner and celebrated alone. I have a standing invitation to Kyra's, but

I hate always intruding on her and her husband. They're practically newlyweds."

"Kind of painful sometimes being around a couple deeply in love when you aren't."

"That's not it. I just..." *Just what?* she asked herself. In truth, Winnie was probably right. Kyra and Michael were always so good to include her in whatever they were doing, but she saw the looks exchanged between them—full of love that excluded everyone else in the room. She'd never had a man look at her like that—not even Greg, who she had thought she would marry one day. "It's not that I want a relationship, but there are times I get lonely."

"We all do. And why don't you want a relationship? You have a lot to offer a man."

Ellie peered at the front door, relieved it was still closed and Colt was outside. "I don't think I'd be very good at it. I've always depended on myself for everything."

"Everything? Not God a little bit?"

"Well, yes. I know He's there, but I'm not sure He's that interested in my day-to-day life."

"Oh, He is."

"Then where was He when I was growing up? Having to raise myself? Take care of my brother because our mother couldn't be bothered?" She finally said the questions that had plagued her ever since she gave herself to Christ.

"Look at the type of woman you've grown into. You're strong. You can take care of yourself. You help others have peace of mind when trouble happens in their life. I for one am thankful you came into my life.

Sadly, an easy road doesn't usually hone a person into what they need to be."

The door finally opened, and Colt hurried inside, stomping his feet. Snow covered his hair and coat. "I forgot something in the Jeep and went out to get it." After shrugging out of his heavy jacket, he put a sack on the table near the chair he settled into. "It's really snowing now. Too much more and we'll have whiteout conditions."

"It sounds like the weatherman got it wrong." Ellie eyed the bag. "What did you forget?"

"A surprise."

"You know a bodyguard doesn't like surprises."

"This is a good one." He quirked a grin, his eyes sparkling. "You and Winnie have to wait until Christmas morning."

"It's a present? I didn't get you anything." An edge of panic invaded Ellie's voice. A gift from him made their…friendship even more personal.

"It's nothing. And I don't want anything. That's not why I'm giving you this."

Winnie laughed. "Ellie, enjoy it. Colt loves giving gifts. He's just like his grandfather. I used to be able to find out what it was before Colt gave it to me. But not anymore. He's gotten quite good at keeping a secret."

"So, Winnie, what are we having for dinner?" Colt combed his fingers through his wet hair.

Winnie gave him a look. "Are you suffering from hypothermia? You want *me* to fix dinner?"

Colt chuckled. "Not if I want to eat anything decent. I was teasing you. Ellie and I will cook dinner for you." He rose and offered Ellie his hand.

She took it and let him tug her up. "You do know I don't cook a lot for myself. I'm not home that much."

"But I cook. We all take turns on the ship, and if we weren't accomplished, we quickly learned or the rest of the crew threatened to toss us overboard."

Ellie examined the contents of the refrigerator. "Grilling is out," she said as she glanced back at Colt. "Which, by the way, I am good at. So I guess the steaks can wait for a less snowy day."

"From the looks of it outside, I don't know that's going to happen before we leave. We can use the broiler in the oven."

"So how are we going to get out of here if it snows that much?"

"We have a snowmobile in the shed out back and skis."

"Winnie skis?"

"She did when she was younger, but she'll use the snowmobile. How are you on skis?"

"Never tried it. I live in flat country."

"We have some cross-country skis. Flat country is fine for that."

"But the way down isn't flat. I might not make a pretty picture on skis, but I'll do what I have to." She took the meat out of the refrigerator. "Okay, steak it is. I can actually prepare them and put them in the broiler. So what are you gonna cook?"

His chuckle spiced the air. "I see how this is going to go. I'm going to do most of the work. I thought you said you could cook."

"Simple things like steaks. Let's say you're the head chef and I'm the assistant. Believe me, you all will be much better off."

"Well then, let's make this simple. Baked potatoes and a salad."

"I'm all for easy."

Surprisingly Ellie found they cooked well as a team, and by the time they sat down to eat she'd laughed more at the stories Colt told her about life on the research vessel than she had in a long time. Her jobs were serious and left little room for the lighter side of life.

"I'm glad you two talked me into coming up here," Ellie said when Winnie finished her blessing. "I've worked a lot in the past few years and have had little downtime. I needed this and didn't even realize it. No bad guys out there stalking a client. That's a nice feeling"

Winnie agreed. "That's how I'm looking at these next three days. A minivacation that I needed a lot. I'm too old to work as hard as I have been with Endless Youth. But it's mostly done, and I've accomplished what Thomas and I set out to do all those years ago. Once the company goes public, I'm stepping down as CEO of Glamour Sensations."

Colt dropped his fork on his plate. "You're finally retiring? I've been wanting you to slow down for years."

Winnie pursed her lips. "I would have if a certain young grandson had decided to use his degree in chemistry and come into the business. I figure Harold can take over the CEO position until he grooms someone for the job."

Ellie picked up on the sudden tension that thickened at the table between grandson and grandmother. She swallowed her bite of mushroom-covered steak and said, "What are you going to do with all your free time?"

"I won't completely turn the company over without keeping an eye on it. But I figure I could knit, read, wait for great-grandchildren."

Colt's eyes popped wide. "Winnie, now I know why you insisted on coming up here. Did you have something to do with all this snow, too? We won't be going anywhere until it stops. Visibility is limited."

His grandmother smiled. "I have a lot of skills, but controlling weather isn't one of them. I figured the circumstances were just right for me telling you this now rather than right before you go back to the *Kaleidoscope*. You'll inherit my shares in the company so you'll have a stake in it."

"What's this about great-grandchildren? This is the first time you've bought that up in a long time."

Winnie pointedly looked at Ellie before swinging her attention to Colt. "Just a little reminder. After all, I'm getting up there. These threats made me realize I won't be around forever. I need to make plans for the future."

Colt's eyebrows slashed downward, and he lowered his head, as though he was enthralled with cutting his steak.

"The threat is over and you should have many years before you, Winnie," Ellie said, trying to defuse the tension vibrating in the air.

"I'm planning on it, but it's in the Lord's hands."

The rest of the meal Winnie and Ellie mostly talked, with a few comments from Colt. What part of the conversation had upset him? Ellie wondered. The part about Harold becoming CEO or the great-grandchildren?

At the end Ellie rose. "I'll take care of the dishes. That I know how to do at least. When I was first in the army I was on mess duty a lot."

"Colt will help you," Winnie offered. "You're our guest. We certainly can't let you do it alone."

As Ellie walked into the kitchen she heard Colt say in a strained voice, "I know what you're doing, and you need to stop it."

"Stop what? If you want, I'll help her."

The sugary sweet sound of Winnie's voice alerted Ellie to the fact that the woman was up to something, and she had a pretty good idea what it was. When Colt came into the small kitchen, his expression reflected his irritated mood toward his grandmother. Ellie worked beside him in silence for ten minutes.

As she washed the broiler pan, she asked, "What's going on with you and Winnie? Are you upset about her retiring and Harold taking over?" She didn't think that was it.

"I'm glad she's retiring, and Harold's a good man. Don't tell her, but lately I've been thinking about what I need to do. I don't see me living on a research vessel for years."

"So you might help with the company?"

"Maybe. I have an obligation that I need to finish first to the research team."

"Then what has you upset? And don't tell me you aren't. It's all over your face."

"She hasn't played the great-grandchildren card in ages. I thought she'd learned her lesson the last time."

"What lesson?"

"Come on. You're smart. Don't you see she's trying to play matchmaker with us?"

"It did cross my mind, but I think it's cute."

"Cute! The last time she did, I went out with the woman to make her happy. On the surface she seemed all right until we stopped dating and she began stalking me. That's one of the reasons I took the job on the *Kaleidoscope*. It's hard to stalk a person in the middle of the Pacific Ocean. It turns out I've enjoyed the work I'm doing and the woman went on to marry and move to New York, but Winnie isn't usually that far off reading people."

"We're all entitled to a mistake every once in a while. Besides, she had your best interests at heart—at least in her mind."

"I told the lady I wasn't interested in a serious relationship. She was and didn't understand why I wasn't. Hence the stalking to discover why she wasn't Mrs. Right."

"Don't worry. I don't stalk. I protect people from stalkers. And I'm not interested in a serious relationship, either. So you're perfectly safe. Your grandmother's wiles won't work on me." Ellie wiped down the sink. "So if you know that your grandmother has done that in the past, why did you talk me into coming this morning when I voiced an objection?"

He blew out a frustrated breath. "Because I like you. I've enjoyed getting to know you, and I didn't like the idea that you would spend Christmas alone."

"Oh, I see."

"Do you? Winnie needs to realize a man can have a friendship with a woman. She keeps insisting Harold is just a friend, so surely she can understand we can be friends."

Ellie laughed. "You don't have to convince me. Just Winnie."

"Yeah. Besides, after Christmas, I'll go back to *Ka-*

leidoscope and you'll go on another assignment. We'll probably be halfway around the world from each other."

"I agree. Forgive the cliché, but we're like two ships passing in the night."

"Exactly." He draped the dish towel over the handle on the oven. "And I think I'll go in there and explain it to her. Want to back me up?"

"Sure."

Colt stalked into the great room and found it empty. He turned in a full circle, his gaze falling on the knitting project in the basket by the chair his grandmother had been sitting in. His forehead crinkled, and he covered the distance to the hall, coming back almost immediately. "She went to bed. It's just you and me, and it's only nine o'clock."

"I think that was her intention."

"I know." A chuckle escaped Colt. "And I'll have a serious word with her tomorrow. In the meantime, want to play chess or checkers?"

"I can't play chess, so it has to be checkers."

Colt retrieved the board and game pieces and set it up at the table where they had eaten their dinner. "I'll have to teach you how to play chess. It's a strategy game. I have a feeling you'd be good at it."

"Maybe tomorrow. After the past few weeks, I don't want too tough a game to play tonight." Ellie took a chair across from him. "After an assignment I go through a mental and physical letdown, and after a particularly hard job, I almost shut down for a couple of days."

"Is this your way of telling me you're going to lounge around and do nothing but eat bonbons?"

"If you have any, I might. I like chocolate." Ellie moved her red checker forward.

"What else do you like?" Colt made his play, then looked up into her eyes, trapping her with the intensity in his gaze. Electrifying. Mesmerizing.

"Protecting people," she somehow managed to reply. "I really do like my work. Making sure a place is secure. Trying to figure out all the ways a person can get to another."

"I can understand liking your job. I like mine, too."

"What do you like about your job?"

"Finding unique species. Trying to preserve the ocean. The challenge of the job. That's probably what I like the most. I want a job that forces me beyond my comfort zone."

"We have a lot in common."

Colt answered her move by jumping her red checker. "You said you became a bodyguard because you want to help those who need protection. Why is that important to you?"

"King me," Ellie said when she slid her first red piece into his home base. "Because my twin was bullied. I wasn't going to allow that to happen to others if I could do something about it."

"He was but you weren't?"

"No. I had a rep for being tough and not taking anything from anyone."

He cocked his head to the side. "How did you get that reputation?"

"By standing up to the people who made fun of my brother. Toby was slow. He was the second twin. He became stuck in the birth canal and was deprived of oxygen, which caused some medical and mental problems."

"When did you start championing him like that?"

"When we started school. Kindergarten."

"What did your parents think?"

Ellie looked at the board and made a move without thinking it through. With his next turn, Colt jumped her pieces until she had to crown his black checker.

"Obviously the subject of your parents isn't one of your favorites," he said. "Like me."

Ellie swallowed the tightness in her throat. Recalling her past never sat well with her. "No. I never knew my father. He left my mother when Toby and I were born. He never once tried to get in touch with us. And for different reasons from your dad, my mother was less than stellar in the parent department. I basically raised Toby and myself. I didn't have grandparents like yours."

"So you and I have another thing in common."

There was something about Colt that drew her. She hadn't wanted to admit that to herself, but she couldn't avoid it any longer. They were alike in a lot of ways even though their backgrounds were very different. He came from wealth and was college educated. She'd graduated from high school and had been educated on the job in the army.

Ten minutes later Colt won the checkers game. She wanted to think it was because her mind hadn't been on the game, but that wasn't true. He was good and she wasn't. She hadn't played since she was a kid and the old man next door used to challenge her. She hadn't won then, either, but she had enjoyed her neighbor's conversation about the different places she could see around the world. So when the U.S. Army recruiter came to her school, she'd thought it would be a good way to go different places.

"Another game?" Colt asked.

"No, one beating in a night is enough. My ego can only take so much."

He threw back his head and laughed. "I have a feeling your ego is just fine."

"Okay, I hate to admit that Winnie has the right idea about going to bed early. What's even nicer is that I don't have to walk through the house and check to make sure we are locked up tight. No one in their right mind would come out on a night like this." Ellie made her way to the window and opened the blinds to look at the heavy snow coming down.

"Near blizzard conditions," Colt said close to her ear.

The tickle of his breath on her nape zipped through her, but she stayed still. There was nothing stopping her from turning around and kissing him. No job. No threats against Winnie. This was her time that she'd chosen to spend with Winnie and Colt. His presence so near to her tingled her nerve endings and charged her, demanding she put aside her exhaustion and give in to the feelings bombarding her from all sides.

"Yes, I haven't seen this much snow in a while." Her reply ended in a breathless rush.

"It makes this cabin feel even cozier." His soft, whispered words caressed her neck.

She tensed, trying to keep herself from leaning back against him.

"Relax. We'll be perfectly fine in here. If we need rescuing, people know where we are and will come when we don't show up the day after Christmas."

His teasing tone coaxed the tension from her. She closed the blind and swung around at the same time she stepped away. "I think I can survive being snowbound in a large, warm cabin with enough food for a week. My boss doesn't expect me to come into the office until the day after New Year's."

"I wish I could say the same thing. I have to get back to the ship."

His comment reminded her of their differences. She was a bodyguard. He worked on a vessel in the middle of the Pacific Ocean. Not conducive to a relationship. "Good night, Colt."

"Coward."

"Oh, you think?" She'd been accused of being many things. Being a coward wasn't one of them.

"When it gets personal, you leave."

"That's what this is?" She drew a circle in the air to indicate where they were standing.

He moved to the side, sweeping his arm across his body. "Good night, Ellie. We'll continue our conversation tomorrow when you're rested."

On her way to her bedroom, the searing heat of his gaze drilled into her back. Every inch of her was aware of the man she'd wanted to kiss but didn't. It was better this way. Now she only had a few more days and she could escape to Dallas.

Ellie hurriedly changed into her sweatpants and large T-shirt then fell into bed. She expected sleep to come quickly. But she couldn't stop thinking about Colt. At some point she must have gone to sleep because the next thing she realized a boom shook the cabin, sending her flying out of bed.

TEN

Ellie fumbled in the dark for her gun she kept on the nightstand out of habit. When her fingers clasped around it, she raced into the hallway at the same time Colt came out of his bedroom.

"Check on Winnie," she said and hurried into the great room. The cabin seemed intact, but when she peered toward the large window that overlooked the front of the place, she saw an orange-yellow glow through the slats in the blinds as though the sun had set in the yard. She yanked open the door, a blast of cold rushing in while flames engulfed the Jeep nearby in the still-falling snow.

Gun up, she moved out onto the porch. When she stepped into the snow blown up against the cabin, she glanced down and realized she had no shoes on. In spite of the biting cold battering her, she scanned the white terrain. Although night, it was light and eerie. The storm had died down some but still raged, as did the fire where the Jeep was.

From behind a hand clamped on her shoulder. She jerked around, her gun automatically coming up.

Colt's eyes grew round, his hand falling back to his side.

"Don't ever come up behind me like that, especially after something like this." Using her weapon, she gestured toward the flames. "I could have shot you."

With her toes freezing and the sensation spreading up her legs, she hotfooted it into the cabin and shut the door, locking it. "How's Winnie?"

"I'm fine."

Ellie glanced over Colt's shoulder. Winnie hovered near the hallway, wrapped in a quilt. "You know what this means."

She nodded. "Mary Ann didn't send those threats."

"Possibly. Or someone was working with her and maybe killed her to keep her quiet. It's possible to make a murder look like suicide. That's what the police wanted to determine when her body was discovered."

"The Jeep couldn't have exploded on its own?" Winnie came farther into the room.

"Not likely."

Colt parted a few slats on the blinds and peeked outside. "The fire is dying down with all the snow falling, and the wind has, too. We need to call the sheriff."

Ellie marched to the phone and picked it up. "No dial tone. This is definitely not an accident."

"So we're trapped in this cabin with no way to get help." Colt strode into the kitchen and peered out the window. "I see nothing on this side."

Ellie checked the other sides of the cabin, calling out from her bedroom, "Clear here." *For the time being.*

"What do we do? Who is behind this?" Winnie's voice quavered.

Ellie reentered the great room. "At the moment the who isn't important. We need to come up with a plan. If he blew up the Jeep, he could try something with the cabin and we can't guard all four sides 24/7. He might have destroyed the Jeep to get us out of the house."

"How can we leave?" Winnie pulled the blanket closer to her.

"The snow is starting to let up," Colt said. "Maybe I could make it down the mountain and get help. You could stay here with Winnie and guard her. I know these mountains and have the best chance of getting out of here."

Ellie faced Colt. "How are you going to walk out of here? Over a foot of snow was dumped on us in the past twelve hours."

"We have snowshoes I can use. Or I'll get to the snowmobile in the shed and use that."

"What if he's out there waiting to shoot anyone who leaves?" This was a situation where she wished she were two people and could stay and protect but also go and get help.

He clasped her arms. "I've fought off pirates. I can do this. Besides, the visibility isn't good because it's still night and snowing."

"Exactly. It won't be good for you, either." Thinking about what could happen to him knotted her stomach.

"But I know this area well. I doubt the person out there does. This is Winfield land. Not much else is up here. This isn't debatable. I'm going. You're staying." A determined expression carved harsh lines into his face.

She nodded. She didn't like the plan, but they didn't have a choice.

Colt started for his bedroom.

Winnie stepped into his path. "Colt, don't do this. I don't like you being a target for this person. You're my only family left."

"I have to go. I'm taking Granddad's handgun with me." He looked back at Ellie. "I'm leaving his rifle in case you need it."

"Fine. Bring it out here with ammunition. I'll keep you covered for as long as I can." The helplessness Ellie experienced festered inside her. Protection was her job, not his.

Winnie turned large eyes on Ellie as Colt disappeared down the hallway. "I'm glad Thomas taught Colt to shoot. At that time it was for him to protect himself if he came upon a bear or cougar in these mountains—not a person bent on killing me."

"You won't die as long as I have a breath in me." Ellie's hands curled into fists.

Nor Colt. I won't let him die, either. He means too much to me. That realization stunned her for a moment, then because she had no choice, she shoved it into the background. She couldn't risk her emotions getting in the way of whatever she had to do.

When he reemerged from the hallway, dressed in a heavy overcoat and wool beanie, carrying snowshoes, thick gloves, goggles and the rifle, he thrust the latter into Ellie's hand then dug for a box of shells and laid them on a nearby table. "More ammunition is on top of my bureau."

He put on his goggles, wrapped a scarf around his neck and lower face, donned his snowshoes and gloves, then eased the back door open. Cracking a window that overlooked the back of the cabin, she took up guard as Colt trudged his way toward the shed two hundred feet away.

Her nerves taut, she shouldered the rifle, poised to fire if she needed to. Ellie scoped the terrain for anything that moved. All was still. Not even the branches of the pine trees swayed from wind now.

"What's happening? I don't hear the snowmobile," Winnie said behind Ellie.

"Nothing. He's inside the shed." *But is he safe?* What if the assailant was waiting for him? Ellie couldn't leave Winnie. That might be what the person wanted. But what if Colt needed—

The side door to the shed opened, and Colt hurried back toward the house, his gaze scanning the area.

"What happened?" Ellie asked at the same time Winnie did when Colt reentered the cabin.

"The snowmobile won't start. Someone disabled it."

"Are you sure? Does it have gas?"

"There's a hole in the tank. The gas leaked out all over the ground. The ski equipment and anything else we might use to leave here is gone. He's cut us off."

Trapped. She'd been trapped before and gotten out. She would this time, too, with both Colt and Winnie. "Okay. For the time being let's fortify the cabin, find places to watch our surroundings while we figure out what we should do."

"I still think I should try leaving here on foot," Colt insisted.

"Maybe. What's up in the loft?" Ellie pointed to a narrow staircase.

"Storage mostly, but it might be a better vantage place to watch the area from," Colt said.

"I'm going to fix some coffee. We need to stay alert. I don't think there's going to be any more sleep tonight."

"Thanks, Winnie. I could use a whole pot." Colt kissed his grandmother on the check.

When she left, Ellie moved toward the stairs. "Keep an eye on her while I look at the loft."

Colt stepped closer and whispered, "Ellie, I don't think Winnie could make it out of here, so all three of us going is not an option. She might have power walked around the perimeter of the estate, but sloshing through the deep snow even with snowshoes is totally different. It's exhausting after a few hundred yards. And snowshoeing can be treacherous going downhill over rough terrain, especially with her weak knees. Not to mention leaving her exposed for the person to shoot."

"And you don't think you'll be."

"What's the alternative? Waiting until we're missed? That could be days. No telling what would happen in that time."

"I'll be back down in a few minutes. Check the windows and doors to make sure they're locked. Put some heavy furniture up against the two doors. Shutter the windows we won't use for a lookout."

"What are you two whispering about?" Poised in the entrance into the kitchen, Winnie planted her fists on her waist. "If you're worried about me, let me inform you I'll do what I have to. I won't let this person win. Any planning and discussions need to include me. Understand?"

Ellie exchanged a glance with Colt before he pivoted and headed toward his grandmother, saying, "We were just discussing our options."

Ellie clambered up the stairs. The whole loft was one large room with boxes and pieces of furniture stored along the walls. Two big windows overlooked the west and east part of the landscape. One person with little effort could keep an eye on over half the terrain. That could leave Winnie and Colt covering the north and south. That might work. But then as she started back down the stairs, questions and doubts began tumbling through her mind like a skier who lost her balance going down a mountain.

The scent of coffee lured her toward the kitchen. She poured a mug and joined Winnie in the great room before the dying fire. She gave the older woman a smile, hoping to cajole one from her.

But Winnie's frown deepened. "I've been trying to figure out who would go to such lengths to get me. I honestly can't imagine anything I've done to cause this kind of hatred. I feel so helpless."

Ellie remembered that exact feeling a little while ago. It never sat well with her. "I've been thinking."

Colt suddenly came from the hallway with his arms full of warm clothing, snowshoes and other items. "If we need to leave suddenly, I want this on hand. I'm separating it into piles for each of us."

"I say we have two options. All of us leave and try to make it down the mountain. Or I go by myself and bring help back." Ellie sat on the edge of the sofa, every sense attuned to her surroundings.

"Those aren't two options in my opinion," Colt said. "I'm going it alone. I can move fast. I should be able to get back with help by dark if I leave right away. The best place for me to try and get to is the estate. I think that's the best—"

"No, Colt. You're not going by yourself. I won't have you get killed because of me. There is a third option. We stay here. That's what I want." Winnie pinched her lips together and pointedly looked at each one of them.

Colt surged to his feet. "Sorry. I love you, Winnie,

but the longer we spread this out the more this person has a chance to accomplish what he wants to do. Kill you and in the process take us all out."

"I agree with Colt about us all waiting, but I'd rather be the one going for help. I know how to avoid being a human target. I was trained in that."

"Winnie is your client and first priority."

"I know. That's the dilemma I—"

Thump!

"What was that?" Ellie rose and started for the window by the front door. She motioned Colt to check the back area.

Again she heard the sound—like something striking the side of the cabin. Ellie parted the blinds to peer outside. Nothing unusual but the sight of the charred Jeep.

Thump!

"That's coming from the north side." Colt rushed down the hallway.

Ellie helped Winnie to her feet and followed him. "Do you see anything?"

He whirled from the window. "We've got to get out of here. He's firing flaming arrows at the cabin."

Ellie stared out at the evergreen forest, which afforded a lot of cover along the north area of the property. Another arrow rocketed toward the cabin, landing on the roof. "He's burning us out. Either we leave or die in a fire."

Colt ushered them out of the room. "Let's go. If we can get away, I think I know a place you two can hide. It's defensible, only one way in. We need to dress as warm as possible."

"He's on the north side. We'll use the window facing south to get out of here. He can't watch all four sides at once."

Winnie halted before her pile of garments. "Unless there is more than one."

"We have to take our chances and pray the Lord protects us." Ellie quickly dressed, then stuffed useful items into a backpack—flashlights, a blanket, matches, weapons, some bottled water and food.

"He'll be able to track us, but the cave system isn't too far away and it's beginning to snow again. I hope the conditions worsen after we get to the cave. The way I have to go is down. I can do that even in less-than-favorable visibility." Colt prepared his backpack then slung it over one shoulder.

The noise of the arrows hitting the cabin increased. The scent of smoke drifted to Ellie as they hurried into the laundry room. A three-by-three window four feet off the floor beckoned her. She pulled a chair to it and opened their escape route. A blast of cold air and snow invaded the warmth of the small room.

Ellie stuck her head out the opening. It was at least six feet to the ground. "I'll go first, then you, Winnie. Colt can help lower you to me."

After tossing her backpack out the hole, Ellie leaped up and shimmied through the small space, diving head-first and tucking into a ball. The snow cushioned her tumble to the ground. She bounced up and positioned herself to guide Winnie, breaking her fall. While Colt wiggled through the opening and followed Ellie's example, she and Winnie put on their snowshoes. Colt donned his as fast as he could.

The thumping sound thundered through the air.

Winnie started to say something. Ellie put her finger up to her mouth. Colt's grandmother nodded that she understood.

Colt pointed in the direction he would take, then set out in a slow pace with Winnie mirroring his steps, then Ellie. The less snow they disturbed the faster the falling flakes would cover their tracks.

When Colt reached the edge of the forest that surrounded the cabin, Ellie paused and glanced back. The stench of smoke hung in the air, but she couldn't see any wisps of it coming from the cabin because of the heavy snowfall. Even the indentations they'd made were filling in, though still evident.

Then the sound of the arrows striking the cabin stopped. Ellie searched the white landscape but saw no sign of the assailant. She turned forward and hurried as fast as she could to catch up with Colt and Winnie.

Fifteen minutes later, the wind began whipping through the trees, bringing biting cold to penetrate their layers of clothing. Even with so little skin exposed to the chill, Ellie shivered and gritted her teeth to keep them from chattering.

A cracking noise reverberated through the forest, followed by a crash to their left. Ellie looked up at the snow-and-ice-burdened limbs on the pines and realized the danger of being beneath the heavy-laden branches. Winnie barely picked up each foot as she moved forward. Her pace slowed even more.

When Winnie stumbled and fell, Ellie whispered, "Colt," and rushed toward the woman.

The wind whisked his name away. He kept trudging forward.

"Colt," she said a little louder as she bent over to help Winnie to her feet, one snowshoe coming off.

He glanced back, saw his grandmother down and retraced his steps as quickly as he could. He assisted Winnie to her feet while Ellie knelt and tied the snow-shoe back on Winnie's foot. Snow-covered, the older woman shook.

Another crack, like a gun going off, resonated in the air. A pine branch snapped above them and plunged toward them. Ellie dove into both Colt and Winnie, sending them flying to the side. The limb struck the ground a foot away from them.

Dazed, Winnie lay in the snow, then pain flashed across her face.

"What's wrong, Winnie?" Ellie asked, pushing up onto her hands and knees next to the woman.

"I think I did something to my ankle," she murmured, her voice barely audible over the howl of the wind through the trees.

Colt knelt next to Winnie. "I'll carry you the rest of the way. The cave isn't far."

"I'm so sorry, Winnie." Ellie peered at the large branch on the ground.

"Don't you apologize. I could have been hurt a lot worse if that had fallen on me."

While Colt scooped up his grandmother, Ellie used her knife to cut a small branch off the big one. She used the pine to smooth out the snow behind them as much as possible and hide their tracks.

Ten minutes later, Colt mounted a rocky surface, went around a large boulder and stooped to enter a cave. Ellie stayed back to clear away their steps as much as possible, then went inside the dark cavern, reaching for her flashlight to illuminate the area. A damp, musky odor prevailed.

Colt set his grandmother on the floor, took a blanket out of his backpack and spread it out, then moved Winnie to it. Kneeling, he removed the boot from the injured foot and examined it. "The ankle's starting to swell. I don't think it's broken. But a doctor will have to look at it when we get home. The faster I leave, the faster you'll get the medical care you need."

Ellie slung her backpack to the ground near Winnie and sat on it. "We'll be fine. I'll make Winnie comfortable then stand guard near the entrance."

"I should be back before dark. If I can get to the house, I can get help. It's a little out of the way, but I think it would save time in the long run. I know I can find help there." Colt started to stand.

Winnie grabbed his arm. "I love you. Don't you dare take any more risks than you absolutely have to. If you have to take your time to be safe, then you've got to do that."

"Yes, ma'am." He kissed her forehead. "I have a good reason to make it safely down the mountain."

Ellie rose and walked with him a few feet. "Ditto what your grandmother said. I have food and water. We have a couple of blankets. We'll be fine." She tied his scarf, which had come loose, back around his neck. Suddenly emotions jammed her throat. She knew the dangers in store for Colt. Not just the rough terrain in a snowstorm but a maniac bent on killing them.

He clasped her glove-covered hands and bent his head toward hers. A smile graced his mouth right before his lips grazed across hers once then twice. Then he kissed her fully. She returned it with all her needs and concerns pouring into the connection that sprang up between them.

In a raw whisper, she said against his mouth, "Don't you dare get hurt. We have things to talk about when this is over."

"If I hadn't been motivated before, I am now." He gave her a quick peck on her lips then departed, striding toward the cave entrance.

Ellie watched him vanish around the corner, then went back to Winnie to make sure she was comfortable before she stood guard at the mouth of the cavern.

"He'll be all right," Winnie assured her. "He knows these mountains well. Hopefully better than whoever is after me."

Ellie nodded at Winnie, remembering the grin Colt gave her before kissing her. The memory warmed her cold insides. "Yes. After all, he's fought off pirates before."

Winnie chuckled.

The warmth died out when a gunshot blasted the air and the mountain over them rumbled.

ELEVEN

Colt exited the cave, scanning the terrain for any sign of their assailant. Through the curtain of snow falling a movement caught his full attention. Suddenly a shadow rose from behind a rock and aimed a rifle at him. Colt dove for cover as the white-camouflaged figure got off a shot, the bullet ricocheting off the stone surface behind him.

A noise rocked the ground—like a huge wave hitting shore in a thunderstorm. Colt had only heard that sound one other time, right before tons of snow crashed down the mountain, plowing through the forest, leaving nothing behind in its wake.

The entrance of the cave a few feet away was his only chance. He scrambled toward it as rock, snow and ice began pelting him.

Winnie went white. "An avalanche!"

Ellie hurried toward the entrance. "Stay put," she said, realizing Winnie didn't have a choice.

As she rounded the bend in the stone corridor, she saw Colt plunge toward the cave, then a wall of white swallowed him up. The force of the avalanche sent a swell of snow mushrooming into the cavern.

When the rumbling stopped, snow totally blocked the cave entrance and she couldn't see Colt. She rushed to the last place he'd been and began digging with her hands. Cold and wet invaded the warmth of her gloves, leaving her hands freezing. She didn't care. Nor did she care Winnie and she were trapped. She had to find Colt.

Please, Lord, let me find him. Please.

Over and over those words zoomed through her mind. But all she uncovered was more snow.

Stunned, with limited oxygen, Colt tried to unfurl his body so he could use his hands to dig his way out before he lost consciousness. But the snow encased him in a cold coffin. He had a small pocket of air, but it wouldn't last long. He finally dislodged his arm from beneath him and reached it toward the direction of the cave, but he could move it only a few inches.

Lord, help me. Winnie and Ellie are in danger.

"I'm in here," he called out, hoping that Ellie was free on the other side.

"Colt!"

The sound of Ellie's voice gave him hope she could dig him out before he ran out of oxygen. "I'm here."

"I can hear you, Colt. Hang on."

He focused on those words and tried to calm his rapid heartbeat, to even his breathing in order to preserve his air. A peace settled around him as if God enclosed him in an embrace.

"Ellie, what happened?" Winnie called out. "It sounded like an avalanche."

"It was. I'm assessing our situation." Ellie kept digging near the area where she'd heard Colt and prayed he wasn't buried too deeply.

If he was almost to the entrance of the cave, he would have been sheltered from the worst of the avalanche. Concerned for Colt, she hadn't thought about their situation till now. They were trapped in the cave. It would be days before a search party was sent out, and then would the rescuers even realize they were trapped in the cavern? And if they did, would it be in time? She had a couple of water bottles and a little food, but what worried her the most was the cold. A chill infused every crevice of the cave.

Although tired from shoveling the snow with her hands, she didn't dare take a break. "Colt, are you there?"

"Yes," his faint response came back and a surge of adrenaline pumped energy through her body.

Her hand broke through the snow and touched him, and relief trembled down her length. She doubled her attack as though sand was running out of an hourglass and she only had seconds left to free him. Soon his arm was revealed. He wiggled it to let her know he was okay. She kept going, uncovering more of him until he could assist her.

When he escaped the mound of snow, Ellie helped him to stand, then engulfed him in her arms. "Are you all right? Hurt anywhere?"

"I feel like an elephant—no, several—sat on me, but other than that, I'm in one piece."

She leaned back to look into his dear face, one she had thought she would never see again. "I heard a gunshot then the rumble of the avalanche. What happened?"

"Our assailant found us and shot at me when I came

out of the cave. That must have triggered the avalanche. I dove back into the cave. He might not have been so fortunate."

"Then he could be buried under tons of snow?"

"It'll depend on where he was and how fast he reacted, but it's definitely a possibility."

"Come on. Winnie is worried." Ellie grasped his gloved hand in hers and relished the connection. She'd almost lost him. That thought forced her to acknowledge her growing feelings toward Colt. There was no time to dwell on them now, but she would have to in the future. Every day she was with him, the stronger those feelings grew.

Winnie's face lit up when she saw Colt. "You're alive."

"Yes, thanks to Ellie." He slanted a look at her before stooping by Winnie. "Are you doing okay?"

"Now I am. What happened?"

As Colt told his grandmother, her face hardened more and more into a scowl.

"I hope he's trapped in the avalanche," Winnie blurted out at the end. "Evil begets evil."

One of Colt's eyebrows lifted. "No forgiveness for the man?"

Winnie pursed her mouth. "I'm working on it, but his actions are making it very hard. It's one thing to go after me, but he was trying to kill you. He needs to be stopped, and if the avalanche did it, so be it."

Ellie sat, her legs trembling from exhaustion. "We need to come up with a plan to get out of here. Colt, you said there's only one way into this cave. You've explored this place completely?"

"There's another way in that is blocked on the other side. This system goes through the mountain we are on."

"What do you mean by blocked?"

"Years ago there was a rockslide. There's an opening, but it isn't big. I'm not sure I can fit through it. For all I know the rocks may have shifted and closed it completely off."

"Or opened it up some more. Would the assailant know about the back way into this cave?" Ellie slid her glance to Winnie, who pulled the blanket around herself, her lips quivering.

"Unless you're really familiar with the area, you wouldn't know about it. Like I said, this is Winfield property."

"Let's hope he isn't because I don't think we can wait around to see if anyone finds us and digs us out."

"Agreed."

"Winnie, if Colt and I help you, do you think you can make it through the cave to the other side?"

She lifted her chin. "Don't you two worry about me. I'll do what I have to. If I can't make it, you can leave me and come back to get me after you find a way out."

"We can't leave you alone." Colt wrapped his arms around his grandmother.

"I'm not afraid. The Lord will be with me."

"It may not be an issue if I can carry you."

Ellie gathered up all the backpacks and supplies and led the way Colt told her to go while he carried his grandmother in his arms. Dripping water and their breathing were the only sounds in the cavern. The chill burrowed into Ellie's bones the deeper they went into the heart of the mountain.

"How long ago were you last here?" Ellie asked as the passage became narrower and shorter.

"At least ten years ago."

Ellie glanced back at Colt. Winnie's head was cushioned against his shoulder, her eyes closed. "Was there any crawling involved?"

He nodded. "Come to think of it, the cave gets tight in one area."

When Ellie reached a fork in the cave system, she stopped. "Which way?"

Colt shut his eyes, his forehead wrinkled. "I think to the right. This probably isn't the time to tell you I'm lousy with telling you the difference in right or left."

"There's no good time to tell me that," she said. "I could go a ways and see what I find."

"No, we'll stay together. If it's the way, you'd have to track back." Colt shifted Winnie some in his embrace and winced.

"Are you all right?"

"I hurt my arm when the whole mountain came down on me."

"Just your arm? Let's take a rest, eat something and drink some water."

"We should keep going."

"Our bodies need the rest, food and water." Ellie plopped the backpacks down on the stone floor and helped Colt lower his grandmother onto a blanket.

"You two don't have to stop for me," Winnie murmured, pain etched into her features.

"We're stopping for all of us." Ellie delved into her backpack and found the granola bars and a bottle of water. "It may be freezing, but we still have to keep ourselves hydrated."

"Just a short break." Colt removed his gloves and rubbed his left arm.

Shivering, Winnie took the first sip of water then passed it to Ellie. When she gave it to Colt, the touch of his cold fingers against hers fastened her attention on him. In the dim lighting his light blue eyes looked dark. Shadows played across his strong jaw. But the sear of his gaze warmed her as though she sat in front of a flaming blaze.

"I wonder if the cabin caught fire." Colt bit into his granola bar.

"If it did, maybe someone will see the smoke and investigate. They might be concerned about a forest fire." Winnie began unlacing the shoe she had put back on when they'd started the journey through the cave.

"Maybe, but we're isolated up here and the conditions down the mountain might be worse than up here." He popped the last bite into his mouth.

Winnie took off her boot to reveal a swollen ankle, worse than before. "I can't wear this anymore. It's killing my foot. Oh, dear, that was a poor choice of words."

"But true. I've had a sprained ankle, and it does hurt to wear close-fitting shoes." Ellie unwound her scarf and wrapped it around Winnie's foot.

"I can't take your scarf. You need it."

"Nonsense, you need it more than me. One layer of socks isn't warm enough. I find feet, head and hands get cold faster than other parts of your body. If you keep them covered it helps you feel warmer."

Winnie smiled, but the gesture didn't stay on her face more than a second. "I can hardly keep my eyes open."

"Then keep them closed. I'm carrying you, anyway." Colt rose. "Ready."

"Are you sure?" Ellie mouthed the question to Colt, touching his hurt arm.

He nodded.

"If the cabin is gone, I won't get to see what you brought in the sack for me and Ellie." Winnie snuggled close to Colt's body.

"What if it isn't burned down?"

Ellie replied, "I think you should tell us, anyway. Don't you, Winnie?"

"Yes."

He exaggerated a sigh, but the corners of his mouth quirked up, his left dimple appearing in his cheek. "Doug carved a German shepherd like Lady for me to give to you, Winnie, and I found my mom's locket in my belongings in the closet when I put my speargun back." His gaze fastened onto Ellie. "I hope you'll accept it."

Her throat closed, emotions she couldn't express rushing to the surface. "I shouldn't. It's your mother's."

"She'd want you to have it. You've gone above and beyond your duties as a bodyguard."

"I totally agree, Colt," Winnie said. "I hope you'll accept it, Ellie, if it didn't burn."

"I'd be honored," she murmured.

Colt cleared his throat. "We'd better get going."

As Ellie continued their trek, the ceiling dropped more until Colt had to bend over while carrying his grandmother through the passage. When Ellie peered at the pair, she noticed Colt's back kept scraping the roof of the cave. Strain marked his features as he struggled to stay on his feet with Winnie in his arms. Ellie rounded a corner in the passageway and came to a stop.

"Does this look familiar, because if it doesn't maybe we should try the other path?" Ellie waved her hand ahead of them at a tunnel about four feet wide and three feet tall.

Colt paused behind her and put his grandmother on the floor. "Yes. I'd forgotten I had to crawl part of the way toward the end. I've been in a lot of caves through the years. They kind of all run together."

"Let me wait here while you two check it out," Winnie said. "I'll be fine. I can catch a catnap. If it turns out to be a way out, you can come back for me. If it doesn't, then we don't have to try and get me through there."

"I don't want to leave—"

"Ellie, we're trapped in a cave with a mound of snow standing between us and the person after me. I think I'll be perfectly safe here by myself."

"I'll go alone, and if it's the way out, I'll come back and get both of you." Colt moved toward the narrow passageway. "Rest, Winnie. It's not far from here so I shouldn't be gone long."

Ellie helped make Winnie more comfortable. Since this ordeal had started, she had appeared to age a couple of years. Ellie was concerned about her. Winnie had been working so hard the past year on the Endless Youth products and then to have to run for her life… It might be too much for even a tough lady like her.

Although her eyes were closed, Winnie huddled in the blanket up against Ellie and said, "Since this began I've been thanking God for sending you to me. Now I'm thanking you for staying for Christmas. I doubt it's your idea of how to celebrate Christmas, but I'm mighty grateful you're here, and if I'm not mistaken, so is my grandson."

"Here we are trapped in a cave and you're match-making."

"You can't blame a grandmother for trying. I've got a captive audience," Winnie said with a chuckle, some of her fight surfacing.

"I like Colt." *A lot.*

"What I've seen makes me think it's more than just like. Or is that wishful thinking on my part?"

Ellie opened her mouth to say, "Yes," but the word wouldn't come out because it wasn't the truth. "No, there is more, but Winnie, I just don't see how…" She didn't know how to explain her mixed-up feelings even to herself, let alone someone else.

"I know you both have separate lives, but even when two people live in the same town and their lives mesh together, a relationship can be hard. Colt needs someone like you in his life."

"You're right about the hurdles between us."

"Thomas and I had hurdles, too, but we overcame them. He'd just divorced his wife a couple of months before we started dating, but we'd known each other and worked together for several years. People took our openly dating as a sign we'd been having an affair while he was married, especially his ex-wife. She made our lives unbearable for a while, then thankfully she decided to move away and we began to have a normal relationship. Thomas was a wonderful stepfather to my son. In fact, he adopted him when we got married."

Marrying. Having a relationship. Where does that fit in my life? She'd spent her years just trying to survive and have a life with meaning. Her work and faith had given her that. But if she gave in to her feelings concerning Colt, everything would change. So much of her life had been one change after another and she had needed some stability, which her vision for her life had given her—until now.

The passageway narrowed even more. Colt flattened himself and pulled his body through the stone-cold corridor. Although pain stabbed his left bicep, he kept going because a freezing wind whipped by him, indicating there was a way out of the cave up ahead. Reaching forward to grasp something to help him slither through the tunnel, he clutched air. Nothing. He focused the small flashlight on the spot in front of him and saw a drop-off.

Dragging himself to the edge of the opening of the passageway, he stared down at a black hole where the floor of the cavern should be. Across from him, not thirty feet away, light streamed into the darkness. He swung his flashlight toward the area and saw the rocks he remembered piled up where the second cave entrance used to be.

So close with a thirty-foot gap between him and freedom.

"What's keeping Colt? He should have been back by now." Winnie's teeth chattered.

Ellie rubbed her gloved hands up and down Winnie's arms. "It might have been farther than he thought. It hasn't been that long." She infused an upbeat tone into her voice because she knew the cold was getting to Winnie. "Tell me some more about your marriage to Thomas. It sounds like you two were very happy."

"Don't get me wrong. We had our problems, especially concerning Colt's father, but we always managed to work them out. As long as we had each other, we felt we could deal with anything."

"That's nice. No wonder you're a romantic at heart."

"Me? What gave you that idea?"

"Oh, the flowers in your house, a tradition your husband started and you continued. The way you talk about Thomas. But mostly some of the products your company sells with names like Only Her and Only Him."

"You aren't a romantic?"

"Never had time for romance in my life."

"Why not?"

Ellie ended up telling a second person about her childhood. "What is it about a Winfield demanding to know stuff I've never shared with others?"

"It's our charm." Winnie grinned, a sparkle in her eyes for the first time since they'd started on this trek hours ago. "That and we care. People sense that about us. Hard to resist."

"That could be it."

A sound behind Ellie turned her in the direction of the tunnel. Colt crawled out of the hole, his features set in grim determination.

"Something wrong?" she asked.

He shook his head. "The tunnel is narrower than I remember, but if I can get through, you two can. Anyone larger than me won't, though. When I reached the other end, there is a sheer drop-off at the opening that wasn't there before, but the hole in the cavern is only four feet deep. I'll be able to lower myself to the floor and make my way to the entrance. It's still partially blocked. I may have to move a few rocks, but I'll be able to get through the hole."

"So bring back some skinny people to help us," Ellie said.

He laughed, then gathered what he was going to take with him—snowshoes, gun, tinted goggles. "I'll keep that in mind. Stay here. It's warmer in this cavern than the other one."

At the entrance to the tunnel, Ellie placed her hand on his arm.

He turned toward her.

"Keep safe. If an avalanche happened once, it can again."

His smile began as a twinkle in his eyes and spread to transform his earlier serious expression. "I like this role of knight in shining armor."

"Well, in that case, here's a token of my appreciation." She produced his scarf he'd left on the floor and put it around his neck. "It's cold out there."

"It's cold in here."

"True, but not as much wind." Her gaze linked with his. "I mean it. Don't take any unnecessary risks."

"Then it's okay to take necessary risks?"

"I'll be praying."

"Me, too, Colt," Winnie said from where she was sitting against the wall of the cave.

Colt stepped around Ellie, made his way to his grandmother, whispered something to her then kissed her on the head.

When he returned to Ellie, he caught her hands and brought them up between them, inching toward her until they touched. "I probably won't be back for a while."

"I know."

He leaned down and claimed her mouth in a kiss that rocked Ellie to her core, mocking her intention of keeping herself apart from him. It was so hard when he was storming every defense she put up to keep people away.

He pulled back, stared at her for a long moment then ducked down and disappeared into the tunnel. She watched him crawl toward the exit, his light fading. *What if I never see him again?* Her heart lurched at that thought.

Lord, keep him safe. Please. You're in control.

Although the temptation was great to check out the front of the cave and the cabin, Colt couldn't. That would eat into time he didn't have if he was going to get help back up the mountain before dark. He didn't know how long Winnie could last in this freezing weather. She had never tolerated the cold like he and his grand-dad had.

When he wiggled himself through the opening in the cave, he emerged into more falling snow, but at least it wasn't coming down too hard. Actually the snow could work to his advantage by covering his tracks if the assailant was still alive and out there waiting.

The scent of smoke hovered in the air. He looked in the direction of the cabin but couldn't see any flames. A dense cloud cover hung low over the area.

In his mind he plotted the trail he would take to the estate. Once there, he could use the phone and call for help. Then he and Doug could start up the mountain even before a rescue team could form and make it up to the cave.

Hours later, only a short distance from the house, Colt pushed himself faster. It would be dark before he could get back up the mountain if he didn't move more quickly. Although his legs shook with fatigue, he put one foot in front of the other, sometimes dragging himself out of a hole when he sank too far into the snow. But once he made it over the last ridge he would nearly be home. That thought urged him to pick up speed yet again.

When he put his foot down in front of him, the snow gave away, sending him tumbling down the incline. When he rolled to the bottom, he crashed into a pine tree, knocking the breath from him. Snow crusted him from head to foot. He wiped it away from his goggles and saw two snow boots planted apart. His gaze traveled upward past two legs and a heavy coat to a face covered in a white ski mask.

"Do you think Colt is all right? What if the bad guy didn't get caught in the avalanche and was waiting for him? I can't lose my grandson." Winnie took a sip from the bottle of water then passed it to Ellie.

"Colt can take care of himself." She prayed she was right.

"I know. I shouldn't worry. It does no good but get me upset."

"In a perfect world we wouldn't worry." Ellie worried, too. So many things could go wrong.

"We're safe in here while he's—"

A roar split the air, sending goose bumps flashing up Ellie's body.

Winnie's eyes grew round and huge. "That's—that's a…" She gulped, the color washing from her face.

"A bear. Nearby."

"In this cave!" Winnie sat up straight, the blanket falling away from her. "What's it doing in here?"

"It's a cave and wintertime. Hibernating?" Ellie

quickly gathered up all their belongings and stuffed them into one of the backpacks.

"What do we do?" Winnie asked at the same time another deep growl echoed through the cave.

"Get out of here."

"How? It sounds like it's coming down the passageway we used."

"We're going through the tunnel. Chances are it can't get through there. It's probably still fat since it's only December." Ellie felt for her gun at her hip. "If I have to, I will shoot it. Do you think you can crawl through the tunnel?"

"If I have to, I will."

Ellie helped Winnie to her feet, then supported most of her weight as the woman hopped toward the escape route. "You go first. I'm going in backward so if the bear follows, I can take care of it. From what Colt said, there is no room to turn around. Okay?"

Taking one of the flashlights, Winnie knelt before the entrance and began crawling forward. Ellie backed into the tunnel, pulling the backpack after her. Through the opening she glimpsed a brown bear loping into the area where they had been, sniffing the air. It released another roar, lumbered to the hole and stuck its head inside.

Colt started to spring up when a shovel crashed down on top of him, glancing off his head and striking his shoulder. His ears rang. The whole world spun for a few seconds. The man lifted the weapon again. Colt dropped back to the ground and rolled hard into the man. The action sent a wave of dizziness through Colt, but toppled his assailant to the snow.

Facedown, Colt fumbled in his coat pocket for his

gun, fighting the whirling sensation attacking his mind. Before he could pull it out, his attacker whacked the shovel across his back. Again, pain shot through his body. Someone yelled right before blackness swallowed him up.

"That's the bear!" Winnie said behind Ellie in the tunnel.

"A big one thankfully. I don't think it can get in here. Keep moving as fast as you can just in case."

Keeping her eye on the bear and her gun aimed at it, Ellie listened to Winnie's struggles as she made her way. Ellie didn't want to go any farther until she knew what the bear was going to do. Even if the animal tried to fit into the narrow passage, it wouldn't be able to do much. She calmed her speeding heartbeat.

Wiping first one sweating hand then the other against her coat, she locked gazes with the beast, giving it the most intimidating glare she could muster. "I'm not letting you pass. Don't make me hurt you." A fierce strength coated each word.

The bear released another growl. Its long teeth ridiculed her statements. The animal pushed forward a few inches but didn't go any farther because the walls sloped inward at that point. Finally it gave one last glower then backed out of the entrance into the tunnel.

"There's a really narrow part," Winnie said behind her.

When the bear disappeared from her view, Ellie scooted backward toward the other end. Sounds of the animal drifted to her, but it hadn't returned to the tunnel. A chill pervaded the passage, especially the closer she came to the exit. The thought that it was even colder than where they had been worried Ellie. Winnie needed medical attention and warmth. Ellie couldn't give her either.

"Colt." A familiar male voice filtered into Colt's pain-riddled mind.

The first sensation Colt experienced besides the drumming throb against his skull was the chill penetrating through his clothing. He opened his eyes to find someone kneeling next to him. With his cheek pressed against the snow, frigid, biting, Colt fought the urge to surrender again to the darkness.

"Colt, I was checking the grounds when I heard a noise and looked up the rise. I saw someone attacking you."

Relief that it was Doug pushed Colt to keep himself as alert as possible. Winnie and Ellie were depending on him. Moaning, he lifted his head and regretted it instantly. The world tilted before him. He closed his eyes, but it still swirled. He didn't have time for this. He forced down the nausea churning his stomach and slowly he rolled to face upward. Snowflakes pelted him, but the storm had lessened. Which meant whoever attacked him could possibly find the other entrance into the cave because his footprints weren't totally covered by the falling snow.

"Winnie and Ellie are trapped in the cave system near the cabin, the one I told you about." Somehow he strung together a sentence that made sense.

Doug looked up at the mountain. "That's the way your attacker fled."

Colt struggled to prop himself up on his elbows, searching for the tracks the man made. If he moved slowly, the world didn't spin too much. "I was coming to the house to call for help. There was an avalanche and it blocked the front of the cave. I used the back way in on the other side of the mountain. It's blocked, but I managed to remove a few rocks and wiggle out of the opening."

"Let's get you to the house and call 911, then I'll go up there."

"No, you go back. We're almost into cell range. Alert the sheriff then follow my tracks. I have to go. If that man finds Winnie and Ellie, he'll kill them. He tried to burn the cabin down."

"But wasn't Mary Ann Witlock the one threatening Winnie?"

"Maybe this guy was helping her."

Taking it slow, Colt tucked his legs under him then pushed himself to stand. Doug hurried to assist him. Colt's body protested with his every move, but he managed to remain upright. Then he put one foot in front of the other and started up the mountain, following his assailant's tracks.

He glanced back at Doug and the man was almost to the fence line at the estate. Help wouldn't be too far behind, but Colt had to quicken his pace if he was going to stop the attacker from harming Winnie and Ellie.

I need Your help, Lord. I can't do this without You. Anything is possible with You.

While Winnie stayed on the ledge at the tunnel, Ellie lowered herself over the cave shelf, clinging to a protruding rock. When her feet touched the floor, she let go of the stone, then positioned herself near the wall.

"Okay, Winnie. I'm going to guide you down and hold you so you don't put any weight on your bad foot."

"I still hear the bear. Do you think it can get through that tunnel?"

"No. It's angry we got away. Come on. We'll find a place to settle down and wait for Colt where we can also keep an eye on the tunnel."

After Winnie made it to the floor of the cavern, Ellie swung her light around to find the best place to wait. Puddles of icy water littered the area. Wind blew through the opening.

"The good news is that the water isn't totally frozen so the temperature isn't much below freezing."

Winnie snorted. "Tell that to my body."

Ellie pointed to a place a few feet away. "It's dry there and it looks like it'll shelter us from the wind. And I can see the tunnel."

Shielded from the wind slipping through the opening, Ellie cocooned Winnie in as much warmth as possible. She even used the backpack for her to sit on. "There. Now it's just a matter of a couple of hours. Everything will be over."

"No, it won't. We don't know who is after me. Who might have worked with Mary Ann?"

"I know we looked into her background and no one stood out. She didn't have a boyfriend, and the couple of members of her family who worked for Glamour Sensations didn't have much to do with her."

"One of the reasons I didn't pick her to be the spokesperson for Endless Youth was the way she always came across as though she were ten or fifteen years older than she was. An old soul but not in a good way. Weary. Unhappy. That wasn't the image I wanted to project for this line. Christy is the opposite of that. Young at heart although she is thirty-two. I didn't want a woman who was too young, but I wanted one who had an exuberance in spirit about her. I was so happy when Christy started dating Peter. She'd been engaged once before, and he was killed in a motorcycle accident." Winnie hugged her arms against her chest.

Ellie needed to keep her talking about anything but the situation they were in. "I understand that Christy became engaged to Peter right after you chose her as the spokesperson. Will that interfere in your advertising plans for the product?"

"No, Peter assured me he would do whatever Christy needed. He's been a great support for her. I was surprised at how fast he moved. They'd only been dating a couple of months. I think secretly—although he would never admit it—that he was afraid once the world saw her another man would snatch her right up. Men and claiming their territory." Winnie chuckled. "But I can't complain. Thomas was just like Peter. We only dated a few months, too. Of course, we worked together for a while before that."

"They know a good woman when they see her," Ellie said over the howl of the wind, its force increasing through the cave.

"Yes, and I'm hoping my grandson follows in his granddad's footsteps."

Even in the shadows created by the dim light, Ellie could see Winnie's gleaming eyes. "I have a very persuasive boss who has tried her best to fix me up with a couple of men she knows in Dallas. So far I've not succumbed to her tactics."

"Colt needs someone like you."

"I refuse to say anything to that. I'm sure there is a better subject than my love life."

Winnie's forehead crinkled. "You know, I've been thinking. Not many people knew we were coming up here. We really didn't make the final decision until we talked with the sheriff yesterday. Remember?"

"Yes. We were having a late breakfast. But only Linda was in the room besides the sheriff and us."

Winnie gasped. "It couldn't be Linda, Doug or the sheriff."

A sound above Winnie drew Ellie's gaze. On top of the ledge stood a man dressed in white wearing a white ski mask with a gun aimed at Winnie.

TWELVE

"Who are you?" Ellie asked the man on the ledge.

He cackled. "I'm not telling you. You two can die wondering who I am, especially after all the trouble you've put me through today."

"Why me?" Winnie lifted her face toward her assailant. "What have I done to you?"

"You continually have ruined my life," he said in a voice roughened as if he disguised it.

"I couldn't have. I haven't done that to anyone. I would know about it."

"Well, obviously you don't," the man shouted, his gun wavering as anger poured off him.

Ellie glanced at her gun lying on the ground next to her. She gauged her chances of grabbing it and getting a shot off before he did.

"Don't think about it. I'd have Winnie dead before you could aim the gun."

The voice, although muffled by the ski mask some, sounded familiar to Ellie. She'd heard him before—recently. Could it be Doug? The sheriff?

"Why me?" Winnie asked the gunman. "Don't you want me to know why you're killing me? What satisfaction can you have in that if I don't know why, especially if I wronged you as you say?" A mocking tone inched into Winnie's voice.

Ellie needed to keep the man talking. "As far as we know you're a maniac who belongs in a mental—"

His harsh laugh cut off the rest of her sentence. "Colt isn't coming to your rescue. I left him for dead and followed his trail to you two. How accommodating he was to show me where you all were."

No, Colt can't be dead. He's psyching me out. Trying to rattle me.

"I guess you should know why, Winnie." He said her name slowly, bitterness dripping from it. "You stole my father from my mother."

Winnie gasped.

"If you hadn't come along, my parents would have gotten back together. I would have had a father who would acknowledge me. Instead, he wouldn't have anything to do with me. You poisoned him. You kept him from me."

"Thomas didn't have a child. Thomas couldn't have one."

"Liar!"

"The doctors told Thomas it was impossible, and we never could have children." The pain in Winnie's voice was reflected in her expression, too.

"I am Thomas Winfield's son. My mama showed me my birth certificate. It was right there on the paper. There wasn't a day that went by that I wasn't reminded I wasn't good enough to be a Winfield. He discarded my mother and me like we were trash."

"Are you talking about Clare, Thomas's first wife?"

"Yes. He decided to divorce her for you."

"No, he didn't. We didn't start dating until after the divorce."

"That's not what my mama told me. Why in the world would I believe you? My father wasn't the only one you took away from me. Everything I wanted you came after. Well, not anymore. I'm putting an end to you." He lowered the gun a few inches and pointed it right at Winnie's heart.

Ellie yanked Winnie toward her at the same time a shot rang out in the cave. Snatching her weapon from the floor, she raised it toward their attacker while putting herself in between Winnie and the man. But Ellie didn't get off a shot. Instead, his arm fell to his side, the gun dropping from his fingers. It bounced on the stone surface, going off, the bullet lodging in the wall. Blood spread outward on the white jacket he wore as he crumbled to the ground.

As Ellie scrambled up, she glimpsed Colt diving through the hole and springing to his feet, his gun pointed at their assailant.

"Ellie, Winnie, are you two all right?"

"Yes," they both answered at the same time.

Ellie swiveled toward Winnie. "Are you really okay?"

She nodded. "At least I'm not cold anymore. Fear will do that to you."

Ellie headed up the sloping side to the ledge above Winnie and joined Colt as he knelt next to the gunman. He removed the man's goggles then his white ski mask to reveal Peter Tyler, blinking his eyes at the light she shone on his face.

Ellie stared at the glittering Christmas tree in the living room at Winnie's house. Although it was Christmas Day, there had been nothing calm and peaceful so far. Winnie had spent time with Christy, consoling her over her fiancé. Harold and Colt had been behind closed doors a good part of the morning, then Colt insisted Winnie rest before the sheriff came this afternoon. He had an update on what Peter Tyler had said after he came out of surgery to repair his shoulder where Colt had shot him. Colt and Doug had gone up to the cabin to see what was left of the place. Colt had wanted her to come, but she'd felt she needed to stay with Winnie. After what had occurred with Mary Ann, she wasn't quite ready to relinquish her bodyguard duties with Winnie until she had reassurances from the sheriff.

Then she would return to Dallas. And try to put her life back together. She finally could admit to herself that she loved Colt, but how could she really be sure? Even if she was, that didn't mean he cared about her or that they should be together. He lived on a research vessel in the middle of the ocean. She could never imagine herself living like that.

When the doorbell rang, she hurried across the foyer to answer it. Stepping to the side, she let the sheriff into the house. "I hope you're here to tell us good news."

"Yes," he said as Winnie descended the stairs and Colt came from the kitchen.

"Would you like anything to drink? We have some cookies, too." Winnie gestured toward the living room.

"Nope. Just as soon as we talk, I'm heading home. My son and grandchildren are there waiting for me so they can open presents. I haven't quite had a Christmas like this year in—well, never." Sheriff Quinn stood in front of the fireplace, warming himself. "I came right from the hospital after interviewing Peter. I laid it on the line. We have him dead to rights on three counts of attempted murder, arson and a number of other charges. I told him the judge would look kindly toward him if we didn't have to drag this out in a lengthy trial. He told me what happened."

Winnie frowned. "What was his involvement with Mary Ann?"

Colt hung back by the entrance into the living room, leaning against the wall, his arms folded over his chest. Ellie glanced toward him, but his expression was unreadable, his gaze fixed on his grandmother.

"He encouraged her to act on her feelings and gave her suggestions. When she was his patient, they got acquainted. He listened to her when she ranted about not getting the spokesperson job, then began planting seeds in her mind about how she had not been treated fairly. The threatening letters were Mary Ann's doing and the stink bombs at the Christmas Gala. He helped her kidnap the dogs because he told her that she could get some good money for them and get back at Winnie."

"Your lead didn't pan out about the dogs. Does he know where they are?" Colt asked, coming farther into the room and sitting next to Winnie.

"Yes, because he connected her with the person who took them to sell in Denver. The police there are paying that gentleman a visit today before he gets rid of them. You should have your dogs home by tomorrow."

"Unless someone bought them for a Christmas gift." Exhaustion still clung to Winnie's face, especially her eyes.

"Then we'll track each purchase."

"Winnie, they're alive. That's good news." Colt took her hand in his.

"So Peter Tyler was responsible in part about the dogs. How about the car left in the middle of the road the night of the Christmas tree lighting?" she asked.

"That was him. He didn't care whether you went off the cliff like Thomas or got upset by the similarities between the two events."

Winnie sat forward. "Wait. He didn't have anything to do with Thomas's accident, did he?"

"No, at least that's what he said, and all the evidence still points to an accident, Winnie. He wasn't even living here at that time. He moved back not long after he saw in the newspaper about Thomas dying. His mother had passed away a few months before your husband. According to Peter, she was still brokenhearted after all the years they were divorced. She fed Peter a lot of garbage about you coming between her and Thomas. I told him that wasn't the case. You two worked in the lab together, but so did my mother and she said it was hogwash what Thomas's ex-wife was saying."

Winnie smiled, and even her eyes sparkled with the gesture. "Your mom is a good friend."

"She sends her regards from sunny Florida. I can't get her back here in the winter. Too cold."

Winnie laughed. "I heartily agree with her. I may go visit her and warm these cold bones."

"We didn't make the final decision to go to the cabin until you told us it was safe. How did Peter know we were there?" Ellie asked Sheriff Quinn.

"He knew there was a chance, based on the talk the night before. He planned ahead, staying in a small cabin not far from you on the Henderson property. Then he came back to watch and see if you went." The sheriff held his hands out over the fire and rubbed them to-gether.

Ellie liked seeing Winnie's smile and hearing her laugh. The past weeks' ordeal had taken a toll on the woman. After the doctor at the house had checked out Winnie, she'd slept for twelve hours last night. Winnie had insisted Colt go to the hospital and have some X-rays on his arm. Ellie had taken him but little was said. In fact, Colt dozed on the trip to the hospital where the doctor told him he would be sore for a while, but he hadn't fractured his arm. Colt had also suffered a mild concussion, but he'd refused to stay overnight.

"Winnie, you could always return with me to the *Kaleidoscope*. We're in warm waters. In the South Pacific, it's summer right now."

"Not if I have to live on a boat."

Colt smiled. "It's a ship."

"Not big enough for me. You know I can't swim. You didn't get the swimming gene from me."

"Speaking of genes. Is Peter my uncle?"

Winnie shuddered. "Good grief, no. I don't know who his father is, but Thomas was sterile. For some reason she used Thomas to blame all her woes on. I guess that was easier for her than changing."

"I'm heading home to salvage a little bit of Christ-mas with my family." The sheriff crossed the room to the foyer, and Colt walked with him to the front door.

Winnie pinned Ellie with an assessing look. "You've been quiet. I imagine you're glad this is over with about as much as I am."

"I'm usually like this when a job is finished. It takes me days to come down from the stress. How's Christy?

She looked much better after she talked with you this morning."

"At first she wanted to step down from being the spokesperson for Endless Youth, but I talked her out of that. I told her she's not responsible for other people's actions. She isn't to blame for Peter or Mary Ann. Christy told me she talked with Peter before he went into surgery. What sent Peter over the edge was that Christy got the job that would demand a lot of her time—time away from him. He came to Bakersville after years of being told I was the one who caused all the trouble for him and his mother. He struggled to make it through school and has a huge debt from college loans he's still paying back. He saw the money he thought he should rightly have as Thomas's only living son. It festered inside him. The trigger was Christy getting the job and getting all the attention. But it was Peter's problem, not hers."

"Can you forgive Peter for what he did?"

"Probably when I recover from the effects of yesterday. Hanging on to the anger will only hurt me in the long run. Look what happened to Peter and his mother when they held on to their anger."

Listening to Winnie's reasonable explanation of why she would forgive Peter made Ellie think about her mother. She hadn't talked to her in years, and that had always bothered her. Maybe she should call her tonight and wish her a merry Christmas.

Colt reentered the living room. "I'm glad this is all wrapped up. I got a message from the *Kaleidoscope*. Doug gave it to me this morning. I'm needed back there to finish up a study we've been running on the seal population in the area where we're anchored."

"When?" Winnie rose.

"Day after tomorrow. I want to make sure you're all right and things are really settled after what's happened."

"At least we have a little more time together. I think I'll take my second nap today. See you two at dinner."

After Winnie left, Colt took the couch across from Ellie. He stared at the fire for a long moment before looking at her. "One thing my grandmother isn't is subtle. For being tired, she can move awfully fast."

"I think she's still trying to process it all. Having not just one but two people angry with you to the point they wanted to harm you is hard on even the toughest person. Imagine Peter's mother lying to him for all those years."

"It just makes me realize how fortunate I've been to have Winnie and my granddad to raise me."

"I'm going to call my mother tonight. It's about time I did. I don't expect warm fuzzies, but I need to take the first step to try and mend our relationship. She's all the family I have. I see the relationship you have with Winnie, and although we'll probably never have that kind, we can at least have a civil one."

"You get a chance to do that. I don't have that. My father is dead."

"You can forgive him in your heart. That's what is important."

"You're right." Colt stood and bridged the distance between them. "Speaking of relationships, what are we going to do about us?"

"Nothing."

He clasped her hands and hauled her up against him. "You can't deny we have a connection."

"No, I can't. But this isn't real. This whole situation

heightened all our senses. I've seen it before with others and their relationships didn't last. You and I live very differently. I couldn't live on a research vessel even if it's classified a ship. I need space. I would go crazy. How could a relationship last with you in the Pacific Ocean and me flying all over the world for my job? I think we should cut our losses and go our separate ways."

"How do you feel about me? Forget about what you just said. All the logical, rational reasons we shouldn't be together." He placed his hand over her heart. "How do you feel in there?"

"I love you, but it isn't enough. A lasting relationship is much more than love. We haven't had any time to think about our feelings. We've been on a roller-coaster ride since you arrived."

He framed her face. "I love you, Ellie. I don't want to let you go. I realized that when I was trying to get back to you and Winnie in the cave. I thought I was going to lose you when I saw Peter pointing the gun at you."

His declaration made her hesitate, her resolve wavering. Finally she murmured, "Someone has to be the logical, rational one. I guess I'm that one. I need time to figure out what I want. You need time. You have a job that needs you right now and so do I."

He bent toward her and kissed her. All the sensations he could produce in her flooded her, making her want to take a risk. When he pulled back, sanity returned to Ellie.

"Why not give the *Kaleidoscope* a chance? You might like it."

She shook her head.

"No, I'm leaving tomorrow morning to return to Dallas. Maybe sometime in the future we'll meet again under less stressful circumstances."

He released a long breath. "You're right. These past few weeks have been unreal. Reality is our everyday lives. Will you promise me one thing?"

"Maybe."

He chuckled. "Why am I not surprised you said that? Where's the trust?"

"That's just the point. I don't trust easily and these new feelings could all vanish with time."

"Winnie will be having an Endless Youth gala to launch the new line on Valentine's Day. In spite of what happened the last time, she'll be having it at the same hotel that evening. Come back. Meet me there if you think we have a chance at what we started here. That's seven weeks away."

"I promise I'll think long and hard on it."

"You do that," he said. "And I hope I'll see you then."

Colt stood at the double doors into the hotel ballroom on Valentine's Day. The event was in full swing. Laughter floated to him. A sense of celebration dominated the atmosphere of the Endless Youth gala. The music, soft and romantic, filled the room. Couples, dressed in tuxedos and gowns, whirled around the dance floor to the strains of a waltz.

None of the gaiety meant anything to him.

The ball was halfway over. Ellie wasn't here. She wasn't coming.

"Colt, why aren't you dancing?"

He forced a smile for his grandmother, but inside his heart was breaking. "You sent Ellie the invitation?"

"For the third time, yes, and I know she received it."

"I gave her the space she wanted."

"Then you've done what you can. Have faith in what you feel, what you two shared at Christmas. I saw how she felt about you. Give her time to work it out. Why don't you dance with your favorite grandmother?"

"You're my *only* grandmother."

"True."

"You know dancing isn't my thing. Harold is so much better than me, and he is your date for tonight."

"Just because Harold and I are dating doesn't mean I should neglect my grandson." She laughed, a sound Colt loved to hear from his grandmother. "I can't believe I'm dating again. I thought that would never happen after Thomas."

"Why not? You're seventy-three years *young.*"

"You're right." Winnie held her hand out to Colt.

He threw a last glance over his shoulder at the hotel lobby. No Ellie. After three days on the *Kaleidoscope* he'd known what he'd felt for her was the marrying kind of love. There was no thrill and excitement in his job. He wanted to share his life with Ellie. He'd completed his research project and resigned. It was time for him to put down roots. Alone, if not with Ellie.

He whisked his grandmother out onto the dance floor and somehow managed to sweep Winnie around the ballroom to some love song without stepping on her foot or stumbling.

Then he saw her, dressed in a long red gown, across the room in the entrance to the ballroom. Ellie had come. He came to a standstill. Their gazes linked together, and his heart began pounding against his chest.

"Go to her," Winnie whispered, backing away from him.

Colt headed toward Ellie at the same time she did. They met on the edge of the dance floor. He was sure he had some silly grin on his face, but Ellie's smile encompassed her whole face in radiance.

"You look beautiful. Want to dance?" He offered her his hand.

She clasped it and came effortlessly into his embrace. The feel of her against him felt so right.

"I'm sorry I was late. My flight was delayed then we had to change planes and—"

He stopped her words with a kiss. When he drew back and began to move about the floor, he said, "You're here. That's all that's important."

They flowed as one through the crowd of dancers. All he could do was stare at her. He never wanted to take his eyes off her again.

"Seven weeks was too long to be apart. When I returned to the *Kaleidoscope,* my life wasn't the same. I wanted different things. I love you, Ellie."

"The same for me. I went back to Dallas. I even went on an assignment in Rome. I love Rome. I stayed a few days after my job was finished, but Rome wasn't the same without you. I tried to talk myself out of my feelings, but I couldn't, not in seven weeks. That's when I knew I had to see you again. Be with you."

The music stopped. Colt grabbed her hand and hurried off the dance floor out into the lobby. He found a private alcove and pulled her back into his arms.

"I want to be with you, too," he said.

"Our jobs—"

He put two fingers over her lips, the feel of them against his skin everything he remembered. Warm. Soft. Her. "I resigned from the *Kaleidoscope.* I'm slowly going to take over for Winnie. She wants to retire completely in a year or so. She says she's ready to lie around and eat bonbons."

Ellie laughed. "That'll be the day. She'll hole herself in her lab in the basement and create some other sensational product."

"As the soon-to-be CEO of Glamour Sensations, I'm hoping she will. What would you say if we hired you as the head of our security? The company is growing. I need someone with more experience than our current guy. Security will become more important than ever before. And there will still be some travel involved so you won't always be confined to here."

She snuggled closer. "I like being confined to here if you're here, too."

"Right by your side. I hope as your husband." Then he kissed her with every emotion he'd held in check for the past seven weeks without her.

"I think I can accommodate that."

* * * * *

Mary Ellen Porter's love of storytelling was solidified in fifth grade when she was selected to read her first children's story to a group of kindergartners. From then on, she knew she'd be a writer. When not working, Mary Ellen enjoys reading and spending time with her family and search-dog-in-training. She's a member of Chesapeake Search Dogs, a volunteer search and rescue team that helps bring the lost and missing home.

Books by Mary Ellen Porter

Love Inspired Suspense

Into Thin Air
Off the Grid Christmas

Visit the Author Profile page
at Harlequin.com for more titles.

OFF THE GRID CHRISTMAS

Mary Ellen Porter

I am the Lord. I am the God of every person on the earth. You know that nothing is impossible for me.
—*Jeremiah* 32:27

To my parents, Ed and Shirley Porter, whose constant love and encouragement have guided all my life choices and underpinned my successes.
Thank you for your unfailing support and for giving me a strong foundation of faith and family.

And to my in-laws, Eldridge and Joyce Grady, for embracing me as your own from the first day we met. I couldn't have asked for a more perfect extended family.

ONE

The Christmas tree had been Arden DeMarco's undoing.

Or, to be more accurate, the decorations on it had.

Not that accuracy mattered. What mattered was that she had to leave. Quickly.

She shoved her sweatshirt into her backpack, the scent of Tide detergent and lavender fabric softener reminding her of her childhood home. She'd hoped to be there for Christmas, reveling in the beautiful predictability of Christmas Eve service, ham dinner, new pajamas worn on Christmas morning.

She was twenty-five years old and she still loved those things.

Unfortunately, in this instance her nostalgia had been her downfall.

She sighed.

What was done was done. For twelve days she'd been safe in this secluded cottage just outside of Lubec, Maine. Now she wasn't.

She hadn't planned to leave, but staying was no longer an option. She'd have to find another place to go to ground. With a quick look around the room, Arden was satisfied she was leaving nothing important behind. No clues as to what she'd been working on, where she planned to go or what her next step would be.

Zipping her pack, she gave the surveillance monitors one more glance.

All clear.

For now. But the odds weren't in her favor.

Grabbing the wearable pet carrier from the hook behind the door that separated the kitchen from the cozy living room, she fastened it around her chest.

"Sebastian? Time to go," she called.

As was Sebastian's way, he didn't answer.

She crossed the room to check his favorite spot, knelt down and peered under the sparsely decorated Christmas tree. Sure enough, he was there, batting at a red bulb.

"Did you learn nothing from the tinsel incident?" she muttered.

He looked at her, blinking large blue eyes and meowing as she scooped him up and placed him in the carrier. Where most cats would have yowled and struggled, he settled in without a fuss, the tips of his dark brown ears barely visible as she pulled the drawstring on the carrier to secure him inside. Like Arden, he was quirky. It was one of the reasons she'd adopted him.

He purred happily against her chest. Poor guy had no idea that he'd brought danger down on their heads.

She'd been so careful when she'd dropped off the grid. Covered all the bases: cash transactions only, no contact with family, prepaid cell phone for emergencies only. There'd been no way anyone could trace her movements.

Or so she'd thought.

Unfortunately, in her panic, she'd forgotten about Sebastian's microchip. Truth be told, if Sebastian hadn't eaten his body weight in tinsel, she'd still be none the wiser. Okay. It hadn't been that much tinsel. After administering an ultrasound, the vet had assured Arden that the cat would be just fine. She'd been happy and relieved until the vet had called an hour ago to check on Sebastian and used Arden's real name.

A name Arden hadn't used in almost two weeks. They'd obviously scanned Sebastian for a microchip and now her assumed alias and the cottage address were linked to Arden's true identity, through the PetID database.

The jig was up. She needed to leave. If she managed to escape with her life, she'd never *ever* hang tinsel again.

A powerful gust of wind whipped in from the ocean, drawing her attention to the window. The sun had set an hour ago, and the full moon should have been rising above the ocean. Clouds covered it, light gray against the dark horizon. Below, the beach lay empty. No lights or bonfires. No people with flashlights digging for clams. This wasn't the time of year for vacationers. That had played to Arden's advantage. Now she felt vulnerable.

She tried to tell herself it was good that she was leaving, but she'd wanted to stay. A quiet cottage far away from anyone who knew her had been the perfect place to hide.

The wind buffeted the cottage's shake siding and howled beneath the eaves, the eerie sound spurring her to hurry. She pulled on her coat, partially zipping it up over Sebastian. He purred even more loudly.

Happy cat.

Unhappy human companion.

Arden shoved gloves into her pockets and yanked a knit cap over her ears. This was it. Time to go. She grabbed her pack, flipped off the lights and dropped the house keys on the desk next to a note about the security system she'd regrettably be leaving behind. State-of-the-art. Expensive. She'd probably need it again before this was over, but it was too heavy and cumbersome for someone who needed to move quickly.

The perimeter alarm chirped, the warning sending her pulse racing. She turned back to the monitors. Three were clear. The fourth showed a lone figure making his way slowly up the steep snow-covered path on foot. She smiled at that. She'd chosen this location well—even a Jeep couldn't navigate the narrow, rock-covered road.

One guy she could handle.

She had the advantage. She knew he was coming.

The cottage was in a large clearing, no place to conceal movement—perfect for seeing what was coming; not so great for a covert escape.

She'd wait until he was on the front walkway, then sneak out the back.

She shrugged the pack onto her shoulders, her attention on the monitor as the man strode up the walkway.

Keeping an eye on the monitor, she crossed the well-worn wood floor to the back door. Heart pounding, hand on the doorknob, she waited for him to reach the front steps. A cold breeze swept in under the door and she shivered. The 1930s cottage, mostly used as a summer rental, was not well insulated. Though it was comfortable enough with both wood-burning stoves fired up, she had extinguished the fires thirty minutes ago in preparation for her departure. Now, with the embers quickly cooling, the cold Maine chill was settling over the house.

The man reached the front steps, eyed the footprints she'd left in the snow when she'd returned from the vet. The image on the monitor wasn't clear enough to see his face, but she didn't plan to stick around long enough to get a better look.

"Get ready for a bumpy ride, Sebastian," Arden muttered, quietly opening the back door. The new storm door stuck, the old frame a poor fit. She should have removed it when she'd first noticed the problem, but she hadn't thought she'd be found. Assumptions could get a person killed. Her oldest brother and decorated FBI agent, Grayson, was always saying that. Hopefully, she wasn't going to prove him right.

She walked outside, letting the door rest against the jamb. No time to wrestle it tightly into place. The yard was a slick sheet of icy snow, but she rushed toward the back corner of the property as quickly as she could. She had to reach the shed, and the motorcycle, if she had any hope of escape. She had minutes. Maybe less.

Bang!

The sound sent adrenaline coursing through her blood.

She glanced back, saw the storm door lifted by the wind.

Bang!

The door slammed again, and a dark figure appeared around the corner of the house. Tall. Obviously masculine. Coming toward her with quick, decisive steps.

She sprinted to the shed.

"Arden DeMarco!" the man yelled, his voice carrying over the sound of the crashing surf and wind.

She reached for the shed door with shaking hands, yanked it open just as he grabbed her shoulder.

Arden was ready for him.

The youngest of five children, and the only girl, she'd learned to hold her own early on—her brothers had made sure of that. And what they hadn't taught her, ten years of mixed martial arts training had. Without hesitation, she pivoted, grabbing his hand and twisting it at an unnatural angle.

He released his hold, giving her just enough space to throw a punch. He dodged at the last minute, her knuckles just brushing his jaw. She pulled back, aiming for his throat this time. She'd practiced this move dozens of times. She knew it cold, but Sebastian hindered her movement and the man was quicker than she expected, grabbing her wrist and yanking her arm down before she could land the blow.

"Enough!" he growled. "I'm just here to—"

She threw a left hook. Her fist connected.

She knew what he was there for. Or she could guess. He was too well trained to be anything but a government operative or a hired assassin.

If he felt the blow at all, he didn't let on. Instead, he raised his arm to block her next punch.

"I said, enough," he muttered, his foot sweeping out, catching her ankle as she dodged. She stumbled backward, managed to somehow regain her balance. He reached for her again, grabbing the sleeve of her jacket and pulling her toward him.

Arden was small, agile and packed a surprising punch for her size. But Kane Walker had spent more than ten years in the Special Forces as part of the army's elite Night Stalkers airborne brigade, and she was no match for him.

Not that he planned to keep fighting her.

He'd come to bring her home.

She was going. Whether she liked it or not.

"Arden, your—" he began, but she was obviously in no mood to listen.

She yanked away, took a stance he'd seen dozens of times when he'd sparred with her brother Jace. She attacked with Jace's signature move. It was almost indefensible.

Almost.

He took a calculated step forward, got his knee behind her leg and swept her toward the ground. If she'd been an enemy, he would have added a punch to the chest or nose to speed her descent; instead, he grabbed her arm as she flew backward, slowing her fall. She hit the ground with a thud anyway.

"How about we call a truce?" he said, holding his hands up in mock surrender. "Jace didn't have me track you down so we could spar."

"Jace?" She got to her feet, eyeing him through the darkness. He doubted she could see his features in the unlit yard. Even if she could, she might not be able to place his face. They'd met a few times in the past. Mostly when he'd joined Jace on home leave.

"Your brother's worried about you."

"And you know this because?" she asked, her shoulders tense, her hands fisted.

"I'm Kane Walker. Your brother's—"

"Business partner," she finished.

"Right."

"So, Kane," she said, sidling along the shed she was backed against. Unless he missed his guess, there was another door in and she was going for it. "Why'd Jace send you when he could have sent any one of my brothers?"

"You've hit the FBI's most wanted list."

"I'm aware of that."

"The Feds are watching your entire family. Since you and I are barely acquaintances, I'm not on their radar."

"Yet."

"Yet," he agreed as she shimmied to the corner of the shed, pivoted and took off.

He snagged her pack, yanking her backward with enough force to throw her off balance. "I thought we were done sparring, Arden."

"You need to leave." She spun around.

"Not without you."

"Let me make this perfectly clear: I'm not going anywhere with you. Make this easy on yourself. Go back to Maryland. And tell my brothers that I'm fine."

"Jace told me to bring you to Grayson—you can deal with the FBI together."

"Jace is going to be very disappointed." She crossed her arms over her chest.

Actually, she crossed them over her bulging stomach. He frowned, eyeing the mound under her coat. It wiggled.

"Carrying a passenger?"

"My cat."

"Might have been a good idea to leave him home. Microchips can make it difficult to drop completely off the grid."

"I'm aware of that," she said.

"Yet you brought him to the vet anyway," he pointed out.

"I was worried," she said defensively, her left hand reaching up to cradle the mound under her jacket. "Though it really was an unfortunate turn of events that the Lubec Veterinary Clinic uses microchip scanners."

"I guess that depends on your point of view." For Kane, it was just the break he'd been waiting for.

She stepped past him, acting like she was going to go ahead and do what she'd been trying to since he'd arrived—leave.

"I hope you're not thinking that you're going anywhere without me."

"I'm not thinking it. I'm doing it."

After nearly six days without a lead, he'd arrived in this snowy ocean-side town under no delusion that getting her home would be simple. She knew how to hide, and she knew how to fight. According to Jace, she also had a tendency to be dogmatic in her approach to things and often unwilling to compromise.

"I'm afraid you've misunderstood. I'm bringing you home, so we're going to have to stick together from here on out."

"Sorry, that doesn't work for me. I prefer solitude to company," she said, tugging open the door to the shed.

He pushed it shut again. "I prefer cooperation to animosity, but we don't always get what we want."

"You're in my personal space," she responded, ignoring his comment. "How about you get out of it?"

He stepped closer, tired of the wordplay and anxious to get her away from the property. "Now you're in mine."

"Personal space is the variable and subjective distance at which one person feels comfortable talking to another. If you want to speak with me, you need to back away."

He almost cracked a smile. Almost.

She wasn't looking for a chat. She was looking for an escape route. He could see it in her eyes. Her body language.

She was Jace's sister through and through. If the black hair and blue eyes weren't a dead giveaway, the stubborn set of her jaw certainly was.

"Let's take the FBI out of the picture for a minute. What are you running from?" he asked, his right hand still holding the shed door closed. His arm just above her shoulder blocked escape from her left.

"Trouble," she replied, glancing to her right as if calculating the likelihood of dodging out of his reach.

"Better to face it with a support system than alone."

"I can't involve anyone else. It's too dangerous."

"You can explain that to your brother when you see him."

"Returning to Maryland isn't an option."

Kane shook his head. "From where I stand, it's the only option."

"Well, if you'd just back up about a foot and take a few steps to your left, *my* preferred option will become a little clearer to you."

He could have laughed if he'd let himself. Jace had said his sister was brilliant. He hadn't mentioned her sense of humor.

"Sorry. That's not going to happen. I promised Jace that I'd find you and bring you home."

"You should never make a promise you can't keep."

Her back against the door, she slowly edged her way toward the right corner of the shed.

He grabbed her left arm just below the elbow, and stopped her in her tracks. "We're wasting time," he said. "I found you—it's safe to assume someone else will, too. If you don't want to tell me why you're running, maybe you can tell me who you're running from."

"I'm running from so many people, it would almost be easier to tell you who isn't after me." She tucked a few strands of hair under her hat, her gaze shifting from him to a point beyond his shoulder.

"Go ahead."

"And leave? I was thinking about it, but it's hard to do with you holding onto my arm."

"Go ahead and list the people who aren't after you."

She sighed, tried to yank her wrist away. "Look, I know you're trying to do what Jace wants, but I can handle this alone. I won't drag him, Grayson or even you into this."

"We're already in it," he pointed out, and she frowned.

"You don't have to be. You can walk away and let me go back to what I was doing."

He was tempted to do just that.

He didn't have time for games. After twelve years of active duty, he'd left the army in August and spent the last three months getting his and Jace's fledgling business off the ground.

Shadow Wolves Security, named after their Army unit, was finally up and running. It had taken a lot of work. With Jace's tour not up for another four months, the bulk of it had fallen on Kane. He'd spent countless unpaid hours making certain things were ready. He'd even managed to land their first contracts, set to start in less than a month.

With that under his belt, he'd planned to leave the business in the hands of his other business partner and Chief Operations Officer, Silas Blackwater, and take a long, relaxing weekend. Jace's phone call had changed his plans. When he'd asked Kane to help Grayson locate their sister, Kane couldn't refuse.

Yeah. He might be tempted to walk away and let Arden deal with her problem alone, but he wouldn't do it. He owed Jace a lot. More than he could ever repay.

"Let's go." He still had his hand around her wrist, and he started walking, dragging her along beside him, not caring that she was yanking against his hold.

"You don't understand the ramifications of me going back," she muttered, digging in her heels and putting all her weight into trying to stop their forward momentum. There wasn't a whole lot of weight to her, so it barely slowed Kane down.

"Explain it to me then."

"The people who are after me are dangerous and they've got deep pockets. They'll stop at nothing to get what they want. They don't care who they hurt in the process."

"Grayson can work with the FBI to clear your name and protect you."

"I trust Grayson, but I can't ask him to put his career on the line and take my side against the FBI. Besides, there's no way to be sure they don't have someone in the FBI on their payroll."

"Who, exactly, are *these people*, and what do they want from you?"

"That information is need-to-know." She tucked another loose strand of hair beneath her hat. A nervous tic? he wondered.

"I need to know."

"You are an intermediary. You only need to know that I'm not returning home. Not yet. Tell my brothers—"

A loud chirp interrupted her words. Two more followed in rapid succession.

He didn't ask what it was.

He knew.

She'd set up a perimeter alarm and it was going off.

"What quadrant?" he asked as she pulled a cell phone from her coat pocket.

"West. Looks like the same way you arrived. You'd better go—"

The phone chirped again.

"Sounds like they have an army coming for you." He sprinted back to the shed, pulling her along with him. She'd been trying to get inside since he'd arrived.

Now, she seemed determined *not* to enter.

She tried to twist away, but his fingers easily locked around her slender wrist. He dragged her into the shed, easing the door closed and sealing them inside. It smelled like sawdust and gas fumes.

"You have a vehicle in here?" he asked, keeping his grip on her wrist tight. He didn't want to hurt her, but he wasn't going to let her leave. Not on her own.

"That would be a likely scenario, since I've been trying to get in here since you arrived," she grumbled, jerking away and moving toward the center of the shed.

"How about you show it to me so we can get moving?" he demanded, his gaze shifting to a lone window that looked out over the beach. It was too dark to see much, but a light bounced along the shore. He doubted it was a beachcomber looking for treasures.

"It's under the tarp," she responded, motioning to the center of the room.

"Then let's go." He crowded in beside her, blocking her path to the door. She had her reasons for continuing to run. He had his reasons for bringing her home. They could hash all that out, come up with a plan that would work for both of them. Later.

After they escaped whomever it was she was running from.

TWO

Someone had breached her security perimeter.

Someone else was on the beach.

Through the shed window, Arden could see the light moving along the shore—a small dot of white in the blackness. She doubted it was just one person. And she doubted it was the FBI.

Grayson probably told Kane to monitor the PetID database for a potential hit on Sebastian's microchip, but there's no way her brother would have shared that information with the FBI.

Arden's ex-boyfriend Randy Sumner was another story.

He knew about Sebastian, and he'd have no qualms about tipping off GeoArray Corporation. He was in this deep and had just as much to lose if the company went down. And he, more than anyone, knew Arden could bring them all down.

She hadn't been exaggerating about GeoArray's power, resources and reach. The corporation *was* an army of sorts, and it would send its best soldiers to bring her in.

Soldiers? Thugs was probably a more accurate descriptor, and unless Arden missed her guess, they were trying to hem her in.

But she'd be gone before whoever was on the beach managed to make it up the bluff. Kane would be with her. She wasn't happy about it. It would be easier to leave him behind, but he had no idea what Arden was up against; what *he* was now up against.

Arden knew. They'd killed before. They wouldn't hesitate to kill again. No, she couldn't, in good conscience, leave Kane to face off against them.

Sure, he was former Special Forces and looked like he could take care of himself. She'd seen him sparring with her brothers at the gym while he and Jace were on home leave one summer. She knew he was quick, sharp-minded and lethal, but GeoArray had money and power behind it. So did its CEO, Marcus Emory. They wouldn't fight fair and could afford to hire the best fighters and trackers to hunt down what they wanted.

At this moment, what they wanted was Arden.

They were desperate to get their hands on her and the files she'd taken from their networks.

She'd given them a golden opportunity, thanks to her love for Christmas and Sebastian. Now, she had to get out of their reach, and she needed to get Kane out, too.

She dragged the canvas tarp off the motorbike her landlord had left in the shed. A 1952 Vincent Black Shadow. Admittedly, the bike had seen better days. But Arden appreciated the handcraftsmanship of the vehicle and the fact that, in its heyday, the model broke speed records. Very few had been made.

Arden suspected the property owner had no idea of the value the bike would bring if restored. If he did, he might not be so quick to leave it in an unlocked shed for his renters to use.

"A motorcycle?" Kane pressed close to her back, in her space again. Usually, she despised having people that close. Currently, she didn't have time to worry about it or to tell him to back off.

"Does it look like something else?"

"It looks old."

"It is."

"Does it work?"

"Yep. It came with the rental—it's a way residents can get up and down the access path to the parking area more quickly."

"I'm afraid to ask how loud it's going to be when you start it up." He glanced toward the window. "There's someone out on the beach. I can't tell if he's alone."

"It's too far down with no easy way up. Anyone on the beach shouldn't pose much of a threat. The bigger threat is whoever's coming up the access path. The shed's in clear view of it. Once we're in the open, we'd be easily picked off by anyone with a high-powered rifle."

"What are you suggesting?"

She turned her attention back to her phone, scrolled through the live video feed from her security system. "They've got no clue I know they're coming. Logic says they'll head for the house. As soon as it's breached, we can start her up and head for the trail at the back of the property. We'll be out of the line of fire before they can make it to the back door."

He glanced at the phone in her hand. "You've set up an elaborate monitoring system."

"Wouldn't you?"

"Yes, but I'm in the security business."

"I am, too. It's just a different kind of security."

Kane cracked open the shed door, his broad back blocking her view.

"See anything?" she asked. She'd have edged in closer, stuck her head under his arm to get a look, but Sebastian was getting restless. His fuzzy ears poked through the top flap of the carrier and bumped against her collarbone as he tried to figure out what was going on.

"Just a lot of darkness, but I don't like the way it feels."

"Darkness has a feeling?"

"Danger does." He grabbed the bike's handlebars, tugged the motorcycle forward and out of her grasp. "We need to move."

She could have argued, but she'd heard her brothers talk about going with their guts so many times, she didn't think it would be prudent to ignore Kane's instincts.

"The trail's kind of hidden. It's just behind the shed and winds toward the bigger path you walked in on." She leaned past, poked her head out the door and pointed at what looked like driftwood and scrappy bushes covered with a fresh layer of ice-crested snow. She wasn't sure if the owner of the property had meant to provide a quick escape, but she'd known as soon as she'd seen the narrow trail that she'd have one if she needed it.

She hadn't expected to need it.

Maybe that was part of her problem. She trusted in her intelligence a little too much. She relied on herself more than she relied on anyone else. She'd been one of the guys for as long as she could remember—the ultra-capable younger sister of four ultra-capable men. She'd never been in a situation she couldn't handle on her own, and she hadn't expected to find herself in one. She'd expected to go off the grid, get the proof she needed to take GeoArray down and go right back to her life. That wasn't how things were turning out.

She found that more irritating than alarming.

"You've ridden a motorcycle before, right?" she whispered, pocketing her phone as Kane pushed the vehicle outside, putting the shed between them and the access path to the cottage. The wind stole her words, but he must have heard.

"Not one this old," he responded.

"The age of the vehicle is irrelevant," she said, ignoring his sarcasm. She loved old vehicles and had restored several of them with her dad while helping out in his shop during the summers. She'd ridden this one enough to know it was in good working order. It was also fast. That was going to be an asset.

"Its working condition is *not* irrelevant."

"It works." They'd reached the brush, and she skirted past him. Not an easy feat considering his size, but there was no way she was letting him drive them out. She knew the trail. She knew the bike. She'd be the driver.

She brushed his hands from the handlebars and climbed on, balancing the bike as she scanned the dark path and the beach below. The light was still there. Farther away and moving at a steady pace, parallel to the shore. Whoever it was wouldn't find a way up from there, but night vision goggles and a long-range rifle could make a long-distance kill easy.

GeoArray wanted her alive. For now. That was one thing she had in her favor.

Kane, on the other hand, was simply in the way.

Her phone chirped, the sound chilling her blood.

"They're in," she muttered.

Kane climbed on the bike, wrapping his left arm low around her waist. "Just be careful," he warned. "The temperature's dropped and the snow's crusted over with ice. If we wreck, it's over."

"Warning duly noted." Arden zipped her jacket up to her chin, completely covering Sebastian. She didn't need Kane to tell her to be cautious. Wrecking the bike and getting herself caught was not on her agenda. Seeing her brother's business partner—one of his closest friends—killed wasn't, either.

She was sorry Kane had been dragged into this, but she wasn't surprised her brothers called for reinforcements. Grayson and Jace were cut from the same cloth, both willing to do anything to help those they cared about. It would be hypocritical to fault them for that. After all, that's how she ended up in this mess in the first place. Of course, Juniper Westin wasn't just anyone. She was Arden's best friend, the sister Arden had never had.

They'd met halfway through first grade. Juniper had walked into the classroom, and Arden had known they were kindred spirits—two oddball mavericks sitting in a room filled with average Joes.

The whispering had started right away, and Arden had felt the overwhelming need to stand up for the new girl the way she'd always had to stand up for herself. It wasn't Juniper's glasses or curly black hair that had all the kids talking; it wasn't her light brown skin—even though there hadn't been many kids of color in their elementary school.

No, it was the dark purple bruise on her cheek that accompanied the healing split on her lip. And the too-big sweater she'd had on with well-worn jeans that were almost too short. Jeans that had bright red patches with pink hearts carefully sewn on the knees. During recess, Robby Dixon had laughed at her for those hearts, and Arden had done the only thing she thought she could. She'd punched him right in the middle of his smug face. She'd earned herself a three-day suspension, the respect of every kid in the school and a life-long friend.

Since then, she and Juniper had been through good times and bad times together. There was nothing Arden wouldn't do for her friend—including hacking into Geo-Array's secured network—which, unfortunately, had led to this.

Kane leaned in, his breath tickling her ear. "I just saw a light go on in the house. If we're getting out of here, now's the time to do it."

"Right." She cranked the engine, the sudden roar drowning out the sound of the surf. No doubt everyone within a mile radius had heard. She gunned the motor, and the bike charged forward, speeding through the narrow space between old shrubs, bits of leaves and branches breaking off as she raced along the trail.

To Kane's credit, he had no problem holding on and keeping his balance. He didn't shout instructions or tell her to watch out for the rocks and debris that littered the narrow trail.

And he'd been right about the ice. It coated every-thing. The bike's nearly threadbare tires barely held on as she sped around a curve.

She thought she heard shouting, but she couldn't be certain. The engine was too loud, the wind too wild.

They'd be at the parking area soon. It was a small lot used by a few seasonal residents whose cliff-side cottages weren't easily accessible by car. It was mostly unused this time of year. Her Jeep was there. Kane's vehicle must be, too. She wasn't sure they'd be able to get to either of them. GeoArray's thugs probably had the area staked out.

"Pull off here," Kane shouted.

She almost ignored him.

She wanted off the trail and on the open road. The more distance they put between themselves and their pursuers, the better. Then again, if guys with guns were waiting in the parking lot below, she'd have to drive straight into their trap before she could get out on the road.

She coasted to a stop and cut the engine, her pulse racing.

"Is there another way out?" Kane asked, his voice tight.

"We can head up the bluff." She nodded toward the south and the scraggly pines that dotted a steep hill. She'd walked there a couple of days ago, trying to clear her mind after hours in front of the computer. "But I don't know how far we can take the bike. The terrain's steep and icy and the bike's tires have definitely seen better days. We need a vehicle, and mine's in the lot."

"I parked off the street. About a half-mile from the lot."

A light flashed at the head of the trail, there and gone so quickly Arden would have missed it if she hadn't been looking in that direction.

"A signal," Kane muttered. "They're going to try to trap us. Can we make it to the road, or should we ditch the bike and try to make it out quietly? You know the area best. It's your call, Arden, but make the right choice. We're probably outmanned and outgunned."

"We can make it out on the bike." It would take a little finesse and a whole lot of guts, but their odds were better on the bike than walking out.

She started the engine and took off again, leaving the trail and bouncing onto ice-coated grass, speeding between spindly pine trees as she raced up the bluff and toward freedom.

Kane had been in a lot of dangerous situations, but riding on an ancient motorbike behind a woman who seemed more daredevil than computer whiz was right up at the top of his list of experiences he never wanted to repeat.

He was concerned about the icy conditions, Arden's driving skills and the fact that whoever was after her might have already spotted his rented Chevy Tahoe. It was unlikely, though. He'd parked behind a small copse of trees, and the vehicle would be difficult to spot from the road.

Still, if the people who were after Arden were as desperate as she seemed to believe, they might have been scoping out the area, looking for signs that someone besides Arden was around.

The bike bounced over an exposed root, and he tightened his grip on Arden's waist. He'd have preferred to drive, but this arrangement left his gun hand free. Arden navigated the rocky, snow-covered bluff with surprising ease.

Kane leaned forward, his chest pressing against Arden's backpack. The wind whipped at strands of hair peeking out from her hat, the soft tendrils brushing against his cheek.

She slowed as they reached the crest of the hill. Even at this speed the cold air was merciless on their exposed skin and eyes. They needed to get to the Chevy. He had a duffel of supplies there, hats and gloves, an extra jacket.

His work required preparedness, and he'd tried to think of all the possibilities when he'd set off to find Arden. He'd been hoping to be a few steps ahead of whoever was after her, but the army that was following her seemed to have a lot of tech power behind it—they'd been able to access the PetID database and register the hit on the microchip just as he had. They also had at least some knowledge of Arden's private life. Kane had only known about her cat and its microchip because Grayson had told him. Was it possible someone Arden knew well had set her up?

He glanced over his shoulder, his arm still tight around Arden's waist.

Bright lights illuminated the path they'd left, what looked like an ATV zipping along the narrow passage.

"They're coming. Looks like they have a vehicle that can make it," he warned.

"Hold on," she shouted, hitting the throttle and propelling them over the top of the bluff. The way down was as steep as the trip up, but the bike managed to cling to the rocky, ice-coated ground as Arden wove her way through sparse pine growth.

There weren't enough trees to provide adequate cover, and the hair on his neck stood on end. He may as well have had a bull's-eye on his back. One well-trained sniper, and he'd be down.

He glanced back. The ATV had crested the hill and seemed to be idling there. It was a good vantage point, and the shot would be easy enough to take.

Arden must have sensed the danger.

"Hang on!" she shouted. Hitting the throttle once more, she increased their speed and veered sharply to the right, steering the motorcycle toward what looked like a shallow ditch. Beyond that, the road curved across the landscape.

The first shot rang out as the motorcycle jumped the ditch. Bits of bark flew into Kane's face as the tires hit the snowy pavement. The motorcycle wobbled dangerously, yet somehow remained upright.

"Left!" he shouted, calculating their distance from his Tahoe, the likelihood of the next bullet hitting its target, the chance that Arden would make it out of this situation alive if something happened to him.

He'd promised Jace he'd get her home in one piece.

He'd do it.

A second shot rang out, and the pavement behind them exploded. A high-caliber rifle, but the gunman couldn't seem to hit his mark.

There are always blessings in the trials.

His grandmother had reminded him of that dozens of times when he was a kid. Maybe she'd been right.

He could see the patch of trees where he'd parked the Tahoe, and the dull gleam of the street sign he'd used as a marker just ahead.

A bullet hit it, bouncing off the metal with a loud crack.

"Just past the sign. Behind those trees," he barked, and Arden veered in the direction he'd indicated, the motorcycle slowing as she bounced off the road and into knee-high grass.

She cut the motor as they reached the Tahoe.

The night had gone silent except for the wind that howled through the trees. No engines roaring, people shouting, bullets flying.

"I don't like this," Arden whispered as she clambered off the bike.

"Get in!" he urged, opening the driver's side door. "They're probably coming from the parking area." Before the words were out of his mouth, she was scrambling across the bench seat; he rushed in after her, pulling the door shut behind him.

Shoving the keys in the ignition, Kane cranked the engine and hit the gas. The SUV lurched out from behind the trees and screeched onto the road.

"Keep down!" Kane ordered as he floored it.

He didn't know how many vehicles were coming from the parking area, but he could already see a set of lights in his rearview mirror. He might be able to outrun them.

Might.

He'd flown into a small airfield three miles away, just outside of Lubec. Bringing the Cessna had been faster and easier than driving or booking a commercial flight.

With the weather getting bad and the enemy on his tail, he wasn't sure it had been the right decision. The airfield shared space with Tommy's Truck and SUV Rentals, the town's only car rental business; the pickings had been slim—mostly older model pickup trucks— and he'd thought he'd been fortunate enough to rent the Tahoe. Now he wished there'd been a faster vehicle to choose.

Arden shifted, and before he realized what she was doing, she was on her knees, peering out the back window.

"They're gaining on us," she commented.

There didn't seem to be any panic in her voice. So far, she'd been unflappable. That was good. Panic only ever caused people to make mistakes that could get them killed.

"Get out of your pack and get your seat belt on." He issued the order and ignored her comment.

"Are you expecting to crash?" But Arden shrugged out of her backpack and fastened the seat belt around her waist, carefully positioning the shoulder strap behind her so it wouldn't bother her cat.

"I'm expecting that they won't give up easily," he responded.

"Logic agrees."

"Does it?" he said drily as he sped around a curve in the road. The light disappeared from the rearview mirror. Gone for now, but not for long. If they hadn't been on a two-lane highway that overlooked a twenty-foot drop to the ocean, he'd have looked for a place to pull off and hide until their pursuers passed.

"Of course," Arden replied. "Now that they've used their weapons and shown their hand, they can't let us escape. They'll need to kill you to keep you from contacting the police once they've gotten their hands on me, so any way you cut it, they're not going to give up easily."

"Kill me, huh?"

"Does that surprise you?"

"No, but I'm curious."

"About?"

"Their reasons for wanting to take you alive."

"It's complicated."

"Yeah?" He glanced at the speedometer, its needle hovering around eighty-five. Any faster and the vehicle would start shaking like it was in need of a front-end alignment.

"Very." She answered absently, giving no further explanation.

"Care to tell me exactly *who* wants to keep you alive?"

"In actuality, there are several entities who might be responsible for this. I *am* on the FBI's most wanted list."

"You're avoiding my question."

"No. I'm just avoiding giving you an answer."

"Why?"

"My reasons are not your concern."

She obviously didn't trust him. He'd drop it. For now.

Arden twisted once more in her seat, looking out the back window. "Can this thing go any faster? I'm pretty sure I see headlights behind us again."

He could see them, too, but he'd already accelerated as much as the Tahoe could. "We've still got some distance between us."

"Not enough. Lubec's less than a mile away. If you avoid Main Street, we might be able to give them the slip."

"It's a small town, and there aren't many places to hide. I won't feel safe until we get you out of Lubec, and Maine altogether for that matter."

"That's unrealistic. If we can't beat them on this curved and twisting road, we can't beat them in a race on the open highway."

"You're assuming I'm planning to drive us out of here."

"Is there another option?" Her voice was sharp.

"I left my Cessna at the Coastal Airstrip just outside of town."

"Cessna?" she said a little too loudly, her voice tight. "*That's* your plan?"

"Yes."

"I don't fly," Arden stated firmly.

"You're about to." He took a sharp curve in the road. The turn into the airport access road was up ahead, and the headlights behind them had disappeared again. If he was fast enough, he could turn onto the road, cut the lights and wait for their pursuers to pass.

As the SUV approached the turn, he cut the headlights and swung into the access road, tires squealing as they tried to gain traction.

"This is the airport," Arden said.

"I told you. We're flying out."

"I told you, I'm not."

She was.

Even if he had to throw her kicking and screaming onto the Cessna. He'd committed to getting Arden back to her family. He was going to do it. No matter who was after her. No matter what kind of trouble she'd gotten herself into.

No matter how determined she was to keep him from doing it.

He didn't back down from challenges. That was one of the reasons Jace had asked him to do the job. It went deeper than that, of course. They'd served together, fought together. They'd saved each other's hides more than once. Their bond was a brotherhood, and it couldn't be broken. They'd do anything for each other.

Even fly a Cessna through a storm with a passenger who obviously didn't want to be there.

THREE

Intellectually, Arden knew that the one-in-ten-million chance of being killed in a plane crash was much lower than the one-in-one chance of being killed if GeoArray got its hands on her. Once GeoArray got what it wanted, her pursuers would have no use for Arden and no reason to let her live. She'd been on the run for almost two weeks and was certain that with a few more days, she could crack the encryption that protected the files. If she was caught and the files confiscated before she had the chance to extract the information she needed, she'd have no way of proving Marcus Emory was a murderer—and maybe worse. She'd also have no way to prove her innocence.

Yep. Her chances were better on the Cessna, but she wasn't boarding it. She didn't fly. Not ever. She'd find another way out of the mess she'd gotten herself into. Of course, to do that, she had to lose Kane.

She shot a quick look in his direction. He was focused on the icy access road, concentrating on getting them to the death trap of an airplane before their pursuers. If he'd been driving a little more slowly, she would have chanced opening the door and jumping. She probably had a good shot of landing without injury—but not when they were traveling nearly blind in excess of fifty miles an hour, and not with Sebastian strapped to her chest.

She'd have to make a break for it after they reached the plane. Even if she weren't terrified of flying, there was no way she could let Kane bring her home.

As much as Grayson wanted to help her, until she could prove her innocence, she couldn't ask him to take her side against the FBI. Law enforcement was his calling and she would not be the one who caused him to lose his job with the FBI. She wasn't sure what story Marcus Emory had fed the FBI, but his clever move had made her an enemy of the state. She was wanted by the United States government and, by now, possibly a half-dozen other entities.

She had to finish what she'd come to Maine to do.

She had to decrypt the files she'd intercepted from GeoArray. The fact that GeoArray was willing to engage the FBI in its search for her meant that Emory was desperate. Any doubt she'd harbored about the importance of those files was gone. Her gut told her the content of the files would expose the criminal activities behind GeoArray.

She glanced out the back window and saw a vehicle pass the airport access road.

"You can slow down," she said. "They've passed us."

"Not if we want to get to the plane before they realize we've turned off."

"What's the plan once we reach it? We can't just climb aboard and leave."

"Sure we can. It's unlikely other planes are flying out of here tonight. I can be cleared for takeoff in minutes."

"If there's anyone at the tower." And she hoped there wasn't.

"There is. I put in a flight plan for this evening and was given a three-hour window to fly out. We're within that time frame."

"I don't like it," she muttered. "How about you come up with a different plan? Because I already told you, I'm not flying out of here."

He didn't respond.

"Did you hear me?"

"I heard."

"And?"

"I don't change plans. Not when they're good ones."

"Often, it's opinion that determines whether or not something is good," she pointed out. "Your opinion and mine are very different on this issue."

"Are you aiming for an argument, Arden? Because now isn't the time for it."

"There's no time like the present for me to state irrevocably that I think your plan stinks." She didn't care about the argument. She didn't care about his plan. She needed him to think she did. That would put him off guard when they reached whatever death trap, winged vehicle he thought they were flying out in.

He didn't take the bait.

"Who's after us?" he asked instead.

"You asked me that before. I chose not to answer."

"I asked who you were running from. Now I want to know who's behind us."

"Sorry, I—"

"If I'm going to go head-to-head with an enemy, I want to know who the enemy is."

"Ever heard of GeoArray?" she asked. She'd let him

think she was cooperating. If he believed she was going along with his plan, he'd be a lot less likely to anticipate her escape.

"GeoArray is after you?" he answered. Obviously he'd heard of the defense contractor.

"Yes."

"Why?"

"I was…helping a friend and I stumbled on some information that GeoArray would rather I not have."

"What kind of information are we talking about?"

"The kind that could get you killed if you knew about it."

"There isn't a whole lot going on tonight that couldn't get me killed," he responded, glancing in the rearview mirror and frowning.

She looked over her shoulder. "Do you see them?"

"No, but once they realize they've lost us it won't take long for them to figure out that we turned into the airport access road." He parked the SUV near a hangar, grabbing her arm before she could jump out.

She could have pulled away. He wasn't holding on that tightly, and she knew how to break someone's grip, but the look in his eyes held her in place.

"Don't try it," he said quietly.

"What?"

"Whatever you've been planning. We don't have time to fight each other."

"We aren't fighting. I'm—"

"You're going to get us both killed, Arden. Is that what you want? Because, if you run, I'm going after you. That will slow us down and give whoever's following us plenty of time to catch up." He released her arm, reached over the back seat and grabbed an army duffel bag, then opened his door.

She opened hers as well, stepping out of the vehicle and shivering as a few flakes of snow landed on her cheeks. She didn't fly, and she especially didn't fly when the weather was bad.

Her plan had been to run as soon as her feet hit the ground, but she couldn't ignore Kane's warning and feel good about it. She glanced at the road running parallel to the airfield, spotting a vehicle creeping along it. It had to be them. It wouldn't take them long to figure out she and Kane were at the airport.

But…

She didn't fly.

She'd have to run, and she'd have to hope that Kane was intelligent enough to stick with his escape plan.

"Don't worry," Kane said quietly. "I've got your pack."

She swung toward him.

She'd forgotten that she'd slipped out of the pack. That wasn't like her. Hesitating wasn't her style, either. She always had a plan. She always followed through on it, and she almost never forgot anything.

Especially not something as important as that pack.

"I'll take it," she said, rushing around the front of the Tahoe to where he was waiting and grabbing one of the straps.

"We're wasting time. I've got it. You want what's in it, you'll have to come with me." He walked away, his strides long and purposeful.

Arden needed that backpack. More precisely, she needed what was inside it. Her laptop. She had, of course, hidden away a second copy of the files for safekeeping, but that laptop contained days of work. In fact, she knew she was close to breaking the encryption wrapped around the files. She couldn't afford to lose all that work. Starting over was not a scenario she wanted to entertain.

"Let's be reasonable about this, Kane," she said.

"If by reasonable you mean we work together to solve your problem, I'm all for it," he responded, stepping into the hangar, his duffel slung over his shoulder, her pack still in his hand.

She had no choice but to follow him right into the belly of the beast.

At least, that's what it felt like when she saw the little tin coffins disguised as airplanes lined up and ready for takeoff.

She felt sick, the thought of getting on a plane and flying into the snowy night making her light-headed.

"You're better than this," she muttered, annoyed with her own weakness.

"What's that?" Kane glanced over his shoulder as he reached the front of the line of planes.

"Nothing."

"You're sure?"

"As sure as I am that I am about to die," she responded.

He either didn't hear or he ignored her.

"We're in front of the queue. That's the good news."

"What's the bad news?" she asked, eyeing her pack and wondering how tightly he was gripping it.

"We're running out of time. Come on. Let's get on board."

The large aluminum hangar door was already open, the Cessna Skyhawk ready to go, having been kept inside the bay to keep ice and snow from accumulating before takeoff. No sign of the dispatcher, but Kane wasn't going to let that slow him down.

He stepped back and took Arden's arm, ignoring the tension in her muscles and the paleness of her face.

"You ready to take off?" someone called.

He turned, watching as the dispatcher walked toward him, a sub sandwich in one hand, clipboard in the other.

"No," Arden responded.

"Yes," Kane corrected.

"Good. Good. You leave now and you'll beat the storm. Otherwise, you'll probably be stuck here for the night."

"That won't work for us," Kane said, with a sense of urgency. "My friend's ex is hot on our heels. I need to get her out of here quickly."

The man nodded his head. "Understood, no problem. Go ahead and load up. I'll contact the tower and tell them you're waiting to be cleared for takeoff." He rushed to his desk, taking a bite of sandwich along the way. Once he'd settled into his chair, he turned to his computer and began typing.

Kane pulled Arden the remaining short distance across the hangar's concrete floor to his plane. There was no sign of the sedan through the open bay doors, but he was certain it would be only a matter of minutes before it would reach the airfield. They needed to be on the plane and on their way before then. "Let's go," he said, sidestepping one of the main wheels and tossing her pack and his duffel onto the rear bench seat of the plane.

Arden stopped short, planting her feet. "Go on without me. I'll find a place to hide."

"That's not going to happen."

"Yeah. It is." She darted away, but he'd anticipated the move and snagged her arm, then, in deference to the cat still hiding under her coat, in one quick motion he hefted her into his arms like a groom carrying a bride over the threshold. He could feel her trembling. This was no joke. She was terrified, and for about two seconds, he thought about finding another way.

Unfortunately, doing that would probably get them both killed. It would more than likely get the guy with the sandwich killed, too.

Kane wasn't in a dying kind of mood, and he sure didn't need any more innocent blood on his hands. He'd had enough of that to last a lifetime. It'd been thirteen years since Evan Kramer had died in his arms and he could still remember the sticky slickness of his second cousin's blood on his hands, the harsh rasp of lungs as he gasped his last breath. A moment in time, a lifetime of regret.

He hoisted Arden up through the open doorway. She was lighter than he expected and, despite her struggling, he still managed to set her down gently on the floor of the plane's cargo area before jumping in after her. Forcing her to do something that obviously terrified her made him feel like the worst kind of jerk, even if his options were less than limited.

"Get out of your coat, and get that carrier off your chest."

Stooping in the threshold of the plane's open door, Kane yelled out, catching the dispatcher's attention once more. "We don't want to bring any trouble down on you, but her ex is dangerous. Be on the alert."

"Got it. I'll lock it down after you leave. And your

return flight plan's been approved by air traffic control, so you're good to go. Let's get you out of here before he shows up."

Kane yanked the plane's door shut; the hatch clicked in place as he locked it. When he turned back, Arden was still rooted to the same spot. He quickly unzipped her coat, dropping it on the bench seat with their bags, then helped her remove the carrier from her chest. Cradling the cat in his left arm, he guided her to the front passenger seat, gently pushed her into it and strapped her in with the safety harness. Arden remained quiet as he set the cat's carrier in her lap and wove the lap belt through the blue carrier straps to secure the animal.

Her silence was disconcerting.

She hadn't been at a loss for words since he'd found her at the cottage. The fact that she wasn't talking now was something he'd worry about after he got them in the air.

He stowed Arden's pack and his duffel behind the bench seat, retrieved her jacket and draped it over her lap and chest. She'd closed her eyes and was breathing deeply, mumbling something he couldn't hear.

That was better than silence, but it still wasn't good.

Being ten thousand feet in the air with a woman in full-out panic wasn't much better than being on the ground with a couple of thugs who wanted them dead.

"It's going to be okay," he said, dropping into the pilot seat and starting the engine.

"I told you, I don't fly," she responded, her eyes still tightly shut.

At least she was talking and coherent.

"You do now." He checked the flaps and instrument

control panels then pulled the safety harness over his shoulders.

"Oh Christmas tree, oh Christ-mas-tree," she sang, her voice high-pitched and a little off-key.

Maybe she wasn't coherent after all.

"Arden?" He touched her shoulder. Her muscles were taut, her entire body tense.

"Thy leaves are so un-change-ing," she continued. Her voice warbled on the last note, but she kept right on singing. "Oh Christmas—"

"Arden? Are you going to be able to keep it together?"

"I am trying to get to my happy place." Her eyes flew open, and he was looking straight into her sky-blue irises. "*You* are making it very difficult."

"Your happy place is Christmas?"

"It sure isn't this dinky tin can that you plan to fly us out in." She closed her eyes again, continuing her song. "Not only green when sum-mer's here…"

She hit the last note and the cat yowled, joining the song with earsplitting intensity.

At least neither was trying to claw a way out.

He guided the plane out of the hangar, radioing the dispatcher for permission to take off. They began taxiing down the runway. With this load, the plane required about eight hundred feet of runway for takeoff. Maybe a little less if the conditions were perfect.

Tonight, the wind was blowing, a light mix of sleet and snow splattering the windshield.

In the distance, the sedan sped through the airfield gates, then veered toward them, high beams on, picking up speed as it approached. He could only hope they'd beat it down the runway. The plane picked up speed.

Six hundred feet. Seven hundred. Kane pulled back on the controls just as the sedan reached the runway. It stopped and the doors flew open.

But Kane was past them, the wheels lifting from asphalt, the plane soaring into the sky. Below, the men were firing. The distinctive metallic pings as several bullets pierced the plane's fuselage left no doubt that some of the rounds had hit their mark.

"Oh Christmas tree, Oh Christmas tree, such pleasure do you bring me!" Arden was nearly screaming the song now, the cat still yowling, the engine roaring.

But they were up, so far away from the gunmen the bullets were ineffective. Whatever damage had been done was done. He assessed the instrument panel, looking for potential trouble.

Arden had stopped her quirky rendition of "O Christmas Tree." The cat had stopped yowling. The only sound was the whir of the engine. It sounded smooth. No coughs or hiccups, but the fuel pressure gauge dipped and a red light flashed ominously on the panel.

"That," Arden said, jabbing her finger toward the light, "does *not* look good."

"We'll be fine." He hoped. There was a problem with the left flap on the wing of the plane. For now he could still fly, but depending on the issue, his ability to control altitude and speed of the aircraft could definitely be affected—the higher they flew, the worse it would be. More of a concern was the fuel pressure gauge that was definitely reading lower than it should. If they lost fuel pressure, they'd have no choice but to make an emergency landing.

"Define fine," she demanded, her face so pale even her lips were white. She had the bluest eyes he'd ever seen, and a face that was more intriguing than beautiful. She also had a brain that rivaled anyone Kane had ever met—she'd definitely give his academically focused parents and those in their social circle a run for their money.

Lying to her wasn't going to work.

Even if it would have, he wasn't going to do it. Truth was always the best way. Even if the truth was sometimes difficult to swallow.

"A bullet may have hit the wing flap," he said, bracing himself for Arden's full-out panic.

To his surprise, she simply nodded.

"That's what I thought. I suppose you have a plan?"

"Yeah. Get the plane back down and fix the problem."

"Is there another airport close by?"

"It doesn't matter. I won't run the risk of landing anywhere in Maine if I can help it." GeoArray seemed to have connections and resources. He was pretty sure the company could quickly mobilize the troops wherever he put down.

"What if you can't make it out of Maine?"

"We'll cross that bridge when we come to it." And if Kane was reading the gauges correctly, they'd be fortunate to make it across the border into New Hampshire.

FOUR

The plane was definitely listing to the right.

Arden decided not to mention that to Kane. She was certain he'd already figured it out.

"How much time do you think we have?" she asked.

Kane didn't answer, but it didn't take a genius to realize that their time was limited. The red flashing light, the heavily listing fuselage, the slight side-to-side motion—she'd never flown before but she was pretty certain none of that was supposed to be happening.

She took a calming breath. *Mind over matter*, she told herself, and glanced out the window, immediately wishing she hadn't.

The plane continued its ascent over the trees that surrounded the airfield. The lights of the runway were small specks on the ground below them. The town a distant pattern of lights and darkness. It would have been beautiful if she hadn't been terrified.

She had never liked heights and always had an unexplainable and insurmountable fear of flying. Yet here she was, in the cockpit of a small plane, sitting next to a man she'd met a handful of times, probably already more than a thousand feet above the ground. Flying. Something she'd told herself she'd never do.

Desperate times really do call for desperate measures, she supposed.

On her lap, Sebastian stirred. Arden folded down the jacket Kane had draped over them for warmth, unfastened the carrier's safety flap and peeked down at the cat. Typical of her furry friend, he popped his head up, took in his surroundings and ducked back into the carrier, snuggling into the warmth of her lap.

She'd adopted him when he was almost two. He'd been a nervous cat then, but she recognized the deep-seated curiosity that was kept at bay by his timid personality. She'd known at once he would be hers. The ladies at the shelter had tried to dissuade her, pointed out several friendlier and more confident kittens. But she instinctively knew that no one would be as accepting of Sebastian as she would be. Her own idiosyncrasies had made her more tolerant of differences in others. He deserved a good home with someone to love him despite his quirks. Everyone did.

For the past six years, she had been his family. They'd done everything together.

Now, it seemed like they might die together.

She shouldn't be scared. She knew where she'd spend eternity. The problem was, she had a lot more living she wanted to do before then.

And then there was the little matter of GeoArray, the fact that without her intervention the company would continue whatever underhanded deals it was making with no one the wiser.

Not only that, but there'd be no justice for Juniper's husband, Dale, and his death would always be considered a suicide, leaving Juniper unable to claim his life insurance policy. Without Dale's income, Juniper would need that money to make a comfortable life for her and their unborn child.

She reached in and petted Sebastian's head, humming a few bars of "O Christmas Tree." It wasn't her favorite song, but it reminded her of childhood, of family nights spent watching Christmas specials with her parents and brothers. Of comfort and love and acceptance.

Christmas was coming.

Would she be spending it with her family?

Or would they be spending it at her grave?

"Death isn't the worst thing a person can face," she said, more to herself than to Kane. "But I'd prefer to not experience it tonight."

He must have heard, despite the loud drone of the engine. "You're not going to die."

"What evidence do you have to support that theory?" Feeling a chill, she pulled the jacket up over her chest and shoulders again, then glanced over at Kane, who was adjusting a headset on his ears with his right hand, his left never leaving the yoke. He grabbed a second set of headphones, passed them to her.

"Put these on. We'll be able to talk without having to yell over the sound of the engine."

A diversionary tactic.

Obviously, he had no evidence, but he didn't want to admit it.

She put the headset on anyway, adjusting the mouthpiece.

The sound of the engine was muffled, and she could suddenly hear the frantic thudding of her heart. Listening to it throbbing in her ears only made her fear more real.

"Can you hear me?" she asked. She was sure he could, but she needed the distraction.

"Loud and clear."

"Can air traffic control hear me, too?"

"Nope, your headset is isolated to this plane. Mine is the only headset that has direct communication with the tower." Kane tapped the instrument panel with his finger, then adjusted some gauges.

"How bad is it?" she asked.

"It's under control, for now." His vague answer was less than satisfactory.

"Can you explain what under control means?"

"Do you always ask for explanations?"

"No. Sometimes I ask for evidence or stats. This time, I want an explanation."

"The plane is maintaining altitude," he said, apparently not alarmed by the fact that they were listing to one side.

"At an angle that doesn't seem conducive to flying," she pointed out.

He met her eyes. "We *are* flying, Arden."

"Stating obvious points isn't helping your cause."

"I think I preferred your rendition of 'O Christmas Tree' to your questions," he muttered, adjusting another gauge.

"I prefer fact to speculation. If we're going down—"

"Every plane goes down eventually."

"That is *not* comforting." She hugged the cat-filled pet carrier to her protectively.

"I'm planning a controlled landing," he responded.

"Planning?"

"I'm also afraid a bullet may have hit a fuel line, so our flight may be cut short." He looked over at her then, his eyes dark, expression guarded.

The dim lights of the instrument panel cast red, orange and green shadows across his face and his dark brown hair. He'd had a military buzz cut the last time she'd seen him; his hair was longer now, falling across his forehead and curling at the nape of his neck in that messy casual way models strove to achieve. On Kane, it looked natural and he didn't seem to be the kind of guy who'd spend time preening in front of a mirror.

"Is that why the light is flashing?"

"That's a warning that the plane's left aileron is malfunctioning. In other words, the flaps on the plane's wing aren't controlling the plane's roll like they should."

"So, the plane can't turn properly?" she guessed, putting the information he'd provided together with other things she'd read over the years. Things about how planes functioned.

And how they failed.

Having a near photographic memory was both a blessing and a burden.

"It can turn. I just have to compensate and allow a much wider turn radius—and a much bumpier ride."

"Human error is the number one cause of small plane crashes," she said, spouting off another bit of information that she'd read years ago. "Most commonly, they run out of fuel because pilots miscalculate distance or fuel efficiency."

"I don't plan to make an error."

"No one ever does," she responded, the fatalistic words ringing in her ears. "JFK Jr. died because of pilot error. John Denver ran out of fuel because he couldn't access a very important fuel selector valve." She'd be better off singing, but she couldn't stop remembering every story she'd ever read about small plane crashes and spouting off the horrible endings like some kind of macabre recording.

"I've got some good news for you, Arden," he said.

"We're landing?"

"This plane has two fuel pumps, and I've already switched to the auxiliary, so you don't have to worry that I don't know how to do it."

"I wasn't worried about that. I was just providing examples and evidence to support my position."

"Which is that we're doomed?"

"I didn't say that."

"Arden, how about you go back to singing?" He adjusted a gauge and frowned. "It looks like we're still losing fuel. I was hoping the bullet hit a tank, but it looks like it hit a main line."

That did *not* sound good.

As a matter of fact, it sounded really, really bad.

She glanced out the window, saw cars and houses far below. "Where's the nearest airport?"

"Behind us."

"But we can't turn around."

"Right."

"So we're going to—?"

"Keep flying and pray we find a spot to land." Kane finished her sentence.

She wished he hadn't.

She would have preferred to create a fictionalized version of what they were going to do. Like—somehow turn and land on the airfield they'd just left. Or—strap on parachutes and jump from the doomed vehicle.

Although, she wasn't sure she had the guts for that.

Still, anything would be better than sitting in a plane not much bigger than a Barbie Dream Jet waiting for it to go down.

She glanced out the window again; she couldn't help herself.

They were high above the tree line now, tiny lights twinkling through the darkness. House lights. Street-lights. Cars. Hundreds of people going about their business while she and Sebastian and Kane went about the business of dying.

Not that she wanted to be melodramatic about the situation. She was a facts gal. Numbers and figures and stats.

And right now, all those things pointed in one di-rection.

"I don't suppose you have parachutes on this plane?" she asked casually. At least, she tried to sound casual. She didn't want Kane to know that she was on the edge of full-out panic mode.

"No, but we're not going to need them."

Give me some evidence to support your supposition, she wanted to say, but she kept her lips pressed firmly together, afraid she wouldn't like the answer.

Arden was taking the news better than he'd expected.

He could let that worry him or he could concentrate on getting them both out of this situation alive.

Kane checked the gauges and eyed the instrument panel. The plane was off its intended course and fly-ing much lower than his flight plan specified. There was nothing he could do about it except search for a place to land.

There were a few lights in the darkness below. Maybe houses or streetlights, but nothing that gave any indication of a clearing big enough to land the Cessna.

Flakes of snow pelted the windshield, cutting down on visibility. He glanced at the GPS to keep his bearings. His original flight plan routed his plane around congested airspace used by commercial flights over coastal Maine, New Hampshire and Massachusetts, then parallel to the Appalachian mountain range, turning back toward the coast as the plane approached Maryland. But Maryland was hundreds of miles away and Lubec was behind them. The malfunctioning aileron made it nearly impossible to change course.

It would be nearly impossible to land, too, but they'd have to do that before they reached the mountain range that was directly in their path. The tallest range in Maine was just over five thousand feet high. Once they hit New Hampshire, the White Mountains would be a threat. At over six thousand feet, those peaks would require him to ascend even higher. Taking the plane's current condition into account, he didn't think that would be safe.

"Is that a mountain range in our path?" Arden was looking at the navigation screen displayed on the instrument panel.

"Yes."

"How close are we?"

"About twenty minutes out."

"Maybe you should call the air tower and find out where we can land before then, because from where I'm sitting, it looks like our chances of getting over the mountains are slim to none."

"I'd rather not contact air traffic control at this

point." Or at all, if he could avoid it. Whether Arden liked it or not, his plan was to get them on the ground undetected if possible, call his business partner, Silas, for a ride back to Maryland and deliver Arden DeMarco to her brother.

"Um, okay…why not?"

"Given who's after you, it's safe to assume someone may be monitoring the dispatch system. I don't want to give away our location."

"It's going to be given away when we crash into the side of that mountain," she muttered.

"We'll find a place to land," he assured her. "And we'll probably be better off than we'd be if we'd stuck to my original flight plan and headed back to Maryland."

"You think they'll have people waiting there?"

"They had people in Lubec."

"Right." She hummed a few bars of "O Christmas Tree" and then fell silent.

She'd have probably been happy if he let the conversation die. But to keep her safe, he needed answers.

"Arden, you need to come clean. According to Grayson you're wanted for suspected espionage."

She remained quiet.

"You said you were helping a friend," he prompted.

"Yes."

He waited for more, but she just sat staring at the instrument panel, her coat pulled up to her chin.

She looked young.

She *was* young. Even if there was only a five-year age difference between them, he'd seen things in combat that made him feel a lot older than his thirty years.

She didn't look scared, though. She looked determined and resigned. Maybe a little annoyed that her plans had been derailed. Jace had told Kane to expect that; that she liked to do things a certain way and didn't much care for change.

"What friend?" he prodded, and she met his eyes.

"Look, Kane, it might seem like we're in this together—"

"We *are* in this together."

"Right now, we are. But once we've landed, we don't have to be. You can go back to whatever you were doing before my brother talked you into coming after me."

"No. I can't."

"Sure you can. It's easy. You just rent a car or call for a ride and go back home. I'll go back to what I was doing, and we'll both be fine."

"*You* were hiding from the FBI," he pointed out. "And from a company that seems to want you dead."

"They don't want me dead. Yet."

"What do they want?"

"Encrypted files that I took from them."

"What kind of files?"

"That's a good question. I won't know until I decrypt what I have. That takes time. A lot of it. Which is why I went off the grid. I needed solitude to work."

"And safety."

"That, too. And I was doing fine on both counts. I still would be, if it weren't for Sebastian." She pulled the jacket down and eyed the cat. "And Christmas," she muttered.

"Christmas?"

"Only the best time of the year," she responded, covering the cat again and leaning forward in her seat to peer out the windshield. The snowfall was heavier now, the flakes sliding off the windshield almost as quickly as they landed. "Although, tonight, I'd be happy if it were the middle of summer. The weather is getting worse."

"Yeah. That happens this time of year. Your family has big Christmas celebrations every year, don't they?" Kane began carefully, knowing that he was about to do something he'd probably regret later. He wasn't big on manipulating people. He didn't like using information to get what he wanted, but he wanted to make very sure he and Arden were playing for the same team before he landed the plane and helped her get back to her family.

He'd agreed to find her because of his friendship with Jace. He'd assumed that she had as much integrity as her brother, but she'd admitted she'd essentially stolen encrypted files. Files that he could only presume were classified. GeoArray was one of the largest defense contractors in the country. Much of what the company did was top secret and well guarded.

Arden was on the FBI's most wanted list because of those files. She didn't want to tell him how she'd gotten them or why she took them. If he had to manipulate her to get the answers, so be it.

"What does my family's Christmas celebration have to do with anything?"

"I heard Jace might be home this year."

Her expression didn't change, but he knew the news had gotten to her. He could read it in her quick intake of breath and the sudden tension in her muscles. She knew her brother wasn't scheduled to return from his tour for several months, and she had to know that his early return meant something was wrong.

"What happened?"

"He was injured in an attack a little over a week

ago. Their helicopter went down just outside of Syria. Three of his men were killed. He'll be getting an early discharge."

"How bad is he?" she asked.

"He didn't give me many details, and he wasn't sure when he'd be on the medical flight back. He was more concerned about you than he was about his injuries," Kane responded, purposely keeping the extent of Jace's injuries from Arden. His friend hadn't wanted his family to worry.

"He wasn't supposed to be in contact with the family for the next few months. How'd he find out I was gone?"

"Tell you what." Kane adjusted something on the instrument panel and frowned. "How about you ask your brothers?"

"My brothers aren't here. You are."

"I don't know, Arden. Jace called me from a hospital in Munich. He asked me to get in touch with Grayson, said he'd been injured and would be coming home and that he needed me to find you. That was the extent of our conversation."

"I wish I'd known," she muttered.

"You weren't around."

"Are you trying to make me feel guilty?" Her voice trembled, and he thought tears pooled in her eyes, but she didn't let them fall.

"I'm trying to make you see that you're not the only one who is being impacted by the decisions you've made. Jace is returning home. He's planning to be surrounded by his family. He needs to be. He needs time and rest to heal. Not added stress. Plus, if you're picked up by the FBI and tossed into federal prison, you're not the only one who's going down. I am, and maybe Grayson, too."

"That's why I've stayed away. I'm sure they're already watching him. Grayson's like a dog with a bone. I don't want him getting hurt or jeopardizing his job because of me."

"Then give me something to go on. Some information that will help me get you off that list and get Grayson out from under the veil of suspicion."

She hesitated, but he knew he had her. The thought of her brothers suffering because of her actions wasn't something she could live with. All the DeMarcos were like that—all about family, about being part of a team built through shared experience and a lifetime of affection.

As an only child, Kane had never experienced that firsthand. And with parents who preferred their careers to raising a child, he spent more time in boarding schools and later reform schools than he had with his own parents. Aside from summers and school breaks with his grandparents, family bonds and holiday traditions were things he knew little about. He'd been pulled into them through his connection to Jace, but he'd never fully understood them.

"My best friend's husband, Dale Westin, killed himself last month while on a business trip to Boston. He was a network administrator."

"For GeoArray Corporation?"

"Yes."

"What does that have to do with the encrypted files?"

"My friend didn't think he killed himself."

"This is the friend you were helping?"

"Yes. Juniper. She said there was no way Dale killed himself. I knew Dale. I agreed with her."

"Depression can be masked," he said gently. "Some people are very good at putting on happy faces for the people they love." Kane had seen firsthand the devastation that suicide brought down on survivors. It was hard being left behind, wondering if there was something you could have done to prevent it. For years after Evan's death, Kane blamed himself for missing the signs. And they'd been there. Evan had been in a downward spiral since the night his sister drowned, but he'd masked it until the end.

"I know the facts and the figures, Kane. I did the research. But Dale had none of the markers. Not even one, and the way he died, the reason he supposedly committed suicide? It just didn't make sense."

"To people who aren't depressed, suicide rarely does."

"That's not what I mean. According to GeoArray, Dale had been having an affair with his married boss and she'd coerced him into building a backdoor on the network so she could transfer files outside of the network without detection. Files that she was selling to the highest bidder."

"And they were caught, so Dale killed himself?"

"Supposedly."

"What'd his boss say?"

"She died in a car accident the night before Dale's body was found."

"That's convenient." Kane didn't put much stock in coincidences. Someone was hiding something.

"Yes. All the loose ends were tied up—nice and tidy. By the time I got my hands on Dale's laptop, it was clean. Too clean. Someone had deleted his work-related email and files from his hard drive."

"If the files were already deleted, what was left to find?"

"Getting rid of computer forensic evidence is not as simple as hitting delete and emptying the trash bin. I won't get into the technical aspects of it because I've been told it bores most people. But I was able to find evidence that Dale had discovered the backdoor on the company's networks and immediately reported it to his boss. The email chain I found eventually made it all the way up to GeoArray's CEO, Marcus Emory. Emory asked Dale and his boss to meet him in Boston. They both died on that trip."

"Why not just report what you found on his computer and let the authorities take it from there?"

"I didn't think the email evidence was strong enough to bring to the authorities, so I accessed GeoArray's network, located the backdoor and intercepted some files that were being exfiltrated along with some encryption software I found."

"Exfiltrated?" Kane asked. "Like a military op?"

"Exactly. Just like that." She smiled. "Only instead of sneaking a person out of a hostile environment, I was attempting to sneak the files out of the backdoor without being discovered."

"So you basically hacked into GeoArray's secure network and stole proprietary files."

"Yes."

"And that's why the FBI's after you."

"That's a likely possibility," she agreed.

"What's in the files?"

"I don't know yet. I'm working on decrypting them."

"You didn't think to go to the FBI with what you found—let them decrypt the files?"

"I thought about it, but first, there's no one more qualified than I am to decrypt the files. Second, it's obvious Marcus Emory has the ear of someone in the FBI. I have no idea if that person's an unwitting pawn or a paid accomplice. Going to the wrong person could have meant even more trouble."

"I'm not sure how you could be in any more trouble than you already are," he responded, eyeing the fuel gauge and then the darkness below.

"If I'd trusted the wrong person, I could have ended up in jail with no access to the files, no way to prove my innocence. It could have also implicated Juniper—after all, she suspected GeoArray was behind Dale's death and gave me access to his computer. Sooner or later, they'll put two and two together and see her as a threat, as well."

"If everything you've said is true—"

"Of course it's true."

"—then it stands to reason that, witting or not, the FBI could pull strings to get the dispatcher in Lubec to track the plane's geo-location beacon."

"So they can get men on the ground before we arrive?"

"That would be my guess."

"If GeoArray catches us, we're both dead. You first, and me after they get their files back. I know you know that, Kane, but I feel the need to reiterate the point. We die. The company gets away with two more murders."

No need for reiteration. He knew exactly what they were dealing with now. And it wasn't good.

He kept the thought to himself.

There were other things to think and worry about. Like the rapidly dropping fuel level. If they didn't descend soon, GeoArray would get exactly what it wanted—the files back and Arden dead, with whatever secret she was trying to uncover buried with her.

FIVE

They were going to have to land soon. Either that or run out of fuel.

The word *crash* came to mind, but Arden didn't voice it. She didn't want to speak into the silence. She was afraid of what she might say.

She'd told Kane as much as she could. Probably more than she should. There were other things—things that she suspected and still hadn't been able to prove—that she wouldn't say. Not to him or her brothers or to the FBI. Even if she said them, no one would believe her.

But she knew what she'd seen: an email exchange between Dale and his boss discussing concern for the security of an unnamed research program. Dale had thought an insider was behind the backdoor he'd found—that someone may be trying to steal GeoArray's research for their own gain. His boss had agreed.

Now they were both dead.

Logic told her they'd been right. Arden just needed to prove it.

It didn't take much digging for her to find that Geo-Array had been awarded a groundbreaking United States government contract to develop a self-improving weapons control system. Arden suspected the research for that system might be concealed under the layers of encryption surrounding the files she'd taken. In her experience, people didn't bother placing that level of encryption around their data unless they were protecting something significant.

Someone had been transferring files outside GeoArray's secure network. Someone was behind Dale's death.

But while she believed that someone was Marcus Emory himself, she couldn't prove it. Yet. As CEO of GeoArray, he definitely had the access and resources to orchestrate the crime. But that alone didn't make him guilty. She needed solid evidence before she could come right out and accuse him, and possibly others in the company, of espionage.

She needed to decrypt the files fast. If she was right, the nation's weapons systems could be compromised and the nation left vulnerable to attack. But it was all speculation. She needed the truth. She needed proof.

Yeah. Running had been her best and only choice.

Taking Sebastian with her had been her mistake.

She scratched him between his soft ears and felt him purring against her chest. If they died, they'd do it together. Cold comfort, and not really any comfort at all.

She needed to finish what she'd started, and then she needed to get home. Jace had to be severely wounded if he was returning from the Middle East. She knew her brother, and there was no other way he'd come home in the middle of a tour. Though he'd never ask for help, she wanted to be there for him.

But the muted roar of the plane engine, the flashing warning lights and Kane's silence were making her wonder if she'd ever see home again. Kane made another adjustment to the panel, and the plane shuddered.

"What was that?"

"We're descending."

"You've found a place to land?"

He didn't respond, and she knew exactly what that meant: he hadn't.

"If you don't have a place to land, why are we descending?" She wanted an answer that would make sense, one that would make her feel better. One that would hopefully make her believe that they weren't about to crash.

"The low fuel light just came on."

"That isn't the answer I was hoping for," she said aloud, then bit her lip to keep from saying more.

Impulse control. It was a thing. Usually she possessed it, but when she got nervous, she tended to forget that.

He glanced her way, his expression grim. "Would a pretty lie make you feel better?"

"Tell me how I can help," she responded, because admitting that she might have preferred a pretty little lie wasn't going to solve their problem.

"Right now, there's not a whole lot you can do."

"There has to be something," she responded, eyeing the control panel and wondering if there was a user manual somewhere inside the cockpit. If so, she might learn some information that could help. She might be terrified, but she wasn't giving up.

There's a solution to every problem. Pray about it, look for it and be willing to accept it when God finally reveals it to you. Her mother had told her that dozens of times when Arden was a kid—gawky and awkward and too tomboyish to ever fit in with most girls her age.

Following her mother's advice had been easy enough to do when she was a tween and teen. It wasn't so easy to do when she was sitting in a plane that was running out of fuel.

"Is there a user manual somewhere?" she asked, desperate for action.

"You think a user manual is going to solve our problems?"

"It might." She glanced out the window. It seemed like the ground was getting closer, the dark outline of trees visible through the snow.

"How about we stick to my plan instead?"

"I'm willing to consider it. If I knew what your plan was," she managed to say, her heart pounding so hard she thought it might jump out of her chest. They were definitely descending. Just like Kane had said. Only there didn't seem to be any place to land.

"According to the GPS, we're closing in on Berlin, New Hampshire. If memory serves me, there's an abandoned airstrip about ten miles east of town. If we can find it, we'll land there."

"If it's abandoned, it might not be safe to land on."

"It's safer than flying a plane that's running low on fuel. Keep an eye out for lights, okay? We should be approaching the town soon."

It was busywork. The kind teachers had once given to keep Arden from asking questions and being annoying while other students were finishing their assignments.

She needed the distraction, so she stared out the window, trying to see through the snow. All she saw was gray-black night and swirling flakes.

Please, Lord. Help us find a place to land. Please, get us out of this alive. Please, get me back home to my family.

She felt like a child begging for favors. A child who'd spent a little too much time going her own way this past year. How many times had her parents asked her to attend church service with them recently? How many times had Grayson?

She'd always been too busy with her budding computer consulting business or too tired.

At least, those had been the excuses she'd given.

The reality was, she hadn't wanted to go, because she hadn't wanted to see her ex-boyfriend, Randy. She was afraid if she did, she'd be tempted to call him a lying, thieving fraud. She didn't think that would go over well in the middle of Sunday service. Plus, she hadn't told anyone in her family exactly what he'd done. She'd been embarrassed that she'd fallen for his act. Believed he cared for her when all he really wanted was her brainpower.

When she'd told her family she'd broken it off, they'd all been sympathetic and understanding. She knew that they'd also been secretly relieved and happy about the breakup. Her parents had never clicked with Randy. Her brothers hadn't, either.

She'd met him just before she turned twenty. Having taken university courses while in high school, Arden had already earned master's degrees in both math and computer science and had been invited to the university's cutting-edge research program while she worked on her PhD.

Randy was nearly eight years older, intelligent and heading up one of the university's most prestigious projects. He was just beginning to make a name for himself in the field and she'd been so impressed by his credentials she'd pushed aside her parents' concerns. They'd dated for just about three years, the entire time they worked side-by-side on innovative research projects for the university. She'd thought they made a good team.

Even now, the truth was hard to swallow. Randy was arrogant and self-absorbed. He loved making other people feel stupid. If she hadn't been so enamored with the idea of falling in love, she'd have seen that long before they became a couple.

Too late for self-recrimination, and much too late to go back and change things. She'd learned a valuable lesson from Randy—she wasn't the kind of woman men fell deeply in love with. She was the kind of woman they used.

She scowled, leaning closer to the window, determined to find lights and a place to land, because she did not want to die in this tiny excuse for a plane.

"There!" Kane exclaimed, motioning to the left. "See that?"

"What?" She leaned closer to him, trying to achieve the same line of vision. Just ahead and to the east, tiny lights glimmered through the snow. "Is that the town?"

"Yep. It should be Berlin." He maneuvered the plane carefully, trying to adjust its trajectory. He shifted the controls, and the plane shuddered before quickly stabilizing.

"Are we going to make it to the airfield?" she asked, her voice shaky. She hated that. She also hated that she couldn't help. That she was just sitting there like a ninny while Kane tried to save both their lives.

He didn't respond. He reached past her, his arm brushing her cheek as he pushed a button on the instrument panel and zoomed in on the navigation system.

She caught a whiff of leather and outdoors. It made her think of childhood and the camping trips she and her family had taken. It had been too many years since she'd slept under the stars and listened to the night's music—crickets and owls and leaves rustling in warm summer breezes.

She'd lost her way somehow. She'd gotten offtrack and forgotten that her work wasn't the most important thing. Randy had been part of the reason for that. Dating Randy had been easy. He never complained about her work; in fact, he'd encouraged it.

And of course that all made sense now.

She'd broken it off with Randy when she suspected he'd taken her code and sold it to the highest bidder. Some of that code had ended up embroiled in a child-trafficking case Grayson had worked on. She couldn't prove Randy was behind it then, but if she survived this plane ride, she was certain Randy's hands would come up dirty this time—his operational signature was all over the application she'd taken from GeoArray.

The plane shuddered again and every thought of Randy fled.

Below, lights sparkled, barely visible through the swirling snow. Then the town was behind them, and the area below was dark again.

The engine sputtered, and Arden's heart seemed to sputter with it.

"Are we out of fuel?" she asked, the panic she'd been

holding at bay threatening to spill out. She could hear it in her voice, and she was certain Kane could, too.

"No." *He* sounded calm. He *looked* calm, his movements confident as he eased the yoke to the left.

"Are we about to crash?"

"I prefer to call it controlled impact," he countered, obviously distracted by the sputtering engine and listing plane.

They were dropping in altitude. She didn't know much about flying planes, but she knew how to read gauges and instrument panels. She'd always been fascinated by mechanical things, and she'd studied airplanes like she'd studied everything. She might be afraid to fly, but she wasn't completely ignorant of how it worked.

"We're going to die," she sighed, the statement popping out before she could stop it.

"Everyone dies," he responded.

"That's obvious."

"It's the truth. If it makes you feel any better, I'm not planning on either of us dying tonight."

"There are three of us on board."

"Cats have nine lives. Your kitty will be fine. We do have a problem, though."

"One?"

He glanced her way, what looked like the beginning of a smile tugging at the corners of his mouth. "A few, but the one I'm currently worried about is our altitude. I can't descend any more quickly without risking the engine stalling. At the speed we're going, we'll overshoot the landing field."

"You're right. That is a problem."

"It's good that we're finally agreeing. That will make things easier when we land."

Probably not.

As much as she appreciated what Kane was trying to do, there was no way she could go back home until she had the proof she needed. And he'd made it quite clear that's what he wanted. Of course that would only be an issue if she and Kane made it out of this alive.

She mentally corrected herself. *When* they made it out alive, she was going to find a way to go off the grid again. She'd been close to decrypting those files. A few more days. That's all she needed. If she could have that, she knew she could get justice for Juniper and Dale, prove her innocence and possibly uncover a plot that could put national security at risk. Then she could go back to Maryland, turn the proof and the files over to Grayson, and let him take it from there.

Kane hadn't missed Arden's lack of response. He was pretty sure she was still planning to run as soon as she got the opportunity. He could have told her that would be a waste of their time, but he had other things to worry about.

They'd already passed the airfield, and the plane was running dangerously low on fuel. He maneuvered the Cessna carefully, trying to adjust its trajectory slowly without stalling the beleaguered engine.

He peered out the window into the darkness below. The abandoned airfield would have been the perfect place to land. Or as perfect as any place could be for a plane in the Cessna's condition. Now that that wasn't an option, he had to reconfigure his thinking, try to come up with another solution to the problem.

The engine sputtered, and Arden nearly jumped out

of her seat. She probably would have if she hadn't been strapped into it.

"Relax," he said, keeping his voice calm and even. One of the things he'd learned in the military was that panicking never did anyone any good. Clear precise thinking; clean precise action. That was the way to get out of a deadly situation.

"Relax? You're a funny guy, Kane. I didn't realize that about you." Her voice wavered, but she was trying to stay calm. He'd give her credit for that. Her hands were fisted around the arms of her seat and she was leaning forward, staring out the window. But she wasn't screaming, she wasn't crying and she wasn't getting in his way. And blessedly, she wasn't singing, either.

"I'm full of surprises," he responded automatically, his focus on the approaching ground, the trembling engine and the listing fuselage. He angled the plane slightly, trying to keep it steady for landing. The plane shook and dipped, protesting even the most subtle of adjustments.

It wasn't a good situation.

He needed to land the plane now before the fuel tank emptied. He scanned the ground, looking for a clearing that would give him the best chance of landing safely.

Arden took a heaving lungful of air.

"You okay?" he asked, not taking his eyes off the approaching ground.

"I forgot to breathe."

"That's never a good thing," he said drily.

Apparently, she didn't catch his sarcasm.

"You're right," she agreed. "You stop breathing and you tense up. It's always best to just relax and ride the punch."

"Right," he responded, only half listening.

He glanced at the GPS, and his pulse jumped. A narrow blue line curved near the top right edge of the map. He eased the aircraft in that direction, fighting the broken flaps and the weather. The riverbanks in places like this weren't easy to land, but he'd navigated worse. He'd flown many rescue missions in Iraq, Syria and Afghanistan. The circumstances of those landings hadn't always been the best, either.

"It's physics simplified." Arden was still talking, spewing facts like she was on a game show trying to win a prize. "In a collision, an object experiences a force for a specific time period that results in the mass of the object changing velocity. That's the basic theory supporting airbags in cars—they essentially minimize the effect of the force by extending the length of the collision. In boxing, it's called riding the punch. When a boxer knows he can't stop a punch to the head, he'll relax his neck and let his head move backward on impact to minimize the force of the blow."

"Arden?" He'd finally managed to fight the plane onto the correct course.

"Think about it this way." She just kept talking. "If you were to—"

"What I'm thinking about is landing the plane. How about you do the same? With both of us focused and paying attention, we have a better chance of walking away from this."

That seemed to do the trick.

She stopped talking, her silence as loud as her voice had been.

He almost felt guilty for cutting off her nervous chatter. Everyone had his or her own way of dealing with nerves. Apparently, when she wasn't singing, she was spouting facts.

"It's going to be okay," he said, trying to reassure her.

"You can't know that. Statistically—"

"Sometimes you have to forget statistics and just trust that God always works everything out for His good." That was a truth Kane had always struggled with. It had taken years to accept that God cared and that He was there. Even in the hard times. Even in the ugliness. And there'd been plenty of that in Kane's younger years. He'd had two deaths on his conscience before he turned eighteen. He'd been the ringleader that night, egging Evan on. The party had been Kane's idea. If he hadn't pressed the issue, Evan would have been watching his little sister more carefully. Lexi would still be alive. Evan, too. Two families had been shattered by that one lapse in judgment. He wouldn't be responsible for shattering another.

"You're right. I know you are."

"So let's focus, okay? There's a river straight ahead of us. I should be able to land there."

"On a river?"

"Do you have a better idea?" Kane pulled back slightly on the controls, forcing the nose of the plane up as he struggled to level it. The landing lights illuminated treetops that rushed toward them at breakneck speed. The effect was dizzying.

Just then, he spotted an opening in the trees almost directly ahead.

The river.

Wide and dark, it loomed ahead. Their only hope. A slight adjustment had the plane angled perfectly, lining up with the flow of the water. The river was wider than he'd hoped, the banks blanketed with more than a foot of snow—remnants of an earlier storm. If they were fortunate, the snow would help cushion their impact.

Reducing the Cessna's speed further, he peered through the falling snow, past the range of the landing lights into the darkness, and prayed for an ideal spot to attempt a landing.

Finally, he saw it. A lazy curve in the river that would allow him to skid the plane over the water. The drag would hopefully bring them to a stop on the banks just before the tree line.

Arden had gone completely silent. No gasping breaths, off-key singing or spouted facts. He could feel her tension, and he could feel his own, the weight of what he was about to do, the responsibility of it, making his muscles taut.

Stay calm.

Stay focused.

That had been pounded into him when he trained as part of the Night Stalkers helicopter regiment.

Pulling back on the steering column, he angled the Cessna's nose up slightly, dropped the aircraft lower and further reduced the plane's speed. The Cessna bumped along the river as its landing gear skimmed the water, bouncing away, then skimming again.

They were moving too fast, the damaged flap making the fuselage list dangerously. He tried to compensate, but they were already down, water spraying, the engine choking. He thought he heard Arden scream, but the sound was masked by the screech of metal as the hull of the craft scraped against low-hanging branches.

They slammed into the riverbank, the explosion of sound deafening, the jarring impact stealing his breath.

Get up! Gather supplies! Get out!

He could almost hear his commanding officer yelling the orders. With the faint scent of fuel spurring him to action, he unbuckled his straps and was up and moving before the metal carcass of the Cessna settled into silence.

SIX

They were alive.

That was Arden's first thought.

Her second was that they needed to get out.

She fumbled with the straps, but her hands were shaking and Sebastian was yowling and she couldn't free herself.

Were they in the river? On the bank?

The headset had flown off. She could hear water splashing against metal and the creaking groan of the wreckage. Cold air flowed in from somewhere, and she shivered, yanking at the strap again.

"Let me." Kane brushed her hands away, and she was free in seconds. He pulled her to her feet and shoved open the mangled door. Water was already lapping at Arden's hiking shoes, licking at the cuffs of her pants.

Were they floating on the river?

"Is there a life raft?" she asked as Kane leaned out the open door.

"We won't need one. Half the cockpit is onshore. Come on." He grabbed her hand, dragging her up beside him.

He was right. They were beached, the tail of the

plane dipping into the flowing river, the nose of it pressed into snow and earth.

The plane shifted, tugged by the force of the water. Eventually, the tail would break away or the shore would release its hold, allowing the plane to drift down the river. They needed to be off the plane before that happened.

Kane motioned to the bank. "You think you can make the jump from here to shore? It's not far. Maybe four feet."

"Sure," she affirmed.

She didn't mention that she'd never been much of an athlete. Self-defense? She'd aced it because it was all about physics and movement, but she'd only ever been picked for a team in school because Juniper had so often been team captain.

They'd always looked out for each other.

Always.

And, if Juniper had been there, she'd have been whispering in Arden's ear, telling her that a woman who could throw a two-hundred-pound man could jump three or four feet.

"Are you certain?" he asked.

"No, but I'd rather try and get wet than float down the river in a leaking fuselage." She slid her arms through the carrier straps, tightening it securely to her chest. Sebastian had calmed and settled into the carrier contentedly, obviously unaware of the fact that he'd just used up another one of his nine lives.

"If you land in the water, you're going to be hypothermic in minutes. Want me to jerry-rig a ramp?" The plane shifted again, and Arden was certain she could feel the force of the water shoving it backward.

"It's simple physics," she muttered to Kane or to herself or, maybe, to Sebastian. "Force. Velocity. Gravitational pull."

"How about you tell me the science behind it after we're out of here?" he asked, reaching into a small cabinet and pulling out a parka and gloves. He put both on, then tugged her hat more firmly over her ears before grabbing her backpack and his duffel. "Do you have clothes in your pack?"

"Yes." Not much, but she could get dry if she needed to.

"Shoes?" He turned off the plane's lights.

"No, but my feet are already soaked. Missing the shore and landing in water isn't going to make them any wetter."

He frowned, reaching back into the cabinet and pulling out several plastic bags. "Wool socks. Gloves. Hats. We can put the bags over your feet after you change socks."

"What about you?"

"My boots are waterproof. I'll be fine. Ready?" he asked. "I'll jump first. You follow."

"Right. Sure." She leaned a little farther out, the frigid air stinging her cheeks. The river in this area was shallow, the glossy rocks beneath its surface shimmering in the crystal clear water. The pebbly snow-dusted shore wasn't far. Beyond that, dense forest blocked the sky. No lights. No houses. Nothing but trees and snow and silence broken only by the rush of the river.

"Arden," Kane said, touching her chin and forcing her to look straight into his face. "If you're too scared—"

"I'm not scared," she said, more to convince herself than him. "Go ahead. I'll follow," she assured him.

She sounded confident.

She sounded capable.

She felt like the kid she'd been in grade school—terrified of public speaking but forced to give oral book reports in front of a hostile audience.

Kane nodded, tossing his duffel onto the shore. He slipped into her pack, and she thought about warning him to be careful, but he was already leaping out, landing lightly on wet rocks.

Effortless.

For him.

She had an odd feeling it wasn't going to be nearly as easy for her. She balanced on the edge of the doorway, took a deep breath and another.

"There's no way to disable the plane's internal GPS," Kane said calmly. "Every minute you stand there is a minute that the FBI or GeoArray could be using it to find us."

She jumped, taking off like a fledgling bird prodded out of the nest by its mother. No grace. No finesse. Just tumbling through the air and landing, feet slipping, arms windmilling, body trying to go in fifteen different directions.

She'd have landed on her butt in the water if Kane hadn't snagged her wrists and jerked her forward onto solid ground. He released her as soon as she was steady, turning to grab his duffel.

"Nice job," he said, tossing her a couple of the plastic bags and some dry socks. "Take off those wet socks and dry your feet. Then let's get out of here."

"I'm thinking we're about ten miles from town,

right?" she asked, pulling off her wet shoes, changing socks and slipping the plastic bags over her now dry feet. She was back in her shoes in seconds, standing up and eyeing the wilderness that surrounded them. If she could get him to relinquish her pack, maybe she could give him the slip and go to ground. It would be easy to drop off the grid out here.

"That's a good estimate," he affirmed.

"Given that the average person walks three or four miles per hour on flat ground, if we factor in the snow and the uneven terrain, our speed will probably be closer to two and a half miles per hour, tops. At that pace, we should hit Berlin in about four hours."

"I won't argue with your math." He smiled, unzipping a pocket in the duffel and pulling out a compass and a couple of flashlights.

"Do you think it's safe to use these?" Arden asked, taking the flashlight Kane offered her. "Assuming the plane's internal GPS is still active like you said, it might not take long for them to pinpoint our location. GeoArray could have helicopters. The FBI definitely does."

"That's a valid concern, but we'll be in the cover of the trees. Besides, we're out in the middle of nowhere and should be able to hear their vehicles coming. Plus, we'll be able to move faster if we can see where we're going."

Arden eyed the dense tree line. "I suppose that's a reasonable assumption. And since there are over seventy species of trees in New Hampshire, with the deciduous varieties less prevalent in the mountains, we should have plenty of cover."

"Now that's a piece of trivia I could never pull from

the recesses of my mind." Kane grinned. "I'm impressed."

Although he didn't look like he was poking fun at her, she felt her cheeks redden and was thankful for the cover of darkness. Why couldn't she keep her little factoids to herself?

Kane stepped closer, pulled her hood up over her knit hat and zipped her jacket to her chin. "Let's move," he said, turning and heading toward the tree line.

She followed, biting her lip to keep more inane facts from spilling out. She was better off spending her time finding a way to get the backpack away from Kane. Once she had it, she could take off. She knew the direction they'd been flying. She knew about how far they were from town. She could make it out on her own, keep Kane from being dragged more deeply into her mess.

First, though, she needed her backpack.

"That duffel looks heavy," she said.

Kane ignored her.

Probably because the duffel didn't actually look heavy, and *he* actually looked like the kind of guy who could have handled it if it was.

"I can carry the pack. That'll make things a little easier for you," she offered.

"No. End of discussion."

"What's that supposed to mean?"

"Jace says you're a genius. I'm pretty certain you know what that means."

"Jace exaggerated." Sort of.

"It doesn't take a genius to understand the word no." He was moving quickly, covering ground at a steady pace.

She kept up, but not as easily as she'd have liked. His

legs were longer, his stride covering a lot more ground than hers. She tried to speed up as they reached the tree line, her foot slipping across snow-covered leaves and rocks. She went flying, slamming into Kane's back. She grabbed the pack to steady herself and thought for three seconds about trying to yank it off.

"Not going to happen, Arden," Kane said, and she let her hands fall away.

"If you lose that pack—"

"I won't."

"I'm not sure you understand how important this is."

"I understand perfectly. Now, how about we both quiet down? I'd like to hear anyone who might be approaching."

Fine. She could be quiet and she would be. Eventually, he'd put the pack down, she'd grab it and be on her way. It was a simple plan and an effective one.

If he'd just cooperate with it.

There was no way Kane was going to let Arden wander around in the New Hampshire wilderness alone.

She might think she could find her way back to civilization on her own, but most people who eventually got lost, hurt or killed in hostile environments thought the same. Add GeoArray, the FBI and anyone else who might want to get their hands on her, and Arden's chances of survival became even slimmer.

He'd keep the backpack for now, and probably for the remainder of the time they were together.

Snow was already coating his parka and hat. They needed to move fast, and not just because they were being pursued. Ten miles was a long way to hike in frigid temperature. He'd survived worse, but Arden didn't look like the kind of person who spent a lot of time hiking through snowstorms.

"You doing okay?" he asked.

"Dandy," she muttered.

"How about the cat?"

"Snug as a bug in a rug."

"The terrain is flat through here. Hopefully, it will be the same for the rest of the hike." He pulled his flashlight out, letting the beam dance along the forest floor. The snow was sparser there, the tree canopy holding back some of the swirling flakes.

Behind him, Arden snapped her light on, as well. "The underbrush is thicker than I thought it would be, more deadfall," she commented. "It would definitely be slower going without these flashlights."

"Yeah, we'll make better time with them, that's for sure." His light glanced off a thick wall of brambles, the thorny branches like a barbed wire fence blocking their path.

"That doesn't look good," Arden said, her arm brushing his as she eyed the thicket. "Maybe we should go back to the river and follow it to town."

"We'd be too exposed," he answered. "We'll use the river as a handrail, keeping it in our sight while we stay in the trees. The underbrush is always thickest at the wood line, but once we get a few more feet in, it should be easier going."

She didn't respond, and he pushed into the brush, thorns and twigs snagging his parka as he broke through. She followed close behind, pressing in against his back but not grabbing for the pack again.

She kept up. He'd give her that. No complaints, either. They moved through the densest part of the undergrowth, sticking close to the tree line. The terrain was flat, the ground sprinkled with snow and dead branches. Berlin would be at the mouth of the river, nestled in the lush New Hampshire landscape. A safe haven or a death trap. Kane wasn't sure which.

If they were fortunate, they'd find an old homestead before they hit the town limits. One that had a barn or an abandoned house on it. Somewhere they could warm up while he fine-tuned the plan. If he had reception, he could call Silas to pick them up, but staying anywhere close to the plane wreckage would be a mistake.

They'd been making steady progress for an hour, ducking under branches, climbing over fallen trees, moving as quickly as they could.

He knew Arden's energy was fading. Her pace was slowing, and she was falling farther behind. She still didn't complain. She didn't ask him to slow down. She just kept hiking. Once or twice, he thought he heard her singing, but when he looked back, she fell silent again.

"Getting cold?" he finally asked, worried about how quiet she was.

"I passed cold twenty minutes ago," she responded, and he thought her teeth chattered on the last word. He stopped, turning to face her, and grabbed her waist when she nearly stumbled into his chest.

"Sorry," she murmured, her face pale in the darkness.

"Why don't you put on a few more layers? You said you had clothes in the pack, right?"

"We don't have time for that."

"We also don't have time for you to become hypothermic."

"As long as we keep moving, I'll be fine." She tucked

a strand of hair beneath her hat and offered a smile that was about as fake as the neon pink Christmas tree his mother used to put up in her sitting room.

"Arden, don't try to be a hero." He slipped out of her pack and would have unzipped it, but a soft sound carried over the rush of the river.

He cut off his light, telling Arden to do the same. He shrugged back into the pack and tugged her close to his side.

"Helicopter," he said, and she nodded, her body stiff, her muscles taut.

The hum of the propellers grew louder. Through the trees, he could see a searchlight arcing over the river. The light swept back and forth across the banks, reaching a few feet into the tree line. The pilot was flying a grid, crossing over the river and then back again. Searching for the plane or for them.

"We need to go!" Arden said, trying to pull away.

He held her still. "We move, and someone on the chopper might spot us. The best thing we can do is stay put until they pass."

"That's counterintuitive," she argued. "If that spotlight hits us, they can land that thing faster than we can run to safety."

"We've got the tree canopy, the snow and the underbrush to hide us. Spotting something on the ground in these conditions is difficult."

"There's such a thing as thermal imaging."

"That's a good point, but with the fresh snow falling, our clothes should be the same temperature as the air, which should make it difficult to spot us." He pulled her down so they were crouching, huddling together in the shadows of a pine tree. The astringent scent of pine filled his nose, the cold air seeping through his coat and pants. He was cold, but Arden must have been colder. He could feel her trembling, hear her teeth chattering.

"That just leaves our faces and of course our breath which will condense and turn to water which is warmer than snow," she said. "We should probably duck our heads down and breathe into our coats."

"Great idea. I wish some of the soldiers I've served with would have thought like you." If they had, he thought wryly, some of them might not have died. He put an arm around her shoulder, dragging her in closer as the helicopter swooped low. They ducked their heads as the spotlight zipped across the forest floor, illuminating dead leaves and white snow. It passed and then returned, seeming to hover yards from where they were.

Arden was still shaking as the searchlight moved across the forest floor, and he wasn't sure if it was from the temperature...or from fear.

SEVEN

Arden wanted to be home. Decorating for Christmas. Calling her mom to ask for cookie recipes. She wanted to be shopping for Christmas presents for her brothers, parents and friends, and for the new nephews that she'd have next month. She wanted to be anywhere but there—shivering with cold, the rotors of the helicopter sending twigs and debris flying.

Kane pressed close to her side, totally in her space, but he was blocking the chopper wind and some of the snow, and she couldn't bring herself to move away.

Finally, the helicopter moved on, zipping above the tree line, its light slashing across the gray-white forest.

"We need to move," Kane said, pulling her to her feet.

"We can't outrun a helicopter," she responded. Sebastian wiggled in the carrier, probably as anxious to be freed as she was to put this nightmare behind her.

"No, but we need a better position. Someplace that will offer more protection. They may have been getting something on thermal and that's why they were hovering for so long."

"Even covered in snow, we're warm bodies in a very

cold landscape," she pointed out. "Of course there *are* an estimated five hundred species of vertebrate animals in New Hampshire, so there are certainly other mammals out here with us. It stands to reason that we could conceal our heat signatures enough to pass as deer. Or moose. There are also bobcats. Foxes. Coyotes." She started listing all the native mammals, the words spilling out like they always did when she was anxious.

"Good point," he agreed, pulling back a heavy pine bough and holding it so that she could walk past. "Hunkering down bought us a little time, but eventually, they'll have troops on the ground as well as the helicopter in the air. It might not be long before they'll send their ground crew to investigate."

He had a point.

She refrained from explaining how good of one it was. She had a bad habit of talking too much about too many things. Or so her ex had said. Then again, Randy had been quick to point out all of her quirks. He'd also been good at telling her the reasons why she needed to change.

In hindsight, she should have kicked him to the curb long before they'd ever become a couple. But she'd wanted what Juniper had had, what her parents cherished. She'd wanted to be part of something more than just herself. She'd wanted to be in love, and she'd convinced herself that she was.

Her fault. Not Randy's.

She was too smart to have fallen for him, but she'd let herself fall anyway. Not that he hadn't helped her along. He'd been so charming when they'd met, so filled with admiration and compliments. He'd bought her flowers and books on string theory.

They'd met at the University Christmas Gala. She'd been uncomfortable in a black cocktail dress and heels that Juniper had insisted she wear. She would have been more comfortable wearing a casual skirt with one of her infamous ugly Christmas sweaters. But Juniper had put her foot down. As a compromise, Arden accessorized with earrings shaped like Christmas bulbs. They did not improve her comfort or confidence level.

When Randy had introduced himself, he'd complimented her on those earrings; she thought that he'd noticed her because of them.

Turned out, he'd noticed her long before that.

She'd been new to the research program but already nipping at the heels of his accomplishments. He'd wanted her in his corner, part of his achievement. He'd wanted her help, her insight, her brain.

He'd wanted her encryption algorithm.

And he'd taken it as his own, using it as a base to create his own encryption application and key. It was the encryption wrapped around the files she'd appropriated from GeoArray. She was confident whatever was on those files had gotten Dale killed.

And Randy was up to his neck in it. He was dirty and she knew it. She intended to prove it. She just needed a little more time.

She tripped over a thick tree root, and Kane grabbed her elbow, holding her steady.

"You okay?" he asked.

Had Randy ever asked her that?

All she could remember was him asking her about work, about projects, about her ideas and programs.

"Fine."

Except that she felt like a fool. A fool who was now

running for her life because of something her ex-boyfriend had done.

The sound of the helicopter had faded; the forest was still again. Fat flakes of snow drifted through the canopy, layering Kane's coat with white. He didn't seem to be hurrying. If anything, they were moving slower than they had been before the helicopter arrived on the scene.

"Shouldn't we speed up?" she asked.

"You said yourself that we can't outrun a helicopter. It's going to swing back around. When it does, I want to be well hidden."

"We're two ninety-eight-point-six-degree pillars moving through a twenty-eight-degree forest. Without a structure to cover us, hiding completely from thermal imaging is a near impossibility."

"Nothing is impossible. I'm looking for anything that can give us enough cover and keep them from pinpointing our location." He pushed through a thicket, holding back thorny branches as she moved through.

A true gentleman. One that held tree branches even when there was no one around to see him or to praise his impeccable manners. Randy had only ever been a gentleman when other people could witness it.

"I really was an idiot," she muttered, stepping over a fallen log, her feet heavy and cold. She was cold all over. Even with Sebastian pressed up against her chest, she could feel the chill of the winter air.

"You are far from an idiot, Arden," Kane said, pulling her to a stop. They stood there for several seconds. She wasn't sure what he was doing, but *she* was listening to the sound of the returning helicopter and to something else. A subtle buzz that seemed familiar. A motor of some sort, maybe.

"What's that?" she whispered.

"A snowmobile, I think." There was no hint of emotion in Kane's voice, no change in his expression. He scanned the area around them.

"It doesn't sound close."

"They'll be here soon enough. The helicopter probably spotted the plane and sent people to check it out." He was moving with a renewed sense of urgency, his hand around her wrist, tugging her through the foliage. They were sprinting now, pushing deeper and deeper into the forest as the distant sound of snowmobiles grew louder.

They were moving fast, but it wasn't going to be enough. Kane knew that, but he wanted to put as much distance between them and the snowmobiles as possible. It was bad enough having the helicopter to contend with. The possibility of being shot by a sniper aiming from somewhere above was a real one, but being apprehended by men on snowmobiles seemed more likely.

If the people tracking them were from GeoArray, they may want to keep Arden alive—at least until they were sure they had their files back. If they were from the FBI, they'd only shoot after they announced themselves.

Arden had gotten herself into some seriously deep trouble. He had to get her out of it. First, though, he had to get them out of this—the forest, the wilderness, the cold.

The sound of the snowmobile was still muted and distant, but the helicopter was heading their way again, the rhythmic thud of propeller blades announcing its return.

Glancing over his shoulder, he saw the searchlight

illuminating the trees about two hundred meters behind them. Up ahead, there was nothing but thick tree growth. A large elm had fallen across their path, and he clambered over it, pulling Arden with him.

The root system had left a deep hollow in the ground. Covered by leaves and snow and dead roots, it was a perfect place to hide until the chopper passed.

"Quick, Arden, this way." He jumped into the hole. Reached up to help her down. "Press your back up against the roots of the tree and cover your legs with some snow," he instructed, as he brushed snow over his own legs.

"Cover your face and mouth," she reminded him. She pulled her coat up over her nose and mouth and covered the rest of her face with her gloved hands, leaving just enough space between her fingers to peer out. He did the same.

Within moments, the searchlight from the helicopter was almost on them. "Be still," he cautioned.

He knew from experience that the pilots would be looking for motion, reflective clothing, bright colors— something that was out of place. From their vantage point in the sky, and with the tree cover and snow falling as it was, the pilot's visibility would be limited.

Dressed in dark clothing, with snow covering their legs and boots, Kane and Arden pressed into the shadowy web of roots and waited for the searchlight to reach them.

EIGHT

A wide beam of light swept in a large arc to the left, then right, passing over their hiding place. Kane and Arden remained concealed in the shadows. The strong scent of damp, decaying wood permeated the air.

Arden didn't move, but he could feel her anxiety radiating out. She was scared. She should be. They were mere moments from being discovered.

Hopefully, the roots, snow and old wood would keep their thermal temperature from registering. Hopefully, the chopper would keep going. Hopefully, the snowmobile driver wouldn't happen upon the tracks they left and would have no idea where they were. They'd have even more time to put distance between themselves and trouble.

Hopefully, but Kane wasn't counting on it.

One thing he'd learned during his years in the military: never take safety and security for granted. Anything could happen at any time. He'd learned to be prepared for it.

Somewhere close by, a small herd of deer was startled from hiding. The animals bolted through the darkness just ahead of them, jumping over logs and stumps, weaving through the snow-coated trees and disappearing deeper into the woods. A few passed close enough to jump over the downed tree where Kane and Arden took refuge.

The movement of the deer was caught in the searchlight. The beam of light passed quickly across Kane and Arden's hiding place, shining briefly on one or two of the fleeing deer before it continued its probing search.

The light moved farther away. They were no longer in the direct path of discovery. The rhythmic thump of propeller blades receded.

Kane stood cautiously, motioning for Arden to remain concealed.

The searchlight was barely visible through the trees. The forest around them was once again dark. Kane pulled himself out of the hole, then reached down to help Arden climb out.

"What should we do?" she asked. "They're going to assume we're headed downriver—they'll probably be waiting for us on the outskirts of town."

Kane had been thinking the same thing. Once their tracks were discovered, it would become evident that he and Arden were paralleling the river and heading to town. Even if their tracks weren't found, that course seemed the only logical choice.

And that's because it was the only logical choice.

Upriver was away from the closest town. Crossing the river was out of the question. One thing was certain: they couldn't stay where they were. Not only because the woods offered no protection from the elements, but because there was no doubt in his mind that the helicopter had left a trooper or two on the ground. It's what he would do if the situation were reversed. Between the ground troops and the snowmobiles, it would be very difficult to escape detection.

Kane surveyed the area. Up until this point, their chosen path had been relatively flat, minus a few drainages that ran off the mountain into the river. Deeper in the woods, the terrain sloped gradually up as the mountain rose from the valley.

It would not be an easy hike.

It would also not be an obvious choice.

If they headed into the forest and away from the river, the heavy snowfall might cover their tracks before anyone on the ground reached this area. The assumption would be that he and Arden had continued along the easiest route. Doing the unexpected would buy them time and, possibly, allow them to escape.

"You're right. I think we need to change course," he said.

"You're thinking of heading up the mountain, right? Doing what we shouldn't and hoping that throws them off our trail. Buys us some time."

"It's the best plan I can come up with on short notice," he said honestly.

"It's better than my plan," she responded.

"Which is?"

"Click my heels together three times and repeat, 'There's no place like home.'" She smiled, a quick curve of the lips that was echoed by the amusement in her eyes. She might be half frozen and running for her life, but she still had a sense of humor. Not something he was used to seeing in the high-stress environment he'd worked in. Stone-cold seriousness or morbid sarcasm seemed to carry his comrades through. Arden's kind of humor—the soft and easy and light humor—was a refreshing change of pace.

She was refreshing.

She was herself and nothing else.

That's how Jace had described her when he'd asked Kane to track Arden down. Obviously, he hadn't been exaggerating.

"You're an interesting person, Arden," Kane said, heading away from the river and toward the mountain slope.

"So I've been told," she muttered.

"That's a compliment."

He glanced her way, met her eyes, saw her smile again.

"In that case, thanks. Although, I'm surprised you didn't notice when you were at family functions with Jace."

"I was noticing other things."

"Like?"

"How kind your family is to one another. How talk-ative they are. How deeply connected you all seem to be." But of course he'd noticed her, too. She'd intrigued him from the start, though he wouldn't let himself go there. She'd been Jace's younger sister after all— dressed in crazy Christmas sweaters or bunny-eared hoodies, flitting from one person to another, completely unaware of her allure, her cold-eyed boyfriend hover-ing nearby.

"You don't have a family?" she asked, her breath puffing out into the snowy night.

"Most people do," he said, wishing he hadn't men-tioned her family and that she hadn't asked him about his. His parents were good people. They tried. But he'd never lived up to their academic standards. He'd never been the kind of kid who'd craved knowledge, who'd aced tests, who'd been at the top of his class.

"Hmm, another nonanswer I see," Arden said, panting a little, struggling a little.

He knew he was moving fast, and he knew she could barely keep up, but the buzzing engines of snowmobiles were growing louder. Keeping ahead of the enemy was paramount to survival.

"Tell you what," he responded. "We can discuss my family once we're safe. For now, let's conserve our energy for the hike."

She didn't argue.

He was worried about what that might mean. He had no idea when she'd eaten last, how much she'd slept the previous night. He knew she'd had self-defense training with her brothers, but he had no clue as to how fit she was.

He could push her as much as he wanted, but her body would only go for as long as it could. Then she'd be down, and he'd have to carry her and her cat out of the wilderness. Not impossible, but it would complicate things a lot.

Getting out of this mess alive was already complicated enough.

Arden followed closely behind Kane, matching his quick pace step for step. She didn't want to slow them down any more than necessary. It was bad enough that Kane was in this predicament because of her. If she got him caught and killed, she'd never forgive herself.

Of course, if she were dead, she wouldn't have to worry about that.

And, she knew if they were caught, she would die. Eventually. Once GeoArray had the files, eliminating her would drastically reduce the company's chances of being exposed.

Cold wind whipped at her cheeks and sliced through the fabric of her pants. She gritted her teeth to keep them from chattering and kept walking. She had no choice.

This wasn't just about Kane's life. It wasn't about hers. If she was right, and the research Dale and his boss referred to in the email was related to the self-improving weapons control system, it was about national security. And that could mean it was about the lives of millions of people.

Even thinking it seemed melodramatic. She couldn't imagine speaking the suspicion out loud. She needed proof, and she needed time to get it.

She wasn't sure they were going to get that.

She could hear the snowmobile moving closer. More than one by the sound of it. She could picture half a dozen armed men and women speeding across the snowy landscape while she and Kane trudged along.

"We need a vehicle," she panted, surprised at how breathless she was.

"True," he responded.

Short. Simple. Abrupt.

"We need a plan to get one."

"Arden." He stopped short, swinging around so that they were face to face. The snow had turned to pellets of sleet, and they pinged off his shoulders and hat. He had a strong face and gorgeous eyes; the kind of looks that most of her friends would have gone crazy over.

The kind of guy that would never give a tomboyish computer nerd like Arden a second glance.

"What?" she asked.

"You need to save your breath. We've got a long hike ahead of us, and you're wasting energy talking."

"If we had a vehicle—"

"We don't. We're in the middle of the New Hampshire forest. The town is miles away."

"There are other places we could get a vehicle. We're in the White Mountains after all—even though much of it's national forest, there's still a lot of acreage owned by private citizens. There could be vacation cabins nearby, active timber operations, campgrounds."

"You're right, but without a map of the area we're running blind. Without divine intervention, we could search this forest for days and never stumble on any signs of civilization. We don't have time to do anything but stay the course. We need to keep moving until we're certain it's safe to angle back toward town. There's no question we'll be able to get our hands on a vehicle then."

"There's always time to pray."

Kane smiled. "Right again. And we don't need to voice our prayers for God to hear them."

She couldn't help but smile back. "Point taken. I'll save my breath."

He started walking again. Jogging really. His pace even more brisk than it had been. The ground and vegetation were slippery with ice. The temperature had dropped significantly since they'd landed. Maybe as low as twenty degrees. Thankfully, with the pace they were keeping, she'd warmed up. She imagined any wildlife that thrived in the brutal New Hampshire winters had hunkered down for the night, curled up against the storm.

Right about now, she wished she were curled up with a nice thick quilt and a cup of vanilla bean tea. Unfortunately, at this exact moment, the best she could do was pray for divine intervention and, barring that, hope they'd be able to slip into town unseen and find a warm place to take shelter until they could rent a vehicle and get away.

Kane pressed forward as Arden sent up her silent prayers. He was right, of course. They needed to conserve their energy.

Well, *she* needed to. She wasn't sure about him. He seemed to be moving along without effort, no gasping breaths or stumbling steps. Definitely fit. But why wouldn't he be? The company he and Jace had started was all about training security forces and offering protection to a variety of clients. That meant being fit, smart and ready for trouble.

She was smart. As for the other two things... She obviously would not get a job on their team.

Which was fine. She had no desire to go into that kind of physical security. She was more interested in computers. The hash analysis she'd run yesterday had been something most people would have no clue about.

She knew Randy took shortcuts in his work and she figured he'd used a public key system as the base for the second layer of the encryption program wrapped around the files. After running the hash analysis, she'd identified some known code that she'd modified and applied to her first attempt at a decryption algorithm. It hadn't worked, but she believed she was almost there—a breakthrough was imminent.

Randy and Arden had collaborated on a number of research projects and she understood his thought process like no one else. She also understood his weaknesses. His codes would be impenetrable for most analysts, but they would not hold up against Arden's scrutiny.

And they both knew it.

It probably pained him to tell GeoArray's CEO, Marcus Emory, that the files were in her hands. But she was certain Randy had told him because it hadn't taken the company long to send someone to ransack her town house. There was no other person that could have recognized her operational signature so quickly.

The snowmobiles were getting closer, the sound louder in the hushed stillness of the snowy forest. The sloping terrain was difficult, her feet constantly slipping on ice-crusted snow. Arden struggled to control her breathing.

Kane reached back, grabbing her and pulling her along. He still wasn't out of breath, and he still didn't seem cold or tired.

He dragged her onto a narrow deer trail that wound its way through thicker foliage. The ground had been trampled down and their footprints would be more difficult to see there. At least, that's why she thought he'd headed that way. They sure weren't going to be less difficult to spot. Not from the air.

The deer trail was definitely easier to follow. Kane took advantage of this by pushing them harder. They were almost running through the woods. As much as anyone could run contouring up an icy, snow-covered side of a mountain.

A sudden flash of light through the leafless trees in

the forest below caught her attention. "They're coming," she panted.

He looked over his shoulder. "I see them. They're not going full speed and there's definitely more than one. They haven't spotted our tracks yet. But when they do, they'll be able to follow them easily."

They raced through the woods, following the deer trail as it wove up the mountain. Within minutes, the snowmobiles were directly below them. Kane pulled her behind a tree while the vehicles continued to move steadily forward, the drivers shining handheld lights on the ground and into the trees.

"They're definitely searching for footprints," he said quietly, leaning his head toward hers. The warmth of his breath touched her cheek. She felt comforted by that and by him. Odd, because she usually liked to handle problems alone. She didn't care to have other people messing with her plans, and she sure hadn't ever thought she'd need anyone to save her life.

Right now, though, she needed Kane, and he needed her to keep her head screwed on straight. No panicking. No chattering. No singing. No running straight into more trouble. She had to be smart. She had to think.

"It isn't going to take them long to catch up," was all she managed.

"Don't worry, I've got an idea."

"Good. Great. Want to explain before they arrive?"

"That," he said, pointing into the sky, "is my plan."

"What? Sprout wings and take off? We already tried the flying thing. It didn't work out."

"Not flying. Climbing." He stopped beneath the broad branches of an oak tree.

She skidded to a stop beside him. Lungs heaving, legs trembling, thankful to not be moving.

Until she finally saw where he was pointing.

There was a structure in the tree. Some kind of wooden platform pounded into thick branches about eight feet off the ground.

"That looks rotted. And dangerous."

"There's no time to second guess. It will hold. They're closing in fast, and we need to get off this trail before they follow our tracks right to us."

Icy snow was still falling, layering fresh white over their very visible footprints. He was right. This was their best chance.

She followed Kane around to the far side of the tree. A few ice-covered two-by-fours had been hammered into the trunk, forming a makeshift ladder of sorts. The person who'd built it was obviously tall. The bottom rung was a good three and a half feet off the ground, with the rung above it just out of her reach.

She didn't have time to ponder how she was going to get on the two-by-four. Kane grabbed her waist and lifted her up, setting her feet on the lowest rung. She felt her boot slip as she steadied herself, grabbing the slippery rung above with her gloved hand. Somehow, she managed to hoist herself up.

She reached the last rung of the ladder and scrambled up onto the platform.

Kane wasn't behind her.

He wasn't climbing.

In fact, he was moving away. She crawled to the edge of the deer stand and looked down. Sebastian let out an unhappy meow. Poor guy was probably hungry. He was always hungry.

She patted his head, searching the area beneath the tree until she found Kane. "What are you doing?" she whispered as loudly as she dared.

"I'm covering our tracks here so they can't tell we left the trail. Then I'll run up the trail a bit before curving off into the trees and circle back," Kane replied. "There won't be enough snow to cover our tracks completely, and I don't want them to realize we bailed here."

"What if they catch you?"

"You'll be fine."

"I'm not worried about me. Well, I am, but I'm also worried about you. They don't need you. You'll just be collateral damage."

"They aren't going to catch me." He sounded confident. He looked it, too, silhouetted in the gray winter night, his shoulders broad, his body muscular. He looked like a hero from one of those action movies she'd watched when she was a kid—tough and rugged and ready to walk through a barren wasteland to save the world.

Only this wasn't a movie. If GeoArray's thugs were on those snowmobiles, he'd be killed. "Kane—"

"No singing, Arden." He'd already turned away, was heading back toward the trail. "No humming. No clicking your heels together. Stay quiet until I get back."

That was it.

He was there and then he was gone. She thought she saw his shadowy form moving along the trail, but she wasn't sure if it was him or trees blowing in the gusty wind.

She shivered, pulling Sebastian a little closer, forcing her mind to something other than Kane—the computer system. The encrypted files. The headway she'd made.

She started spinning programs through her mind, mentally testing variables, imagining their results on the encrypted file. The sound of snowmobiles grew louder. The snow fell in even heavier sheets and covered the trail and the trees and the little hunting stand where she and Sebastian waited.

Kane sprinted up the path, mentally counting his paces and tracking his direction of travel. He didn't want to get lost. He couldn't afford the time it would take to use his compass and get himself back on course. He also couldn't afford to leave Arden for too long. She was smart, funny, quirky. Unpredictable. That last one worried him.

He wanted her to stay where he'd left her.

He wasn't sure if she would.

He also wasn't sure how well she'd be hidden. The tree stand was great as long as the guys on the snowmobiles weren't looking too carefully. If they shone searchlights toward her location in the trees, they might just see some of the tracks he and Arden had left as they ducked off the deer path. It had been impossible to obscure them all.

He ran up the trail about seventy meters before taking a sharp left, leaping from the path into the thicker tree cover and doubling back. Jumping deadfall, breaking through the ice-covered snow, he sprinted all out.

He found the base of the tree where he'd left her. Scrambled up, relieved to find her there. Her black clothes blended with the darkness, but her face was stark against the night, and he could see her eyes widen as he climbed onto the platform.

"You made it," she whispered. A smile curved her lips, softening the angles of her face.

Something about that smile reminded him of all his childhood dreams of having someone to come home to. Someone who'd be happy to see him when he returned. It had never been that way with his parents. He'd always been the third wheel to their partnership, the unexpected surprise that had changed everything.

He'd thought he'd finally found that someone to come home to when he met Ellen.

He'd been stationed in Georgia for flight school. She'd been waiting tables in the officer's club and studying accounting at the community college. Beautiful and outgoing, she'd had an infectious laugh. He'd fallen for her. Hard. They'd maintained a long-distance relationship during his first tour of duty. Gotten engaged while he was on home leave.

But it didn't take long for rumors to surface. When he'd confronted Ellen, she'd admitted she needed someone to be there with her, and for her, every day. Something he just couldn't do. Not then.

He'd joined the military to atone for Evan's death. For Lexi's. When push came to shove, Kane's obligation to Evan's family was stronger than his love for Ellen. His obligation to them was a driving factor in every decision he made.

After breaking off the engagement, Kane had jumped from relationship to relationship, woman to woman, avoiding commitment. Afraid to put his heart into something that just wouldn't last. After a while, he'd gotten tired of that.

He and Jace had met by then, and Jace had set an example of gentlemanly honor, of respect, of work ethic.

He'd talked to Kane about things that mattered—faith and hope and believing in a God who was bigger than every failure.

Those things had sunk in deep.

Kane had stopped playing the field, but never met the one woman he could share his life with. He figured he might never settle down with a family of his own. He was fine with that, but sometimes he wanted more than an empty apartment when he returned home at night. He wanted more than silences at dawn when all the memories woke him. Of Evan and Lexi. Of others lost later, in combat.

He wanted something like what he saw in Arden's smile.

He frowned, pressing in close so that they were shoulder to shoulder. The tree stand was small but sturdy.

"I can see their lights," she whispered.

He shimmied past her along the large branch that hung out over the trail. "They're almost here. Get to the ladder, stay hidden and be ready to move when I do."

She nodded, carefully maneuvered her body around the trunk of the tree and lowered herself onto the topmost two-by-four. She waited, poised to descend at his signal.

The hum of engines grew louder. The light from an approaching vehicle reflected on the adjacent trees just before it rounded the bend. He remained motionless, silently calculating the vehicle's speed as it rounded the curve in the trail. It sped by the tree, the driver unaware of their presence.

Kane watched until it disappeared around another curve in the trail. Moments later, a second vehicle approached the bend. He readied himself. He'd have to time his move perfectly if he wanted to pull this off.

The snowmobile approached, this driver taking the curve more cautiously—clearly not as confident in his driving skills. The slower speed would work to Kane's advantage.

He waited until the guy was right behind them, and then he moved, launching himself out of the tree. The driver must have heard him. He looked up, reached for something beneath his jacket.

Too late.

Kane was already on him, the force of his movement sending both of them skidding across the snowy trail, colliding into a young tree. The other man took the brunt of the impact, his helmet glancing off the tree, his left shoulder taking most of the blow.

With the tether switch ripped from the snowmobile, the engine cut off abruptly. The vehicle's forward momentum carried it a few feet farther up the trail before it skidded to a stop.

Kane pulled himself off the driver, who lay motionless in the ice-crusted snow—his left shoulder lodged against the tree. Crouching over the fallen man, Kane removed his glove and checked for a pulse. It was there, strong and steady. The man's helmet, scraped on its left side, appeared to have deflected the initial hit to the tree.

The high-end black tactical gear the man wore screamed of private security. There was no time to check for identification or to wait to see what they could learn once the man gained consciousness.

Kane guessed he was a GeoArray-hired thug, but

he couldn't know. And he didn't dare wait around to find out.

Arden had already climbed on the snowmobile.

Kane reached down and quickly unhooked the kill switch tether cord from the man's belt and tossed it to Arden.

Ahead on the trail, the hum of the first snowmobile abruptly stopped.

"That's not good," Arden muttered, turning the key in the snowmobile's ignition. The vehicle sprang back to life.

"Let's get out of here." Kane hopped on behind her, sliding an arm under the cat carrier and around her waist.

"Where to?" she asked, turning in a tight U and facing back the way they'd come.

"There was a fork in the trail a while back. Go there. We'll take the right branch and hope we can lose him on it."

"All right," Arden responded. "Hold on."

She gave it full throttle, navigating the snowmobile back along the deer trail. Totally focused. No singing. No humming. No list of things that could go wrong or right.

He imagined this was the way she did her job—with absolute dedication.

She found the fork without any help from him, the snowmobile skidding to the right. The steep trail would bring them farther up the mountain and turn them back toward town. They'd lost some time backtracking, but they had a vehicle now. They'd ride the snowmobile as far as they could, then go it on foot. If they could stay ahead of their pursuer, they just might make it out of this without any blood being shed.

Kane prayed that would be the case. He was prepared to do whatever was necessary to keep Arden out of the hands of GeoArray Corporation, but he'd rather avoid a shoot-out. GeoArray wasn't the only entity after Arden. The FBI wanted her. Local authorities might be pulled in to apprehend her. At a distance, it would be impossible to distinguish the law from the lawless.

He'd been a sharpshooter in the military. He was well trained. He could hit his target. But he had enough innocent blood on his hands.

His memories were vivid and unrelenting. Lexi's blue lips, the gray tint of her skin as he pulled her from the bottom of the pool. The strong scent of chlorine. Water dripping from his face as he'd tried to breathe life into her.

Through Evan's tears and pleading to God, through their friend Tyler's panicked phone call, Kane had counted breaths. Counted compressions. He could never forget. Every moment was etched in his mind. She'd been four years old. Even his dreams were not safe from remorse. He'd prefer not to add an officer of the law to his list of regrets.

Arden slowed the snowmobile and gestured farther up the mountain. "See that? Looks like someone cleared the trees. Do you think it's a road?"

He could see the area. The trees were sparse against the black-gray sky. These mountains had once been filled with logging camps, so it was likely that old logging roads still crisscrossed the landscape. If they were looking at a road, there might be a cabin at the end of it. Maybe an old vehicle with enough gas in it to hot-wire and drive.

"If you think you can get this thing up there, we can check it out."

She nodded, gunning the engine again.

They left the deer trail, bounced along snow-covered leaves and over thick root systems and deadfall, and finally burst out onto a road. Although coated in a layer of snow, it showed signs that vehicles had passed through earlier in the day. Tire tracks were coated with a fresh layer of icy snowfall. He wasn't sure if it was an actual paved road or some sort of access road, but it was definitely a road.

If they went downhill, it would probably bring them to Berlin faster. The thought of making it to town was appealing. Arden was cold. Running on fumes. But in reality, going downhill might bring them closer to danger. For sure, it was the direction anyone following them would think they'd gone.

"Up or down?" Arden asked, her voice tight with tension.

The first snowmobile had gone silent. The driver had either stopped to help his fallen comrade or he'd come up with a different plan of attack. Either way, Kane and Arden needed to keep moving.

"Up," he said.

She gunned the engine again, speeding along the road, passing old wooden signs that pointed the way to camping areas.

As they rounded a bend in the road, the road forked off in two directions. At the intersection, three wooden arrows on a painted post pointed them in different directions. Two of the arrows pointed up the mountain, identifying Milan Hill Picnic Area and the fire tower. The third arrow pointed left and announced the camp- ground office. It was off-season; the office would likely not be staffed.

"Left?" Arden asked, heading in that direction be- fore he answered.

They were finally in sync, working together as a team, thinking in the same direction. He'd experienced the same on the battlefield, the connection between the men and women there almost mystic in its intensity.

The need for survival trumped just about everything else.

Except love. He'd seen how powerful that could be, and he knew how much people were willing to sacri- fice for it.

Arden pulled up in front of a small wood-sided cabin. Several outbuildings were scattered nearby. A free- standing display case stood near the cabin—a map of the campground inside it. Nearby, a long carport housed three pickup trucks. Two were new, with shiny paint and gleaming windows. Both were Parks and Recre- ation vehicles.

The third truck was older, with a dented hood and cracked windshield. There'd once been a New Hamp- shire Parks and Recreation logo on the door, but some- one had sprayed a light coat of green paint over it. The words *For Sale* had been scrawled across the top of the front window, the lettering old and nearly worn off.

If it worked, they could take that. Its age should make it easy to hot-wire. If Kane had to, he could syphon gas from one of the other two vehicles.

He hopped off the snowmobile and tried the truck door. Unlocked. Just like he thought it would be. The interior was as worn as the exterior, but the inside light came on. Hopefully an indication that the battery was in working order.

He tossed his duffel bag behind the seat, then slid into the driver's seat, pulling out his Swiss Army knife.

"What are you doing?" Arden peered into the truck, her face dripping with melting snow, her hat listless and sopping wet. She'd unzipped her jacket and freed Sebastian, holding the giant animal in both arms.

"Big cat," he commented as he opened the ignition switch.

"That's not an answer to my question."

"I'm hot-wiring the truck."

She frowned. "We can't steal a truck, Kane. It's against the law."

"Would you rather stay here and get caught?"

"No." She set the cat down. "Do your business, Sebastian, and be quick about it," she said, then tugged at the pack Kane still wore. He grabbed her wrist. No way was she getting the pack. Not until he had her somewhere safe.

"We don't have time for this," he muttered, looking straight into the bluest eyes he'd ever seen.

"I'm just grabbing some cash." She pulled back, waving a wad of bills at him. "How much do you think this thing is worth?"

"Arden—"

"Seriously, Kane. How much?"

"A couple hundred. At most."

"Okay." She pulled out a few bills and shoved the rest back in the pack. "I'll be back."

"Don't go far," he warned. "I'll have this started in a moment."

"I won't." She was humming as she jogged away, the cat scurrying along beside her. She shoved the money through a mail slot in the cabin's door. He tracked her movements as she walked to the display case.

She must have felt the weight of his stare. She met his eyes again.

She was lovely. The unwelcome thought popped into his mind. He pushed it out just as quickly. Arden's brother was his best friend. There was no room for thoughts like that.

"You're not going to ever get done if you don't get started," she pointed out. "And you really do need to get started. I think I hear the snowmobile again."

He did, too, the distant hum of the engine echoing through the snowy clearing.

It took him seconds to get the truck started, the engine sputtering for a few moments before it sprang to life.

He checked the gas gauge. Over half filled. That was plenty to get them past Berlin. There were other small towns interspersed through the region. They could fill up when they reached one. He shrugged off the pack and tossed it behind the seat with his duffel.

A flash of light caught his attention, and he glanced at the tree line. Definitely a light, there and gone as it was blocked by trees and revealed again.

"Arden!" he shouted, but the passenger door was already opening and she was sliding into the vehicle. Cold air and snow seeped in with her. Sebastian was in his carrier again, eyeing Kane balefully.

"Hurry," Arden huffed, slamming the door shut.

"I plan to," he responded. He pressed on the gas and prayed that the old truck was more reliable than it looked—and that it could outrun a snowmobile and whatever else might be waiting for them when they got off the mountain.

NINE

Arden was scared.

She could admit it.

She'd seen the campground map. She'd memorized it. She knew exactly how far up the mountain they were and exactly how sharp the horseshoe curves were that would lead them down.

In the best of weather with the best of road conditions, they'd have to take those curves slowly. The weather was horrible. The road was icy, and Kane was racing along like they were on an open stretch of highway in the middle of the desert.

Yeah. She was scared, so of course she opened her mouth and started talking.

"Velocity is the change of position relative to time. Based on the speed we're going and the fact that the first horseshoe curve we'll encounter is roughly three miles from the campground, we have a good shot of becoming airborne in the next couple of minutes." The words just kind of spilled out, and she was certain Kane's lips curved. His focus was on the road, though. He didn't even glance in her direction.

"Are you asking me to slow down?"

"Statistically speaking, the chance of you making the first curve at this rate of speed is slim to none." There she went again. She pressed her lips together, sealing in more information that wasn't going to help their situation at all.

Kane was smart. He could have figured it all out without her spiel.

To his credit, he just nodded, easing off the accelerator and slowing down.

"You know, Arden," he said, and she braced herself to get an earful. How many times had Randy pointed out that she'd embarrassed herself and him by saying too much, offering too many details, talking incessantly? Too many.

But he was a jerk, so she really shouldn't care.

Except that she knew he'd been right. She did talk a lot about the things she liked. And she liked a lot of things.

"What?" she finally asked. She told herself she wasn't going to care about Kane's opinion any more than she should have cared about Randy's. But of course she was lying.

"Until tonight, I'd never met anyone who could make me smile while I was running for my life."

"I'm glad I could amuse you," she replied, her cheeks hot with embarrassment. Amusing other people was something she excelled at.

"I didn't say I find you amusing, Arden. I find you pleasantly surprising," he continued. He took the first steep curve without difficulty, the truck only shimmying a little on the ice- and snow-crusted road. "I knew you were smart, but you're so much more. The way you handled the snowmobile back there, the fact that you took the time to leave money for this beat-up truck just because it's the right thing to do. The way you've pushed yourself all night. It's refreshing. You're refreshing."

They'd reached a long stretch of gently curving road, and he did glance her way. Just a quick look, but she saw something in his eyes that made her breath catch. She'd never ever seen it in Randy's. Admiration mixed with respect. That's how she'd describe it if she was asked.

She looked out the window, focusing on the grayish night, the ice-covered trees, the swirling snow. Anything but Kane. There was something different about him. Something down to earth and honest that made her want to talk more, ask questions, find out who he really was when he wasn't hanging at the edge of her family's holiday celebrations.

She wasn't going to do it.

He'd be too easy to fall for. And she wasn't ready for another relationship. Being made a fool of once was more than enough.

"There's another horseshoe curve coming up," she said, eyeing the dark stretch of road. There was no sign of the snowmobile, but the truck's engine was loud enough to mask any sound of pursuit. She glanced back. The road was empty and still.

"Thanks," he said, taking the sharp curve easily.

"Where are we headed? Town?" Arden asked, pulling Sebastian out of the carrier and depositing him on her lap.

"Not Berlin. We'll need to stop for gas at some point, but we'll do it when we're farther away."

"You really are very good at avoiding my questions," she said.

He smiled. "We're going to Massachusetts. Cape Cod, to be specific."

Arden's heart jumped, her pulse racing. "You do realize GeoArray headquarters are in Boston, don't you?"

"Yes."

"And you want to go to Massachusetts because…?"

"It won't be expected, and because I have a cottage there."

"You have a cottage?"

"It belonged to my grandparents. They left it to me. I haven't been out to it in over a decade, but my parents use it in the summer, so it should be in decent shape."

"Decent shape for what?"

"Laying low until we can come up with a better plan."

She almost protested. She had no intention of staying anywhere near GeoArray. She sure didn't plan on staying in a cottage with Kane. It was only a matter of time before someone linked Kane to that plane. Any property that could be traced to him would be the first place they'd search.

The words were on the tip of her tongue, but for once common sense won out. Until she had a better plan, she'd just have to go along for the ride. Let him think she was cooperating. It was becoming increasingly clear that giving him the slip was not going to be easy. Perhaps she should try another tactic. Get him on her side, then convince him that she'd be safer going off the grid again. Alone.

"You've gone quiet," Kane said. "You don't like the plan?"

"I'm tired." She sidestepped the question, and she was certain he noticed.

He didn't comment. Just turned up the heater that was blowing lukewarm air into the cab. He pulled the sopping knit cap from her head, his fingers brushing against her ear and the side of her neck.

He'd taken his gloves off at some point, and his fingers were warm and calloused against her cold skin.

"Go ahead and close your eyes for a while. We've got a long ride ahead of us, and you're probably going to want to work on those files once we reach the Cape."

She did want to work on the files, but she wasn't planning to rest now. She had too much on her mind and on her heart.

Juniper had trusted her to prove her husband's innocence and to clear his name. Arden had foolishly promised to do it. She'd had no idea what she was getting herself into, and she had no way of letting Juniper know what she'd learned. She also had no way of letting her friend know that she was safe.

"Juniper is probably worried sick," she murmured.

"So are Jace and Grayson. I'd put in a call to let them know you're with me, but the FBI is probably monitoring their cell phones."

"Right." She sighed, leaning her head back against the cracked leather seat and closing her eyes. Not because she planned to sleep, but because she didn't want to talk.

She was afraid everything would spill out. All her dramatic speculations about just how dangerous those files might be, about what they might be hiding, was better left unsaid. The less she told Kane, the better off he'd be. Two people were already dead because of those files. She was certain Juniper's husband had been murdered and that his boss had suffered the same fate.

She just had to prove it.

She had to decrypt those files.

Most of all, she had to make sure that whatever Geo-Array had started was stopped.

And she'd really like to do it all before Christmas. She missed her family. She missed baking with her mother. She missed shopping with Juniper. She missed being home where she knew exactly what each day would bring.

She sniffed back unexpected tears, disgusted with herself. She wasn't a crier. She'd never been a crier. Even when she'd discovered the truth about Randy, she hadn't cried. She certainly wasn't going to cry now. She sniffed again, trying to prove that truth to herself.

"Are you crying?" Kane asked.

"Why would I be?" she asked, not opening her eyes. She was afraid a tear might slip out.

"Because you've been running for weeks? Because you're tired? Because it's almost Christmas and you're far from home?"

Yes. To all those things.

"I'm this close to decrypting those files, Kane. I just want to get somewhere where I can concentrate on doing it," she responded.

He didn't say anything. Just let the truck fill with their silence.

That was fine.

She was fine.

Or she would be. Once she fulfilled her promise to Juniper and made it back home.

Please, God, let that happen. Please, she prayed silently, her eyes still closed as the truck descended the mountain.

* * *

They made it down the mountain in twenty minutes with no sign they were being followed. Kane fished his cell phone out of his pocket and dialed Silas. The call went directly to voice mail.

"Hey, it's me. I've got Jace's sister. The plane's down just outside of Berlin—I'll need you to handle it for me. We're headed to the Cape. Give me a call when you get this."

Another few hours, and they'd be at the Cape.

Unfortunately.

He hoped he was making the right decision.

His name wasn't on the Cessna's title and hadn't been used to file the flight plan. The plane was owned by Shadow Wolves Security. They'd purposely not tied any of their names directly to the company to help maintain anonymity for the benefit of their clients. Discretion would be paramount to their future success.

It would be difficult for anyone to put his name together with Arden's but it wouldn't be impossible. If the FBI tied Kane's name to the company and the plane, they'd be able to quickly figure out that he owned the cottage.

A good reason to stay away, but he figured it would take time for the Feds to realize he and Arden were together. He could use that time to make plans.

For now, the Cape was his best option, but he didn't want to go there.

He'd left it almost thirteen years ago, and he hadn't looked back. There were too many memories, too many regrets.

He'd been a stupid punk when he'd spent summers and winter vacations there with his grandparents. His parents had never had time for more than a couple of days off during school break. They'd had busy lecture schedules that took them to many universities, hospitals and research facilities around the globe. None of those engagements would be considered fun for an active kid like Kane.

So when he wasn't in boarding school, he'd been shipped off to his grandparents at the Cape. Seventeen years of hanging out with the same spoiled summer crowd. Seventeen years of being Mr. Popular, Mr. Cool, Mr. Least-Likely-to-Get-Caught.

Seventeen years, then it all changed.

One bad decision. One stupid choice. One moment forever etched in his mind.

Like Kane, Evan had never forgiven himself for Lexi's death. The party had been his idea. They'd been distracted and it had cost Lexi her life. Two months later, Kane was left shouldering the guilt alone. Facing Evan's mom and siblings across another mahogany casket. Knowing he was one of the reasons they were grieving. There was no way he wanted to face Arden's family under similar circumstances.

He'd caused enough harm to last a lifetime. He'd enlisted in the army, both to honor Evan's plan to join the military and to atone for his role in Lexi's and Evan's deaths. Evan had intended to send money to his mom to help support his siblings. Instead, Kane did that for him. Every month. While in the army, Kane had found God. He'd been forgiven, but he'd never been able to forgive himself.

His hands tightened on the steering wheel, his heart pounding painfully.

That summer had altered the course of his life for the

better. He knew that. But he'd still give anything to go back, to change what had happened, to make a different decision. He'd lived with those regrets for thirteen years. He definitely didn't need any more.

The drive into Cape Cod took longer than it should have. Sudden winds and icy snow hampered their progress along I-93. The blinding, relentless storm didn't let up for more than an hour.

Arden was silent for most of the four-hour ride.

She'd handed him cash when he'd stopped in a small town to fill the tank, asked once how many miles stood between them and the Cape. Other than that, she didn't speak.

Though she'd dozed on and off, she'd stayed awake for the majority of the trip. He felt her tension as he crept along the nearly empty highway. He hoped she wasn't planning her escape.

She could plan all she wanted, but she wasn't going to succeed. The more he knew about what she'd gotten herself into, the more dangerous it seemed. She needed help and protection. Whether she wanted to admit it or not.

"We'll be at the cottage in less than ten minutes," he said quietly, and she opened her eyes, straightening in her seat and stretching a kink in her neck. Sebastian protested as she disturbed his sleep.

"Silly boy," she said, patting the cat's fuzzy head. "I'm sorry I woke you. Just a little while longer and you'll be able to freely roam about for a bit."

"He's been a pretty good traveling companion."

"Running-for-our-lives companion is more like it. I should have left him at home, but I'd have had to ask someone to watch him, and that would have meant explaining why I needed to leave. Plus, he'd have missed me."

"And you'd have missed him?"

"Of course. Aside from my dad and brothers, he's the only guy who's ever been loyal to me." She must have realized what she said. "What I mean is, he and I have been buddies for a long time."

"Randy isn't loyal?" he asked, not really surprised and not really disappointed that she must have finally seen the guy for what he was. Kane had met him a couple of times, and that had been a couple of times too many. The guy was an arrogant blowhard who seemed to get a kick out of poking fun at Arden. All Arden's brothers had thought the same.

"He's not part of my life anymore, so how about we change the subject?"

"To?"

"The weather seems like a safe choice. The storm is breaking. It should be a good night for coding."

"Or sleeping," he suggested.

"I'm too wound up, and I'm way too close to accessing what's in those files."

She leaned her forehead against the window as they crawled through town. The roads were lightly layered with snow, the businesses decorated for the season with bright lights, wreaths and ribbon. "I've never been to Cape Cod, but I like it. They know how to do Christmas right."

"So there's a way to do that?"

"Sure." She pointed at several pine trees decorated with colored lights and red bows. "That's the right way. Bright. Fun. Happy."

"I'll take your word for it."

"You're not a Grinch are you?"

"What?"

"A Scrooge? A Christmas curmudgeon?"

"I like Christmas as much as the next person," he said, turning onto a side road that would bring them closer to the beach.

"You don't sound very enthusiastic about it."

"My family never made that big of a deal about the holidays."

"No big family celebrations when you were a kid?"

"I mostly celebrated with my grandparents. It was nice. Quiet. A good meal and a couple of gifts." And parents who'd called around noon to ask if he liked whatever they'd given him.

Kane could only remember one or two times that his parents had been home during the holidays. Even then, they'd shipped him to his grandparents during his school breaks and joined him on Christmas Day.

"That sounds…lonely."

"It wasn't. I always had a good time. My grandparents were great."

"Did they raise you?"

"Mostly. What they didn't do, boarding school took care of. My parents were busy."

"Doing what?"

"Being internationally renowned geneticists. They spent a lot of time traveling to hospitals, labs and universities." He turned onto Sea Street and followed it to the end. His grandparents' 1835 cottage sat on two acres there. Surrounded by tall evergreen trees on three sides, it was bordered on the fourth by a sandy section of beach. He'd spent a lot of time there. He thought he knew it and remembered it well, but it looked different now—the cottage more quaint than he remembered, the yard larger.

"Is this it?" Arden asked as he pulled into the snow-covered drive.

"Yes."

"It's cute. It would be even cuter with some Christmas lights, a Nativity scene, a wreath."

He followed the driveway around to the back of the house, driving under the boughs of an overgrown spruce. Everything was locked up for the winter. His parents used the place a few times a year. Usually in the summer and spring. Other than that, it stayed empty, the skeleton key that opened the back door hidden in a faux rock that sat at the edge of the flower bed.

He pulled up to the detached garage. A motion-activated light above the garage door flicked on and illuminated the area. There were no footprints in the pristine snow, no tire tracks on the paved drive. Kane cut the engine.

"Here's how it's going to go," he said, reaching over the seat and grabbing Arden's backpack. "We'll go in the back door. You'll stay in the house. I'll get the key for the garage and move the truck into it."

"Okay," she responded.

"You're agreeing that easily?" he asked. He eyed the back of the cottage. His grandmother's gnome was still standing guard in the barren flower bed. Beside it, the cement birdbath stood empty. The place had an air of neglect that bothered him. Sure, it was still charming but in a few years, it would look like so many forgotten properties—lonely and old.

"Of course. I've got work to do, remember?"

He remembered. He also remembered that she didn't want to go back to her family. She didn't want other people involved in her trouble, and she'd been wanting to lose him since the moment he'd found her.

He grabbed his duffel as well, and got out of the truck, listening to the winter silence. Cape Cod was busy in the summer, but this time of year, it quieted down. Mostly locals and a few die-hard visitors who loved the beach in the winter.

"It's quiet," Arden whispered as she climbed out of the truck, Sebastian in her arms.

"The quieter the better," he responded. He put a hand on her back and urged her to the rear stoop. He stopped at the flower bed, lifting the rock his grandfather had bought decades ago. His grandmother used to constantly lock herself out of the house.

Thinking about what a great couple they'd been, how committed to each other and to their only daughter and to him, made him smile.

"Are you planning to break a window?" Arden asked, eyeing the rock as he turned it over in his hand. The compartment that housed the key opened easily, and he dumped the key into his palm.

"Not unless this key doesn't do its job."

"I hope it does. It's freezing out here."

"I can't promise it'll be any warmer in the house." He shoved the key into the lock and turned it. He opened the door and held it so that Arden could walk into the mudroom at the back of the house.

He followed her inside, pulling the door closed and turning the lock. The mudroom was small, the kitchen just beyond it pitch-black. He expected the place to have the closed-up musty smell of a house that hadn't been used in a while, but it smelled like…

Christmas?

Cinnamon for sure.

Pine.

Something else that he couldn't quite place. Cookies maybe. Or bread.

Whatever it was, it didn't belong. He grabbed Arden's arm, pulling her back.

"Something isn't right," he muttered, the hair on his nape standing on end. "We need to get out of here."

Too late.

A floorboard creaked and the kitchen light flicked on.

Kane stepped between Arden and the threat, dropping her pack and pulling his gun in one quick movement.

TEN

Arden had always wondered if a person's heart could actually stop from fear.

Now she knew.

It could.

Hers had.

It started again when a woman screamed, the high-pitched sound like a jolt of electricity to Arden's flagging cardiac muscle. Arden jumped, her grip on Sebastian loosening. Sebastian yowled and twisted out of her arms.

Arden grabbed for him. Missed. Started after him as he rushed across the room.

"Sebastian!" she yelled, her heart pounding over the sound of other voices.

"Stop!" Kane commanded, and Sebastian did, plopping his furry body down on a pretty throw rug near the kitchen sink. Arden skidded to a standstill a couple of inches from Sebastian.

"What in the world," a woman said, "is going on here?"

Arden whirled around, found herself three feet from an older couple. Flannel pajamas, bare feet, salt-and-pepper hair. They were a matched set. The man clutched a baseball bat. The woman held a huge tome that probably outweighed her by several pounds.

"Is that *The Iliad*?" Arden asked, and the woman glanced down at the book.

"Why, yes! It is," she responded.

"Light reading before bed, Mom?" Kane asked, slipping his gun back into the holster beneath his coat.

"Mom?" Arden repeated, but no one seemed all that interested in responding.

"This was one of your grandfather's books. It was the first thing I could find that could be used as a weapon." The woman set the book down on the counter. "We were certain we were about to get murdered in our beds."

"Except that we're not in our beds, dear," the man pointed out. He leaned the baseball bat against the wall and let it rest there. "We would have been murdered in the kitchen. It's good to see you, son. It's surprising, but good."

"I'm as surprised as you are." Kane ran a hand over his hair. "I thought you were overseas."

"We flew back a few days ago," the woman said, her gaze darting to Arden. "We got to our place and a pipe had burst. They're fixing it and drying everything out, so we decided to stay here until the work was finished. You did say that we could use the cottage any time."

"Right. I did."

"So…" Arden cut into what seemed like an awfully awkward conversation. Shouldn't they be hugging? Throwing themselves into each other's arms and talking about how much they'd missed each other? "I guess these are your parents?"

"Julia and Henry Walker," Kane said. "Mom and Dad, this is Arden DeMarco."

"DeMarco…" Mr. Walker mused. "Why do I know that name?"

"Because my business partner is Jace DeMarco, Arden's…"

"No, no. That's not it," Mrs. Walker interjected. "Remember, Henry? That paper we read on quantum computing?"

"Oh, that's right! Superb work. Real cutting-edge stuff." Mr. Walker smiled broadly. "Are you *that* Arden DeMarco?"

"Yes," she admitted, surprised that they'd read any of her work. "It was part of my dissertation."

"Your theory on error-correction algorithms was groundbreaking. Were you really able to use only four qubits?"

"To a point," Arden answered. "Unfortunately, as you are probably aware, interference is still an issue, even with the use of trapped ion qubits with intense magnetic fields."

"So true, yet the technology is promising," Mrs. Walker added, smoothing her hair and smiling at her son. "Kane, we're infringing on your time with your *friend*. Your father and I will pack our things and go to a hotel."

"Why would we do that? This place is plenty big enough for all of us, and I want to talk to Arden about her research," Mr. Walker said.

"As do I, but I think that Arden and Kane would prefer to talk to each other."

"Statistically speaking, after traveling here together, they are probably both ready for a break from each other. Why, just yesterday, I read a study on couples. Genetics aside, we tend to be attracted to that which is both different and familiar." Mr. Walker was off chasing rabbits, and Arden had a moment of clarity, a moment of absolute vivid truth—Kane's parents? They were her flannel-clad, tome-carrying people.

"Wow," she breathed, and Kane grinned. He took her elbow and led her through the kitchen and out into a cozy living room.

"I figured you'd like them," he murmured, his lips so close to her ear that she could feel the warmth of his breath.

"I like you, too," she responded, the words out before she could stop them. Her cheeks were suddenly hot. "What I mean—"

"Don't ruin the moment," he replied, smiling.

And she couldn't make herself say what she'd been going to. Not while she was looking into his gold-flecked eyes, seeing the humor there.

"How far did you two travel today? Miles or kilometers is fine," Mrs. Walker said.

"Longer than either of us planned to, Mrs. Walker," Arden said. As much as she loved talking shop and chasing intellectual rabbits, she was more interested in decrypting files, finding her answers and shutting down GeoArray. "I'm exhausted," she added. Just in case the older woman hadn't gotten the hint.

"Call me Jules. And my husband answers to Henry. Your father and I are in the room at the top of the stairs, Kane. That leaves the blue room and the yellow."

"Let's give Arden the yellow," Kane said.

"It *is* the larger of the two." Henry stepped into the room, Arden's backpack over his shoulders, Sebastian cradled in his arms. "My son has always been a gentleman. Is that one of the things that attracted you to him?"

"We're not—"

"Henry! What a thing to ask!"

"It's a valid question, honey. Remember that piece we read two months ago?" Henry started upstairs, continuing on about the article as he went. Jules followed, the two of them batting around statistics.

Henry disappeared into a room down a wide hallway and reappeared at the top of the stairs seconds later without Sebastian or the backpack. "Do you need me to grab luggage from your car?" he asked.

Kane shook his head. "I'll take care of it."

"Then I'll head to bed. You know how I've always been. Early to bed and early to rise. Statistically speaking, people who live by that pattern have longer, healthier lives." Henry offered them a quick smile and went into his room.

"I really need to turn in, too," Jules said. "The bathroom is at the end of the hall, Arden. Linen closet is stocked with toiletries if you forgot anything."

She'd *forgotten* everything.

She couldn't tell Jules that, so she just nodded and smiled and said good-night. She followed Kane up the stairs, past the Walkers' bedroom door to her own room. The room was large, with a full-size bed, dresser, single nightstand and one window facing the front of the house.

It was definitely called the yellow room for a reason. Pale yellow walls and white bedding with yellow and orange flowers and throw pillows screamed of an era long gone. A yellow area rug under the bed covered most of the scratched wood floor.

She sat on the bed. "The room's been aptly named."

Kane stood at the threshold of the room, watching as she pulled her laptop from the backpack that Henry had left on the bed.

"It lacks a yellow brick road, but I hope it will do."

She laughed. "Well, there's no place like home, but this does have a homey feel."

He smiled. "My parents being here complicates things."

"Should we leave?"

"We're both running on fumes, so it's best if we stay, at least for the night. Hopefully, they won't call the neighbors to brag about their houseguest and her dissertation work."

She laughed and flicked on her computer. Her mind was already sprinting ahead, working through the files. She wouldn't work yet, though.

Kane was correct—his parents being in the house added a whole new dimension to the problem. She definitely did not want them pulled into the mess she was in. There was no time to convince Kane to let her walk away. But this cottage just might offer her an unexpected chance to give Kane the slip. She'd let him think she was working, let him get settled in. Once he was asleep, she'd take Sebastian and go.

It was safer for everyone that way.

"You laugh, but the guy who lives at the end of the street is an astrophysicist. He'd love to meet you, and my parents would love to be the ones to make the introduction."

"I'm sure they mean well."

"They do, but we need to be as unobtrusive as possible."

"You do realize they think we're dating, don't you?" Arden asked.

"Yes. There's no sense arguing with them. They hear what they want to hear, especially at two in the morning." Kane gave her an easy smile and leaned against the doorframe.

Tall and muscular, he exuded confidence, affability and strength. They were a winning combination, and if she let herself, she could imagine seeing him at her family's Christmas celebration again this year. Instead of pretending to hang on every word Randy spoke, she'd be doing her own thing, free to talk to whomever she wanted.

"You're staring," he said. His hair was just long enough to curl at his nape, his eyes a light brown that looked almost gold in the soft yellow light.

"Sorry. I was zoning out." And being an idiot. Kane probably dated models and actresses and NFL cheerleaders. Not geeky computer experts.

"It's been a long day. A little zoning out is to be expected."

"A long couple of weeks," she admitted.

"Things will get easier from here. My associate, Silas Blackwater, can help us with GeoArray. I've already asked him to handle the plane."

"Teamwork is great, but this part—" she tapped her computer keyboard "—is something only I can do."

"Why you?" he asked, and she realized she'd said too much.

"I've been doing this for years," she hedged. She focused on the still-blank screen and pretended to type.

"You obviously aren't working, Arden. And you obviously aren't telling the truth."

"I *have* been doing this for years."

"Lots of people work in computer forensics. Lots of people know how to decrypt files. If you turned the files over to the FBI, they could put a team of people on it. It seems like that might be more effective. What is it about this encryption that makes it so difficult?" He sounded angry. She couldn't blame him. He'd risked his life for her, and she was withholding information from him.

His eyes never left hers as he waited for her response, the silence in the air heavy between them.

"It's complicated," she began, still hesitant to let him in.

"Try me."

"Aside from the person who encrypted the files, there's likely no one who can decrypt them as quickly as I'll be able to."

"Okay, I'll take the bait—why?"

"Because I developed the base encryption code that's wrapped around the files." She saw the surprise register in his eyes. Wished she could stop his next question before he said it.

"How did your code end up around those files?"

There it was. She could either lie or let him in on what a sham her relationship with Randy had been. As mortifying as the truth was, she couldn't bring herself to lie to him. Randy had used her. The facts were the facts. There was no use sugarcoating it. "Because when Randy and I worked at the university together, he had access to my research, stole my code, then passed it off as his own."

"Your boyfriend?"

"*Ex*-boyfriend," she corrected.

"Does he work for GeoArray?"

"He's apparently a consultant for them now. A very highly paid consultant."

"Which probably means they're willing to pay a hefty price to ensure the security of those files."

"Exactly," Arden agreed. "I think those files are somehow connected with GeoArray's one-hundred-million-dollar contract to design and build a self-improving weapons command and control prototype."

"Self-improving?"

"In the loose sense of the word, it means artificial intelligence or machine learning."

"I thought that was mostly academic conjecture?"

"It has been, but inroads have been made lately. For instance, in credit card fraud recognition programs. The concepts are definitely becoming more mainstream."

"So this application will do what?"

"Without getting my hands on the research, I can't know for sure, but there are numerous possibilities. It could be programmed to learn if-then scenarios to have weapons change course after launch based on real-time data."

"So that means a nuclear missile, for instance, could be made to abort or self-detonate?"

"Yes. It could even change targets on its own based on the programmed scenarios."

"That could be catastrophic."

"I agree—a system like that could turn one of our weapons against an ally or ourselves."

"Do you think they may be close to completing the application?"

"The government picked up the contract's option years last October without recompeting it—" she stifled a yawn "—so there's a pretty good chance that's the case."

"You're probably right." Kane straightened. "But maybe you should think about getting some rest tonight. Start fresh in the morning. You might have better results."

"I won't work too long. I just want to try something I've been thinking about," she said.

He started to leave, but turned back. "Remember, we're in this together now. You worry about decrypting those files and I'll take care of everything else."

"Got it," she said to his back as he closed the bedroom door behind him. Kane said all the right things, but she knew what she had to do. In the long run, everyone would be safer once she dropped off the grid again.

She was going to try to leave.

There was absolutely no doubt in Kane's mind about that.

He was going to stop her. There was no doubt about that, either. Whether or not she'd still like him when it was over? That was something that remained to be seen.

He jogged downstairs, grabbing the keys to the garage from the hook near the front door. His grandfather had made a habit of putting the keys there to help his grandmother. She'd always been forgetful, but things had been worse during the last decade of her life.

I can't have my best friend feeling bad about forgetting, so let's make it easier for her to remember.

Kane could almost hear his grandfather's words ringing through the quiet house. They'd been a team, putting up the key hooks, purchasing a high-tech oven that turned itself off if left on for too long.

He'd not thought much of it then, but looking back on it he could see that those times with his grandparents had shaped the man he would become. It was fact that he'd spent the first seventeen years of his life running after acceptance and popularity and fun. But that summer before his senior year had changed all that.

It had been a typical Friday night. Evan was stuck watching his siblings while his mom worked a second job. Kane insisted a party would be a good idea. By the time they'd found Lexi in the pool, it was too late.

That decision haunted him. Now he chased after things that had meaning and eternal value. But Kane had long ago resigned himself to the fact that he'd likely never find that one person who would fill his heart with joy.

I like you, Kane, Arden had said. For some reason, that meant more to him than any compliment he'd ever received from any woman he'd ever dated.

Maybe because she'd said it without any desire for reciprocation. She hadn't asked for a response. She hadn't seemed to even want one. She'd simply been stating another one of her facts.

He frowned, stepping outside and letting the cold, crisp air fill his lungs. He could smell the ocean in it, the briny water and moist air. He'd always loved this place. Even tainted by the memories of what he'd done, it felt more like home than any other place ever had.

He crossed the yard and unlocked the two-bay garage. His parents' car was on the left. The right bay was empty, his grandparents' old Chrysler long gone. He pulled the truck into place, then took out his cell phone and tried to reach Silas again.

This time Silas picked up.

"Silas, we've got a problem." Kane explained Arden's theory as succinctly as he could. If what Arden believed was true, keeping her safe while she decrypted the files had become more than just a personal mission. It was a matter of national security. As was his way, Silas listened without commenting, until Kane was through.

After they discussed their next move, Kane hung up, satisfied backup was on its way. He'd have called Grayson, but that was too dangerous. He couldn't risk his call being intercepted by the Feds. He'd promised Arden the time she needed to decrypt those files.

He tucked the phone into his pocket, got out of the truck and closed the garage door.

One less thing to worry about.

A few dozen more to take care of.

Like his parents.

He glanced up at the cottage, eyeing the window of their room. No light, and he assumed they'd done what they'd said they would and gone to bed.

Tomorrow morning would be soon enough to ask them to keep quiet about his "girlfriend." Hopefully, they'd cooperate.

Hopefully, they wouldn't ask a million questions.

He didn't want to lie, but there was no way he could tell them the truth without endangering them.

He did a perimeter check of the property, the velvety silence of the early morning enveloping him. No sign of movement on the street in front of the house. Nothing to the rear. No lights. No vehicles. There was no reason to believe they'd been found, and every reason to believe they would be eventually.

Their time was limited by that, and by whatever was in those files.

He reached the area of the cottage beneath Arden's window. She'd turned off her light. Maybe she thought that he'd assume she was asleep. Maybe she just hoped it.

No sense making her wait too long to try her escape.

He went back inside and walked up the steps loudly enough for her to hear. Opened and closed the door to his room with just enough force to be convincing.

Once the sounds settled into quiet, he walked back downstairs, avoiding the creaky tread on the third and fifth steps, the groaning floorboard near the kitchen. He pulled a chair away from the table where he'd once eaten breakfast, lunch and dinner with his grandparents and sat, waiting for Arden to make her move.

ELEVEN

Arden's eyes drifted shut for what seemed like the fifteenth time in as many minutes. She forced them open again and got to her feet. It was now or never. If she didn't make her escape, she'd accidentally fall asleep and lose the opportunity.

She strapped on Sebastian's carrier, then slipped into her coat. Shrugging the straps of the pack onto her shoulders, she glanced at the antique clock sitting on the dresser. Nearly three in the morning. The house had been quiet for almost an hour.

Time to go, but she really didn't want to.

Being part of a team working to take down GeoArray seemed so much easier than going it alone. But Kane's parents were now in the equation. Two people were already dead. She couldn't risk more lives.

Arden plucked Sebastian from his cozy spot between the pillows and deposited him in the carrier.

She crossed the room in darkness, cracked open the door. Head cocked, she strained to hear signs that her movement had disturbed anyone. Hearing nothing, she stepped into the hallway, keeping close to the walls and praying she could avoid the groans and creaks from the old, worn floor.

At the top of the stairwell, she paused and peered down into the darkness below. With Kane's room toward the rear of the house, the front door gave her the highest probability of slipping out unheard. Of course, once she got the truck started, he'd wake up.

If she got it started.

She'd read about hot-wiring cars. So she had all the steps memorized, but she'd never done it.

She crept silently down the steps, crossed the foyer and fumbled with the lock on the front door. Turning the handle, she slowly eased the door open and looked out into the dark morning. It would be hours before the sun rose. That gave her time to make her way back through town and out onto the interstate again before the town woke. The less people who knew she'd been there, the safer it would be for Kane's parents.

She'd find a place somewhere far away, she'd decrypt the files, and then she'd pass the information to Grayson and let him take it from there.

First, though, she had to get the truck started.

She scanned the yard and the street beyond it. Everything looked just like it had when they'd arrived—pristine snow blanketing grass and driveway. Across the street, a pretty little cottage was tucked away from the road, the lights off, the driveway empty. There was an SUV parked on the street in front of it. Had it been there when they'd arrived?

She couldn't remember seeing any vehicles on the street, but she'd been tired and distracted. She leaned farther out the door, staring hard at the SUV and the shadowed driver's window.

Was someone in there?

The vehicle's door swung open and a man got out. He stood near the driver's door, looking in her direction.

There were no streetlights, no moonglow, nothing to illuminate his face or eyes. But she was absolutely sure he was looking right at her. And she was absolutely positive he was about to head her way.

He took the first step, and she jumped back into the house, knocking into something firm and warm.

A hand slammed over her mouth.

She screamed.

Or tried. All that came out was a muffled squeak. An arm slid around her waist, and Sebastian—traitor that he was—started purring.

"Not a good idea, Arden," Kane said quietly.

Because, of course, it was Kane.

He'd set her up. He'd known she was going to try to leave, and he'd given her the opportunity.

She shoved his hand away, whirling to face him. Angry that he'd made her look like a fool. Terrified that guy who'd been crossing the street was still coming.

"There's someone out there," she managed to say, her voice shaking with emotion.

"I know," he said simply. "That's Silas Blackwater. He's Jace's and my business partner."

"You could have warned me about him before I opened the door. It would have saved my heart some effort," she snapped, and he frowned.

"You're angry."

"Of course I am. You made a fool out of me." She *was* angry. She'd lost count of the number of times Randy had made her feel the fool. "You pretended you believed me, made a big show about your nighttime routine, then sneaked down here and basically lay in wait for me when all you needed to do was—"

"Stop," he interrupted, pressing three fingers gently to her lips. "First of all, I only found out an hour ago that Silas decided to head to the Cape rather than New Hampshire. Second, it would be impossible to make you look like a fool. You're too intelligent to ever be mistaken for one." He dropped his hand from her mouth, stepped closer and removed Sebastian from his carrier. The little Judas purred loudly as Kane scratched behind his ears.

"And lastly, I didn't tell you I was onto you because that wouldn't have stopped you from hatching your next plan. You're too determined. You know what you're up against and you don't want to put anyone else in danger. Not Juniper, my parents or me. That's one of the things I admire about you. But I needed you to understand that you won't be able to slip away from me. We're in this together. Whether you like it or not."

He set Sebastian on the floor. The cat wove between her legs, then Kane's, before climbing the stairs toward the yellow room without so much as a backward glance.

Arden's anger started to melt away. He'd just spent an entire night up close and personal with all her little foibles, yet he thought it would be impossible for her to look like a fool?

The door clicked shut softly behind her. Arden whirled around with a startled yelp and found herself face to chest with Kane's associate, his arms laden with kitty litter and a plastic shopping bag brimming with supplies. She was touched by Kane's thoughtfulness.

She took a step back, looked up into a pair of heavy-lidded green eyes. He was easily over six feet tall with straight black hair tied in a short, low ponytail. Lean and muscular, his swarthy skin, high cheekbones and aquiline nose all spoke to his Native American heritage.

"Sorry, I didn't hear you come up behind me," Arden said.

"You weren't supposed to," he said simply.

"This is Silas Blackwater. He's with us from now on." Kane's tone left no room for argument. He reached around Arden and took the shopping bag from Silas. "Now let's come up with a plan of action we can all agree on." He turned toward the kitchen, clearly expecting Arden to follow. With Silas behind her blocking the front door, she didn't have much choice.

If she was honest with herself, she was warming up to the idea of being part of a team. Maybe it was time she stopped relying on herself and started taking advantage of the resources God placed in front of her. And she couldn't deny that Kane made her feel safe. Like it was okay for her to be her. Like he wouldn't have it any other way.

She shrugged out of her pack and followed Kane into the kitchen. She'd give the whole team thing a shot, but first she needed to break the code that protected those files, and that was something she'd have to do alone.

Kane placed the bag on the table and started unloading the supplies. In addition to a plastic litter pan and a bag of cat food, he'd asked Silas to bring some breakfast food. He was pretty sure Arden must be starved. He knew he was. Kane pulled the last item from the bag, held it up and looked at Silas. "Hershey's Kisses?"

"Don't all girls like chocolate?" Silas shrugged.

"This one does," Arden piped up, snatching the bag

of assorted chocolate kisses from Kane's hand and ripping into it. "And I can definitely use the sugar right about now." She popped one in her mouth. "Mmm. So good. Thanks, Silas."

"No problem." Silas had the decency not to gloat as he placed the box of kitty litter on the floor. "Dutch is in the yard taking care of business," he said, walking toward the back door. "Do you mind if I let him in?"

"Go for it," Kane responded.

"Dutch?" Arden booted up her laptop and reached for another chocolate.

"My dog." Silas opened the back door and gave a piercing whistle. "He served in combat with us."

"He's retired?" Arden asked, typing on her keyboard.

"By default," Kane explained. "When Silas decided to get out, Dutch was supposed to be placed with another handler, but no one could get the Sioux commands quite right."

"At least that's the theory." Silas grinned. Dutch crossed the threshold into the kitchen. Silas shut the door behind him.

"Are you sure he's a dog?" Arden pulled her earbuds from her bag, eyeing Dutch from her seat at the kitchen table.

"He's a Czechoslovakian Wolfdog, to be exact." Silas gave a command in Sioux. The dog immediately lay on the rug by the back door.

"Looks like more wolf than dog to me," Arden mused before shoving the earbuds into her ears. "The chocolate's given me a renewed burst of energy. I'm going to see if I can get this algorithm working before dawn."

"I'm not sure if my parents had time to call and get

the Wi-Fi switched on yet, but you can use my cell phone as a hot spot if you'd like."

"The Wi-Fi's active," she responded, popping another chocolate into her mouth.

"Great, let me know if you need the password for it," Kane said.

"No need. I'm in already."

"How'd you get around the password?"

She met his eyes across the table. "Have you forgotten what I do for a living?"

Silas snickered.

"I just didn't realize you could hack in so quickly. You've only been sitting there for a few minutes."

"It's a known fact that people tend to choose passwords that are easy to remember and mean something to them. In this case, your last name, the word *home* and the house number were used. You should probably consider changing it."

"I'll do that," Kane responded drily, but Arden didn't seem to hear him. She was lost in her work, her jet-black, shoulder-length hair tucked casually behind her ear, thick-lashed eyes focused on the screen in front of her.

She was the exact opposite of every woman that had even remotely attracted him in the past, but he found himself drawn to her. She was extremely intelligent, but that was only part of the person she was.

Truth be told, she drew him in from the first time he met her, but his friendship with Jace and Arden's ever-present jerk of a boyfriend gave him plenty of reasons to tamp those feelings down. One of those reasons was now out of the picture. His friendship with Jace, on the other hand, would not be easy to get around.

Jace knew Kane before he became a Christian. He'd accepted him for all his past mistakes and helped him find his faith. But that didn't mean Jace would ever see Kane as good enough for his little sister. Kane wouldn't blame him there.

A rapid succession of buzzing tones came from Arden's laptop.

"That didn't sound promising," Kane commented.

"It's not great news, but on the plus side, I got past the first level of encryption. It's only a matter of time before I break the last."

He admired her confidence.

Nearly an hour later, Kane had filled Silas in on the events of the evening while making some breakfast sandwiches. Arden had scarfed down her food with a quick thanks, barely taking her eyes from the computer screen. Kane wondered about the progress she was making but didn't want to distract her from her task.

"Yes! Thank You, God!" Arden exclaimed happily.

"What?" Kane and Silas both came around the table and peered over her shoulder.

"My decryption application is loaded and ready to test." She stretched her arms and yawned. "We'll know in a few moments if it works." Her fingers ran over the keyboard. "Here goes nothing," she said and pressed Enter to launch the program.

"Is it working?" Silas asked.

"Yes. Yes. Yes!"

Kane tried to focus on the rows of code that scrolled quickly across the dark screen. He had no idea what he was looking at, but judging by her enthusiasm, he predicted success. "How long will it take to run?"

"It's almost complete." As if on cue, a tune erupted from the computer—a tune that sounded suspiciously like the fanfare in one of his retro video games that signaled a player had found an important item. Typical Arden. Kane couldn't help but smile.

Arden pulled up the first of the decrypted files and began reading. Kane and Silas attempted to read over her shoulder.

"I can't keep up. She's reading way too fast," Silas commented.

"I'm in the same boat," Kane said, still trying to skim the contents of the files as Arden clicked from page to page.

"Houston, we have a problem." Arden focused on the screen in front of her, still scrolling through documents.

"What is it?" Kane asked.

"Oh, no," she said flatly. She leveled her gaze on him and shut her laptop. "It's worse than I thought. Marcus Emory is not just selling research—he's planning to sell the code for the prototype of the self-improving weapons control program that GeoArray developed for the Department of Defense."

"To who?" Kane asked.

"It's not clear, but my guess is it's a foreign buyer. The first payment was wired to an offshore account about a month ago. The rest will be paid on delivery of the weapons control system. The trade is scheduled for two days from now. We don't have much time."

Kane thought Arden was probably spot-on. She'd been right to this point, so it was likely Marcus Emory was planning to sell United States secrets to the highest bidder. Likely a nation-state entity that could threaten world peace.

A low growl sounded from the corner. Dutch was standing alert by the back door. "Someone's out there," Silas whispered.

"Let's check it out."

Arden started to get up from the table.

"You stay here, Arden, and keep away from the windows," Kane said. "Silas and I will handle this."

For a moment, Arden looked ready to argue the point, but Kane decided to beat her to the punch. "Someone needs to remain here and be ready to warn my parents if needed."

"You're right, of course." She sat back down, began to pack her computer. "But just be careful."

Kane and Silas left through the front door.

"You take the left and I'll take the right." Kane was only slightly mollified by Arden's promise to stay put. He'd hated to leave her alone in the kitchen, but nothing else could be done.

Silas headed toward the front corner of the house, Dutch at his heels. Kane didn't bother to warn him to keep quiet. If Silas didn't want you to hear him coming, you wouldn't.

Kane saw fresh footprints in the snow leading to the back of the house. Someone was here.

He slipped around the corner, saw a shadowy figure advancing toward the kitchen window, something dark in his hand. A gun?

Kane rushed forward and tackled him, the impact sending them both reeling into the side of the house. Something black fell from the man's hand. Kane jumped up and grabbed for it. A tactical flashlight? Oh, boy.

Within seconds, Silas and Dutch were at his side.

Kane shined his light on the man who was still sprawled facedown in the snow.

Silas turned him over. Snow coated the man's uniform and stuck to his face. "You just knocked out a cop, bro."

Kane looked at the nametag on the man's department-issued jacket. Deputy C. Moran. Great.

"Deputy Moran, this is dispatch. Please report findings from the Walker place. Over." A woman's voice crackled through the radio holstered to the officer's belt. Kane looked at Silas, whose expression likely mirrored Kane's thoughts. Not good. "Deputy Moran, do you copy? Over."

"We need to get your girl and book it before dispatch sends backup. I'm guessing that the local cops are checking out the place as a favor to the FBI. It probably won't be long before either GeoArray or the FBI show up."

Kane had been thinking the same thing. The FBI had somehow connected him to the plane. The Cape was no longer safe for any of them. He handed the flashlight to Silas and hoisted the deputy on his shoulder.

"What are we going to do with him?"

"I haven't thought that far ahead, but we can't just leave him here in below-freezing temperatures. Let's get him to the house."

TWELVE

Three minutes, ten seconds.

Three minutes, eleven seconds.

Arden watched the second hand on the old grandmother clock creep to twelve, thirteen, fourteen.

Every second seemed like an eternity. Every minute that passed brought them closer to disaster. Someone had been outside. Silas's dog had made that clear. If it were one of GeoArray's thugs, there'd be more assassins waiting in the shadows.

She shuddered, sliding the laptop back in her pack. Now she understood why GeoArray had been so desperate to retrieve the files and stop her from opening them.

She understood, and it terrified her.

There had to be a way to keep them from releasing the information, and she planned to find it. Standing around waiting for Kane and Silas to return wasn't helping her do that.

Besides, she wasn't just terrified. She was worried.

Logically, she knew that Kane and Silas didn't need her help, but logic had nothing to do with the heart. And her heart was telling her they might be in trouble, that even with all their combined training and expertise, they might have run into a situation they couldn't get out of.

She grabbed the baseball bat that Henry had abandoned earlier and walked to the back door. She peered out the little window beside it.

The light above the garage door was still glowing, illuminating footprints and tire tracks left in the snow. A shadow moved near the corner of the garage, and a man appeared. Tall. Broad shoulders. Moving toward the house, a dog beside him.

Silas. It had to be. The dog wouldn't be walking beside anyone else.

She unlocked the door and stepped onto the back stoop, still clutching the baseball bat.

"Where's Kane?" she asked, and Silas gestured toward the back corner of the house.

"Coming. You need to get your things. We need to move out."

"My things are ready to go." She stepped back as he walked up the steps, crowding into her space and making no apology for it.

"Go back inside, Arden. It isn't safe out here."

"Did you find the person who was out there?" she asked, peering around him and finally catching a glimpse of Kane.

He was moving across the yard, something flung over his shoulder. A bag of some sort? An animal?

The closer he got, the more it looked like…

A person?

"In the house," Silas repeated, and somehow he had her moving backward, across the threshold and into the mudroom.

Once she was inside, he moved past her, the dog trotting along beside him.

Seconds later, Kane appeared in the doorway.

"You were supposed to stay inside," he growled. He closed the door with a little more force than she thought was necessary.

"Shh!" she cautioned. "You're going to wake up your parents."

"You were supposed to stay inside," he repeated, his eyes flashing with irritation as he strode past. The person he was carrying hung limply over his shoulder.

A man.

She could see that now.

In a police uniform.

"Is he dead?" she asked as Kane set the guy in a chair.

"No." Kane's response was terse. He grabbed Arden's backpack and was sliding into it. "Did you leave anything upstairs?"

"Just Sebastian. I'll get him. He's not going to be happy when I put him back in the carrier. I think he's sick of traveling. Cats aren't known for being fond of it. I read an interesting article about—"

The floorboards in front of the kitchen doorway creaked, cutting off the rest of whatever babbling diatribe Arden had been about to deliver.

Nerves.

Because she knew Kane was upset, because there was an unconscious police officer in a chair at the kitchen table, because everything was riding on them being able to stop GeoArray before the company transferred the system to a buyer and she was scared they wouldn't get the opportunity.

"What's going on?" Henry asked, walking into the kitchen. Jules was right behind him. "Why is Chuck Moran here?" His focus jumped from the officer to Silas. "And who are you?"

"Silas is my business associate," Kane explained, taking the baseball bat from Arden's hand and setting it on the table. "The officer ran into some trouble."

"What kind of trouble?" Jules hurried across the room, lifting the officer's wrist and checking his pulse.

"He was outside the house. I thought he was trying to break in. I knocked him out before I realized he was law enforcement."

"Did you also think he had something to do with whatever Arden has gotten herself involved in?" Jules asked.

Arden met Kane's eyes. He looked as surprised as she felt.

"What are you talking about, Mom?" he asked.

"Arden was on the evening news last night. That's one of the reasons why Henry and I remembered that article so well. Right, honey?" She plugged in the coffeepot and filled the reservoir.

"Right. They even had a picture of you, Arden. Apparently, the FBI has you on its most wanted list. Someone spotted you at an airport in Maine. I heard your name and remembered you from that article, so I looked it up online to refresh my memory. Very interesting read, Arden. Very interesting."

"Why," Kane began, and Arden thought he was doing everything in his power to hold onto his patience, "was the local evening news running a story about Arden, Dad?"

"It was a short piece, really. Simply said the FBI

believed Arden to be traveling with an unknown male companion and that they were likely headed toward Massachusetts and one or both could be armed. Once you showed up here, we realized that the FBI was totally wrong about whatever they think Arden did. You have too much integrity and honor to ever get involved with someone who deserves a spot on the most wanted list, Kane."

"So you didn't call the police?" Kane asked, glancing at the officer.

"Good gravy train! Why would we do something like that?" Jules exclaimed. "We trust you to know what's going on and to find a way out of it."

"That's not going to happen if we stay here much longer," Silas grumbled.

"Right. Logic dictates that if there's one police officer here, more are probably coming," Henry said. "You three go do what you need to do. We'll take care of Chuck."

"If he realizes we were here, you both could be in trouble," Kane warned.

"He's still out cold. We'll wake him up after you leave and tell him we heard a noise and went out to investigate. That we found him unconscious in the snow, poor man, and dragged him into the house out of the cold."

"He's going to ask about me," Kane said.

"We haven't seen you and have no idea what's going on." Jules pulled a bag of corn from the freezer.

"And that last part, of course, is true. We're clueless. When it's all over, I hope you'll fill us in." Henry took Arden's arm and walked her through the mudroom to the back door.

"I need to get Sebastian," she said, pulling away and not promising anything. She wasn't sure if she'd be able to tell the Walkers what was going on. She wasn't even sure if she'd see them again.

"The cat? Is he really going to want to ride in the car with that dog?" Henry asked.

"He's not going to have a choice."

"He will if you leave him with us. We'll take good care of him until you return," Henry offered.

"I can't. He'll think I abandoned him." Arden turned, ready to get Sebastian, but Kane blocked her path.

His expression was grim. "Chuck is starting to come to. We need to move out."

"I *need* to get Sebastian."

"I know you love the cat, Arden, but you're going to have to make a decision here." He opened the back door, letting cold air blow into the mudroom. "You walk back into the kitchen, and you're going to be seen by a guy who is going to be happy to tell every police officer in the area that you were here. There'll be blockades up from here to Boston, and we'll be fortunate to make it onto the interstate before we're caught."

He was right.

She knew it.

She still didn't want to leave Sebastian.

"Arden?" He touched her cheek, and she found herself looking into his eyes. Found herself thinking about all the ways he and his parents could be hurt if she was caught.

She loved Sebastian, but he'd be fine without her for a few days.

"Okay."

He smiled, tucking a strand of hair behind her ear,

his fingers lingering for a moment. She could still feel their warmth after he stepped away, after they walked outside, after they climbed into the back seat of Silas's vehicle.

That should have bothered her.

It should have made her nervous. It should have set off alarms and warning bells, made her toss up walls and create boundaries.

Should have, but all it really did was make her wonder why she'd spent so much time with Randy when he'd never ever made her feel what Kane did.

"Where to?" Silas asked as he started the engine and pulled away from the house.

She hadn't thought about it. Not much. She'd been too busy thinking about decrypting the files, escaping GeoArray, outwitting the FBI.

Now, though, she'd accomplished her first goal. She knew what GeoArray planned. She also knew exactly what she needed to do to stop it.

"Boston," she answered. "We need to get into Geo-Array's offices and take down its network before the system prototype is transferred in two days."

"No way." Kane didn't hesitate. He didn't think it through. He didn't need to. There was no way he was bringing Arden anywhere near GeoArray.

"Hear me out, Kane," she said calmly.

"I'm listening." But listening didn't mean he was going along with her plan.

"The day after tomorrow, GeoArray is getting paid to deliver the weapons control system. Once that's leaked, our own weapons systems can be used against us and our allies. We need to take down GeoArray's network system to prevent that from happening."

"Then remotely log onto the network and take it down. You hacked in before, you can do it again."

"I can't. Once I took the files from their network, they knew it had been breached. They took their system off the net. It's completely inaccessible to anyone outside their facility."

"So we'll take the information to the FBI and let them handle it."

"They may not be able to get a search warrant quickly enough to give them time to stop this from going down," she argued. "Plus, we know Emory has the FBI's ear. Someone could tip him off. By the time they get into the GeoArray systems, the information could be out, and our national defense will be compromised."

"They'll move quickly. They'll have to. We take the evidence to Grayson, he'll know who to trust," Kane said grimly.

"Even then, the government doesn't always move quickly," Silas said. "I'm going to have to take Arden's side on this. We should move in now while there's still time. Take GeoArray by surprise."

"I disagree," Kane argued. "There has to be another way."

"There isn't. If I'd had time to leave a worm while I accessed their system, I could have wiped out their network. Unfortunately, their network monitoring system found me too quickly. There is absolutely no way to wipe out that system except from the inside. We go in, or we allow the country's entire defense system to be vulnerable."

"Then you tell us how to do it. Silas and I will go in. You call the shots via phone."

"Statistically speaking, there's more chance of a meteorite falling on GeoArray and taking out the system than there is of that plan succeeding."

"Ouch!" Silas said. "You don't have much confidence in us."

"I have plenty of confidence in you, but this will only succeed if we work together. If you go it alone, you'll be in enemy territory, talking to me over a phone, trying to do something it took years for me to learn. All I need you to do is get me in the building. I can do the rest."

She had a point.

Kane didn't want to admit it.

But they'd need to get in and get out quickly and silently. Stay under the radar. That would be hard to do while trying to communicate with someone on the outside.

"Fine. You win."

"I do?" She sounded shocked.

"Why are you surprised?"

"Because I haven't won a debate with you yet."

"There's a first for everything."

She smiled and leaned her head back against the seat, sighing.

"Tired?"

"No. Just enjoying the victory." She met his eyes, and he found himself smiling right back at her, because she was Arden. She loved cats and Christmas and her country. She was smart, quick-minded and honest as they come, and he liked that. He liked her, and he was starting to think he could feel a lot more than that if he let himself.

"No one should be claiming victory yet. Not until we've gotten in and out of GeoArray without getting ourselves killed," Silas muttered, merging onto the highway.

"You have a point," Arden agreed. "We can't just waltz in the front door and demand access to the server."

"Once we get to Boston, we may be able to track down the blueprint of the building and get an idea of what access we can use." Kane could think of a dozen areas that were probably weak in security: upper level windows, ventilation systems, delivery bays.

One of his company's specialties was identifying physical security weaknesses for clients and shoring them up. Most companies didn't bother hiring outside experts, though. Most thought their security could never be breached.

Most were wrong.

"We can probably do that now." Arden tugged at the strap of her backpack. Kane hadn't removed it when he'd gotten in Silas's SUV. He'd been in too much of a hurry to bother. "Hand me my laptop. I can take a look through city records and see what I can find. I'm sure there's a digital file of it somewhere."

He shrugged out of the pack and pulled out the computer.

Seconds later, she had it open, booted up and connected to the internet through her wireless network card.

They bounced over a rut in the road, but she didn't seem to notice. She also didn't seem to notice the landscape changing, the lights of the city shining in the distance, time passing. She was completely engrossed in what she was doing, and he let her be.

He had things to do, too. Plans to make.

They'd go into GeoArray together. They'd come out together.

That was the goal, but anything could happen.

The company had money, resources and a lot to lose if they were unable to deliver the information in those files. If something were to happen that prevented Arden from taking down the server, GeoArray would successfully pass on information vital to national security.

Kane couldn't let that happen. He couldn't take a chance that they'd fail and that the secrets they'd discovered would be kept. And of course he wanted to clear Arden's name. Give her life back to her and have her home in time to enjoy Christmas with her family.

He had every reason to succeed and he had no intention of dying before he completed the mission. He had no intention of allowing Arden or Silas to die, either. But he'd be foolish if he let them walk into GeoArray without a backup plan.

He couldn't call in the local authorities. They'd stop the operation before it began. He couldn't contact the FBI for the same reason.

He *could* contact Grayson, though. But not yet. Not until right before they went in. He'd need to convince Arden to email him the files, too. That was the only way to be sure the information would get into the hands of someone who would know what to do with it if the mission went south.

THIRTEEN

They reached Boston in less than two hours. Gray morning light filtered through thick clouds and between tall buildings as they crawled through rush hour traffic.

Arden had spent every minute of the drive searching the internet for the blueprints of GeoArray's building. She'd finally hacked into City Hall's database and was searching through a disorganized mess of file folders.

Her eyes were gritty with fatigue, her mind numb. She'd been on the go for days, running on adrenaline and not much else. She couldn't remember the last time she'd closed her eyes. Aside from the breakfast sandwich Kane had made her, she couldn't recall eating anything in the past forty-eight hours.

Yeah. She was a mess.

A mess who had to take down GeoArray's server system in a few hours. She scowled, scrolling through the City Hall files. Her neck felt stiff from too many hours hunched over the computer, and she rubbed the knotted muscles.

"It's got to be here," she muttered, annoyed with the amount of time the search was taking. Usually, she was fast. Then again, usually she wasn't working on no sleep.

"Why don't you take a break, Arden?" Kane asked, turning in his seat to look at her. She looked up, met his warm brown eyes and for a moment was lost in the depth of them. "Arden?" he prodded, and she finally registered the question. She blinked back the exhaustion.

"I've almost got it."

"I'm pretty certain you said that thirty minutes ago," Silas said.

"Studies show that optimists live longer, healthier lives," she responded.

"They also show that people who go into enemy territory blind die." Silas pulled into a public parking garage, grabbed a ticket from the kiosk and tucked it into the glove compartment.

"Aren't you just a stream of warm sunshine on a dreary winter day?"

Kane laughed.

"She's got you pegged, Silas," he said.

"I'm a realist," Silas muttered. "There's nothing wrong with that. I'm thinking we ditch the floor plan idea and do some covert reconnaissance. One of us can do a perimeter search of the building. We might be able to locate an access point that way."

"Just give me another minute," Arden said. She scrolled through the files on another page, and her heart jumped when she finally found GeoArray's name.

She clicked the file, smiling as the blueprint popped up on the screen.

"Got it!" she nearly shouted.

"Can I take a look?" Kane reached through the center

console, pulled the computer from her lap. He studied the blueprint for several minutes, and she studied him.

She didn't mean to.

It just happened.

He was looking at the computer. She was looking at him.

He had a tiny scar above his left eyebrow and a larger one at the corner of his mouth. Both were faded white with time. Next thing she knew, she was noticing the thin white line that ran across the top of his right hand and the deep purplish mark on the side of his neck near his hairline.

He turned in his seat, caught her staring, and she was suddenly looking into his handsome face, his dark eyes. "Everything okay?" he asked.

She nodded, her cheeks hot. "Fine. I'm just tired. A habitual sleep pattern of seven to eight hours a night is thought to be best for peak cognitive performance. Of course, the amount can vary based on an individual's basal sleep need and sleep debt, as well as age. There's also a small percent of people that are their best with only six hours of sleep. It's been scientifically proven. When they exposed rats to high levels of stress and little sleep, they found they were less able to perform tasks."

"That's an interesting data point," he said without rolling his eyes, laughing or otherwise treating her like she was an idiot. She wasn't used to that. Aside from her family and Juniper, there weren't many people who didn't at least smirk when she went off on one of her tangents.

"It's just some silly trivia that I probably read a dozen years ago," she murmured.

"It's very relevant to our current situation," he corrected. "And being exhausted when we go into Geo-Array tonight isn't a good idea. How about you try to rest for a while?"

"I'd rather take a walk and scope out GeoArray's headquarters. I'd like to take a look at the building. See how much security they actually have."

"No," he said.

"We could at least drive past. We certainly can't just sit here. We'll draw attention to ourselves. Plus, it's a waste of time."

"It's a public garage. And not all of us are going to be sitting here." Kane handed the computer back.

"What's that supposed to mean?"

"I'm going to survey GeoArray. You and Silas are staying here."

"What! When was this decided?" Not while she was around to have some input. That much was certain.

"Now," he responded.

"Well, you're going to have to undecide it, because I'm not sitting in this car—"

"Sleeping would be a better idea."

"I'm not sitting, sleeping or staying in this car while you're doing reconnaissance."

"Sure you are," Silas said, opening his door and getting out of the SUV. "We're too close to GeoArray for you to be wandering around. Its people have been looking for you for weeks. You think they're not going to recognize you if you show up on one of their exterior security cameras?"

"They may be circulating Kane's picture by now, too. We know they've connected him to the plane."

"I'm pretty good at being unobtrusive." Kane got out of the SUV, too.

"By pretty good, he means exceptional." Silas closed his door. Kane did the same.

And Arden was suddenly sitting in the SUV with nothing but a dog for a companion. She couldn't make out their conversation, their voices muffled by the closed windows. Admittedly, Kane was probably the best qualified to scout the facility, but that didn't mean she didn't have thoughts to contribute to the plan of action.

She reached for the door handle, freezing when the dog let out a quick, sharp bark.

"Calm down, Cujo," she said. "I just want to get out and stretch my legs for a minute."

The dog barked again, and Kane's door opened. He leaned into the SUV, looking her straight in the eye. "You're supposed to be resting, Arden."

"I just wanted to stretch my legs for a minute." *And hear whatever plans you and Silas were making without me*, she added silently.

"There'll be time for that tonight. Right now, please try to sleep. Assuming we get in undetected, we'll need you to be at the peak of your cognitive ability," he said, throwing her words back at her.

"I guess a little shut-eye couldn't hurt," she grumbled. "Do you think you'll be long?"

"I'm not sure. But you can rest easy. Silas and Dutch will stay with you until I get back."

"How long should we wait before we come looking for you?"

"Forever," he said.

"That's a long time, Kane."

"My point is, I don't want you to come looking. I'll

be back by lunch time. If I'm not, Silas will know what to do."

Be careful, she wanted to say, but he closed the door, stood for a few more minutes talking to Silas, and then walked away, sauntering along like he had all the time in the world.

Getting close to GeoArray wasn't going to be complicated. Kane had been in more difficult circumstances on more dangerous missions. Compared to those, doing a little recon on a traitorous tech company would be a piece of cake.

The complicated part would come later, after the sun went down. He'd studied the blueprints; he knew that GeoArray had an intricate ventilation system. The vent cover should be on the western side of the building at—or very close to—ground level. He needed to make certain it was there. Blueprints were great, but they weren't always accurate.

He jogged down three flights of stairs, exited the stairwell and walked into the lowest level of the parking garage.

Although visible from the public parking garage, GeoArray was across a small side street. Kane walked outside, following the sidewalk to the nearest crosswalk. A crowd of people waited there, most of them on phones, several carrying briefcases. Normal people going about their normal business. None of them had any idea how close the country was to disaster. The information GeoArray planned to release threatened the well-being of the entire nation.

Greed.

It made smart people do evil things.

GeoArray towered over the older buildings that stood nearby. Modern and edgy with sleek lines and reflective windows, the place was huge—a discordant note in an otherwise quaint section of the city. They were close to the harbor here, the glint of water just visible to the east. Lots of people. Lots of activity. That made it easy to blend in.

The light changed, and the crowd swarmed across the street. Adults. Kids. Families. Like DC, Philadelphia and Gettysburg, Boston had enough historical significance to bring crowds of sightseers all year round. He'd come here often as a child, traveling with his grandparents during his breaks from boarding school. Boston had been one of their favorite haunts, his grandfather's passion for history dictating their travel plans.

He frowned.

He didn't have time for introspection. He sure couldn't afford to be distracted.

He stepped onto to the sidewalk with the rest of the crowd, making sure he was in the center of the swarm. There were security cameras near GeoArray's front door and several more at both corners of the building. He noted those and the guard who stood nonchalantly in front of the building. No firearm that Kane could see, but that didn't mean much.

If the blueprint was accurate, the vent was on the east side of the building, close to the back corner. An old cobblestone road led in that direction. He bypassed it, still walking with the crowd. Heading into the alley from the main street would be a red flag to anyone watching. He turned the corner and walked around the city block, grabbing coffee and some pastries from one shop, then stopping at another to buy some cold-cut subs.

Normal things that a normal person walking near the harbor might do.

There was plenty of hustle and bustle, plenty of camera flashes and excited chatter. He followed a small group of tourists past GeoArray. No public entrance on this side, but there were several doors and plenty of security cameras.

The buildings to either side were commercial properties. He used that to his advantage, walking down the cobblestone alley and trying the door of an obviously closed souvenir shop.

He turned back, sipping coffee and scanning Geo-Array's facility. There were several doors. Just like the blueprint had indicated. At the back corner, a vent sat flush against the brick wall.

He walked past as slowly as he dared. Phillips-head screws held it in place. There'd be a fan just beyond it. Easy enough to dismantle and remove with the right tools.

If he knew Silas, the guy would have an entire toolkit tucked away in the rental. He believed in being overly prepared. So did Kane.

He stepped out of the alley, merging with another small group. They were walking slowly, snapping photos of some of the older buildings and plaques that explained the history of the area. He took out his cell phone and did the same, taking a picture of the alley, zooming in on the vent and getting a picture of that. He snapped a photo of a small memorial marker that stood near the street and then turned to snap one of the back of GeoArray's building.

One of the doors was opening, and he lowered his phone, pretending to scroll through photos as two men stepped outside. One was a stranger—tall with black hair, wearing a suit that probably cost a small fortune. The other looked familiar—light brown hair cut short, expensive suit, thin build.

Randy Sumner.

Arden's ex.

The guy looked haggard, his cheeks gaunt, his eyes deeply shadowed. Whatever was going on, he didn't seem happy about it.

Kane gave himself just enough time to notice those things, and then he moved away, merging with another group milling around near a bus stop. He snapped a few pictures of the distant harbor and waited impatiently for Randy and his buddy to make a move. If they returned to the building, he'd go back to the SUV. If they left the area, he'd follow.

Either way, he had information he didn't have before.

Randy was in town.

As far as Kane knew, the guy was a consultant working out of GeoArray's DC office. If he'd flown into Boston, he must be feeling pressure to make sure the cyber exchange went off without a hitch.

The fact that GeoArray hadn't been able to find and dispatch Arden probably had her idiot ex sweating bullets. He knew what she was capable of, and he knew she wouldn't stop until she was forced to or until she achieved her goal.

The door opened again and a uniformed security officer stepped out. He was pushing a cart of luggage, and he didn't look happy about it.

"Where do you want it, Mr. Emory?" he snapped, loudly, rolling it toward the street.

Kane tensed at the name.

Emory and Randy together with a cart full of luggage all sounded like an escape waiting to happen. The two men made their way toward the curb.

"You called a cab?" Emory asked, glancing at his watch and frowning.

"Didn't you ask me to?"

"Don't get smart with me, Henderson," Emory growled. "I don't like it."

"Yes," the security guard ground out. "I called a cab."

"When it gets here, load everything in it and take it to the dock. The *Relentless Journey* is in its usual spot. Just leave the stuff in my cabin." Emory slapped a wad of bills in the guy's hand. "That's for the extra effort. Come on, Randy. We've got a few things to discuss before I leave. Let's grab some coffee."

"What do you mean, leave?" Randy sputtered, his face flushed with displeasure.

As Emory and Randy approached the bus stop, Kane turned away, knowing he was staring and afraid he'd be noticed. He texted Silas to give him an update, his back still to the men as they moved past.

"We're both leaving, Randy. You go your way. I go mine. We knew it might come to this—especially with the elusive DeMarco girl still just out of reach."

Kane fell in step behind them as they passed, keeping within earshot of their conversation.

"The plan was to leave after the file transmission, if we couldn't find Arden and get the files back," Randy whispered. "Why are you packing up now?"

"My wife thinks I'm leaving on a business trip this morning. My girlfriend and I are going out for dinner and I'll likely stay on the yacht tonight. But I'll be ready to launch it tomorrow night in the event that you haven't retrieved those files. Not that I owe you an explanation. I've paid you plenty for your work. Or, should I say, for your girlfriend's work?"

Randy responded, but the words were lost as the men walked across the street.

Kane could have followed, but he'd heard enough. He was more interested in the yacht. If he could get on board, he might be able to figure out where Emory planned to go. Despite what the CEO had told Randy, Kane wondered if Emory planned to leave long before the exchange happened.

Not that the exchange would ever happen.

Not if Kane had anything to do with it.

He texted Silas again and let him know that he was heading to the docks. He tucked his cell phone away, finished the last of his coffee and headed toward the glittering water of the harbor.

FOURTEEN

Arden dreamed of Christmas.

Of family gathered in her parents' large home. Of good food and conversation, of laughter and off-key singing. She dreamed of hot cocoa topped with whipped cream, a fire glowing softly. Kane smiling at her from across the room. Cold wind whipping in from an open door. A dog barking.

A dog?

She opened her eyes, still groggy with sleep, and stared into Dutch's dark eyes. He leaned in so close, his nose touched her cheek and his hot doggy breath fanned her face.

"Are you going to eat me?" she asked.

"Kee-gur'-lah!" Silas commanded leaning into the open front door of the SUV and eyeing her dispassionately. Dutch immediately backed away. "I see you're awake."

"I see you're still grumpy."

Someone laughed.

No. Not someone. Kane. She could see him now, standing next to Silas, his hair covered by a black cap. He had a couple days' worth of stubble and a rugged outdoorsy look that made her wonder if he spent most of his life tromping through forests.

She was stretched out across the back seat of the SUV, her backpack under her head. Her laptop was still open and sitting on the floor, the battery charging in the SUV's power outlet. She'd spent a couple of hours prepping for the night mission and waiting for Kane. She wasn't sure when she'd dozed off, but it hadn't been dark.

Now it was.

Which had to mean that it was almost time.

She sat up too quickly, saw a million tiny stars dancing in front of her eyes as she opened the door. Her foot caught on Kane's duffel, and she nearly took a header on the cement.

She would have if Kane hadn't grabbed her arm, his fingers curving around her biceps. "Slow down, Arden. We've got time."

"It's dark," she pointed out. "And I'm ready."

"Not until you eat." He handed her a paper bag, his hand sliding from her upper arm to her wrist. "I brought back cold-cut subs. I thought you might be hungry."

"I'm starved, thank you." She began unwrapping the sub. "I'm going to love you forever for this, Kane," she said, just like she would have if he'd been one of her brothers.

Only he wasn't.

"We've moved on from like to love pretty quickly, Arden," he said, urging her back until her legs hit the SUV and she was sitting on the bench seat again.

"Just a figure of speech," she muttered. She removed the last of the wrapper from the sub and did everything in her power to *not* look in his eyes.

He was special, and he was trouble, and he was exactly the kind of guy she should *not* be saying things like "I'll love you forever" to.

Because she thought that she *could* do that.

She could also get her heart broken, her dreams crushed and all her silly little fantasies about forever dashed.

Again.

Only this time it would be worse, because this time, she'd be dreaming all those things about Kane. And he was so much more than Randy had ever been.

"I bought it so you could eat it," Kane said quietly. "Not stare at it like it's going to bite you."

She took a bite, swallowed. "This is so good."

"Eat up. We can't afford to have you distracted tonight." He crouched in front of her, brushing strands of hair from her cheek. "I know I don't need to tell you that I'm worried about what we might come up against in there. If I could take down the system myself, I'd leave you here and do it."

"I know what's riding on this. National security—"

"I'm worried about *you*, Arden. Which reminds me." Kane reached into a large pocket in his jacket. "I bought you dessert. It's gingerbread. It seemed appropriate. Since you like Christmas so much."

"You're kidding." She opened the small white bag, got a whiff of spicy ginger and sweet molasses. "You aren't kidding." She took a bite, savoring the lightly iced desert.

"A gun would have been more appropriate," Silas grumbled, polishing off the rest of his own sub.

"We've got those, and the security team at GeoArray doesn't look armed," Kane responded. "Not that that means much."

"Did you see the ventilation shaft?" she asked, finishing off the gingerbread and brushing crumbs from her hands.

"I did," Kane acknowledged. "I also saw your ex and Marcus Emory. Emory has all of his things packed on a yacht. He's ready to leave the country once this deal goes through—unless he can find you and eliminate any threat of discovery."

"Is Randy going with him?"

"Emory may take his girlfriend. Randy's on his own. Both of them are going to be disappointed."

"When they don't get the payoff because they failed?"

"When the FBI takes them in before they have a chance to escape the country," Kane replied.

"That's definitely the best-case scenario," Arden agreed.

"Speaking of the FBI, I think we should fill Grayson in on what we've learned before we head into the facility."

"What! I thought we weren't going to get him involved in this until it's over? If he has knowledge that we plan to break into GeoArray's secure facility, he'll have a duty to report it."

"You've decrypted the files, Arden. We have all the proof we need. Marcus Emory is selling proprietary national secrets. If we weren't under time pressure, I'd turn this over to Grayson and let him and the FBI deal with GeoArray from this point forward."

"We already determined that could take too long."

"Right. We're going in. We're taking the system

down. I'm planning on all three of us getting into that building and getting out of it," Kane responded. "But if that doesn't happen, someone has to know what's going on at GeoArray. I want you to send your brother the files before we leave. He won't see them until it's too late to stop us."

She knew what he was saying.

She understood his fear.

If they were captured and killed, GeoArray would get away with an act of espionage that would rival the Robert Hanssen case, which was the worst in FBI history.

She grabbed her laptop. "I'll send them to his work email. That way I can encrypt them with the FBI's encryption program. We can't take a chance of the files leaking out."

"You have access to the FBI's encryption program?" Silas asked.

"Yes, I've consulted for them before on special cases," she answered. She attached the files to an encrypted email and sent it to her brother. "Done."

"You're quick." Silas opened the SUV's hatchback. "Now, how about we get moving?" He tossed several things in her direction. Somehow she managed to catch them. Black gloves. A black cap like Kane was wearing.

She put them on, then set her computer on the seat, the screen glowing blue-white.

"Are you leaving Dutch?" she asked. The computer had to stay on. If the connection was disrupted, she'd have no way to reset it from inside the building and nowhere to send the command and control application once she removed it from the network.

"He'll stay back here," Silas said. *"Oh-wahn'-kah,"*

he commanded, and the dog hopped into the cargo area of the vehicle.

"If he comes up here and steps on my computer, we're sunk. The connection needs to remain open so I have a safe place to send the files."

"Dutch will stay put. He'll also keep people away from the SUV." Silas shut the hatchback and rounded the side of the vehicle.

"Ready?" Kane asked, offering a hand to Arden.

She took it, allowing herself to be pulled from the vehicle. December wind blew through the parking garage as they made their way to the stairwell, and she wanted to press close to Kane, gather a little of his warmth.

She wasn't just cold.

She was scared.

There was no guarantee they'd be able to make it into GeoArray through the ventilation system. If they did, there was no guarantee that she could accomplish her task before they were discovered.

She didn't say what she was thinking.

For once, her nerves didn't cause a stream of words to spill out of her mouth. She was going through the steps she needed to take, mentally rehearsing the quickest, most efficient way to infect GeoArray's server with a worm that would disrupt system operations. She'd have to be careful to stay out of the system storage to preserve the network's integrity. If she did it right, there'd be no chance that anyone connected to the system could retrieve files from it until she restored the server and turned it over to the FBI.

They stepped out of the parking garage and stuck to the shadows as they approached the rear of the dark-

ened GeoArray facility. Arden waited impatiently while
Kane and Silas unscrewed the vent cover.

They set it against the brick wall, then disconnected
and removed a fan that blocked the ventilation duct.

It took merely moments, but it felt like hours. Cold,
moist air blew in from the harbor and seeped through
Arden's layers of clothes. By the time the fan had been
removed, she was cold to the bone, her teeth nearly
chattering.

"This is going to be a problem," Silas said quietly,
and she moved closer, eyeing the dark shaft that led into
the building. It was small. She'd be able to fit, but there
was no way either of the men would.

"Time for plan B," Kane said.

"Which is?" Arden asked.

"We try to get in one of the back doors."

"You're kidding, right?"

"No." He scowled. "I'm not kidding. There's no way
Silas and I are getting in through this vent."

"You don't need to," she argued. "I can fit through,
and I'm the only one who really needs to be in there."

"You're not going in alone."

"We could stand out here all night arguing," Silas
said. "But that's not going to do us or the country much
good."

"We're not arguing. We're switching gears." Kane
started to walk away, but Arden grabbed his hand.

"We don't have time to switch gears. We don't have
time to try something that might not work. This is our
best chance, and I'm taking it."

"She's right, Kane," Silas agreed. "We try to get in
one of those doors and set off an alarm, and that in-

formation will be out before anyone can stop Marcus Emory."

"No," Kane said again.

"You're letting your heart influence your head. That's a good way to get people killed," Silas responded.

Kane scowled. "What's your point?"

"If I were the one who could fit through there and take down that system, you'd let me go."

"You're a trained professional."

"Who can't fit through the shaft," Arden cut in. She needed to get moving before her nerves got the best of her. "I memorized the blueprints. I know the easiest path to the server room. It should take me forty minutes tops. If I'm in there longer, call the cavalry."

She released his hand and would have climbed into the shaft, but he touched her shoulder.

"Arden," he said quietly. She turned, looked into his gorgeous eyes. Even in the dim alley light, she could see his concern.

"Don't stop me, Kane, okay? This has to be done. I'm the only one who can do it."

He nodded. "You have forty minutes. Not a minute longer."

"Afraid I'll fall through the ventilation shaft and start spouting random facts about espionage and the death rates of spies?" she tried to joke.

He didn't even crack a smile. "I'm afraid of not getting a chance to see your Christmas sweater this year. It's one of my favorite parts of your family's Christmas celebration." His knuckles skimmed down the side of her cheek, and she felt the heat of his skin through the thin fabric of his gloves before he stepped away.

She wanted to tell him she'd be fine.

She wanted to explain facts and figures and statistics that proved it, but her mind was blank, her mouth dry with fear. She tried to smile and failed miserably, so she turned back to the vent.

"Take this." Silas handed her a multipurpose tool. "You'll need it to exit the vent."

"Right." She tucked it into the pocket of her pants, accepted a flashlight he held out to her and crawled into the ventilation shaft.

The floor and walls were coated with a grimy layer of dust. Not something that Arden was expecting. Then again, her only frame of reference came from watching movies where the heroine escaped through shiny, clean and very roomy ventilation shafts.

She was shimmying through what felt like a toddler-sized hole, elbows and legs kicking up a layer of dust that swirled in the beam of her flashlight. Although claustrophobia wasn't currently among the list of her idiosyncrasies, Arden could see how this situation could send her in that direction.

Stay focused.

Stay calm.

Think about the blueprint.

Two left turns. A right turn. Straight ahead until she reached the end of the shaft. The server room should be there.

Please, Lord. Let it be there.

If it wasn't, she'd be dropping down into an unknown room in an unknown part of the building. She'd have to find her way to the server room without being seen.

She took a deep, calming breath—as deep as she dared in the dusty shaft—and pressed on.

After a couple of difficult turns in the vent shaft, Arden's flashlight beam reflected on the vent cover at the other end. She flicked off her light and peered through the vent slats. The hum of the server fans were an audible and very blessed relief.

She was in the right place.

Now she just needed to get into the room without alerting security to her presence. Slipping the multi-purpose tool from her pocket, she shoved it between the vent cover and the drywall and began to pry the cover away. It gave easily, and she barely managed to keep it from falling.

She slid it to the side, letting it rest against the wall as she half crawled, half fell into the room. Snapping on her flashlight, she scanned the server room for the local administrator terminals.

The computer was on, two screens flashing a screen saver with the lock-screen prompts. The last user had forgotten to log off.

Perfect. Now she wouldn't have to come up with a user name, just the password.

She committed the user name to memory and rebooted the system, placing her drive in one of the USB ports and the wireless internet connection in the other. The system came up, detecting both the wireless interface and the external drive.

Bingo.

Her custom password program was now tied in to the computer's start-up sequence. She needed to degrade the system but keep the evidence of GeoArray's crimes for the FBI. Not a complicated process, but it would take time.

Arden watched the progress bar scroll across the

screen. Just like the watched pot that never boils, it seemed to take forever to upload the worm.

Once it was in, she ran the program and removed her external drive and network card. The worm would immediately affect every computer currently logged on the network without leaving any forensic traces behind. The beauty of it was that the shutdown would occur one system at a time, as users logged on, making it difficult to recognize the full scale of the problem until it was too late.

She smiled as the terminal went black.

Done. She glanced at her watch. With a little time to spare.

She pushed out of the chair and started back to the ventilation shaft. The sound of approaching voices stopped her in her tracks. No way was she going to make it into the shaft in time to shimmy out of reach of anyone who happened to walk in.

She moved the vent cover over the opening, then crawled between two server racks at the back of the room. She was hidden well enough if whoever it was just walked by.

The door opened. The light went on.

She held her breath, afraid even the slightest movement would give her away.

"I'm sure we can just reboot the server and the system will come right back online," a man said.

She knew the voice, and the breath she'd been holding threatened to spill out in a great gasping rush. She let it out slowly, her pulse racing.

Randy. Of course.

He must have been working in another area of the

building. Once he tried the admin workstation, he'd know they weren't dealing with an isolated computer.

A few frantic moments of fingers tapping on a keyboard, a soft hiss of frustration and she knew Randy had figured it out.

"What?" another man said.

"I think we've been hacked. The system's been compromised with a worm of some sort."

"What do you mean, hacked? I paid you to make sure this system was impenetrable. If we can't make the file transfer—"

"We'll make it. I uploaded a backup copy of the application to the stand-alone system on your yacht yesterday morning."

"The application wasn't complete yesterday. There've been dozens of man-hours of work on it since then, and it's all lost! If we don't meet that deadline—"

"We have bigger things to worry about. We were hacked. It had to be an inside job. I took the entire system off the web after we were hacked the first time. There's no way someone could have accessed it externally."

"Call security in here," the second man growled. "I want everyone in this building rounded up and brought to this room."

That was her cue to get out.

She was inches from the vent and out of view of the men. They were distracted, and she could either wait to be discovered, or she could try to make a run for it.

The fact that Randy had uploaded a backup copy of the application to an off-site, stand-alone system made the decision for her. She had to find the yacht and infect the system there. Otherwise, the rest of the work she'd done would be fruitless.

Randy was calling for security, his voice ringing through an intercom system. She used the noise to mask her movements as she shifted the vent cover and crawled into the hole.

Her feet scraped against the metal floor of the shaft as she tried to shimmy farther in, the noise echoing loudly.

Someone grabbed her ankle and tugged her backward with enough force to send her flying. She tumbled out of the vent, landing on the floor with a thud that stole her breath.

She bounded up, swinging wildly, connecting with a jaw, a nose, a soft abdomen.

She could have won the fight.

Would have won if it had just been her against Randy.

But the door flew open and two security guards rushed in. Four against her, but she still couldn't quit. She grabbed a chair, would have tossed it at the two guards, but a man stepped between her and them. Marcus Emory. She recognized him from photos posted on GeoArray's website.

"Enough!" he growled, yanking the chair from her hands. "You're done, Arden. It's over. You lost. Take her to the harbor and throw her in," he said, striding to the door.

"If they do that—" her brain clicked along at hyperspeed, making connections so swiftly, her mouth could barely keep up "—you can kiss goodbye any chance you have of meeting your deadline."

"What are you talking about?" Emory swung back

around, his gaze going from her to Randy. "What's she talking about?"

"Don't ask me. She's always talking. Mostly about nothing."

"Randy just told you that nearly two days' work has been lost. Currently destroyed by the worm I uploaded to the system here."

"Get rid of her," Emory spat.

"It will take more than a day to rebuild what I've destroyed. That means you'll miss tomorrow's scheduled transfer time," she continued as one of the security guards grabbed her arm. "I can restore the data in an hour."

Emory turned again. "How?"

"This." She took the drive from her pocket. "I copied everything here. It's encrypted. It would take the best expert in the world months, if not years, to break my encryption." If it could be done at all.

"Take it," he said to Randy. "We'll go to the yacht, and you figure this mess out."

"I can't," Randy grumbled, his cheeks red with anger. "If she encrypted it with a custom program, there's no way I'm going to be able to get the information off of it before the deadline."

"Then I guess she comes with us. Cooperate and you might survive, Arden," Emory said. "Let's go." He grabbed her arm in a vicelike grip and dragged her into the hall.

She didn't bother fighting. She was getting exactly what she wanted. A trip to the yacht and to the server. Once she plugged the drive into the system, the worm would do what it was supposed to.

Randy and Emory weren't going to be happy when they realized it.

Hopefully, Kane would figure out that she was in trouble long before that happened. She had a really cool Christmas sweater to wear this year—a Christmas tree with real lights that flashed on and off with the push of a button. She'd hate for him to miss out on that. She'd hate to miss out on it herself.

But what she'd hate more than anything was dying knowing that she hadn't done what she'd intended.

People like Randy and Emory?

They should never ever win. And if she had it within her power to stop them, she had every intention of doing it.

They had her.

Kane knew it before his cell phone buzzed, knew it before he glanced at the text message that had come through.

There's a black car pulling up in front of the building. Looks like someone's going for a ride. Get the SUV.

Silas's message was brief and to the point.

Kane knew Silas, hidden in the shadows near the building's main entrance, had a clear view of the front door, but there was no way he'd heard what Kane had— the tinny voice echoing through the ventilation system, calling for security in the server room—but he knew trouble when he saw it. Silas had impeccable instincts.

So did Kane.

Yeah. They had her, and he wanted to run into the building to get her back. If he hadn't thought that would get them all killed, he would have.

A car meant they were taking her somewhere. A car meant there was still time. He hadn't heard a gunshot, and he didn't think Emory would be foolish enough to have someone killed in his building.

No. He'd want the dirty work done somewhere else.

Kane sprinted to the parking garage and jumped into the front seat of the SUV. He grabbed the keys and started the engine. He didn't turn on the lights, just sped down the ramp that led to the garage exit.

A dark Mercedes was pulling away from GeoArray, its taillights glowing in the night as it headed east.

Seconds later, Silas emerged from the shadows and yanked open the passenger door. "They're heading to the harbor," he said as he climbed in.

"You're sure?"

"Arden was talking nonstop and loudly enough for anyone nearby to hear. She mentioned the harbor and a server and something about fixing what she'd broken."

"If there's a computer system on the yacht, that would make sense."

"Do you know where Emory is docked?"

"Yes." Kane had done a little research, talked to some people at the marina's fishing supply shop and gotten a pretty good idea. He hadn't been able to access the dock, though. It was guarded during the day, and he hadn't wanted to draw attention to himself by climbing the fence that surrounded it. "How many men were with Arden?"

"Four, including the driver," Silas answered. "At least one is a security guard."

Kane drove them toward the marina, keeping the taillights from the Mercedes at a safe distance to avoid drawing attention.

The thought of Arden being in the hands of Marcus Emory made his blood run cold and he had to push back the worry. He'd flown critical extraction missions in the Middle East for the last seven years, a number of them under enemy fire. But none of those compared to this.

He'd promised Jace that he'd bring Arden home, but there was so much more to it now. There was something special about Arden, something that the world really needed—uninhibited joy and curiosity and intelligence.

She was uniquely beautiful inside and out, and he thought that maybe that was something *he* really needed. He was no longer that dumb kid. He'd spent years atoning for his mistakes. Perhaps it was time to embrace the possibility that God wanted more for him than a life of regret.

Up ahead, a set of modest iron gates were swinging closed, the Mercedes's taillights glowing from the other side of it.

The gate, which was open and guarded during business hours, was unmanned and closed at night, requiring an access code Kane didn't have. Instead, he found a meter on the street and parked. He was out of the vehicle and over the fence in seconds. Keeping to the shadows, he made his way across a sparsely treed patch of snow-covered lawn.

Whispered movement drew his attention. A glance over his shoulder registered the shadow of a dog in motion. Dutch scaled the fence in an impressive leap, his chain collar jingling as his paws touched the ground. Silas followed suit, landing almost silently. Joining Kane in the shadows, he motioned to the dog, who immediately heeled at his side.

"You said you know where the yacht is docked?"

Silas asked. His voice was barely a whisper on the cold night air.

"This way." Kane jogged through the silent marina, passing several piers. He'd struck up a conversation earlier with a couple of retirees he'd met in the bait shop and discovered that the *Relentless Journey* was docked at Pier Six, the farthest from the gate. Ostentatiously extravagant, it had its fair share of detractors. Kane had spoken to more than one person who was less than impressed by both the yacht and its owner.

The guy might have friends. They apparently didn't hang around the harbor.

That had worked to Kane's advantage. The yacht was exactly where he'd expected it to be, the Mercedes parked on the street near the pier. Doors closed, lights off, it looked empty. The yacht was well lit, though. Shadowy figures moved along the foredeck.

Kane motioned for Silas to stay near the Mercedes and headed to the yacht, the soft lap of water against the hull drowning out his footsteps. A ladder to the aft of the vessel led to the foredeck. He climbed it quickly, taking out a guard who'd been smoking a cigarette near the life raft.

He dragged the guy to a dark corner, using tether lines to tie him up and a signal flag to gag him.

This was what he'd spent his military career doing: going in silently, taking out the enemy, making a way for the team to get in and take out weapons caches. Kane dragged the guy to the railing, used his own handcuffs to imprison him there. He grabbed a small Maglite from his cargo pocket and pointed it at the pier, clicking it on and off twice.

He didn't wait for an answering signal. Silas would

board the vessel, search out the rest of the security team and take it out.

Kane was going to find Arden. He was going to get her off the yacht. He was going to stop Emory and Randy, and then he was going to make Arden's ex very, very sorry for underestimating the woman he'd supposedly loved.

FIFTEEN

Arden's nerves were taut, her composure held together by a thread. She had to believe that Kane and Silas knew where she was. She had to believe they were on the way to help. She had to trust that God was in this, that His way was perfect, that she'd get out of the situation and get back to her life. Otherwise, she might just give into temptation and start singing or talking or spouting useless facts.

That would do absolutely nothing except irritate Randy. She wouldn't mind that so much, except that she had to focus. What she needed to do—what she *would* do—was stay calm.

She was where she wanted to be, sitting in front of the stand-alone computer system, watching as Randy logged in as the administrator.

He was nervous. His face was ruddy and glossy with perspiration, his hands shaking as he typed. He looked like an understuffed scarecrow, his suit bagging around his skinny frame, his cheeks gaunt.

She almost felt sorry for him. *Almost*. If he hadn't stolen government secrets and wasn't trying to pass them into enemy hands, maybe she'd have a little more sympathy for his plight.

As it was, she hoped he got every single thing that he deserved.

"How long is this going to take?" Emory asked. He picked up the portable drive that a security guard had taken from Arden's pocket when he'd frisked her. The rest of what she'd been carrying was spread out on a marble counter nearby—wireless connector, flashlight, screwdriver and prepaid cell phone.

The security team had disappeared. She thought one of the guards was standing on the other side of the closed door. She might be able to get past him, but she'd have to get past Randy and Emory first.

After she infected the system, she was going to be running for her life. Literally. There was no doubt in her mind Emory would kill her once he realized what she'd done.

"Be careful with that," Arden warned, her heart in her throat as she watched him flip the drive in the palm of his hand.

He met her eyes, his expression cold. "Do I look stupid?"

"Is that a rhetorical question?"

He slapped her—a quick vicious hit that left the taste of blood in her mouth.

"Hey!" Randy glanced their way. "Careful. If you give her a concussion, she might not be able to access the files. Then what?"

"Sheesh," Arden said, refusing to let either man know how terrified she was. "Thanks for caring, Randy."

"It's nothing personal, Arden. I needed money. This

was the best way to get it." He finished typing in his passcode and took the drive from Emory's hand.

"By selling out your country?" she asked, and he frowned.

"I'm not a traitor."

"You're not a thief, either, but somehow you used my encryption program to help him smuggle classified information to a recipient outside of GeoArray. The initial files that were sent were bad enough, but if the completed application falls in the wrong hands, our national defense systems will be in trouble."

"I didn't steal your program. We collaborated. It was ours."

"Right." She snorted, knowing that that would get a rise out of him. "We collaborated on a lot of things when we worked on the university's research team, but that program was not one of them." She wanted him irritated. Angry was even better. The less time he had to think, the better. She might despise him, but she couldn't deny his intelligence. If he weren't working from a place of fear, he'd have considered the fact that the drive he was holding was infected with the worm she'd used to take down GeoArray's system.

"Enough chitchat. I asked a question," Emory snapped. "How long will this take?"

"It depends on how intricate her encryption program is." Randy plugged the drive into the port, and Arden's heart skipped a dozen beats. She was *this* close to destroying everything these men were working toward.

Please, God, let this work, she prayed silently.

"Let her do it then," Emory said. "I want it done quickly, Ms. DeMarco."

"It will be." She tried to match his tone, use the same

cold, hard inflections he had, but her voice was shaking. She was disgusted to see that her hands were shaking, too.

She knew what she had to do. Fear would not stop her.

Had Kane and Silas seen her taken? Were they trying to figure out a way to save her?

She typed in her passcode incorrectly, knowing how the program would react. It was her fail-safe, her backup plan. If anyone tried to access the files without the code, the worm automatically uploaded to the system thirty seconds after the first failed entry. The only way to stop it was to enter the correct code.

She had no intention of doing that.

"What happened?" Randy asked, leaning in as the passcode prompt appeared again.

"Shaky hands," she lied, typing in another wrong code.

The server was on borrowed time. Unfortunately, Arden was pretty sure she was, too.

The upload box appeared, ticking off the seconds as the worm infiltrated the system.

"Is that it?" Emory asked, leaning close to the screen.

"I...think so," Randy responded, but she knew he was worried. Unlike Emory, he understood computers. He knew that her passcode should have opened a screen with file options that she could choose from. This upload was different. This was a one-way ticket to Randy's failure.

He met Arden's eyes, and she could see the anger there.

He'd been bested at his game.

He knew it.

The upload box filled, then the screen went black. Randy's quiet curse filled the sudden deafening silence. The system had shut down completely. No more soft hum of drive fans. Nothing but the harsh sound of Randy's frantic, furious breaths.

"What just happened?" Emory demanded.

"She compromised the system," Randy bit out. "She uploaded a worm and destroyed everything."

"Were you planning to die tonight?" Emory yelled, dragging Arden from the chair and throwing her against the wall. Every bit of air left her lungs at the impact, but she didn't have time to recover. He was on her again, screaming into her face, demanding she bring the program back up.

She'd been trained for this. Her brothers had made certain she could defend herself. She knew what to do. She just needed her body to cooperate with what her brain was demanding.

She slammed her head into his chin, the force of the blow knocking him backward. The door was just a few feet away, and she lunged for it, praying it wasn't locked, praying she'd make it out.

She turned the knob, yanking on it with so much force the door slammed into the wall, bouncing back as she darted through. The security guard was leaning against the far wall of the captain's quarters, his head down.

He looked up from his cell phone as she raced out, stunned confusion crossing his face.

One more door, and she'd be on the deck. From there, she could jump overboard if she had to.

"Don't just stand there," Emory yelled as he nearly flew out of the server room. "Stop her."

The security guard finally moved, darting toward her, grabbing a handful of her jacket as she raced toward the door.

She swung around, using the flat of her hand against his nose. He cursed and fell back, blood oozing from his nose.

She thought she heard footsteps outside the door, but she didn't have time to worry about it. She had the door open and was running, feet slipping on wet flooring as she raced toward the stairs.

She could see the sky through the stairwell opening. The stars sparkled against the blackness. She could feel the cold air wafting down, smell the briny scent of saltwater. All of it was there, clear and crisp and vivid. Freedom. Just a few more yards away.

An explosion rocked the yacht.

Or, maybe, it just rocked her.

She stumbled, falling onto the stairs. Pain stole every thought as blood spurted from a wound in her shoulder.

Shot. Her mind finally registered it, and she was up again. She dodged this time, weaving and ducking even though the stairs were a straight line up and a bullet could easily find her again.

Another gunshot came from the left, glass shattering as a porthole imploded. She wasn't sure who was shooting at her. She just knew she had to keep moving.

A dark figure appeared in front of her, blocking the sky and the cold. She planned to plow through him because she sure wasn't going to stop. No way was she going to die in the bowels of Emory's yacht.

She slammed into a hard body, felt an arm wrap around her waist. And she knew before she saw his face, before he spoke her name. She knew without even knowing how that it was Kane.

She'd been shot.

Kane could see the blood oozing from a wound in Arden's shoulder, and it infuriated him. Her face was leached of color. She clung to his arm and offered a smile that made his heart break into a million pieces.

"It's done. We stopped them," she said.

"It's not done until I get you off this boat."

He helped her up the stairs, keeping one hand on her waist and the other free. Silas had taken out the guard who'd shot Arden, but Emory and Randy were still on the loose. He doubted Randy had a weapon, but he thought Emory might be carrying. The guy didn't seem like someone who took chances. He also didn't seem like the kind of guy who'd be happy to lose out on millions of dollars.

Arden had destroyed the only possibility Emory had of getting the rest of the money. If nothing else, he would want revenge.

They made it onto the deck. The second guard was still trussed up and handcuffed to the railing, the rest of the area empty and silent.

That should have made Kane feel better, but something was off. The skin-crawling, hair-raising feeling of danger seeped through his pores.

"What's wrong?" Arden whispered as he hurried her across the deck.

"Can you make it down the ladder?" he asked.

"What's wrong?" she repeated.

"I want you off this boat," he responded. The soft clank of feet on metal rungs made his heart race.

Arden must have heard it, too. She lowered herself over the side of the deck, her feet scraping against the hull. Blood was still pouring from her shoulder, and he wanted to tell her to be careful, but she was already moving. She eased herself down one slow step at a time.

He scanned the deck, searching for the danger he knew was there. Metal vibrated somewhere above, and he eyed the bridge, certain someone was there. Pale moonlight filtered down from the clear winter sky. It splashed across the upper deck and silhouetted a man who was walking to the railing.

Not Silas. This guy was shorter, broader, louder. Emory.

He lifted his arm, a handgun glinting in the dim light.

Kane didn't hesitate. He didn't issue a warning. His Glock was out, and he was firing as Emory took aim at the ladder and Arden.

"Arden, watch out!" Kane shouted, his words lost in the explosion of gunfire.

His bullet hit its mark, knocking Emory backward.

Emory's shot pinged off the metal handrail. Arden jerked back, releasing the rail. The muffled sound of her scream was followed by the soft splash of a body landing in the water.

Kane was up and over the railing before the sound faded away. He could see the telltale waves where she'd gone under, the rippling circle spreading into wide arcs that lapped against the hull of the boat.

He tucked his gun in its holster and jumped. Feet first just like he'd done during dozens of training exercises. Only this wasn't training. This was the real deal. If he couldn't find Arden, if she was unconscious, if the bullet had nicked a major artery, if any of a dozen things went wrong, she'd die.

He hit the water almost silently, sliding beneath the inky surface, eyes open in the salty water as he searched the blackness for Arden.

SIXTEEN

She came up gasping and choking, water in her nose and her throat and her lungs. Lights splashed on the surface of the harbor—blue and red flashes of color against the darkness. For a moment, she thought they were Christmas lights and that she'd somehow found her way home.

Except that she was sinking in the black and brackish water of the harbor, her body weighted down by her coat, ski pants and boots. She tried to tread water, but her left arm didn't seem to be functioning.

"FBI! Drop your weapons!" someone ordered.

Whoever it was couldn't be talking to her. She didn't have a weapon. She didn't have a life vest, either.

Which shouldn't have mattered. She was a good swimmer. She'd always loved the water. But the frigid temperature had stolen her energy, sapping her strength so effectively she slid under the water again.

Don't inhale, her sluggish brain screamed, but her body had other plans.

She sucked in a mouthful of water, probably would have sunk to the bottom of the harbor if something hadn't snagged the back of her coat. She was hauled up, and water spewed from her mouth as she gagged up half the ocean.

"It's okay," someone said. "You're okay."

Kane. Of course it was Kane.

He pulled her against his chest, one arm wrapped around her waist, the other paddling to keep them afloat.

"You're my hero," she tried to say. But she was coughing so hard, nothing came out except a horrible croak that sounded like the death knell of an ancient tuba.

"Throw me a life preserver," he called to someone. His voice was hoarse with what sounded an awful lot like fear.

"Are you all right?" she managed to ask.

"You're bleeding like a stuck pig."

"I'll be okay."

"You'd better be," he growled as a life preserver landed in the water beside them. He grabbed it with his free arm and tugged her even closer.

"Are they going to pull us up?" she asked, so cold that the words only barely formed through chattering teeth.

He must have heard. "No. The paramedics have a boat in the water."

"That explains it."

"What?"

"The Christmas lights," she slurred.

"Christmas lights?"

"On the water. I thought that's what they were." She sounded as confused as she felt. Nothing felt real. Not the water or the cold. Not the throbbing pain in her shoulder and chest.

She took a deep breath, trying to ground herself, but

she was floating somewhere between here and there. This world and another one.

"Hey!" Kane said, his voice sharp with concern. "No closing your eyes."

"They're open." Only she couldn't see anything. So maybe they weren't.

"Arden!" he said again, and she did open her eyes. Realized they were still in the water, bright lights moving toward them.

"The boat's almost here," he said. "We'll have you home in front of your Christmas tree in no time."

A fiberglass water rescue boat pulled up alongside them. Kane cradled Arden tightly as they bobbed in the choppy wake of the boat. The pain in her shoulder was getting worse. Every bounce and jostle sent shooting pain through her chest and down her arm.

"Arden!" Kane barked, and she realized she'd closed her eyes again.

"They're open, okay?" she snapped. Or tried. Nothing came out. Not a word or a sound, and she was floating again, the water tugging her out of Kane's arms and into the blackness.

She tried to grab his hand, but she felt paralyzed, leaden.

"Don't fight them, Arden. We've got to get you into the boat," he whispered in her ear, and she realized that she was still in his arms, clutching his coat with her right hand.

Two other men were beside her, a backboard between them.

"Ma'am, try to relax," one of them said, his face pale in the flashing light of the boat.

"Is she conscious?" a familiar voice called from the

boat. She thought she must have closed her eyes and drifted off again. It sounded like Grayson.

"We're going to float you on your back," the man was saying. "And strap you onto the backboard so we can lift you onto the boat. It'll be easier if you let go of your friend."

She did what she was told mostly because she had no strength left to hold on.

"It's okay," Kane said again as if saying it could make it so.

Maybe it could, because she was suddenly on the backboard, floating above the water, cold air flowing across her nearly frozen skin.

She felt the backboard slide up on the boat's access ramp. Hands grabbed the board and pulled it into the boat.

"Hey, kid," Grayson said, his face suddenly in her space, his eyes filled with worry.

"Is this a dream?" she asked as he dropped a blanket over her.

"If it were, it would be a nightmare," he said grimly.

"So...you're really here."

"Yes."

"Where's Laney?"

"Still on bed rest. Aunt Rose is taking care of her until I get back."

"You should be with your wife. Go home to Laney," she tried to demand. The words came out so slurred even she wasn't sure what she'd been trying to say.

"She's losing a lot of blood," Grayson called, and someone shoved in next to him, kneeling beside Arden.

"Ma'am, I'm going to apply pressure to your shoulder. It may hurt a little."

"Logically speaking—" she began, but a finger pressed against her lips, sealing in whatever she was going to say.

"How about we save your logical assumptions for a time when you aren't attempting to bleed to death?" Kane asked grimly. She turned her head. He was right beside her, water dripping down his face, a blanket around his shoulders.

"You saved me," she said.

"Not yet," he responded. He looked…scared. Terrified, really, his gaze sharp, his expression hard.

"You did. Emory was trying to shoot me. I saw him on the bridge."

"Emory is dead," Grayson said bluntly. "And the Feds and local law enforcement agencies are going to want to know why. You're both going to have a lot of questions to answer once we get back to the dock."

"Once she's stabilized, you mean," Kane corrected. His fingers trembled as he brushed damp hair from Arden's cheek.

"It's going to be okay," she tried to reassure him.

"That's my line," he responded with a tender smile.

She wanted to return the smile. She wanted to tell him how thankful she was for what he'd done. She wanted to say a dozen things, but they were all lost as someone pressed against her shoulder.

Pain exploded through her chest, and she was gone again, floating in the black water of the harbor, reaching desperately for something to hold onto.

She was out cold.

No response at all as the EMT put pressure on her bloody shoulder. Kane had felt fear before, but never anything like this. Arden was still, lips blue from cold, her right arm hanging limply from the backboard. He lifted it, holding her hand and praying in a way he never had before, with a desperation he'd never felt before.

Please, God. Save her.

Her fingers twitched, and then she was squeezing his hand. Her eyes were open and she stared straight into his face.

"Don't let me go," she said. "If you do, I'll float away with the Christmas lights."

The words were the first clear, crisp ones she'd spoken.

"I won't let you go," he promised. The boat bumped against the pier as it docked.

Her eyes were already closed again, and he wasn't sure she'd heard.

He'd keep his promise anyway. Just like he kept his promise to Evan.

He could still remember every detail of that night. A lone figure silhouetted on the windy bluff. Evan. A half-empty bottle of vodka next to him. A gun in his lap. Waves crashed loudly on the rocks below. Evan lifted his head. Saw Kane. Pointed the gun at his own chest. There'd barely been time for Kane to scream his cousin's name.

Kane had spent years trying to forgive himself for not being able to save Lexi. And in the end, for failing to save Evan. He'd spent years reliving those moments, hearing Evan's harsh rasping breath, the last words of his dying cousin. "Tell Mom I'm sorry. Make sure she's okay. Promise me."

Kane had joined the military and kept that promise,

anonymously sending money to Evan's mom. It was all he could do. It would never be enough.

He shoved the thoughts away, pushed the memories back where they belonged. The crew lifted Arden's backboard and carried her off the boat.

He didn't release her hand.

He wouldn't. Not until he was pried away from her, and even then, he planned to put up a fight.

The dock was a flurry of activity. Silas was talking to agents, Dutch at his feet. Randy stood a few feet away, handcuffed and haggard, talking rapidly.

Kane couldn't hear what he was saying, but he was certain it was a list of excuses that would take weeks for the FBI to sort through.

Grayson fell in step beside him, his voice clipped and tight.

"Agent Keller from the Boston Office is here."

"And?"

"He wants to speak to you."

"I told Arden I wasn't letting go of her. I'm not."

Grayson frowned, his gaze dropping to his sister. "I'll do damage control, then meet you at the hospital. She's going to need surgery. You let her out of your sight except for when they're working on her, and I will personally make sure you spend the next few days answering useless questions at headquarters."

"It's not nice to threaten people, Grayson," Arden said without opening her eyes.

"It's not nice to let people get shot, either," her brother replied.

"It wasn't his fault. He told me not to go in alone, but I had to." She finally opened her eyes. "Where's my laptop?"

"Still in Silas's SUV," Kane responded.

"I need it." She tried to sit up, but the harnesses held her in place.

"Stop," Kane cautioned. "You're going to hurt yourself."

"I'm already hurt."

"You'll make it worse. I'll have Silas grab the laptop. You rest. We've got things under control."

"Not if the FBI plugs the USB into their computers. It'll take down their system. Don't let them do that, Grayson. Just get the laptop to the hospital. I'll take care of everything from there. I need to get the files—"

"Kane is right," Grayson cut her off. "We'll handle things. You just get better."

"But—"

"Oxygen levels are dropping," a paramedic said, dropping an oxygen mask over her face. "You need to relax and stop talking, ma'am."

"Story of my life," Arden murmured. Her eyes closed again, and her hand tightened around Kane's as if she thought he could keep her from drifting away.

He climbed onto the ambulance after they lifted her in, borrowed the paramedic's phone and texted Silas to bring the laptop to the hospital once the FBI cleared him to leave. There was more that needed to be done to assure national security. The entity that had paid to receive the files still needed to be revealed.

Kane wanted to care. He *did* care, but he was more concerned about Arden. Her vital signs were dropping, her breathing becoming shallower. By the time they reached the hospital, the EMTs were working silently and quickly, keeping pressure on the wound to slow the blood loss, increasing oxygen flow. He could feel their tension and his own.

The ambulance doors opened, and a team of doctors and nurses appeared. They were moving, shifting Arden to a gurney, wheeling her through the hall, and he still managed to hold onto her hand. It was limp now, no desperate grasping.

"She's lost too much blood," someone said. "We're going straight to surgery."

"Sir?" A man touched his shoulder. "You're going to have to let her go."

Probably, but he couldn't quite make himself release her hand.

They reached the double doors that led into the surgical suite, and the same guy stepped in front of Kane, blocking his path.

"There's a waiting room to the left," he said quietly. "I'm Lucas Riggs. Head surgical nurse. I'll keep you updated on things, Mr.—?"

"Walker. Kane."

"We'll take good care of her, Kane," the nurse said, and then the gurney was moving again. Arden's hand slipped from Kane's as she was wheeled away.

Nearly two hours later, and she still wasn't out of surgery.

Kane eyed the waiting room clock and wondered how much longer it would be.

He'd already given his statement, had his firearm confiscated for evidence, given his statement again. He'd used the phone at the nurse's station to call both Jace and Silas, who'd been taken downtown for his statement.

Kane stopped by the large windows that looked out over the courtyard. A dusting of new snow covered the walkways. Icicle lights hung from the windows and doorframes. Arden would love that.

She'd love the snow. The lights. The Christmas carols playing over the intercom.

The doors opened and Grayson DeMarco walked in. His black hair was nearly the same color as Arden's, his blue eyes not nearly as soft and inviting.

"How is she?"

"Still in surgery."

"I'm going to see if I can find someone who knows what's going on." He turned back to the door.

"I've been to the front desk every fifteen minutes. No one's talking," Kane warned him, and Grayson swung back around.

"I don't like being helpless," he growled.

"Join the crowd."

"Since there's only two of us, there's not much of one. The hospital staff's extremely fortunate the snow has grounded my parents at the airport in Baltimore or my mom would take up permanent residence at the desk until someone gave her some answers."

"Maybe I should try that," Kane responded wryly.

Grayson walked to a coffeepot that sat on a nicked Formica counter and poured thick black coffee into a cup. "This stuff taste as bad as it looks?"

"Worse."

"A perfect end to a perfect day," he responded, taking a quick sip and grimacing. "You didn't lie."

"I usually don't."

"We've got men in GeoArray, a team of specialists that may or may not be able to undo what Arden did. I'm really hoping that the two of you have evidence that proves it was necessary to totally degrade a system used by the Department of Defense."

"We do."

"Good. I'm staking my reputation on that."

The door opened again. The nurse stepped inside the waiting room.

"Kane? She's out of surgery. I'll take you back now." His gaze cut to Grayson, sizing him up. "If you're FBI, you're going to have to wait. She's not up to answering questions."

"I'm her brother."

"Then you can come back. But no more than two people at a time in the recovery room."

Kane and Grayson followed him through the double doors down a pristine hallway to a small recovery room where Arden lay. She looked tiny, her body shrouded in blankets. A monitor measured her heart rate and blood pressure. Clear fluid dripped steadily into the IV line attached to her arm.

The doctor, still dressed in surgery scrubs, was making notes on a clipboard. He looked up as they entered the room.

"Are you Ms. DeMarco's relatives?" he asked, pushing his glasses up on his nose and slipping his pen in his pocket.

"Yes," they answered simultaneously.

"The surgery went well. We were able to use a plate and screws to rebuild the clavicle."

"Rebuild?" Kane asked. He pulled a chair over to the bed and sat.

"The bullet went through her humerus and traveled up into the shoulder, shattering her clavicle. She's very fortunate it missed the major arteries in the chest wall. She'll need eight to twelve weeks to recover fully." The doctor attached the chart to the clipboard at the end of Arden's bed. "We'll be monitoring her closely, but the prognosis is good."

"Thanks, doctor," Grayson said, shaking the man's hand.

Kane would have done the same, but the surgeon was already hurrying away.

"Arden?" Grayson said. He touched his sister's forehead. She shifted but didn't respond. "She looks terrible," he said.

"Thanks," she muttered without opening her eyes.

"Sorry, sis. I thought you were still out."

"I wish I were. I really, really do."

"Are you in a lot of pain?" Kane asked, and she finally opened her eyes.

"Is the opossum the only North American marsupial? Are the echidna and the platypus the only mammals that lay eggs?"

"I'll take that as a yes," he said, lifting her right hand and giving it a gentle squeeze.

"You know what would make me feel better?" she asked.

"Christmas?"

"No. Well, yes, but...my laptop. Where is it?"

"We can worry about the laptop later," Grayson said. He pulled a chair over to the other side of his sister's bed.

"We have a twenty-four-hour window of opportunity to catch the buyers. That's when the file transfer was scheduled. If we miss the opportunity, we may never catch the buyer." She was pallid but reached for the button on the bed railing, obviously trying to lever the bed up.

"Stop," Kane said, and she shook her head.

"I can't. There's too much riding on this."

"We've got a team working on it, Arden. All you need to do is work on healing," Grayson cut in.

"It is going to take your team too long. I designed the worm to stay out of the system storage and preserve forensic evidence that could be used in trial. They'll never be able to recover the server in time. I'm the only one that can do it."

She met Kane's eyes. "You know it's true, and you know I can't rest until I do this last thing."

He did.

He also knew that he cared as much about her health as he did anything else. She wouldn't rest. He knew that. She'd lie in bed, her mind working through the computer system even if the laptop wasn't in her hands.

He reached for the bedside phone, ignoring Grayson's scowl. "I'll call Silas for his ETA. Last time we spoke, he planned to return to the SUV from the FBI's Boston office."

"Thanks," she said. She smiled like she had on the yacht, and he knew. Suddenly and clearly. No questions. No angst. No second-guessing.

She was where he'd been heading all his life.

She was the home he'd been searching for.

Her smile? It was the thing that had been missing from his life, and if her brother hadn't been sitting right beside her, he'd have told her that.

Instead, he dialed Silas's number and waited impatiently for his friend to pick up. He knew Arden would never rest until she had her computer in hand. And she needed rest to heal.

SEVENTEEN

Arden's small hospital room was packed. Two FBI agents stood against the wall. Grayson and Kane were sitting near the bed, talking in hushed voices while Arden typed right-handed.

She'd been at it for two hours, and her entire body hurt. She wasn't quite sure where the pain was coming from. She only knew it was there and that she had to ignore it. This had to be done. No pain meds until it was. No sleeping.

No looking into Kane's beautiful dark eyes.

It took every ounce of concentration she could muster to focus on the complex algorithms scrolling across the screen in front of her.

Silas leaned against the wall next to the window, dressed in all black. The medical staff gave him a wide berth, some glancing uncomfortably at him, as they entered and exited the room.

A young nurse in colorful scrubs with rosy cheeks and a nametag identifying her as Lisa, with a heart over the *i*, fussed around the hospital bed, checking Arden's vital signs and the IV fluids.

With a thermometer under her tongue, Arden was

doing her best to ignore the woman and focus on the task. A feat made doubly difficult by the room full of people. Not to mention that the overly chipper nurse seemed more interested in stealing glances at Kane, Grayson and Silas than in recording Arden's temperature.

Arden found herself uncharacteristically annoyed by that.

She was used to women fawning all over the men in her life. Her four brothers commanded attention from the ladies wherever they went. Arden usually found humor in it. But somehow watching the nurse covertly glancing at Kane when she thought no one was looking was irritating.

Of course, she couldn't blame the woman—Kane's quiet confidence and strength filled a room when he entered. Truth be told, Arden had caught herself glancing at him as well, only to find Kane's warm brown eyes fixed on her from across the room.

She took a calming breath and tried to ignore the nurse while she made a few adjustments to the reparation program.

At Arden's insistence, Grayson had called the FBI's forensic specialist, Harriet Clemmons. Together, Arden and Harriet had been able to establish a connection for Arden to remote into the FBI's network from her laptop. Grayson had forwarded the decrypted files to Harriet earlier, but Arden had still needed to transmit all the research files she'd collected, along with the files she'd swiped tonight.

A quick look at the evidence was enough to convince Harriet that Marcus Emory had planned to sell government secrets.

The question remained, to whom?

Arden hoped the answer was somewhere on GeoArray's network, and she intended to help the FBI find it.

Advised of the contents of the decrypted files, Harriet had pulled some strings to get a warrant for Marcus Emory's personal system as well as GeoArray's networks. One of Harriet's techs had retrieved Arden's external drive from the hospital, then met Harriet and the FBI forensics team at GeoArray's headquarters.

Once the USB was plugged into the network and the override code entered, Arden was able to remotely access the system and launch her program to restore it. Arden had already restored the company's networks so the FBI could perform a thorough forensic investigation. She only had one more thing to do before turning the network over to the FBI—discover who was at the receiving end of the stolen files.

"Do you need anything?" the nurse asked sweetly as she removed the thermometer.

"Coffee and doughnuts might help," Arden answered wryly, her stomach rumbling. She'd only been allowed ice chips since she'd awakened.

"Unfortunately, a doughnut and coffee probably won't sit well on a post-operative stomach," the nurse responded. "But I'll see if I can scrounge something up for you that might hold you over."

"Thanks," Arden said absently, her attention on the computer again. She was almost there. She could feel it, the cyber trail she was following, leading her closer to the answer she was seeking.

She shifted uncomfortably, pain stabbing through her chest and shoulder and maybe her arm.

"You need to take a break, Arden," Kane said. He

offered her the cup of ice that was sitting on a table beside the bed.

"I need to figure this out," she responded. She continued to type, scrolling through lines of code one after another. She followed the trail. Just like she always did. Minutes passed, and the nurse returned with chicken broth and Jell-O.

Arden didn't have time for either.

She'd found a signature she recognized, one she'd run across on the darknet when working a forensics investigation a few years ago. It was tied to Alexei Petrov, a Russian citizen and hacker for hire. She pinged his system, located the associated IP address for the file transfer and slipped out the backdoor. Hopefully undetected.

"It's done," she said, pushing the laptop away. She suddenly realized how quiet the room had become. Only Grayson and Kane remained, both of them working quietly on tablets.

"You found them?" Grayson asked.

"I found someone who is affiliated with the email account Emory was communicating with. I was able to trace the backdoor he'd set up to transfer the files. I sent his name and the IP address for the end system to Harriet. My guess is he's hired help, just like Randy. The FBI will have to take it from here to determine if it's a nation-state entity."

"You're amazing, sis," he said, pulling out his phone and sending a quick text.

"I'm also tired." Exhausted really. Her entire shoulder and chest throbbed with pain.

"I can see that," Grayson said, heading toward the door. "I need to make a few calls. I'll go to the lobby so I won't disturb you." He opened the door and looked back. "I won't be long. Kane, you've got watch."

"I'm on it." Kane affirmed.

Arden closed the laptop and leaned her head back on the pillows, shutting her eyes against the ceiling lights.

Cloth rustled next to her, but she didn't open her eyes. She wasn't sure she could. Warm fingers traced a path along her cheek, tucking strands of hair behind her ear.

"You didn't eat your soup or your Jell-O," Kane said, and she realized she *could* open her eyes.

And he was there. So close she could see the tiny scar near his lip and the fine lines near the corners of his eyes. So close she could smell winter on his shirt.

"I'm saving room," she said.

"For what?"

"Christmas dinner," she replied, and he smiled. He moved the laptop onto the table and pulled the blankets up around her shoulders.

"That's a couple of weeks away."

"It's never too early to start planning."

"Probably not."

"Definitely not," she said. Her eyes drifted shut despite her best efforts to keep them open. Somehow, she still managed to speak, spewing out useless facts that she couldn't even blame on pain medication because she hadn't had any. "Studies show that the best Christmas bargains are found during the summer months. Clothes. Shoes. Books. People who buy early save themselves nearly forty percent."

"You know what else studies show?" he asked.

"What?" She opened her eyes, saw his gentle smile and smiled back.

"That patients who rest heal faster."

"I—"

"You don't want to miss Christmas dinner because you're in the hospital, do you?" He crossed the room and turned off the light.

"Are you going to be there?" she asked. The question spilled out before she could stop it.

"With bells on," he replied.

"I'd like to see that," she murmured. Her eyes closed again, the dark room and soft beep of machines lulling her into sweet velvety sleep.

The muted dawn light seeped in through the hospital blinds. The hospital was just beginning to wake, the silence of the evening interrupted by the sounds of rattling carts and the murmuring voices of doctors and nurses making their morning rounds.

Kane stretched and yawned. He debated whether he should go for a cup of hospital coffee or play it safe with a soda from the vending machine. After Arden had fallen asleep, he'd argued with Grayson over who would stay with her and who would find a hotel for the night. In the end, they'd flipped a coin for it and Kane had happily spent a less than comfortable night in the blue pleather recliner.

He glanced over at where Arden lay, a little banged up but safe. To his surprise, she was awake, dark shadows under her eyes, her face drawn.

She smiled, though, just like she always seemed to. "You're still here."

"Where else would I be?" He walked to the bed and lifted her hand. "How are you feeling?"

"Like I've been manhandled, shot and half drowned in the Atlantic Ocean."

"So, pretty good?" he joked, and she laughed, wincing a little at the effort.

"How about you don't be funny for a few days, okay? It hurts too much."

"Sorry." He brought her hand to his lips, kissing her knuckles. He watched as her cheeks went pink.

"What was that for?" she asked, but didn't pull away.

"Does it have to be for something?"

"Statistically speaking? Yes," she responded.

"Then let's call it practice."

"For what?"

"The Christmas party."

"You plan on kissing people's hands at the Christmas party?"

"No, but there'll be mistletoe there, and a stunning, brilliant, funny woman wearing a crazy Christmas sweater. I'm thinking that if I time it right, I just might steal a kiss." It wasn't something he'd planned to say. It wasn't something he'd even meant to say, but it felt right.

Her eyes widened, and she started talking, spewing facts faster than a wood chipper shot out chunks of wood.

"Who says you need mistletoe to steal a kiss? There are other traditions. Like kissing at the stroke of midnight on New Year's Eve, kissing beneath the harvest moon. Some people believe that if you stand on the peak of Mount—"

He stopped the words with his lips, kissing her gently and sweetly and with all the affection he had for her.

Her hand slid into his hair, and she pulled him closer.

The beauty of the moment shivered through him and made him long for more of this and of her.

The door opened, and she jerked back, her eyes bright blue against her fair skin.

"Wow," she breathed.

"I can think of another word to describe it," Grayson said.

"How about you keep it to yourself?" Kane suggested.

"I think I will," Grayson agreed. He walked in the room, his face carefully masking his feelings, a cup of coffee in his hand.

"Sorry for interrupting your…moment. I thought you might need some coffee after a night on that chair." He looked from Kane to Arden and back to Kane again.

"We weren't having a moment," Arden began, her cheeks pink.

"Yes," Kane interrupted. "We were."

"See?" Grayson kissed Arden's cheek. "You were. Which was obvious."

He handed the coffee to Kane. "I just want to know if I need to punch him for taking advantage of my sister or congratulate him for seeing how special she is."

"There's no need to throw any punches, Gray," Arden said, shaking her head.

"Then congratulations, man. I guess I'll be keeping my fists to myself…for now."

Arden rolled her eyes. "How about we change the subject to something more interesting."

"Personally, I find you very interesting," Kane said, just to see her blush again.

She didn't disappoint. "I mean the case. Have you heard from Harriet yet, Grayson?"

"She called this morning. They identified the buyer—it's classified, so all I can tell you is that it's a nation-state entity. We're teaming with the CIA to catch them."

"What about Randy?"

"He was transferred to Massachusetts Correctional Facility early this morning. That little weasel is being held without bond—Harry and her crew found enough evidence to try him as an accessory to espionage."

"What about the deaths of Juniper's husband, Dale, and his boss?"

"The team's still building their case. It could be a while. I'll push a little harder. Just to make sure they keep digging. But I feel confident—" Whatever Grayson was going to say next was cut off by his cell phone.

"Hang on, it's Mom. I asked her to let me know when her flight would get in this morning." He put the phone to his ear. "Hi, Mom...wait, slow down, what? Where are you?" His brows furrowed and he glanced at his watch. "Okay. I'm on my way. I'll call in some favors to get a private flight out and should be there in under two hours."

Grayson hung up, his usual calm demeanor slightly rattled. "Laney's having contractions. Mom and Aunt Rose are taking her to the hospital now. The airport's opened and Dad's on standby—he's hoping to get here later this morning."

"I knew you shouldn't have left Maryland," Arden said. "What if you miss the birth of your kids?"

Kane reached out and grabbed her hand, hating to see her so upset.

"Stop worrying and get some rest, kid." Grayson leaned down and kissed Arden's forehead, then ruffled her hair. "I'll see you in a few days." He turned to rush toward the door, then paused and looked at Kane. "Take care of her for us."

"I got this covered, Grayson."

"Make sure you call with updates," Arden yelled as the door shut behind Grayson.

"The flight to Maryland takes an hour, tops. He won't miss the birth," Kane assured her.

"I know," she sighed. "It's just Laney's not due for another three and a half weeks. She's probably scared and needs Gray to be there for her."

"He will be," Kane said with conviction. He prayed he was right. If Grayson missed the birth of his children, Arden would blame herself, even if it was misplaced blame. She genuinely wanted her family safe and happy. Would sacrifice everything for them. Just like he would sacrifice anything for her.

"But anything could happen," she worried. "Statistically speaking, preterm birth is the greatest contributor to—" He cut her off with a kiss, which ended too soon.

"What was that for?" she asked, her face flushed.

He smiled down at her, losing himself in her eyes. "That one was just for you."

EPILOGUE

Five thirty in the evening on Christmas, and Arden should have been giddy with happiness.

Bing Crosby crooned from the stereo system in the DeMarco home. The smell of ham and pecan pie filled the house. Arden breathed in the familiar smells of Christmas and tried on a smile. It felt as fake as the plastic mistletoe someone had hung above the living room doorway.

She could hear her mom and Juniper bustling around in the kitchen, their laughter and muted chatter barely lightening her mood. It should have made her ecstatic. It had been too long since she'd heard Juniper really laugh. In the days after Emory's death and Randy's arrest, Arden's friend had been looking increasingly drawn and tired. Juniper claimed it was morning sickness, but Arden suspected she was stressed over the ongoing investigation.

Evidence had quickly cast doubt on the circumstances of Dale's death, but her friend was still waiting for Dale's name to be fully cleared and justice to be served. Arden only hoped it would happen soon. The stress could not be good for Juniper or her unborn baby.

Arden rose from her father's favorite recliner and made her way to the large bay window. Her shoulder was still stiff, her arm aching dully as she moved. She'd refused to let it ruin her Christmas. She'd decorated cookies, just like always. She'd helped decorate the Christmas tree. She'd done dozens of things that should have put her in the holiday spirit.

Somehow, none of them had.

She sighed, squeezed in next to the colorfully decorated tree, and looked out into the yard and street. A light layer of snow covered the ground, its surface painted gold with the setting sun. It was beautiful, breathtaking, nearly perfect.

And she still felt glum.

With her arm still in a sling, and doctor's orders to take it easy for another three weeks, Arden had been relegated to light duty. Her mom had also given her the task of keeping Laney's Aunt Rose out of the kitchen while the Christmas meal was prepared.

That should have been easy enough, but Rose loved people, and she'd wanted nothing more than to be in the thick of things. Fortunately, Laney had handed Rose one of the twins. Rose was currently ensconced on the couch talking gibberish to little Aiden.

Laney held Flynn, and the two women sat side by side, sharing and reminiscing like they did every year. Arden could have joined in, but for once, she didn't feel like she had anything to say.

The men were in the family room playing a game of pool. Every now and then, one or the other would exclaim loudly at a particularly good or bad shot. Inevitably they'd argue that someone had cheated and there would be no clear winner.

Arden smiled at the predictability of it all. The family had expanded over the years, but the bonds between them were far from weakened.

Hearing a soft rustling near her feet, Arden looked down to find Sebastian under the tree. He was nestled between two immaculately wrapped Christmas presents and amusing himself by batting at a low-hanging bulb. She carefully knelt down and scooped him up with her right arm. He immediately snuggled his head up under her chin, his front legs wrapping around her neck. He purred loudly.

"I love you, too, buddy, but if you break another bulb Mom will kill me." She rubbed her face against the top of his head and thought about carrying him into her room and taking a nap. That didn't seem very festive, so she stayed put.

After her release from the hospital, and at Kane and Grayson's insistence, Arden had temporarily moved in with her parents. Her mom had been happy to have her home, of course, and Arden had enjoyed the preparations for the holiday, even if she hadn't been able to do much to help.

"Why so glum, doll?" Rose said. Arden glanced her way. Laney had disappeared and both babies were sleeping in their travel beds.

"I'm not glum," she said, her voice as bright and hard as a new penny.

"You think he ditched you, right?"

"Who?"

Rose laughed. "The man who was at the hospital every single day you were in it? The one who has driven you to almost every doctor's appointment you've attended? Kane Walker? Did he tell you he was coming?"

"He was supposed to be here a half hour ago," she responded. "He's not here. I'm not sure what your definition of ditching is, but that kind of seems like it to me."

"Half an hour, huh?" Rose patted her white curls and sighed. "That seems like a long time when you're waiting, but in the grand scheme of life, it's less than the blink of an eye."

"I know." Arden really did. Half an hour wasn't long. Anything could have happened to keep Kane from arriving on time. Her head knew that, but her heart was telling her something different. It was telling her she'd been fooled before.

"Of course you do. Just like you know he's coming because he said he would. Some men are like that. They say what they mean and do what they say. When you find a guy like that, you really should hang on to him."

"I know that, too," she said, setting Sebastian down a few feet away from the Christmas tree.

"Then why are you letting your worries ruin your day?"

"I'm not." Much.

"I'm going to give you some unsolicited advice, Arden. Because I'm old and I can. Do you mind?"

Arden smiled, her first real smile of the evening. "You know I don't, Rose."

"Leave the past where it is. Enjoy the moments that are given to you and the people who are in those moments. Once they're gone, you can't get them back." She smiled. "Now, how's that for Christmas cheer?"

"I kind of liked it," Arden said. She leaned in and kissed Rose's soft cheek. "Thanks."

"If you want to thank me, go see if you can find

some real mistletoe. That plastic crud has got to go."
She waved at the glossy, fake-looking sprig.

"Are you planning to steal a midnight kiss underneath it?" Arden teased, and Rose grinned.

"Stranger things have happened. But not under plastic mistletoe."

"My mom left a box of Christmas greenery on the porch. Maybe there's some in there."

"No need for you to go outside, my dear. I was kidding. Fake mistletoe won't ruin this lovely holiday."

"I don't mind looking, Rose." The box had been sitting there for nearly a week, forgotten in the excitement of the twins coming home from the hospital. Arden had planned to drape the greenery around the porch railing and tack it to the windows. She'd also planned to put up the fresh green wreath with the pretty red bows that her mother had bought from the local Christmas tree farm.

No one had let her touch any of it. She was too weak, too delicate. She was still recovering. The list of reasons had been long, and Arden had been too tired to argue. But now the greenery was still in the box, and it seemed a shame to waste it.

She shoved her feet in boots but didn't bother with a coat. She wouldn't be outside for long.

She stepped onto the porch. Cold wind whistled beneath the eaves, and the air smelled like snow and evergreen and fresh apple pie.

She rifled through the box one-handed and pulled out a long rope of greenery. There were tiny Christmas lights woven through it, and she could picture the porch railing glowing colorfully once the sun went down.

She dragged the greenery from the box and walked down the porch stairs, the chilly winter evening filled with the quiet Christmas hush that she'd always loved so much. There—in that quiet expectancy—she'd always felt God's presence. There, more than anywhere else, she'd always felt at peace.

She wrapped the greenery around the railing, then added more to each of the balusters, humming Christmas carols as she went. Every bit of greenery that went up made her happier. Why not do what Rose had said? Why not enjoy the moments and the people in them?

It was Christmas of *this* year, and she was here to enjoy it.

"O holy night!" she began, belting out the familiar carol. "The stars are brightly shiiiiining—"

"If I'd realized you'd be singing, I would have gotten here sooner," Kane broke in.

She whirled around, saw him walking down the snowy sidewalk. He'd parked up the road, the driveway too filled with family cars for his SUV to fit. She could see the gleaming hood of his Chevy near the corner of the street. A man got out of the back passenger seat. She thought it must be Silas, but she was too busy focusing on Kane to pay much attention.

"You're here!" she said as she walked into his embrace. "Finally."

"Sorry I'm late. I had to take a quick trip to pick up a surprise." He kissed her forehead, shrugged out of his coat and dropped it around her shoulders. "I'm assuming you have a reason for being outside without a coat?"

"Just living in the moment," she responded.

"Could you have done that with a coat on?" he asked.

She smiled and took his hand, pulling him up the porch stairs. "I'm looking for mistletoe. Rose doesn't like the fake stuff my mom hung."

"I'm shocked," he said, tucking a strand of hair behind her ear and smiling.

"That she doesn't like plastic mistletoe?"

"That you don't want to know what the surprise is."

"Logic dictates that surprises are meant to be secrets that are revealed when the presenter is ready."

"What if I'm ready?" he asked. He put a hand on her good shoulder and turned her back to face the street.

Two men were walking toward her, a dog trotting along beside them. She recognized Silas and Dutch immediately. The other man was tall and broad-shouldered, his hair cut in a military style, his face partially covered by a thick layer of white gauze. He was using a walker, easing up the street like an old man, but he wasn't old. He looked about the same age as her brother...

"Jace?" she whispered, her heart recognizing him before her mind did.

"Jace!" She rushed down the stairs and met him on the walkway, her heart pounding in her chest. The last she and her family had heard, he was still in Germany trying to recover enough from surgery to make it home.

She stopped inches away from the walker, afraid to touch him. She wasn't sure where he was injured or how badly he hurt.

"Jace," she said for the third time, and he smiled, his eyes deeply shadowed.

"This is the first time I've ever known you to be speechless, kid," he said, his voice raspy and rough.

"I can't believe you're here. We thought you were still recovering."

"I am. I wanted to do it here." He released his hold

on the walker and pulled her close. "I'm glad to see you're recovering, too."

"Wait until Mom and Dad see you! All they've done is worry about you and wonder when you're coming home." Arden kept her hand on his arm as he held onto the walker again. He was trembling, and she assumed it was from pain and fatigue, but he managed to shuffle along the snowy sidewalk. Silas walked closely behind him.

"You should have had them drop you off in front of the house," she said as they continued up the walkway.

"They tried. I refused. I won't get better letting everyone baby me."

"It's not babying. It's smarts." Silas spoke for the first time.

"We'll see if you say the same if you're ever the one walking around with a metal cage holding you up." They made it to the steps and Arden hurried to open the front door.

Warmth drifted out. Voices. Someone asked about the open front door and the next thing she knew, her family was there, peering out, seeing Jace. The explosion of noise and joy was deafening, and she stepped back, making room for her parents and three other brothers.

Her father grabbed the walker, and her brothers flanked Jace. He made it up the five steps like an old man with achy bones, but he made it.

She let them move past, stepping farther back to give them more room. She bumped into Kane's familiar warmth.

"Are you happy?" he whispered in her ear.

"There are no words to describe how I feel right

now," she responded, her eyes burning with something that was beyond happiness or joy. This was home and family and Christmas and love, every color and sound and scent vibrant and beautiful and heartrending.

"Speechless again?" he teased gently.

She turned in his arms, looking into his dark eyes. "Yes, but it's probably not something you should get used to."

He laughed and leaned down to press a quick kiss to her lips.

"Thanks for the warning." His gaze dropped from her face to her carefully chosen outfit. She'd spent hours deciding what to wear. She'd tried on a few dresses and even borrowed one of Laney's skirts. She'd put on blouses and cardigan sets and a dozen other things that just didn't feel right.

In the end, she'd opted for black jeans and the Christmas sweater she'd bought on clearance last January.

She tensed as Kane's gaze lingered on the fuzzy yarn Christmas tree, tiny blinking lights, pom-pom Christmas balls.

His gaze finally lifted, and he met her eyes with a sweet, tender smile that took her breath away. "Thank you," he said.

"For what?"

"Not disappointing me. You look exactly like Christmas should, Arden. And you are absolutely the most beautiful woman I have ever seen."

She probably should have responded, but she was speechless again. When he took her arm and walked her inside, she still wasn't sure what to say.

She'd always been the DeMarco boys' sister, the tough little girl who never backed down from a fight.

She'd been the computer geek, the bookworm, the quirky woman who wore odd holiday sweaters, but she'd never ever been beautiful.

Until now.

Arden lit up the room. And not because of the flashing lights on her Christmas sweater. Her smile was bright and real and so beautiful it stole Kane's breath.

Every. Single. Time.

He watched as she moved around the room, hugging her mother and her father, sharing their joy in her brother's homecoming. There was no artifice with Arden. Everything she felt was painted in a million nuances on her stunning face.

She glanced his way, and her cheeks went pink, her eyes sparkling. She was what he'd been looking for since he was a kid. The port in the storm. The place to come home.

"Now is as good a time as any," Silas said quietly, catching Kane's eye.

"What are you talking about?"

"Ask her what you need to while her family is around. Make it a memory they all can share. That's what she loves most. Aside from you," Silas continued, his gaze turning to Arden.

"You're making a lot of assumptions, Si."

"Are any of them wrong?"

"No."

"So get to it. I'm starving, and if you start making your declarations of undying love at the dinner table, all the smarmy sweetness of it might kill my appetite."

Kane went.

Not because Silas had told him to, but because he'd

been right—Arden was all about family and memories, tradition and home. She turned as he approached, her smile as bright and tremulous as the shimmering tinsel on the tree.

"We forgot something," he said, and she glanced around, frowning.

"We did?"

"The mistletoe?"

"It's okay. I think Rose has forgotten."

"Maybe, but I haven't." He took her hand, tugging her to the doorway where the shiny plastic mistletoe hung.

"But I'm thinking we shouldn't switch it out," he said. The room seemed to go quiet, the conversation fading as he looked into Arden's bright blue eyes.

"Why not?"

"Logically speaking," he began, and Arden grinned.

"Isn't that my line?"

"Logically speaking," he continued, pulling a small box from his pocket, "plastic mistletoe is better than the real stuff because it lasts forever. Like God and eternal life. Like love." He opened the box and showed her the antique ring he'd found in a little shop in DC.

"Kane—"

"It's just a promise. From me to you. That I will always be there when you need me. That when you're ready, there will be another ring and a wedding and all the things that go with forever." He took out the silver ring, a beautifully crafted dove in the center of a jeweled cross.

"It's…beautiful," she said. Her voice trembled, and he knew she felt what he did—the solemnness of the moment, the power of the bond they'd created together.

"Beautiful and unique. Like you. When I saw it, I knew it belonged on your finger. If you'll wear it."

"It's the only logical thing to do."

Someone laughed, but Kane was too busy looking into Arden's face. Too busy watching a tear slide down her cheek to wonder who it was.

"Don't cry," he said.

"Sometimes, there's just too much happiness to contain," she responded. She held out her right hand since her left arm was still in a sling. He slid the ring on her finger.

"I love you." He wiped the tear from her cheek. "Today and always."

"I love you, too," she replied.

"Then kiss already!" Aunt Rose crowed. "The mistletoe might be fake, but the love's sure not!"

Arden laughed, and Kane leaned down, capturing her joy with a kiss that promised everything he wanted to give her—love, family, happiness. Home. For now and for always.

* * * * *

Thick snow squalls blew down the Toronto shoreline of Lake Ontario, turning the city's annual winter wonderland into a haze of sparkling lights. The cold hadn't done much to quell the tourists, though, Detective Liam Bearsmith thought as he methodically trailed his hooded target around the skating rink and through the crowd. Hopefully, the combination of the darkness, heavy flakes and general merriment would keep the jacket-clad criminal he was after from even realizing he was being followed.

The "Sparrow" was a hacker. Just a tiny fish in the criminal pond, but a newly reborn and highly dangerous cyberterrorist group had just placed a pretty hefty bounty on the Sparrow's capture in the hopes it would lead them to a master decipher key that could break any code. If Liam didn't bring in the Sparrow now, terrorists could turn that code breaker into a weapon and the Sparrow could be dead, or worse, by Christmas.

The lone figure hurried up a metal footbridge festooned in white lights. A gust of wind caught the hood of the Sparrow's jacket, tossing it back. Long dark hair flew loose around the Sparrow's slender shoulders.

Liam's world froze as déjà vu flooded his senses. His target was a woman.

What's more, Liam was sure he'd seen her somewhere before.

Liam's strategy had been to capture the Sparrow, question her and use the intel gleaned to locate the criminals he was chasing. His brain freezing at the mere sight of her hadn't exactly been part of the plan. The Sparrow reached up, grabbed her hood and yanked it back down again firmly, but not before Liam caught a glimpse of a delicate jaw that was determinedly set, and how thick flakes clung to her long lashes. For a moment Liam just stood there, his hand on the railing as his mind filled with the name and face of a young woman he'd known and loved a very long time ago.

Kelly Marshall.

Don't miss
Christmas Witness Conspiracy *by Maggie K. Black,*
available wherever Love Inspired Suspense books
and ebooks are sold.

LoveInspired.com

LISEXP0920

Heartfelt or suspenseful, inspiring or passionate, Harlequin has your happily-ever-after.

With new books published every month, you are sure to find the satisfying escape you know you deserve.

HNEWS2020

Love Harlequin romance?

DISCOVER.

Be the first to find out about promotions,
news and exclusive content!

Facebook.com/HarlequinBooks

Twitter.com/HarlequinBooks

Instagram.com/HarlequinBooks

Pinterest.com/HarlequinBooks

ReaderService.com

EXPLORE.

Sign up for the Harlequin e-newsletter and
download a free book from any series at
TryHarlequin.com

CONNECT.

Join our Harlequin community to
share your thoughts and connect
with other romance readers!
Facebook.com/groups/HarlequinConnection

HSOCIAL2020

DEC 0 5 2020